GIRL
HAVEN

AN ONI PRESS PUBLICATION

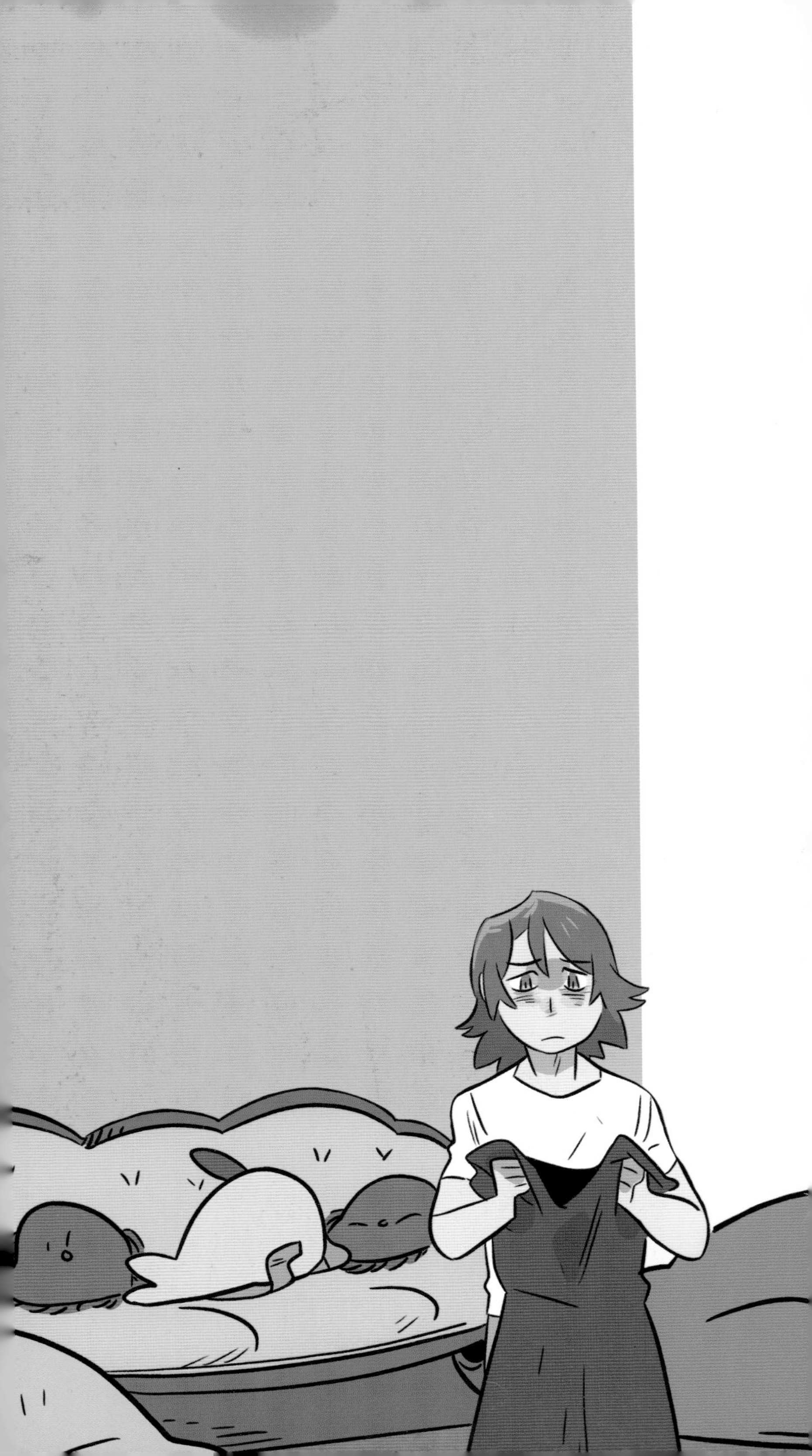

GIRL
HAVEN

WRITTEN BY LILAH STURGES

ILLUSTRATED BY MEAGHAN CARTER

LETTERED BY JOAMETTE GIL

DESIGNED BY SONJA SYNAK

EDITED BY SHAWNA GORE & ROBIN HERRERA

CONSULTING READER
CAP BLACKARD

PUBLISHED BY ONI-LION FORGE PUBLISHING GROUP, LLC

JAMES LUCAS JONES, PRESIDENT & PUBLISHER · SARAH GAYDOS, EDITOR IN CHIEF · CHARLIE CHU, E.V.P. OF CREATIVE & BUSINESS DEVELOPMENT · BRAD ROOKS, DIRECTOR OF OPERATIONS · AMBER O'NEILL, SPECIAL PROJECTS MANAGER · HARRIS FISH, EVENTS MANAGER · MARGOT WOOD, DIRECTOR OF MARKETING & SALES DEVIN FUNCHES, SALES & MARKETING MANAGER · KATIE SAINZ, MARKETING MANAGER · TARA LEHMANN, PUBLICIST · TROY LOOK, DIRECTOR OF DESIGN & PRODUCTION · KATE Z. STONE, SENIOR GRAPHIC DESIGNER SONJA SYNAK, GRAPHIC DESIGNER · HILARY THOMPSON, GRAPHIC DESIGNER · SARAH ROCKWELL, JUNIOR GRAPHIC DESIGNER · ANGIE KNOWLES, DIGITAL PREPRESS LEAD · VINCENT KUKUA, DIGITAL PREPRESS TECHNICIAN · JASMINE AMIRI, SENIOR EDITOR · SHAWNA GORE, SENIOR EDITOR · AMANDA MEADOWS, SENIOR EDITOR · ROBERT MEYERS, SENIOR EDITOR, LICENSING · GRACE BORNHOFT, EDITOR · ZACK SOTO, EDITOR CHRIS CERASI, EDITORIAL COORDINATOR · STEVE ELLIS, VICE PRESIDENT OF GAMES · BEN EISNER, GAME DEVELOPER · MICHELLE NGUYEN, EXECUTIVE ASSISTANT · JUNG LEE, LOGISTICS COORDINATOR

JOE NOZEMACK, PUBLISHER EMERITUS

ONIPRESS.COM 🖪 · 🖸 · 🖾 LIONFORGE.COM

TWITTER.COM/@LILAHSTURGES
INSTAGRAM.COM/MEGACARTER

FIRST EDITION: FEBRUARY 2021

ISBN 978-1-62010-865-9
EISBN 978-1-62010-866-6

1 2 3 4 5 6 7 8 9 10

LIBRARY OF CONGRESS CONTROL NUMBER: 2020937823

PRINTED IN CHINA

Author's Preface

Girl Haven is a story about gender. It tells one kind
of story—and hopefully it's a good one—but it's important to
know that there are lots of other stories to tell about gender
that are just as valid.

There is no one right way to have a gender, and no wrong way.
Some people's genders match what they were assigned at birth, and
some don't. Some people are boys, some people are girls, and some
people are neither. Some people feel their gender strongly, and some
people don't feel it at all. For some people, gender stays constant,
and for some people, it changes over time.

All these ways of being matter, and none of them is more
important than any of the others.

While Girl Haven is mainly about one kind of gender experience, its
central message is true for everyone: your story is your own; you
don't need anyone's permission to be who you are; and when you
accept that, magical things can happen.

Love is stronger than fear.

Lilah Sturges
April 2020

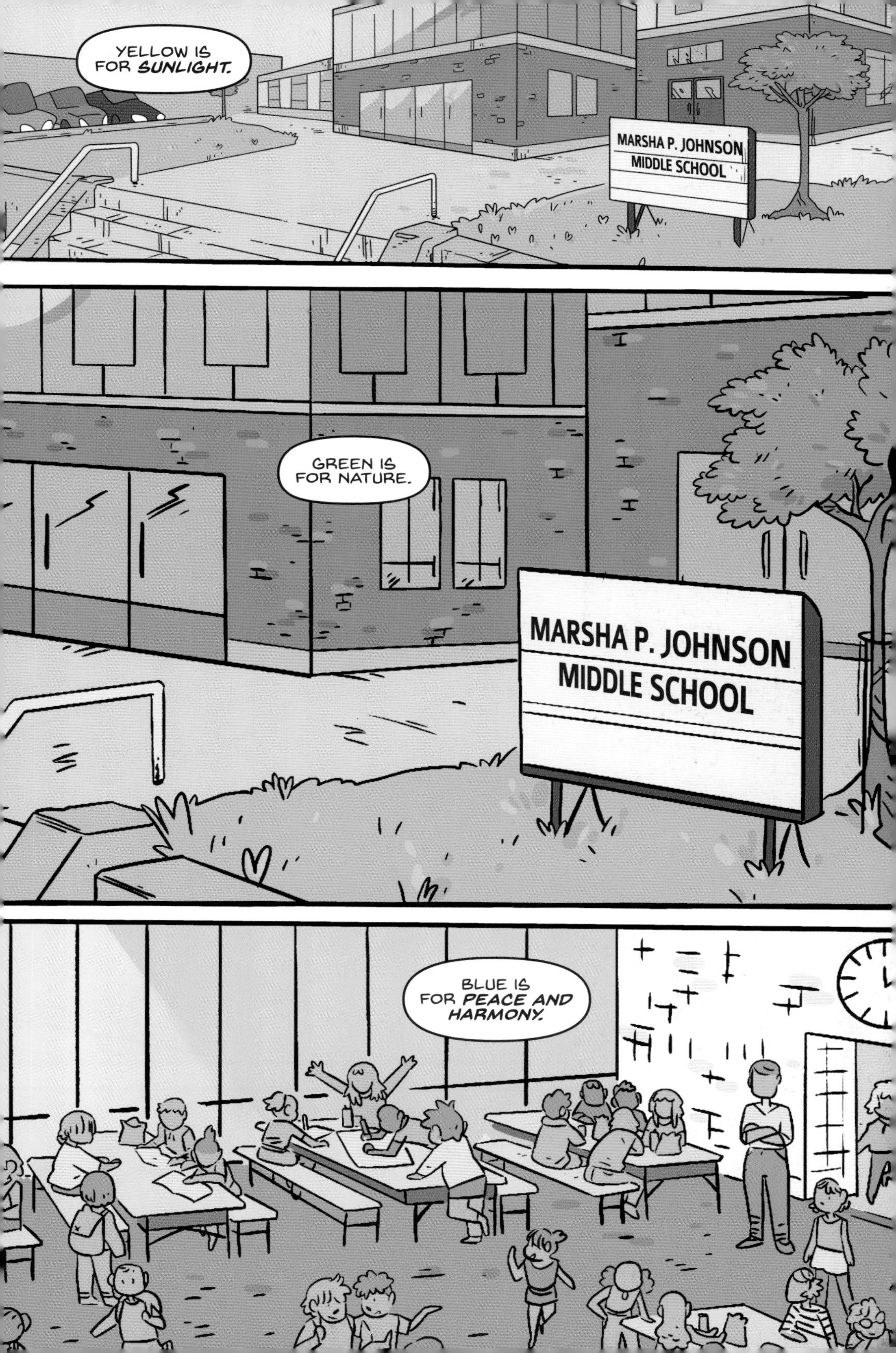
YELLOW IS FOR SUNLIGHT.
MARSHA P. JOHNSON MIDDLE SCHOOL
GREEN IS FOR NATURE.
MARSHA P. JOHNSON MIDDLE SCHOOL
BLUE IS FOR PEACE AND HARMONY.

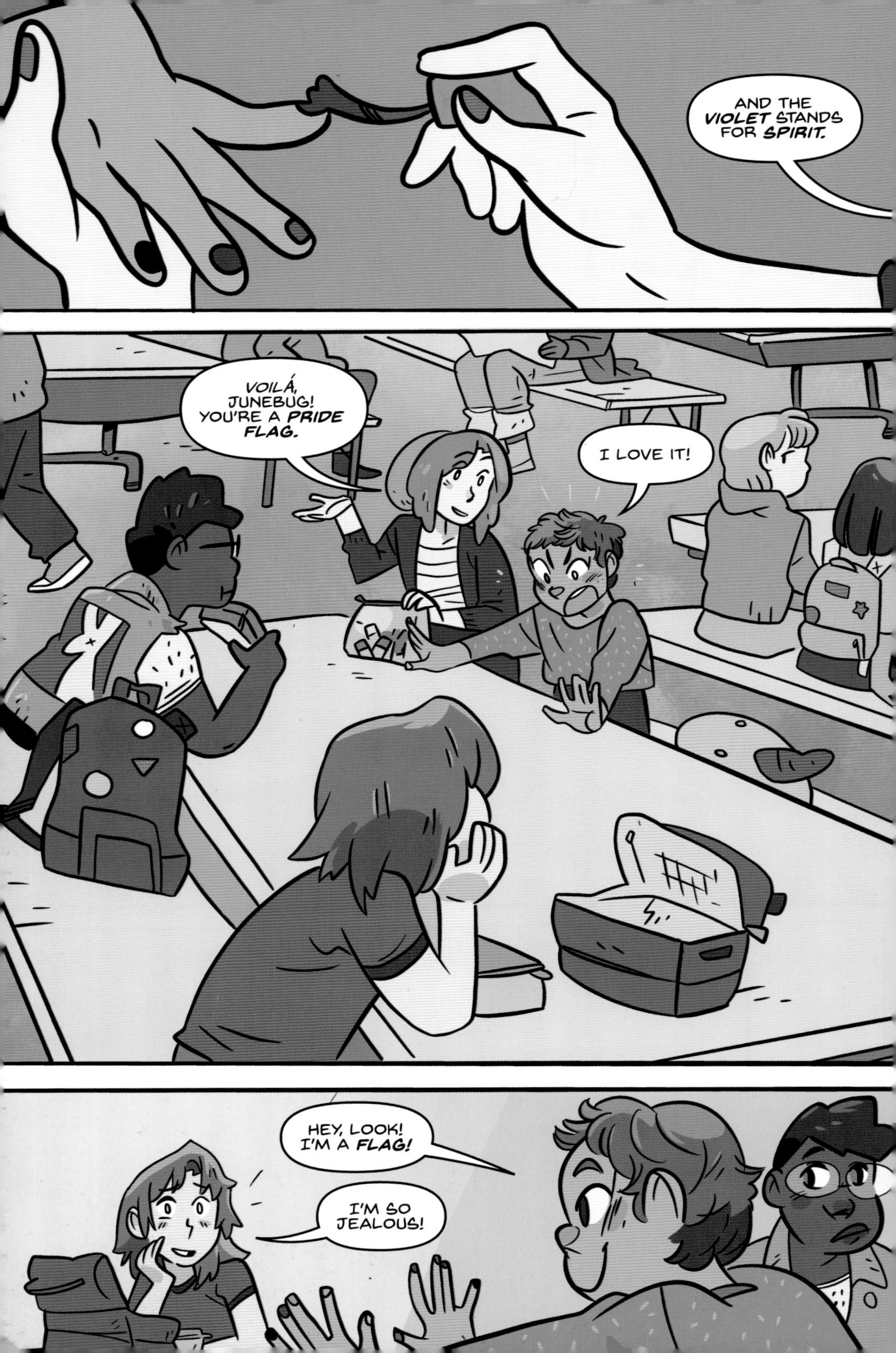

AND THE VIOLET STANDS FOR SPIRIT.
VOILÁ, JUNEBUG! YOU'RE A PRIDE FLAG.
I LOVE IT!
HEY, LOOK! I'M A FLAG!
I'M SO JEALOUS!

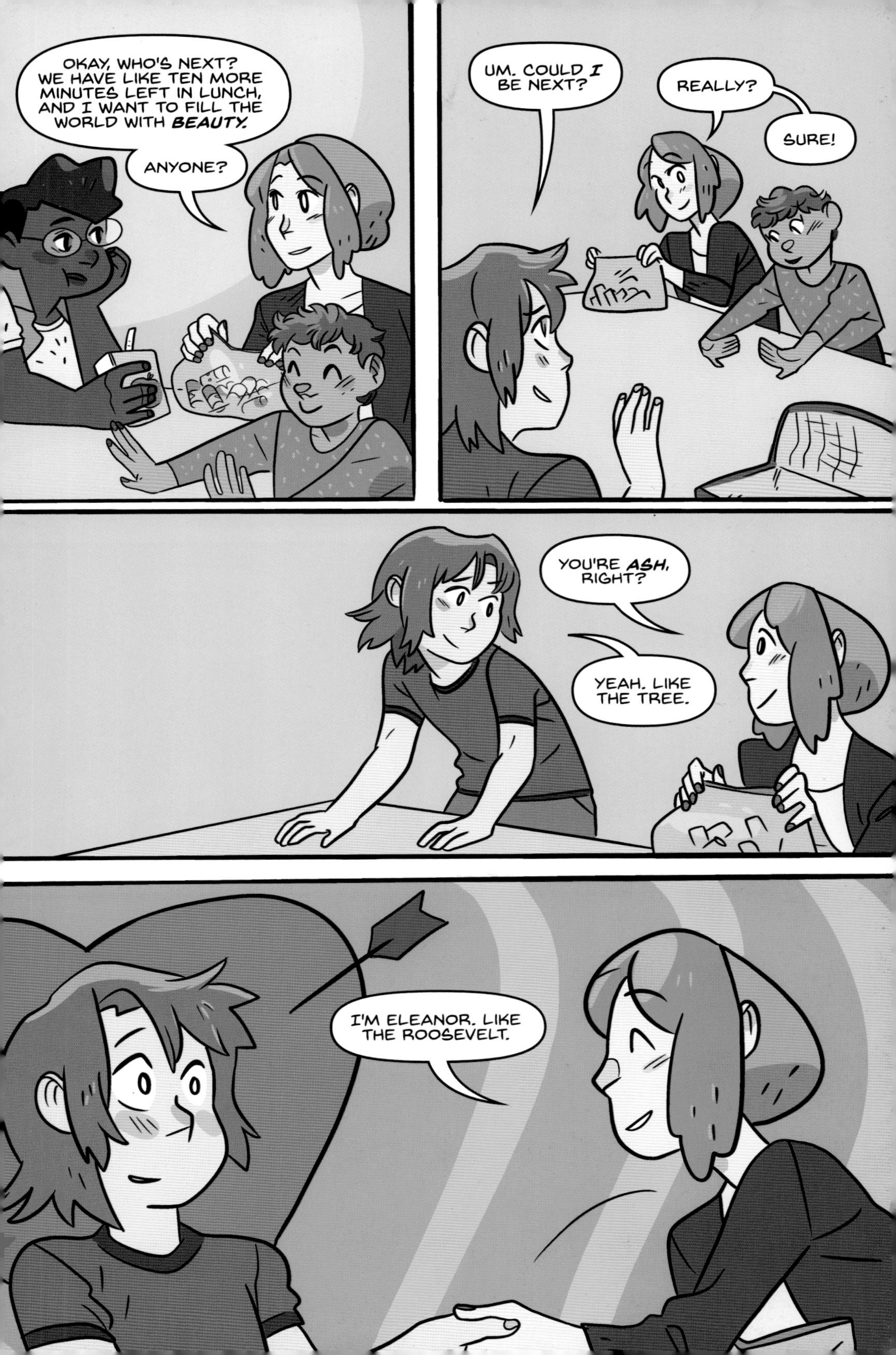
OKAY, WHO'S NEXT? WE HAVE LIKE TEN MORE MINUTES LEFT IN LUNCH, AND I WANT TO FILL THE WORLD WITH **BEAUTY.**
ANYONE?
UM. COULD ***I*** BE NEXT?
REALLY?
SURE!
YOU'RE ***ASH,*** RIGHT?
YEAH. LIKE THE TREE.
I'M ELEANOR. LIKE THE ROOSEVELT.

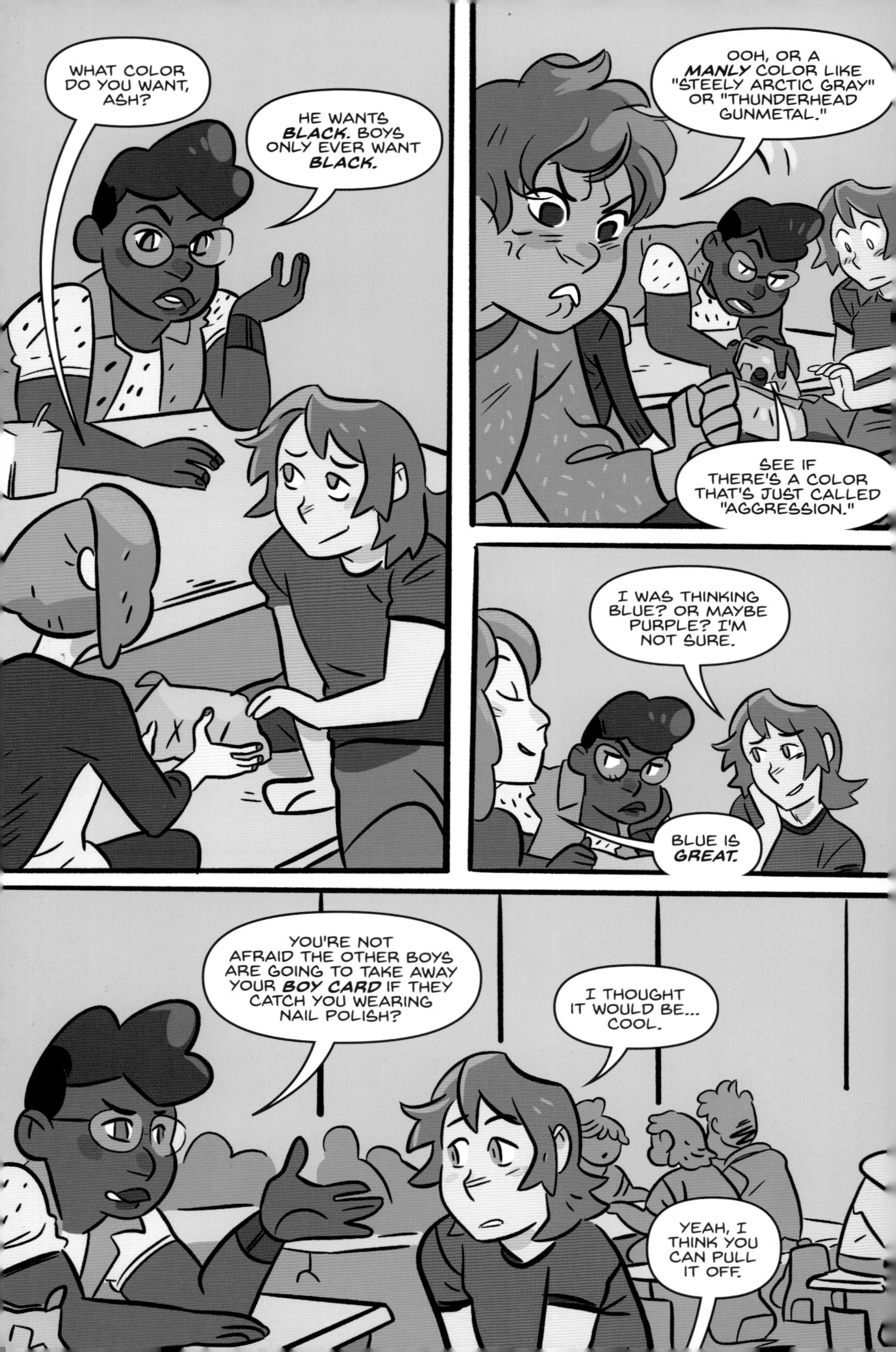
WHAT COLOR DO YOU WANT, ASH?
HE WANTS BLACK. BOYS ONLY EVER WANT BLACK.
OOH, OR A MANLY COLOR LIKE "STEELY ARCTIC GRAY" OR "THUNDERHEAD GUNMETAL."
SEE IF THERE'S A COLOR THAT'S JUST CALLED "AGGRESSION."
I WAS THINKING BLUE? OR MAYBE PURPLE? I'M NOT SURE.
BLUE IS GREAT.
YOU'RE NOT AFRAID THE OTHER BOYS ARE GOING TO TAKE AWAY YOUR BOY CARD IF THEY CATCH YOU WEARING NAIL POLISH?
I THOUGHT IT WOULD BE... COOL.
YEAH, I THINK YOU CAN PULL IT OFF.

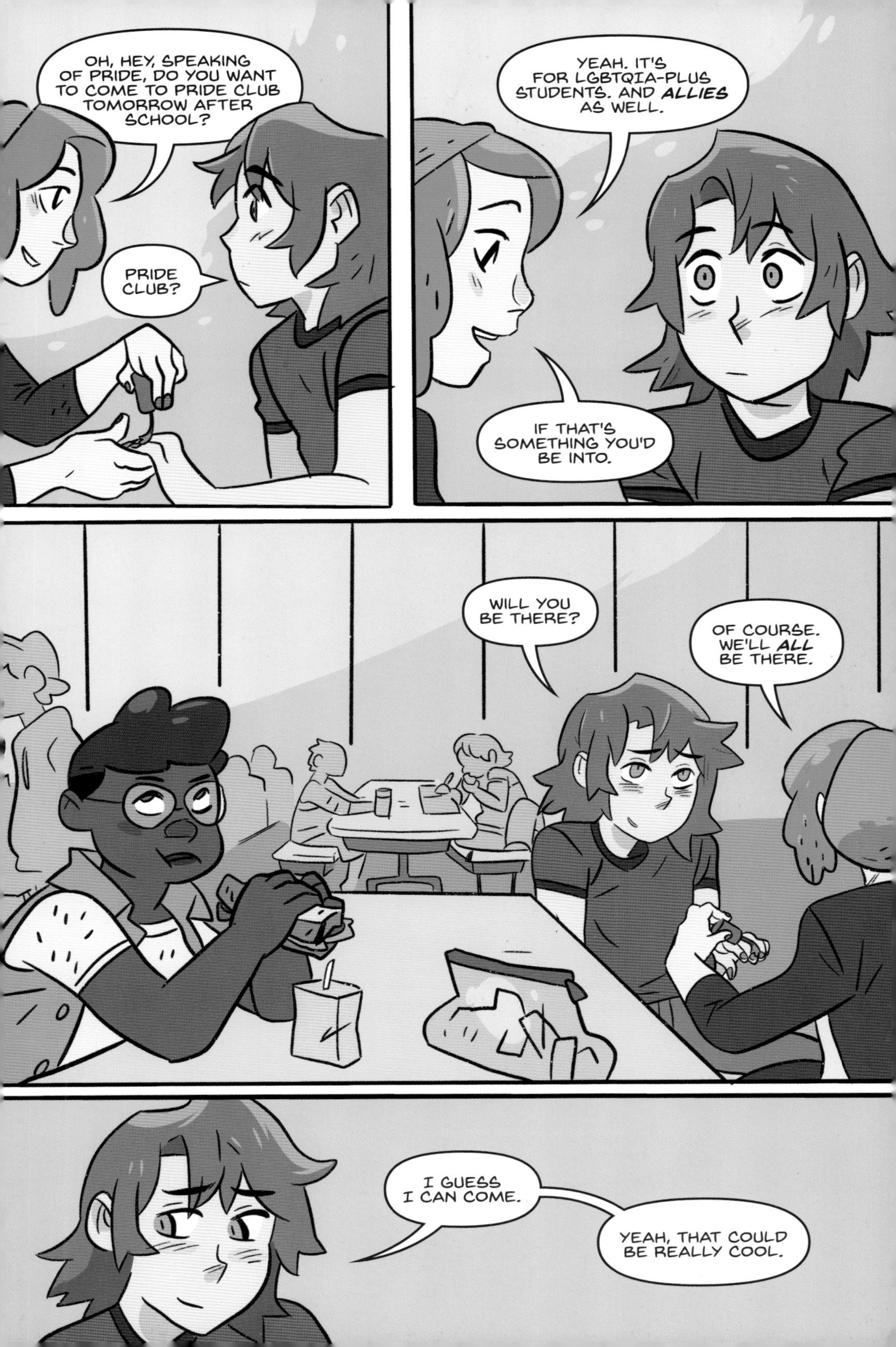
OH, HEY, SPEAKING OF PRIDE, DO YOU WANT TO COME TO PRIDE CLUB TOMORROW AFTER SCHOOL?
PRIDE CLUB?
YEAH. IT'S FOR LGBTQIA-PLUS STUDENTS. AND *ALLIES* AS WELL.
IF THAT'S SOMETHING YOU'D BE INTO.
WILL YOU BE THERE?
OF COURSE. WE'LL *ALL* BE THERE.
I GUESS I CAN COME.
YEAH, THAT COULD BE REALLY COOL.

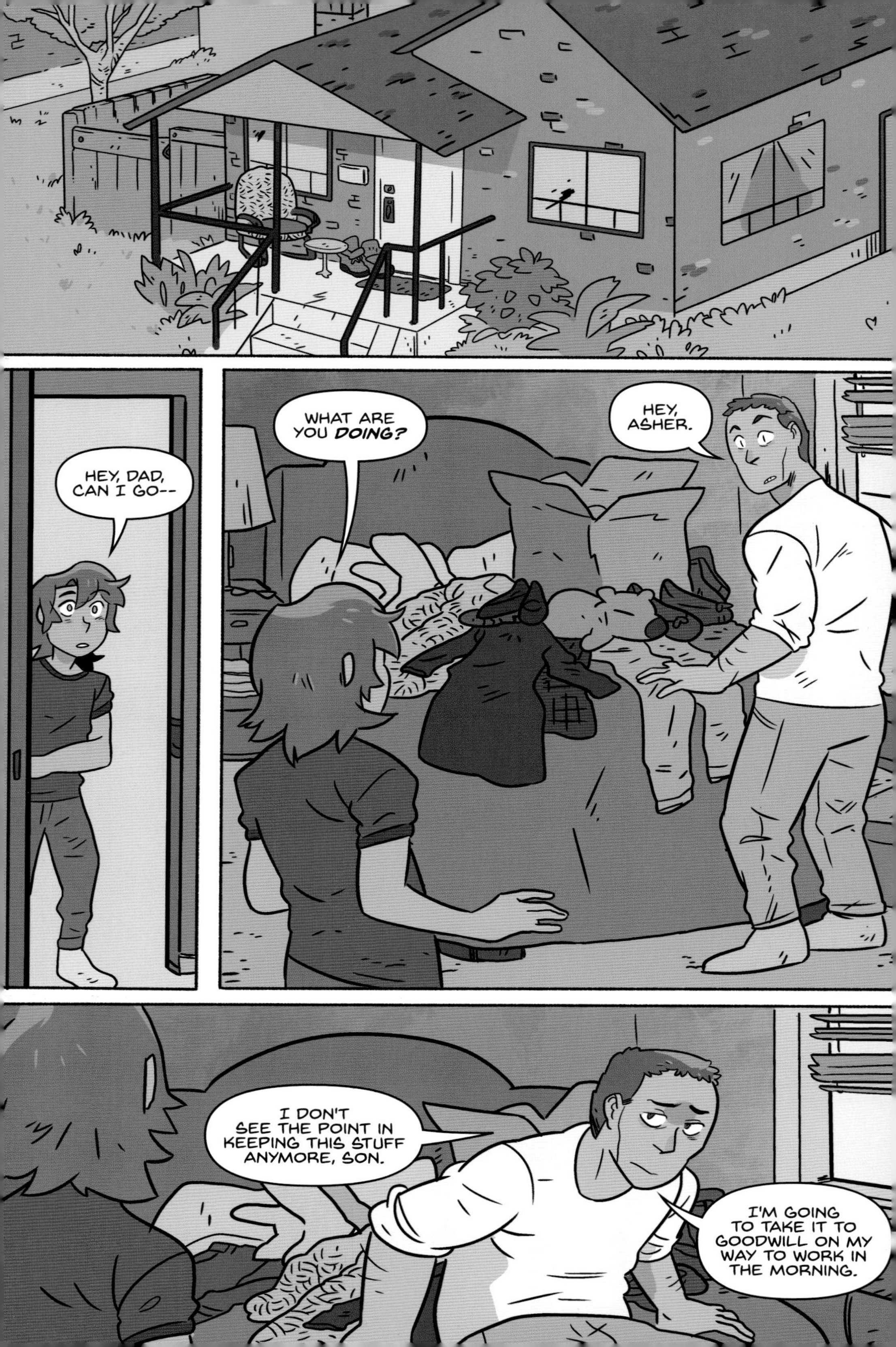
HEY, DAD, CAN I GO--
WHAT ARE YOU *DOING?*
HEY, ASHER.
I DON'T SEE THE POINT IN KEEPING THIS STUFF ANYMORE, SON.
I'M GOING TO TAKE IT TO GOODWILL ON MY WAY TO WORK IN THE MORNING.

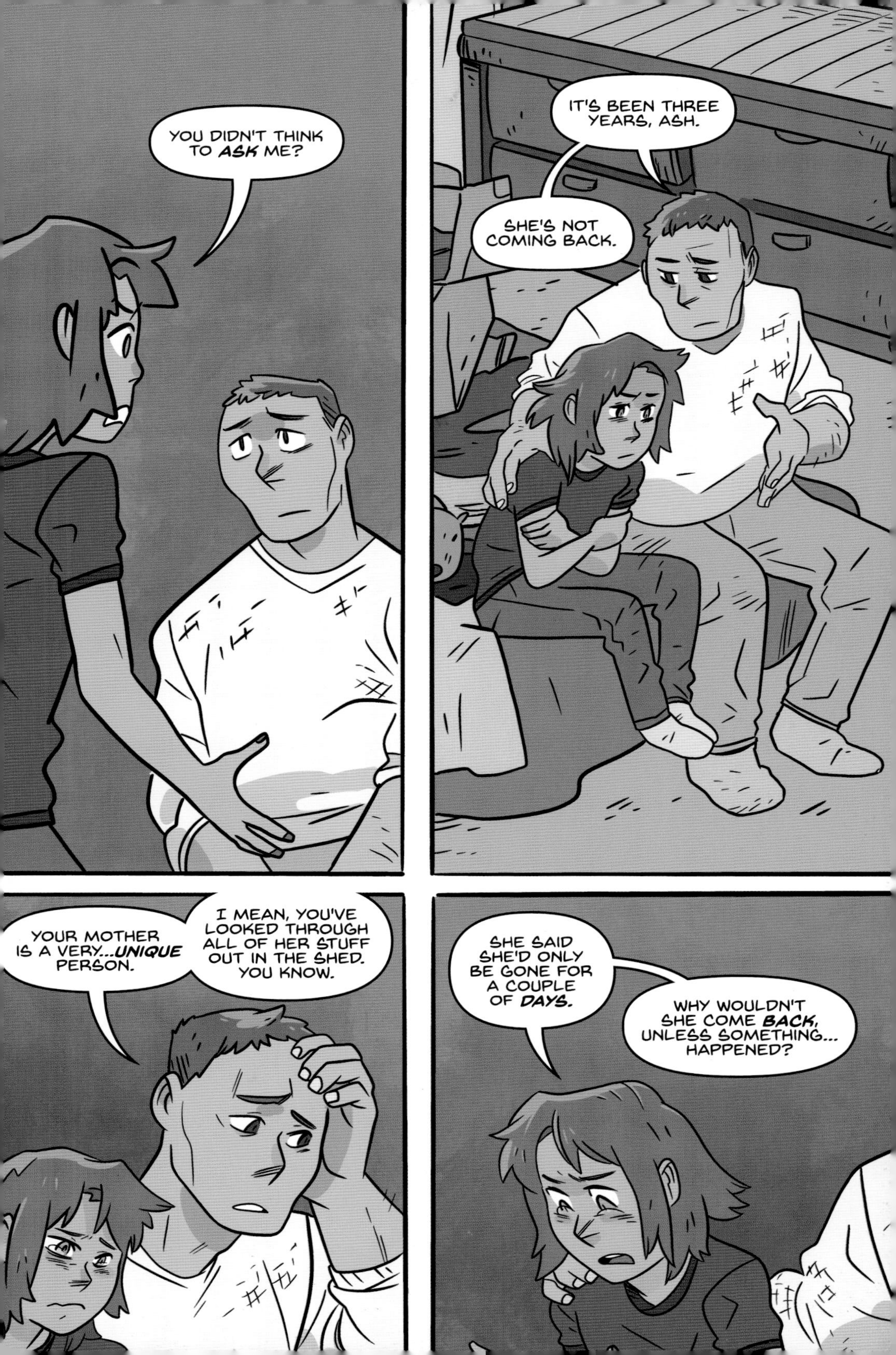
YOU DIDN'T THINK TO ASK ME?
IT'S BEEN THREE YEARS, ASH.
SHE'S NOT COMING BACK.
YOUR MOTHER IS A VERY...UNIQUE PERSON.
I MEAN, YOU'VE LOOKED THROUGH ALL OF HER STUFF OUT IN THE SHED. YOU KNOW.
SHE SAID SHE'D ONLY BE GONE FOR A COUPLE OF DAYS.
WHY WOULDN'T SHE COME BACK, UNLESS SOMETHING... HAPPENED?

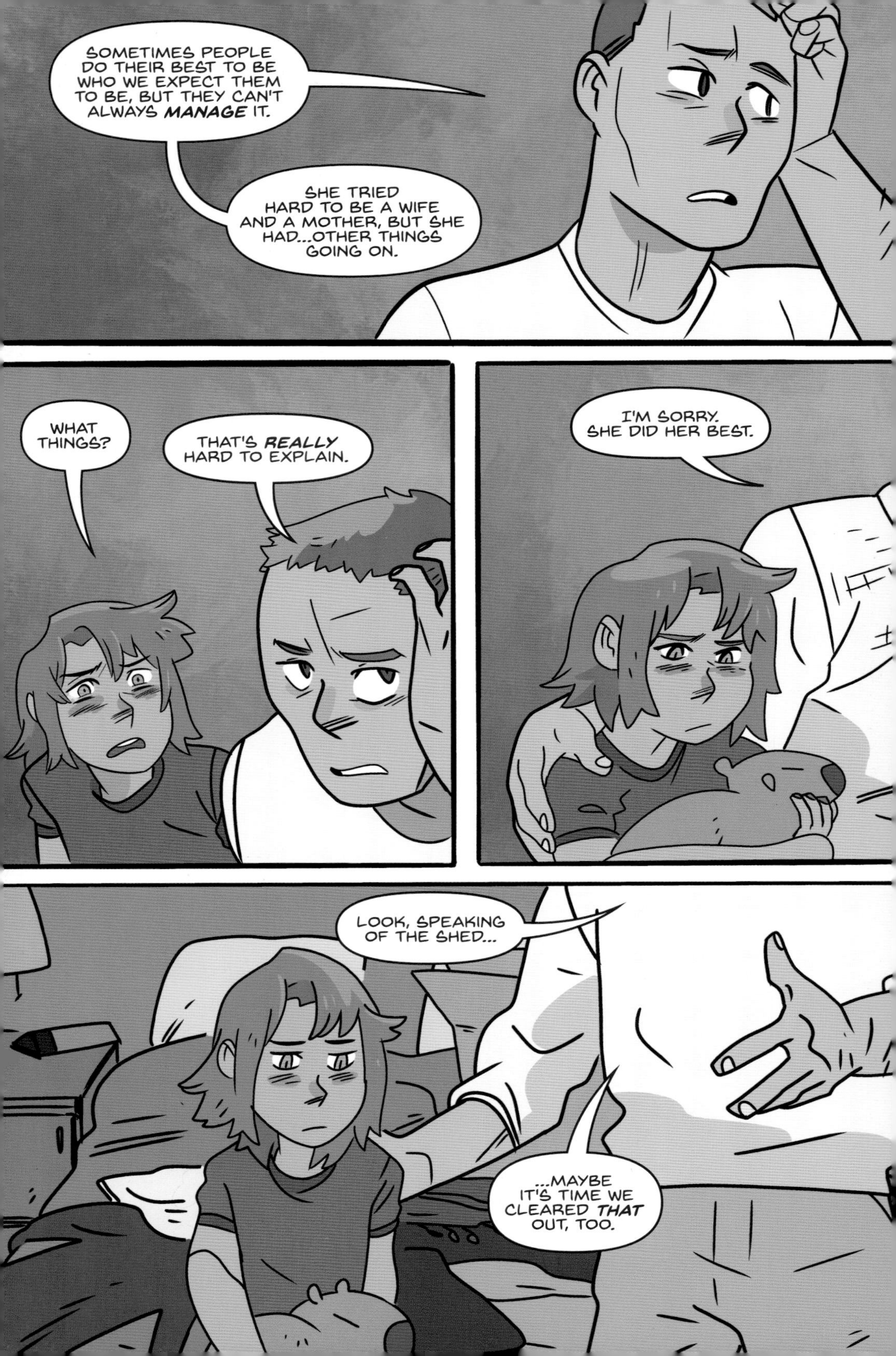
SOMETIMES PEOPLE DO THEIR BEST TO BE WHO WE EXPECT THEM TO BE, BUT THEY CAN'T ALWAYS ***MANAGE*** IT.
SHE TRIED HARD TO BE A WIFE AND A MOTHER, BUT SHE HAD...OTHER THINGS GOING ON.
WHAT THINGS?
THAT'S ***REALLY*** HARD TO EXPLAIN.
I'M SORRY. SHE DID HER BEST.
LOOK, SPEAKING OF THE SHED...
...MAYBE IT'S TIME WE CLEARED ***THAT*** OUT, TOO.

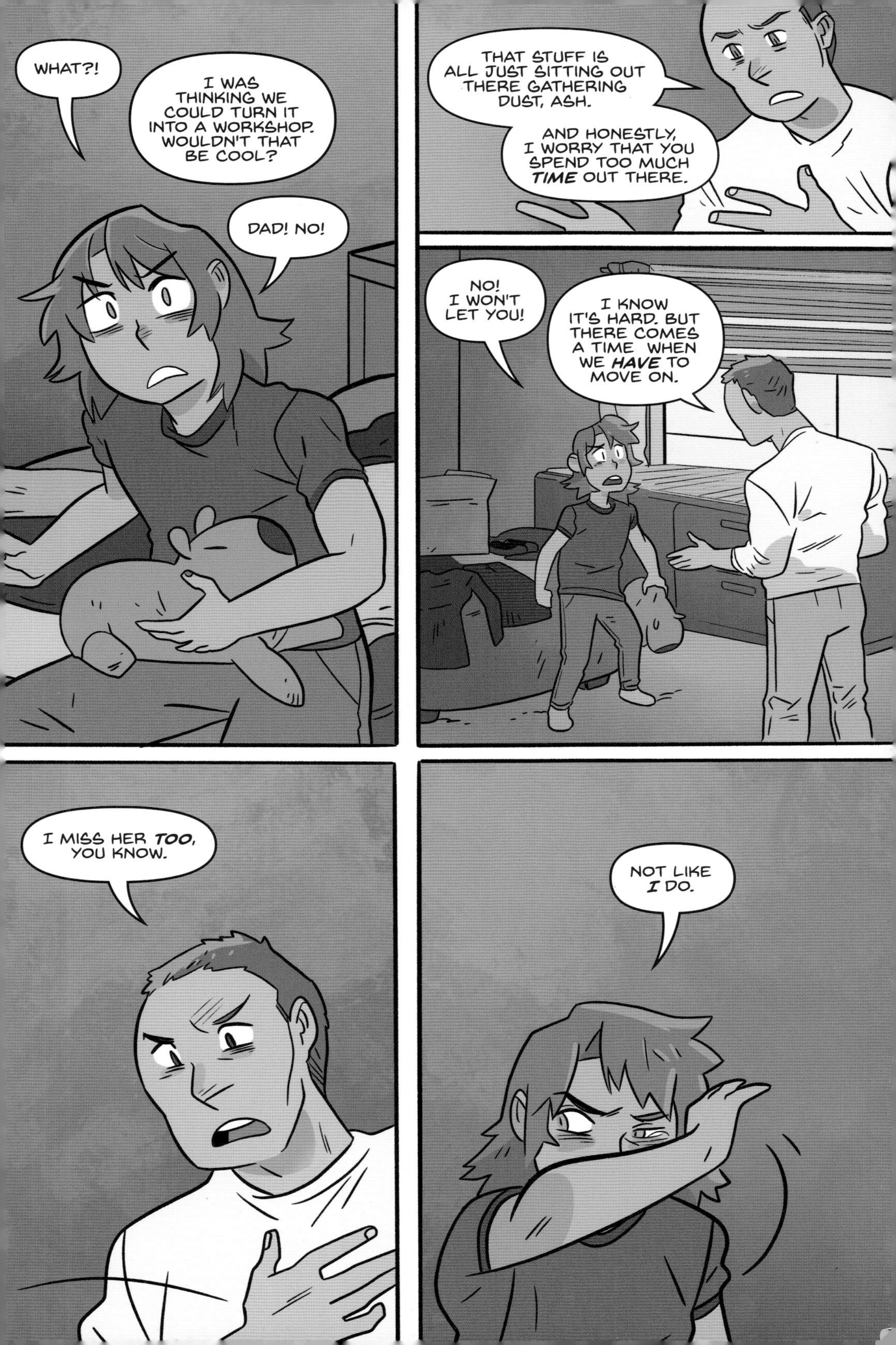
WHAT?!
I WAS THINKING WE COULD TURN IT INTO A WORKSHOP. WOULDN'T THAT BE COOL?
DAD! NO!
THAT STUFF IS ALL JUST SITTING OUT THERE GATHERING DUST, ASH.
AND HONESTLY, I WORRY THAT YOU SPEND TOO MUCH *TIME* OUT THERE.
NO! I WON'T LET YOU!
I KNOW IT'S HARD. BUT THERE COMES A TIME WHEN WE *HAVE* TO MOVE ON.
I MISS HER *TOO*, YOU KNOW.
NOT LIKE *I* DO.

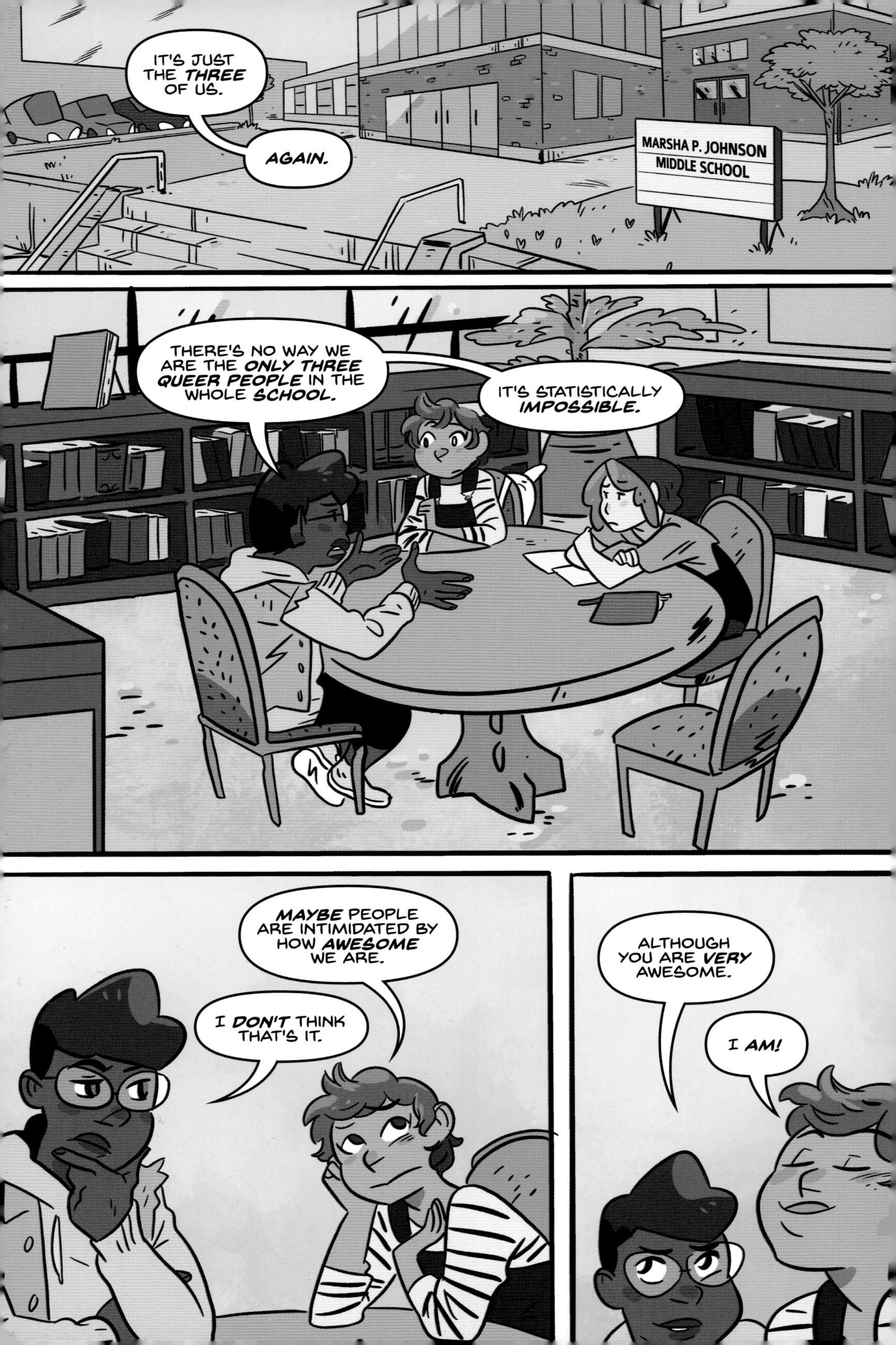
IT'S JUST THE THREE OF US.
AGAIN.
MARSHA P. JOHNSON MIDDLE SCHOOL
THERE'S NO WAY WE ARE THE ONLY THREE QUEER PEOPLE IN THE WHOLE SCHOOL.
IT'S STATISTICALLY IMPOSSIBLE.
MAYBE PEOPLE ARE INTIMIDATED BY HOW AWESOME WE ARE.
I DON'T THINK THAT'S IT.
ALTHOUGH YOU ARE VERY AWESOME.
I AM!

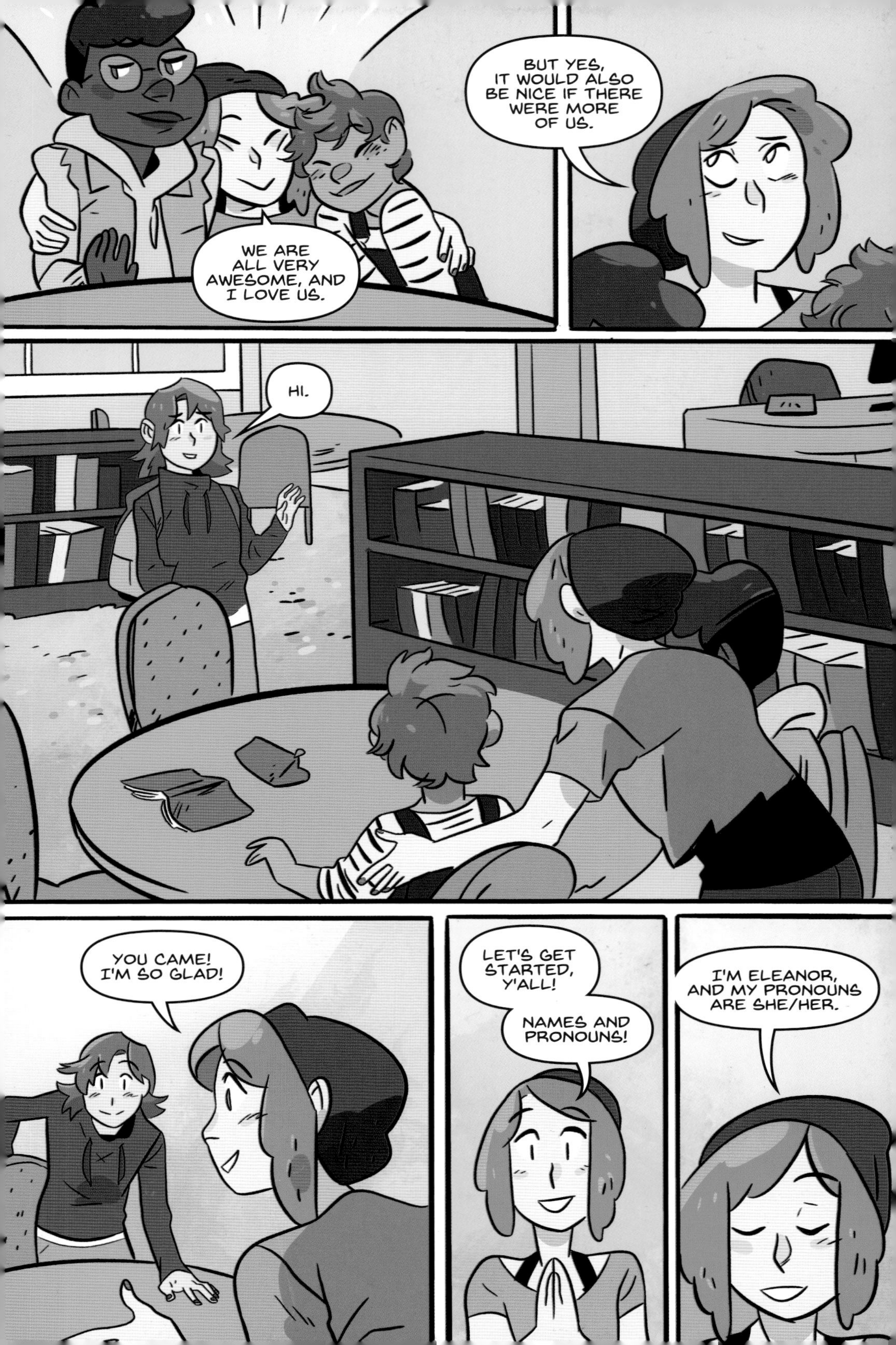

WE ARE ALL VERY AWESOME, AND I LOVE US.
BUT YES, IT WOULD ALSO BE NICE IF THERE WERE MORE OF US.
HI.
YOU CAME! I'M SO GLAD!
LET'S GET STARTED, Y'ALL!
NAMES AND PRONOUNS!
I'M ELEANOR, AND MY PRONOUNS ARE SHE/HER.

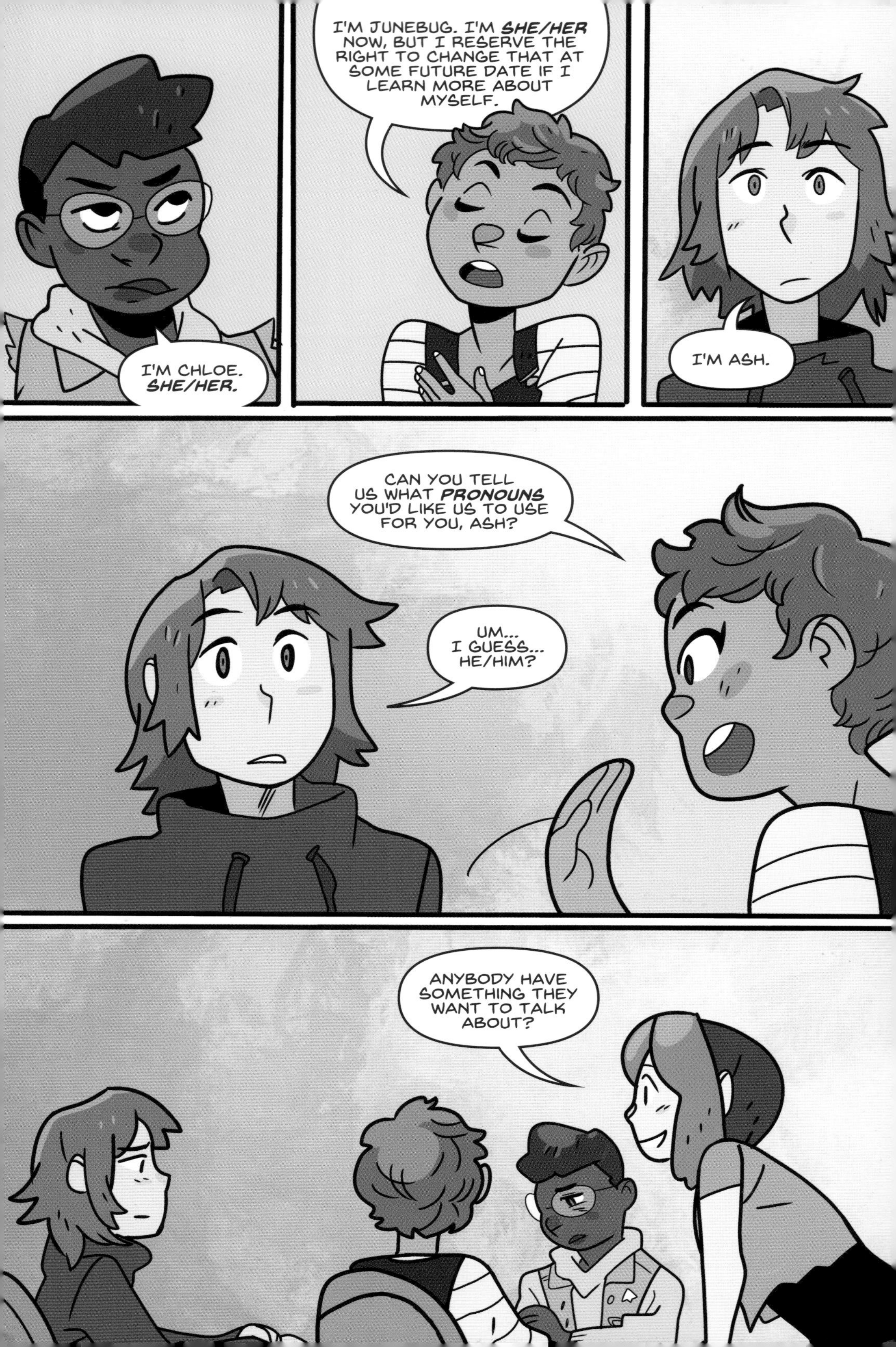
I'M CHLOE. SHE/HER.
I'M JUNEBUG. I'M SHE/HER NOW, BUT I RESERVE THE RIGHT TO CHANGE THAT AT SOME FUTURE DATE IF I LEARN MORE ABOUT MYSELF.
I'M ASH.
CAN YOU TELL US WHAT PRONOUNS YOU'D LIKE US TO USE FOR YOU, ASH?
UM... I GUESS... HE/HIM?
ANYBODY HAVE SOMETHING THEY WANT TO TALK ABOUT?

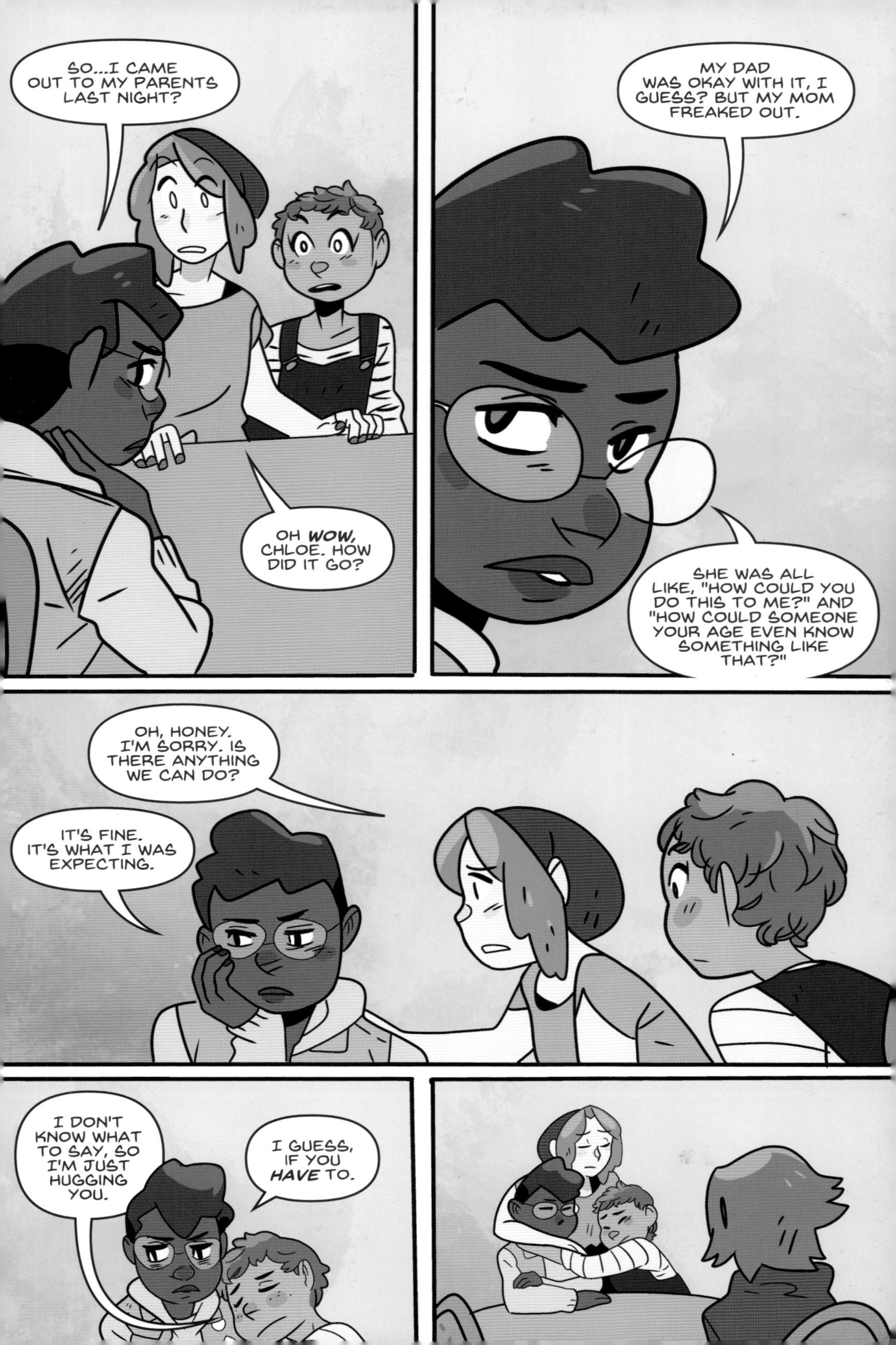
SO...I CAME OUT TO MY PARENTS LAST NIGHT?
OH *WOW*, CHLOE. HOW DID IT GO?
MY DAD WAS OKAY WITH IT, I GUESS? BUT MY MOM FREAKED OUT.
SHE WAS ALL LIKE, "HOW COULD YOU DO THIS TO ME?" AND "HOW COULD SOMEONE YOUR AGE EVEN KNOW SOMETHING LIKE THAT?"
OH, HONEY. I'M SORRY. IS THERE ANYTHING WE CAN DO?
IT'S FINE. IT'S WHAT I WAS EXPECTING.
I DON'T KNOW WHAT TO SAY, SO I'M JUST HUGGING YOU.
I GUESS, IF YOU *HAVE* TO.

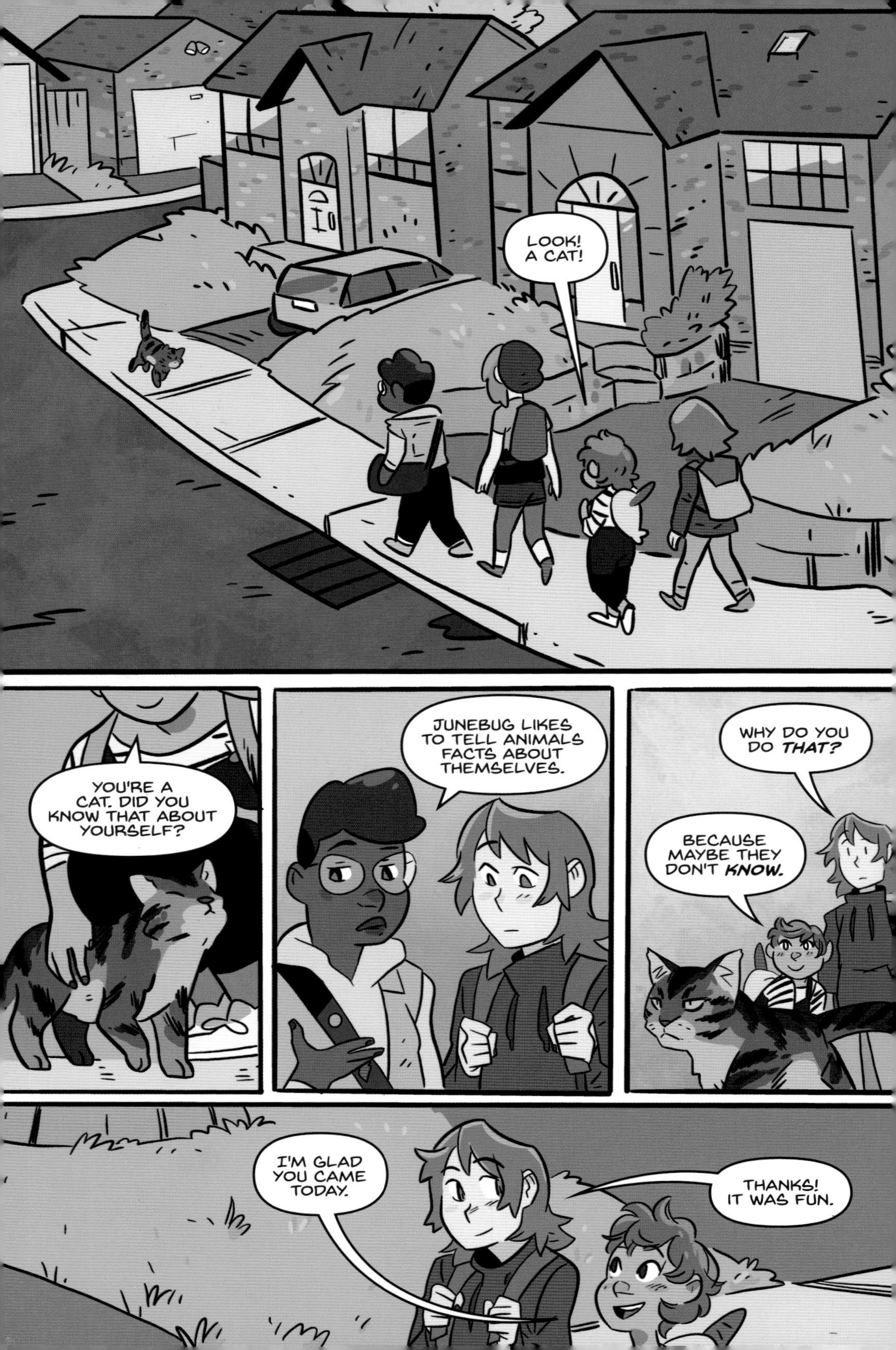
LOOK! A CAT!
YOU'RE A CAT. DID YOU KNOW THAT ABOUT YOURSELF?
JUNEBUG LIKES TO TELL ANIMALS FACTS ABOUT THEMSELVES.
WHY DO YOU DO *THAT?*
BECAUSE MAYBE THEY DON'T ***KNOW.***
I'M GLAD YOU CAME TODAY.
THANKS! IT WAS FUN.

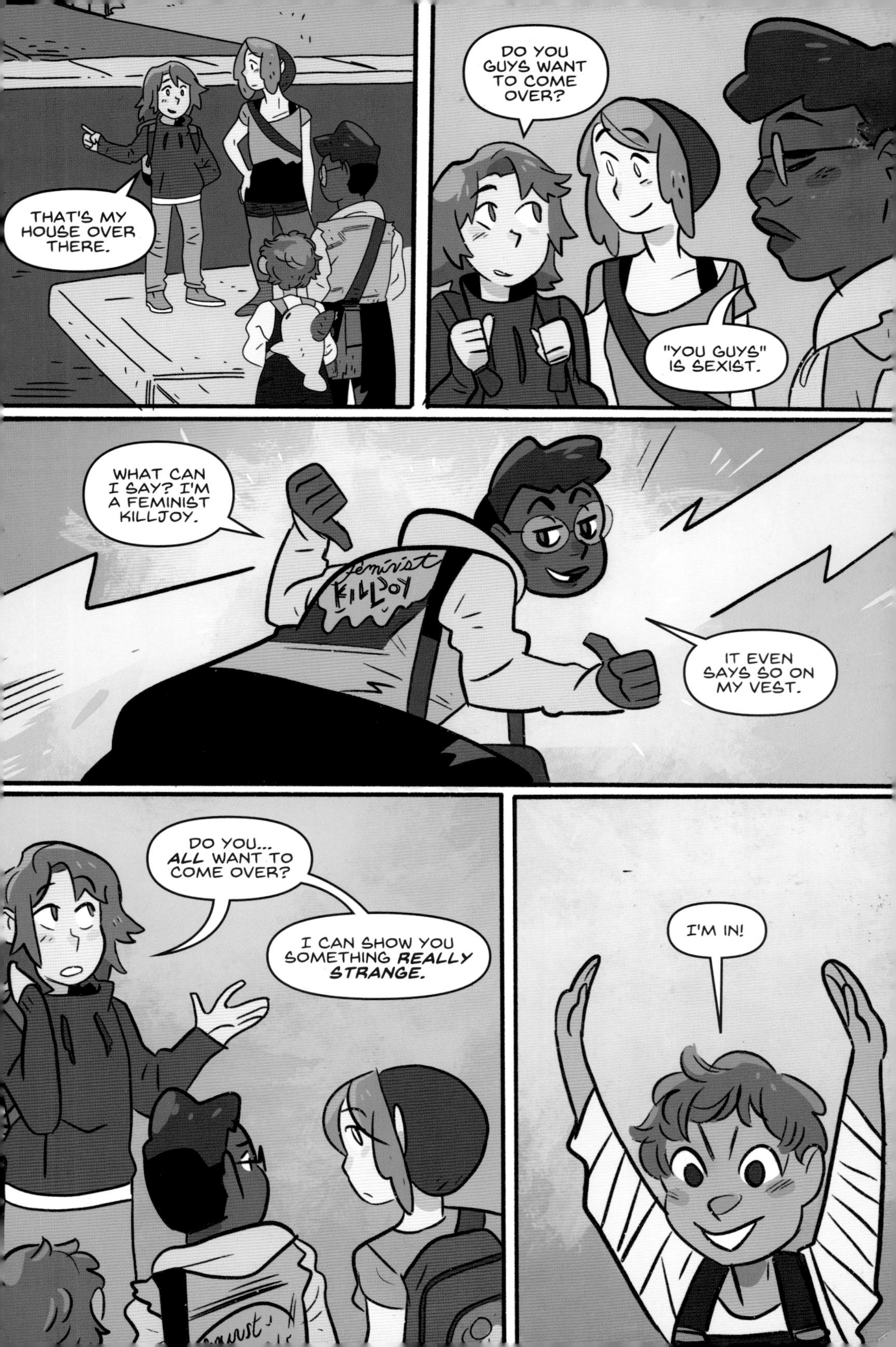
THAT'S MY HOUSE OVER THERE.
DO YOU GUYS WANT TO COME OVER?
"YOU GUYS" IS SEXIST.
WHAT CAN I SAY? I'M A FEMINIST KILLJOY.
feminist KILLJOY
IT EVEN SAYS SO ON MY VEST.
DO YOU... ALL WANT TO COME OVER?
I CAN SHOW YOU SOMETHING REALLY STRANGE.
I'M IN!

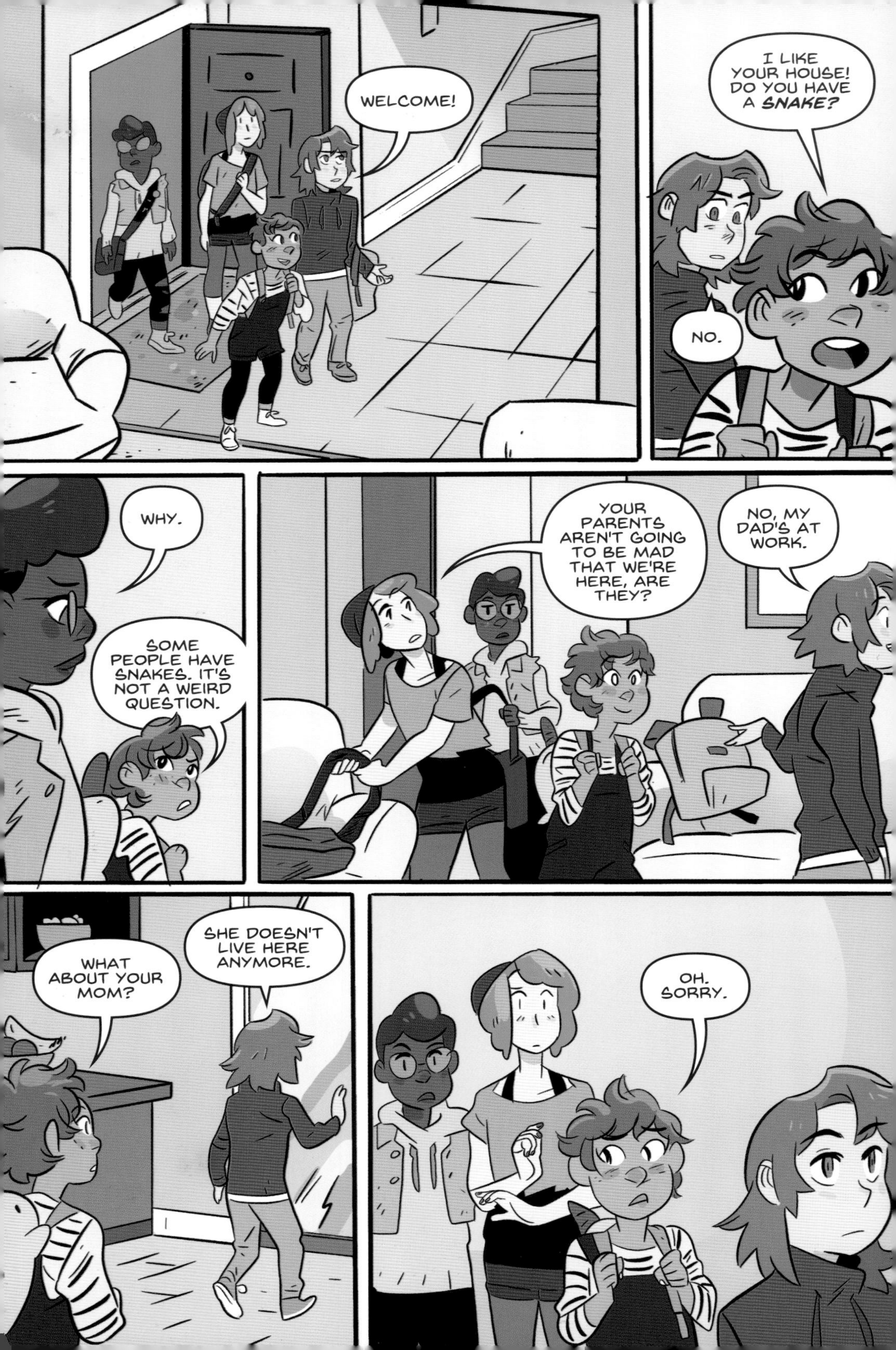
WELCOME!
I LIKE YOUR HOUSE! DO YOU HAVE A SNAKE?
NO.
WHY.
SOME PEOPLE HAVE SNAKES. IT'S NOT A WEIRD QUESTION.
YOUR PARENTS AREN'T GOING TO BE MAD THAT WE'RE HERE, ARE THEY?
NO, MY DAD'S AT WORK.
WHAT ABOUT YOUR MOM?
SHE DOESN'T LIVE HERE ANYMORE.
OH. SORRY.

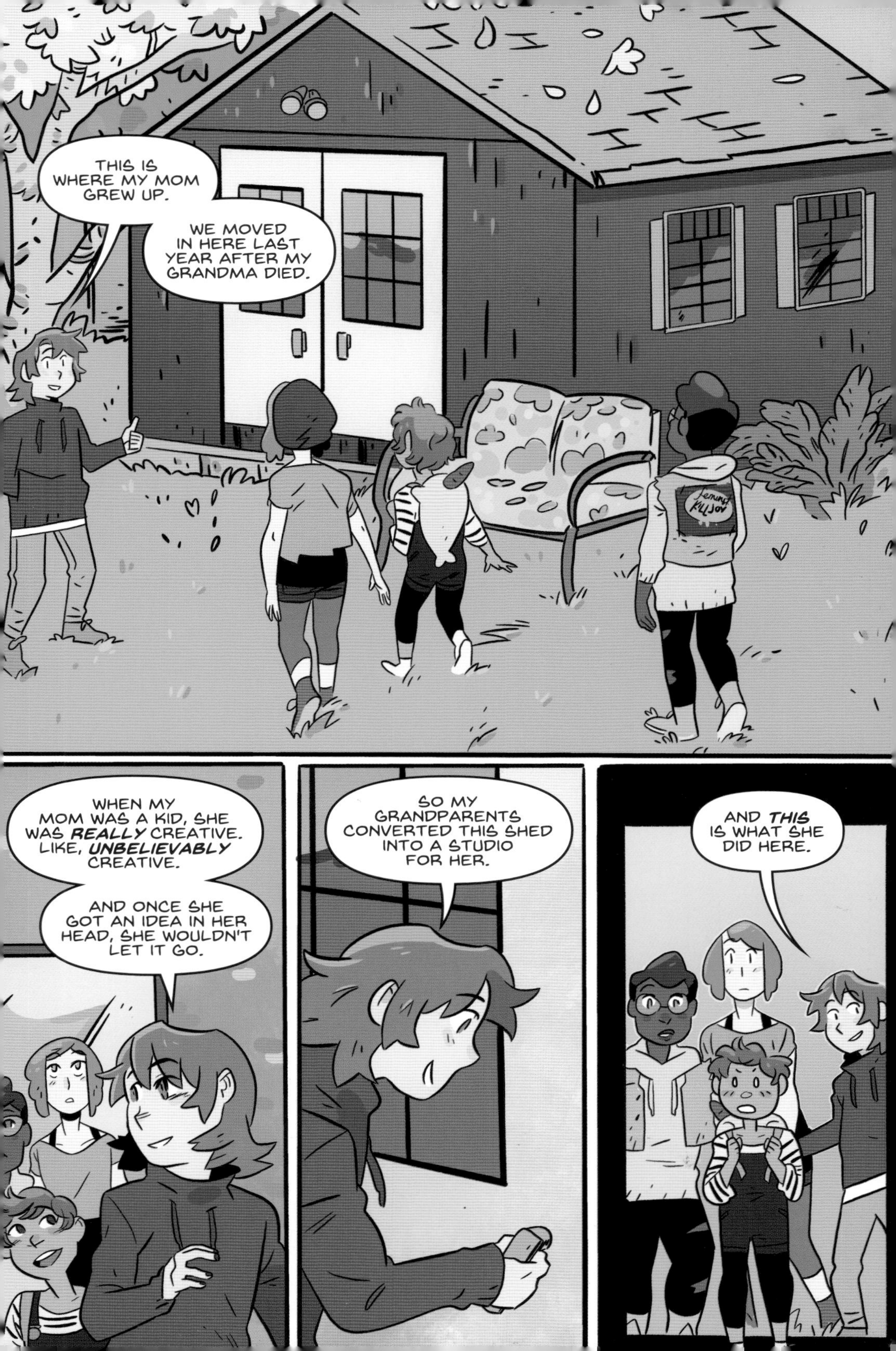
THIS IS WHERE MY MOM GREW UP.
WE MOVED IN HERE LAST YEAR AFTER MY GRANDMA DIED.
WHEN MY MOM WAS A KID, SHE WAS *REALLY* CREATIVE. LIKE, *UNBELIEVABLY* CREATIVE.
AND ONCE SHE GOT AN IDEA IN HER HEAD, SHE WOULDN'T LET IT GO.
SO MY GRANDPARENTS CONVERTED THIS SHED INTO A STUDIO FOR HER.
AND *THIS* IS WHAT SHE DID HERE.

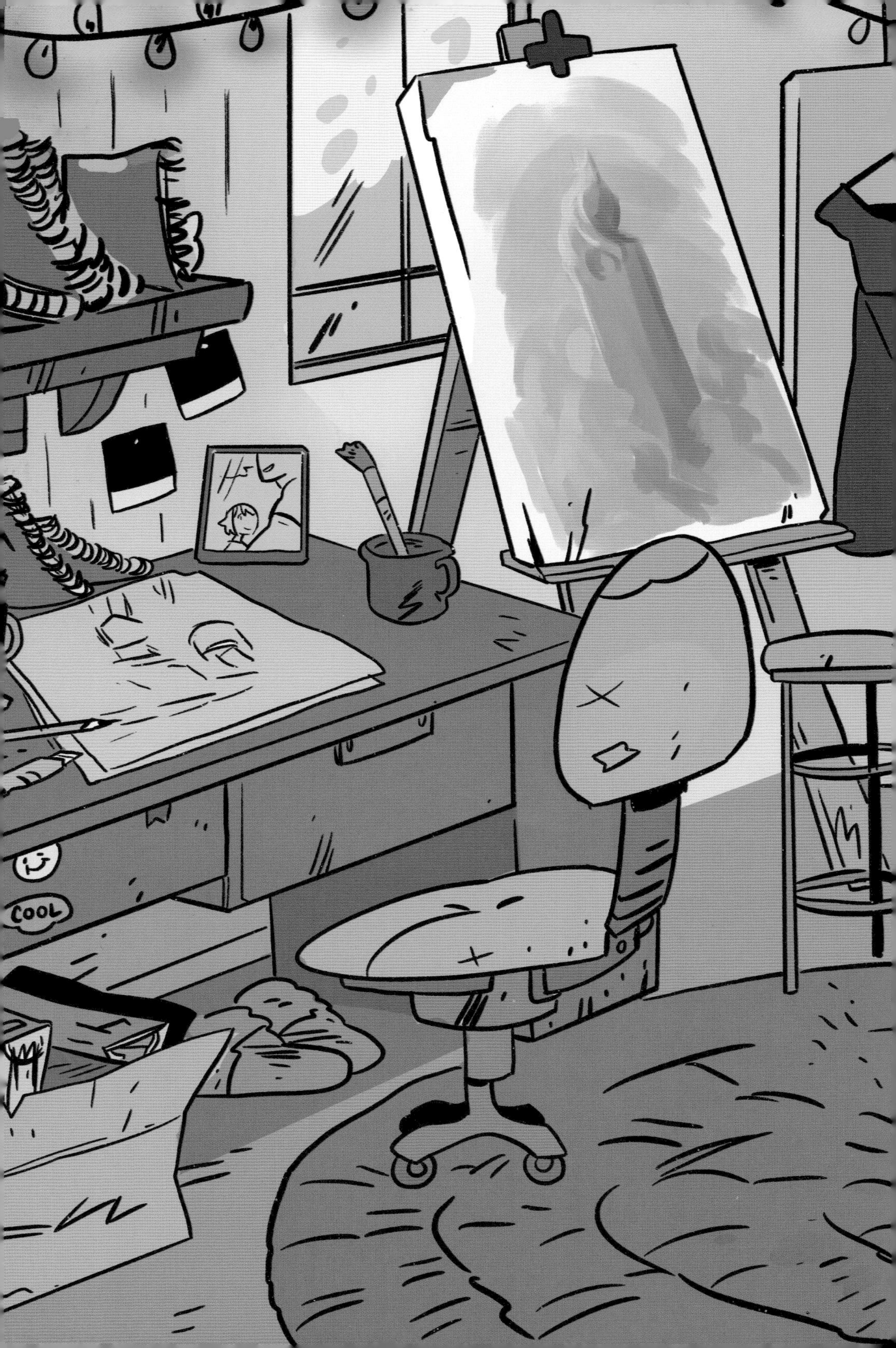
COOL

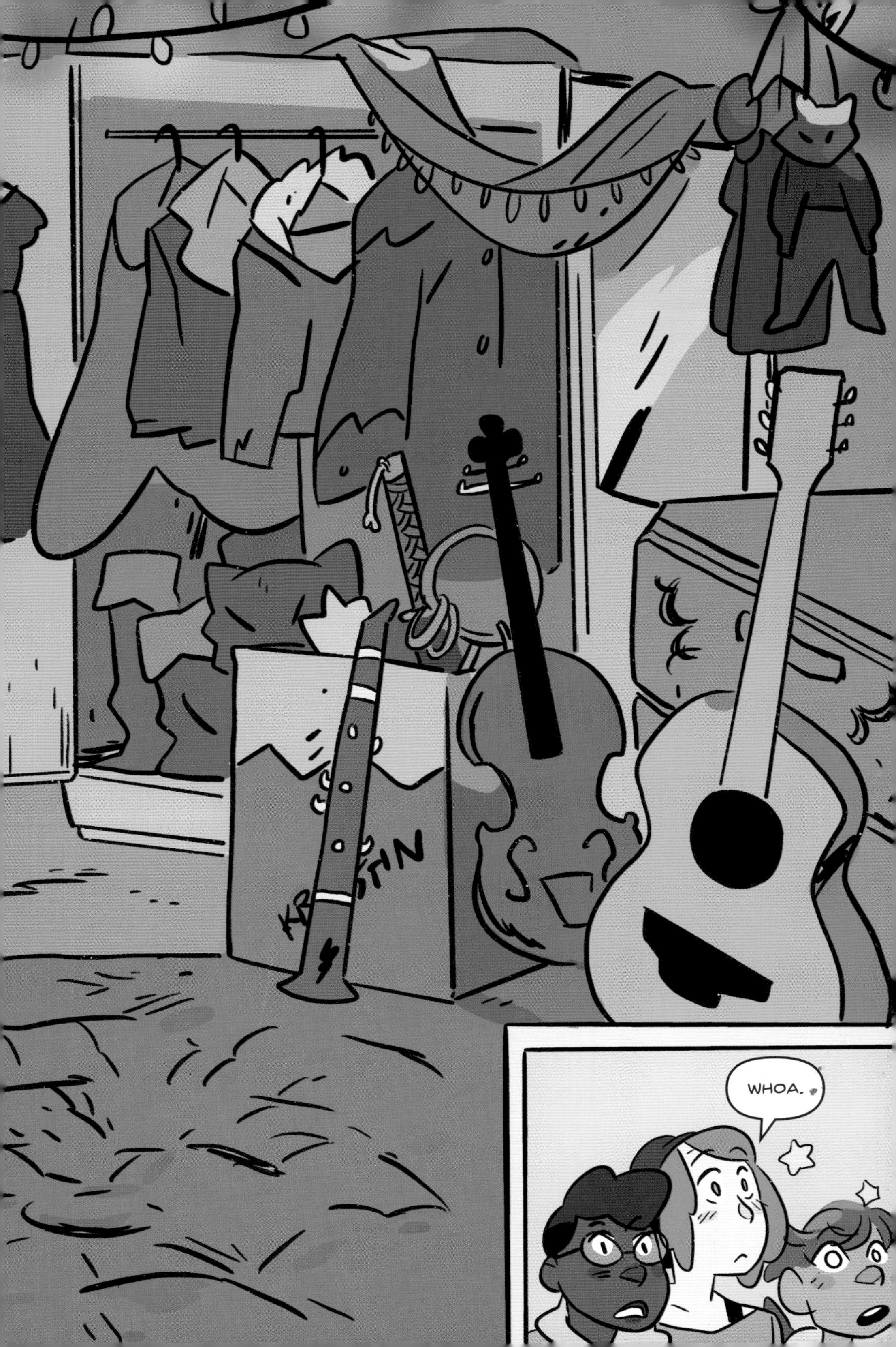
WHOA.

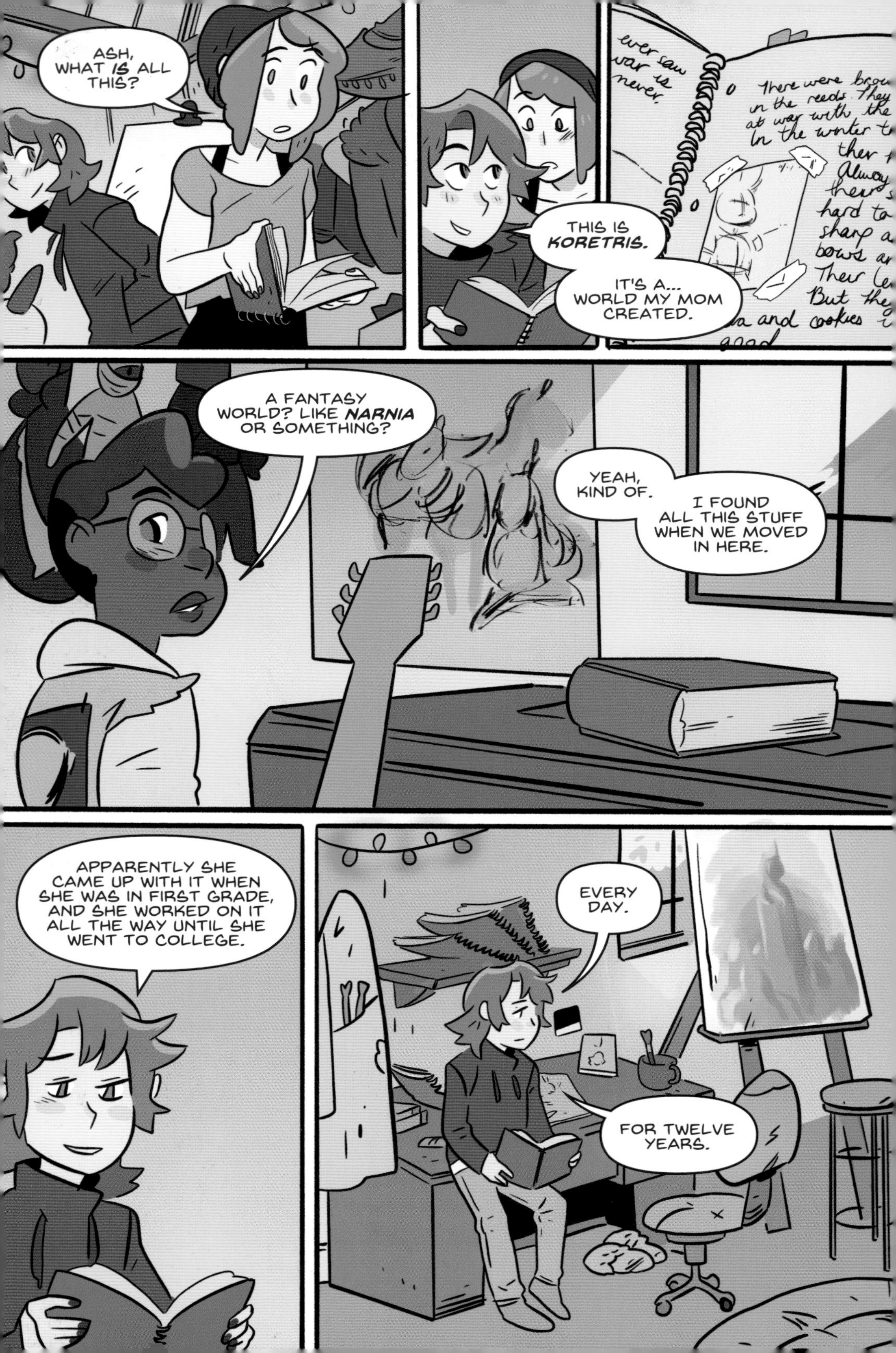
ASH, WHAT IS ALL THIS?
THIS IS KORETRIS.
IT'S A... WORLD MY MOM CREATED.
A FANTASY WORLD? LIKE NARNIA OR SOMETHING?
YEAH, KIND OF.
I FOUND ALL THIS STUFF WHEN WE MOVED IN HERE.
APPARENTLY SHE CAME UP WITH IT WHEN SHE WAS IN FIRST GRADE, AND SHE WORKED ON IT ALL THE WAY UNTIL SHE WENT TO COLLEGE.
EVERY DAY.
FOR TWELVE YEARS.

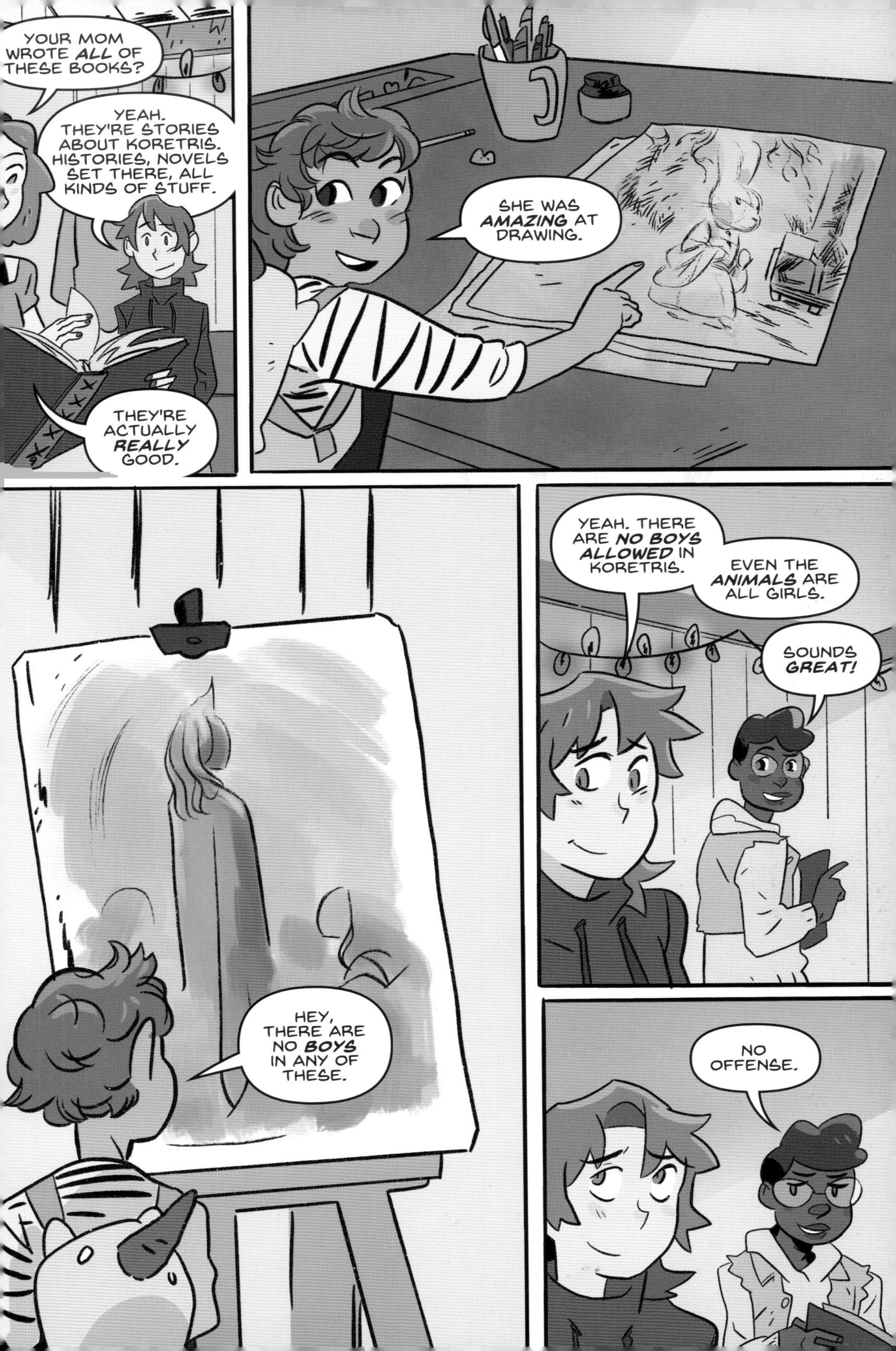
YOUR MOM WROTE ALL OF THESE BOOKS?
YEAH. THEY'RE STORIES ABOUT KORETRIS. HISTORIES, NOVELS SET THERE, ALL KINDS OF STUFF.
THEY'RE ACTUALLY REALLY GOOD.
SHE WAS AMAZING AT DRAWING.
HEY, THERE ARE NO BOYS IN ANY OF THESE.
YEAH. THERE ARE NO BOYS ALLOWED IN KORETRIS.
EVEN THE ANIMALS ARE ALL GIRLS.
SOUNDS GREAT!
NO OFFENSE.

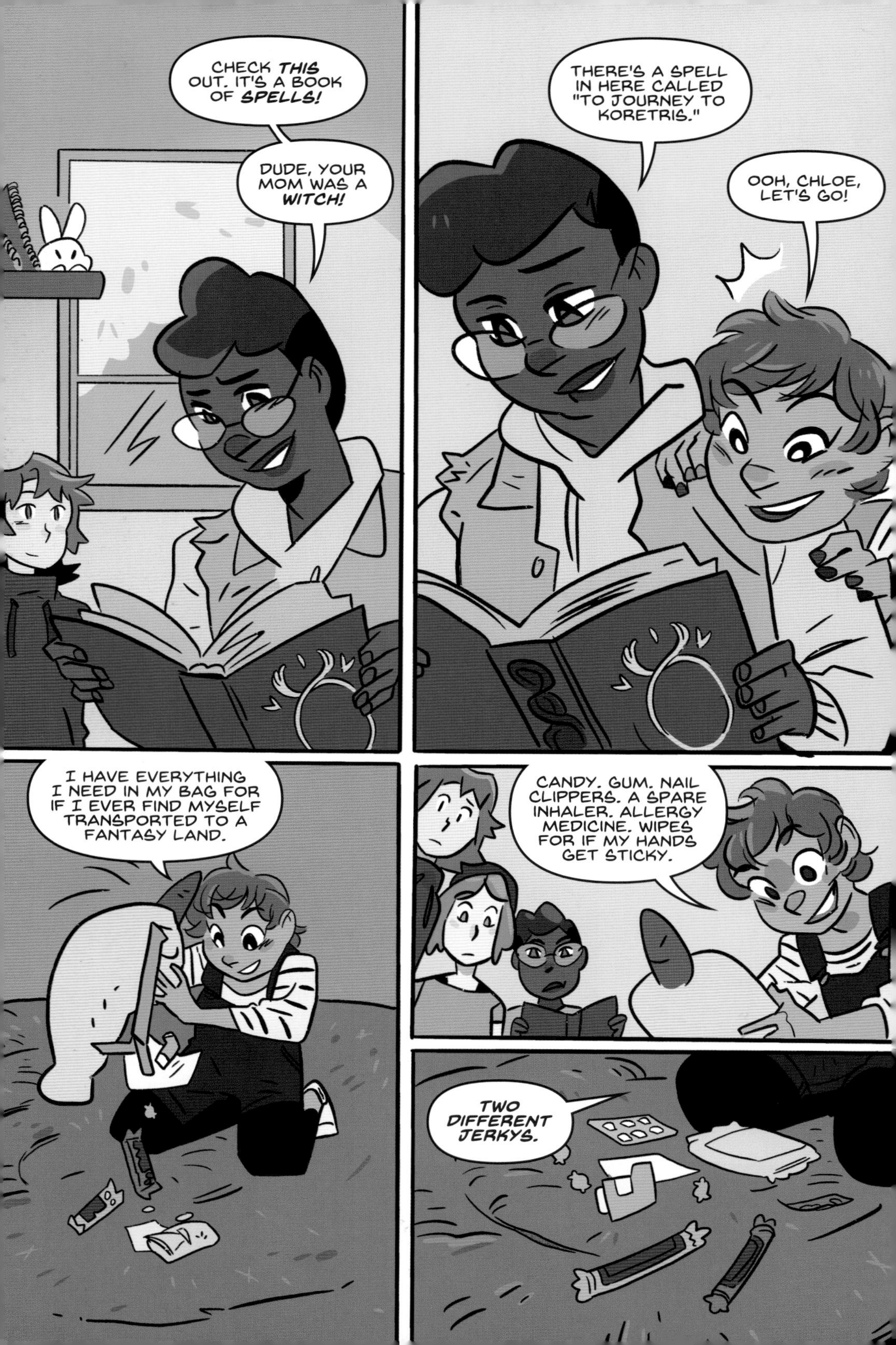
CHECK THIS OUT. IT'S A BOOK OF SPELLS!
DUDE, YOUR MOM WAS A WITCH!
THERE'S A SPELL IN HERE CALLED "TO JOURNEY TO KORETRIS."
OOH, CHLOE, LET'S GO!
I HAVE EVERYTHING I NEED IN MY BAG FOR IF I EVER FIND MYSELF TRANSPORTED TO A FANTASY LAND.
CANDY. GUM. NAIL CLIPPERS. A SPARE INHALER. ALLERGY MEDICINE. WIPES FOR IF MY HANDS GET STICKY.
TWO DIFFERENT JERKYS.

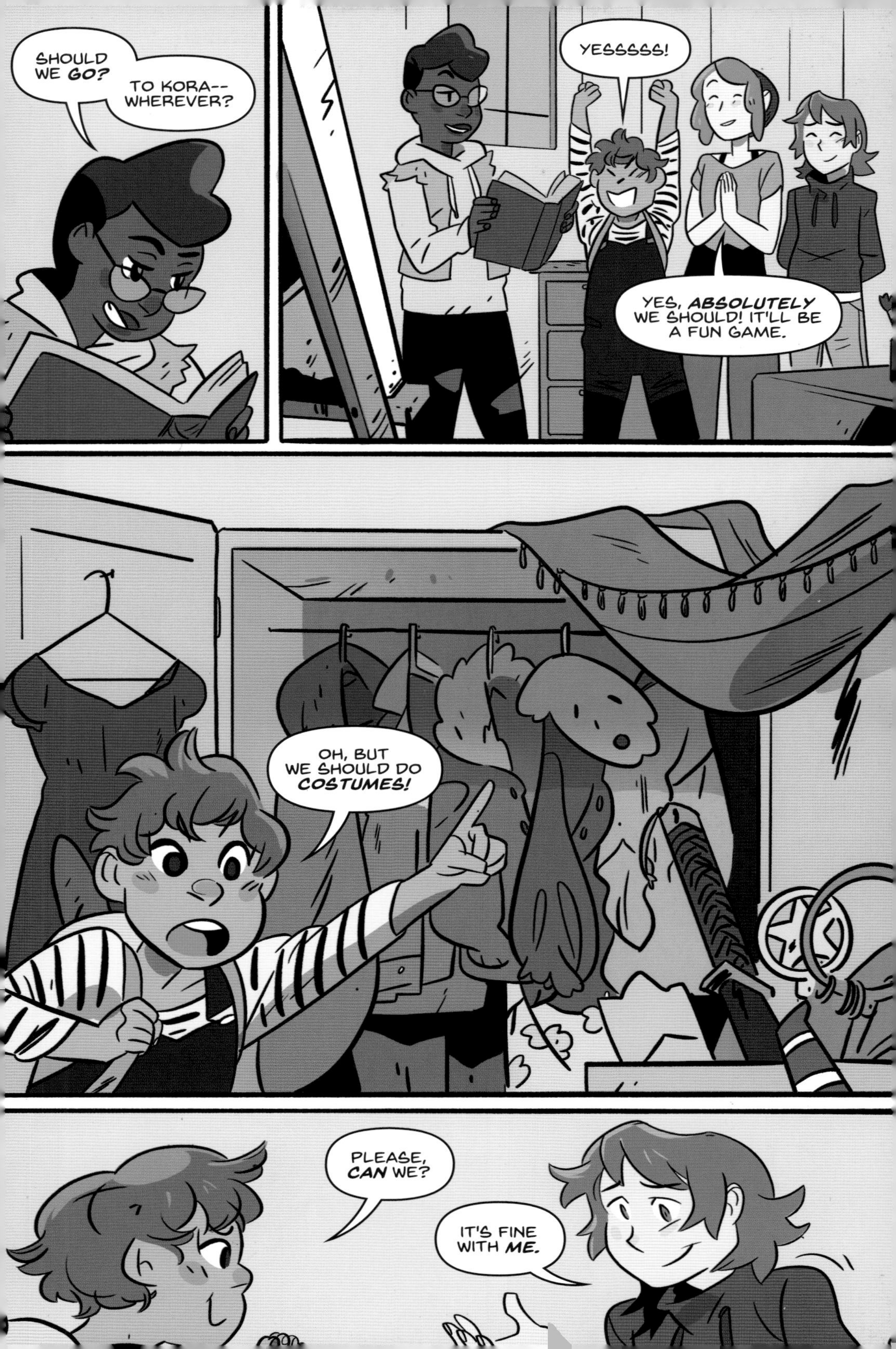
SHOULD WE GO?
TO KORA-- WHEREVER?
YESSSSSS!
YES, ABSOLUTELY WE SHOULD! IT'LL BE A FUN GAME.
OH, BUT WE SHOULD DO COSTUMES!
PLEASE, CAN WE?
IT'S FINE WITH ME.

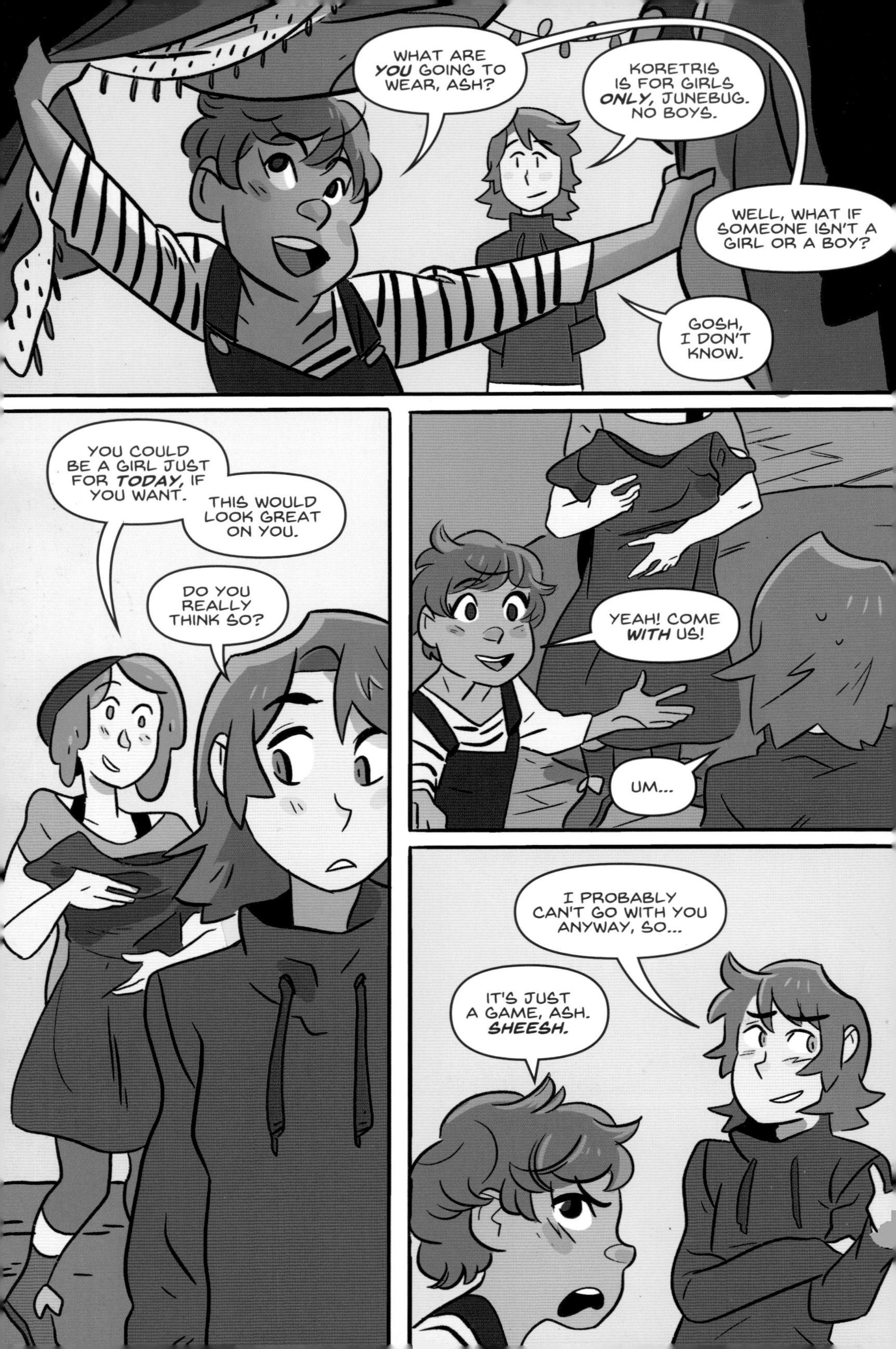
WHAT ARE *YOU* GOING TO WEAR, ASH?
KORETRIS IS FOR GIRLS *ONLY,* JUNEBUG. NO BOYS.
WELL, WHAT IF SOMEONE ISN'T A GIRL OR A BOY?
GOSH, I DON'T KNOW.
YOU COULD BE A GIRL JUST FOR *TODAY,* IF YOU WANT.
THIS WOULD LOOK GREAT ON YOU.
DO YOU REALLY THINK SO?
YEAH! COME *WITH* US!
UM...
I PROBABLY CAN'T GO WITH YOU ANYWAY, SO...
IT'S JUST A GAME, ASH. *SHEESH.*

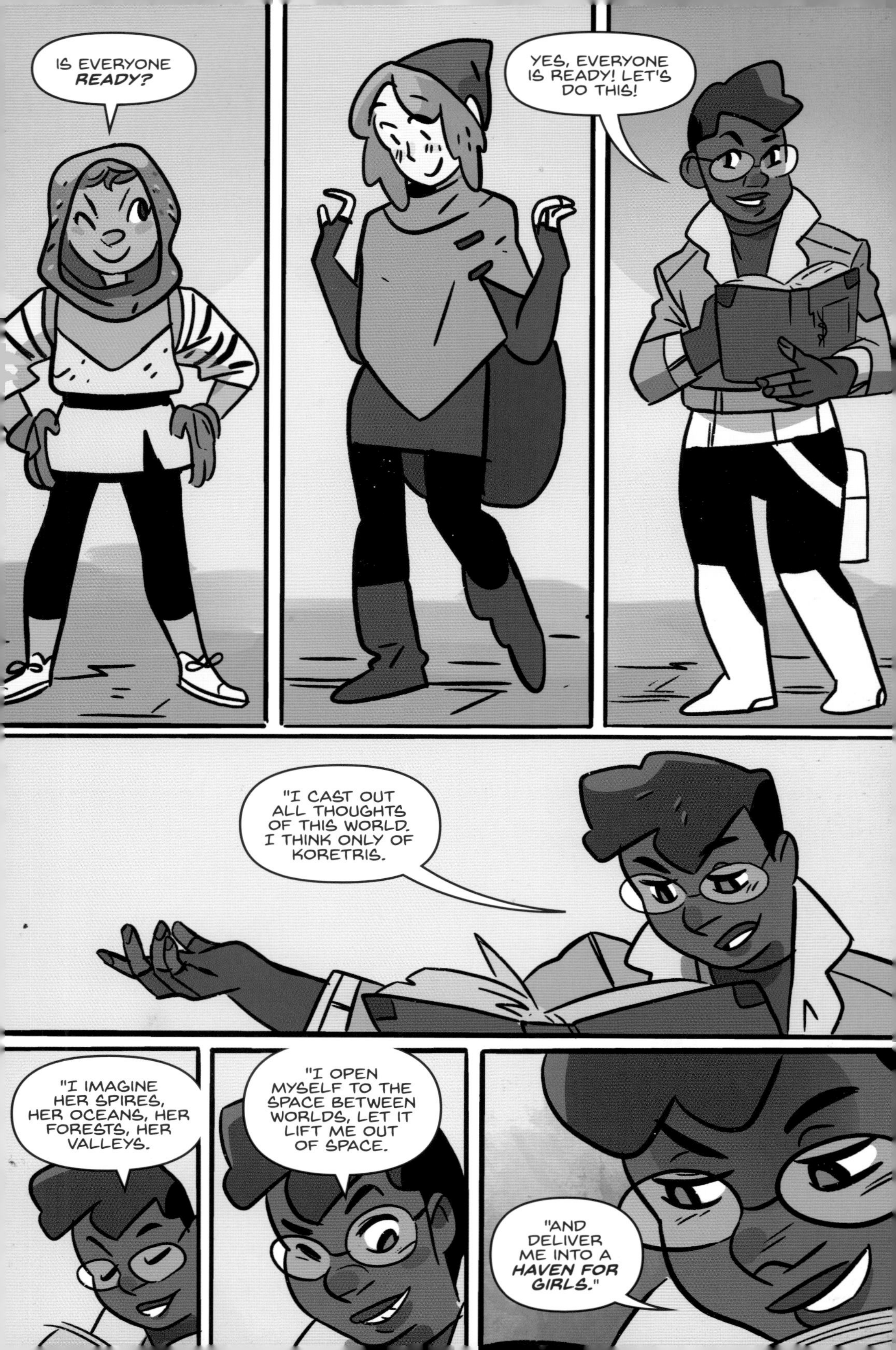
IS EVERYONE *READY?*
YES, EVERYONE IS READY! LET'S DO THIS!
"I CAST OUT ALL THOUGHTS OF THIS WORLD. I THINK ONLY OF KORETRIS.
"I IMAGINE HER SPIRES, HER OCEANS, HER FORESTS, HER VALLEYS.
"I OPEN MYSELF TO THE SPACE BETWEEN WORLDS, LET IT LIFT ME OUT OF SPACE.
"AND DELIVER ME INTO A *HAVEN FOR GIRLS.*"

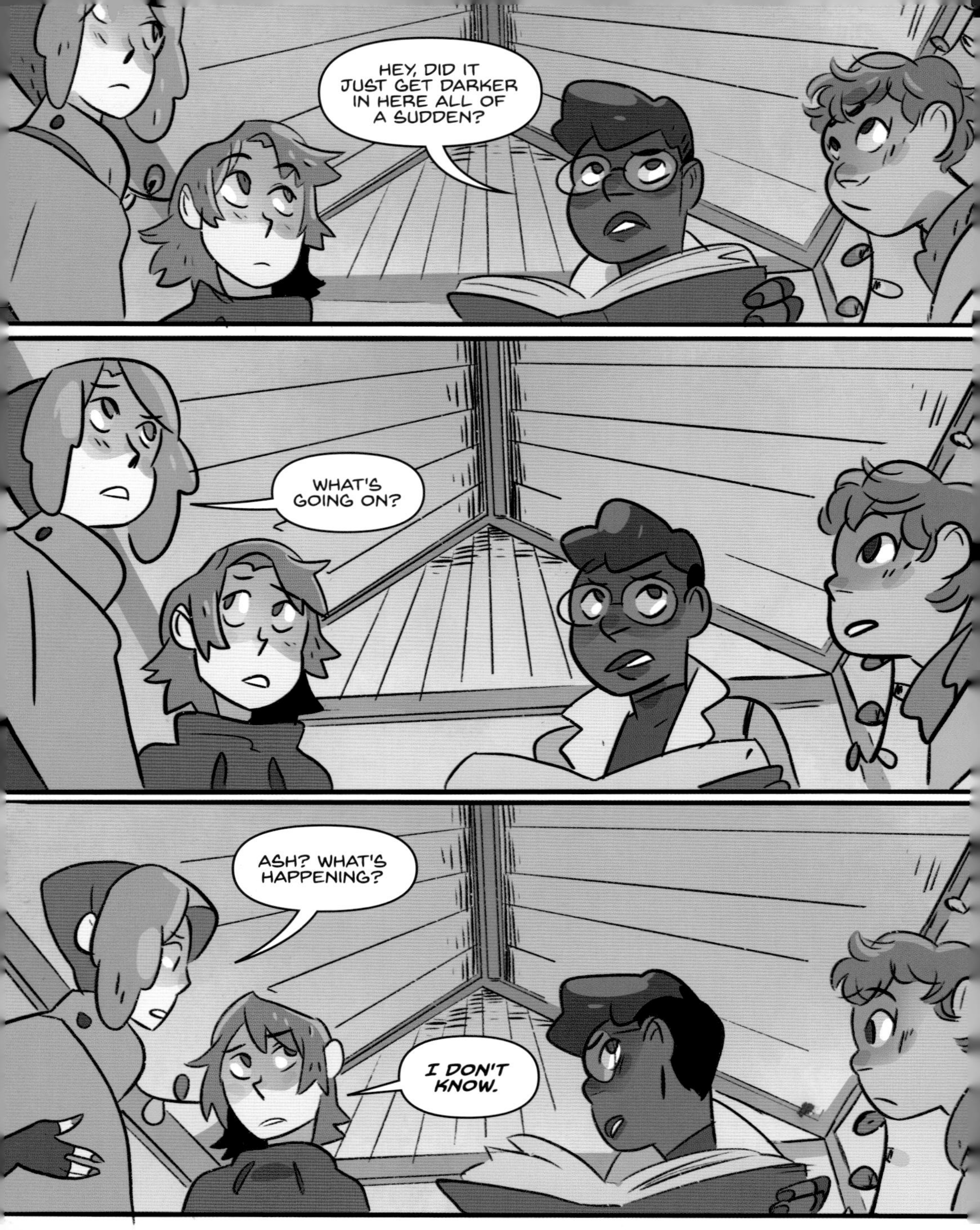
HEY, DID IT JUST GET DARKER IN HERE ALL OF A SUDDEN?
WHAT'S GOING ON?
ASH? WHAT'S HAPPENING?
I DON'T KNOW.

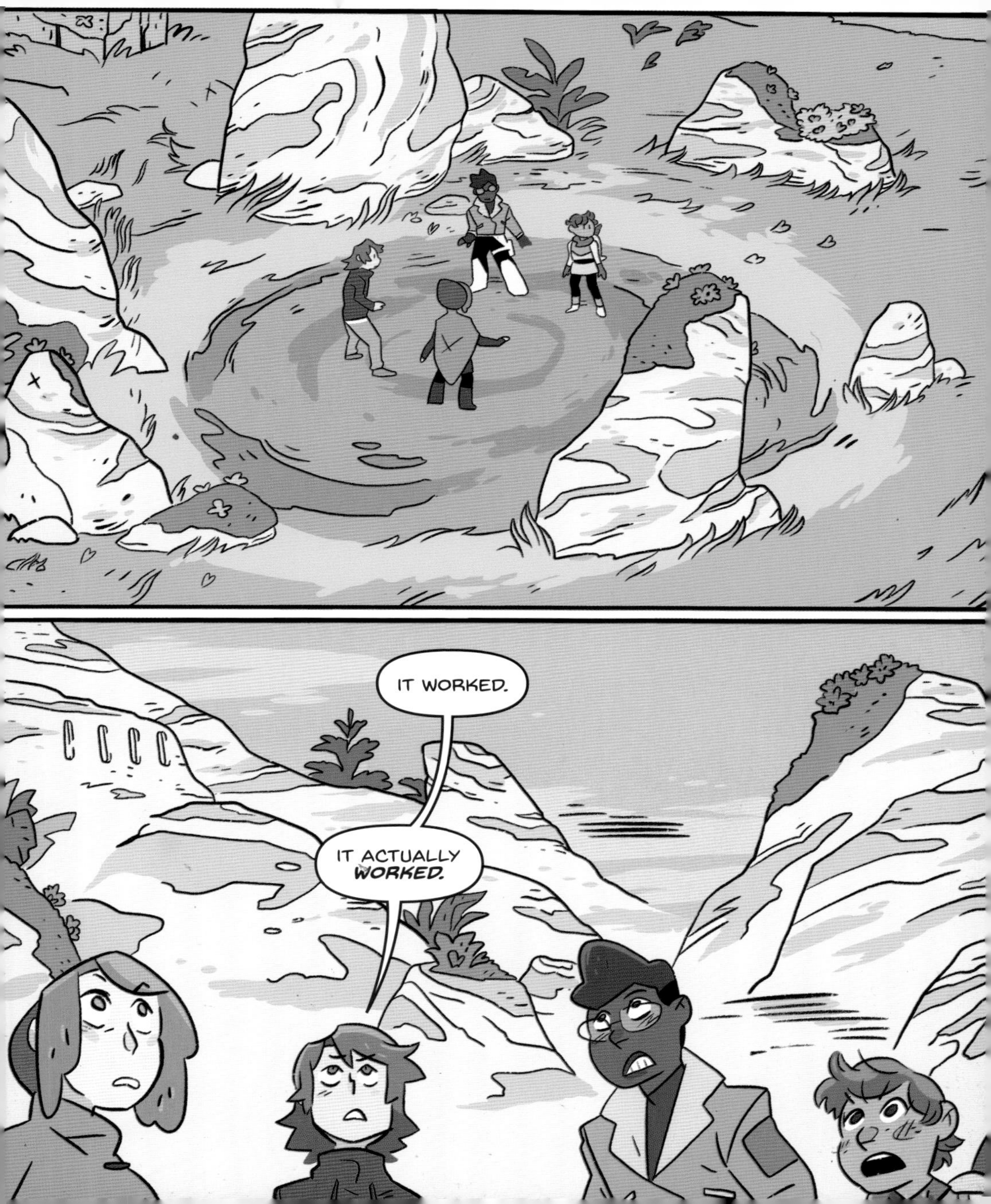
IT WORKED.
IT ACTUALLY WORKED.

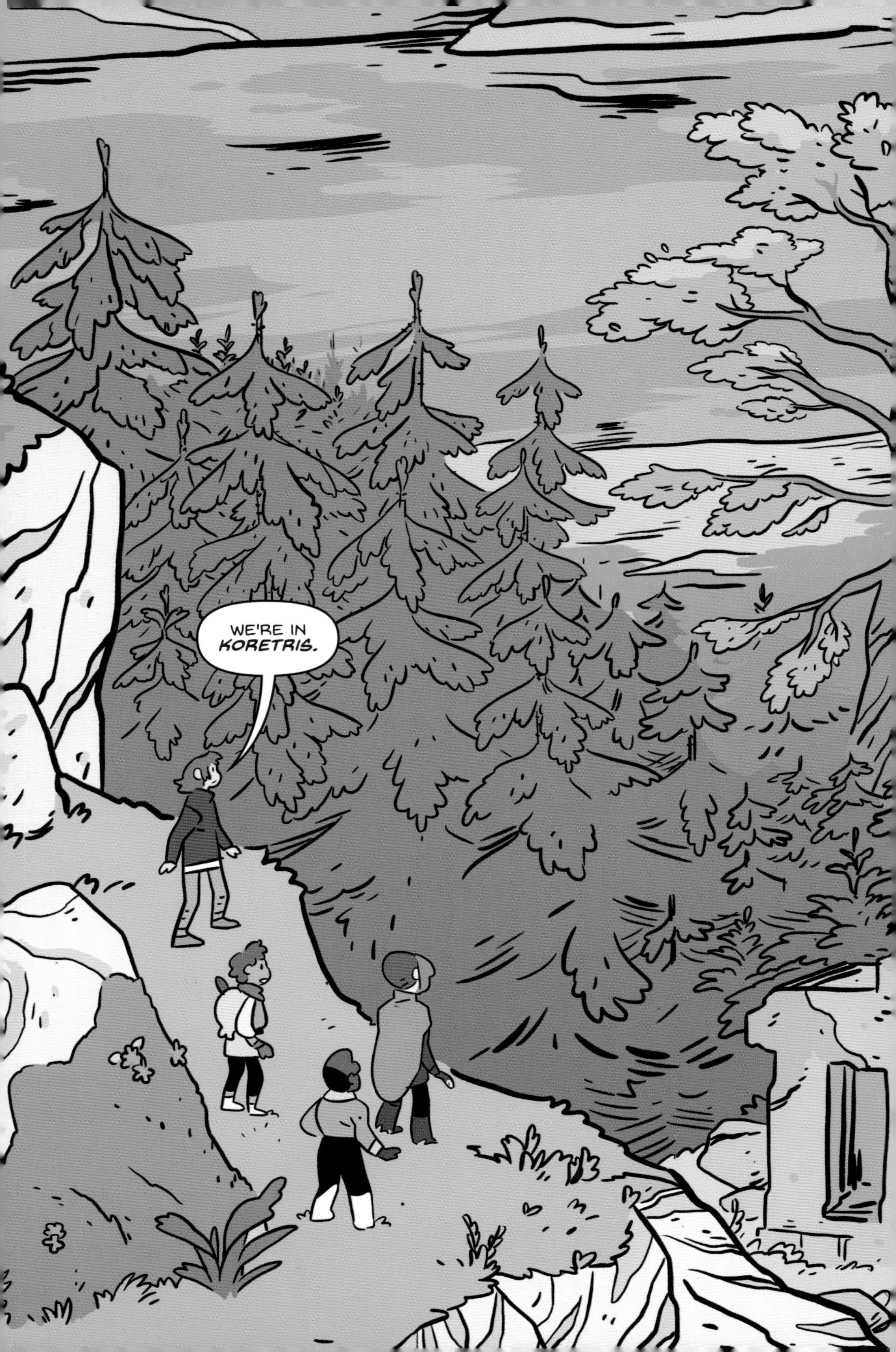
WE'RE IN KORETRIS.

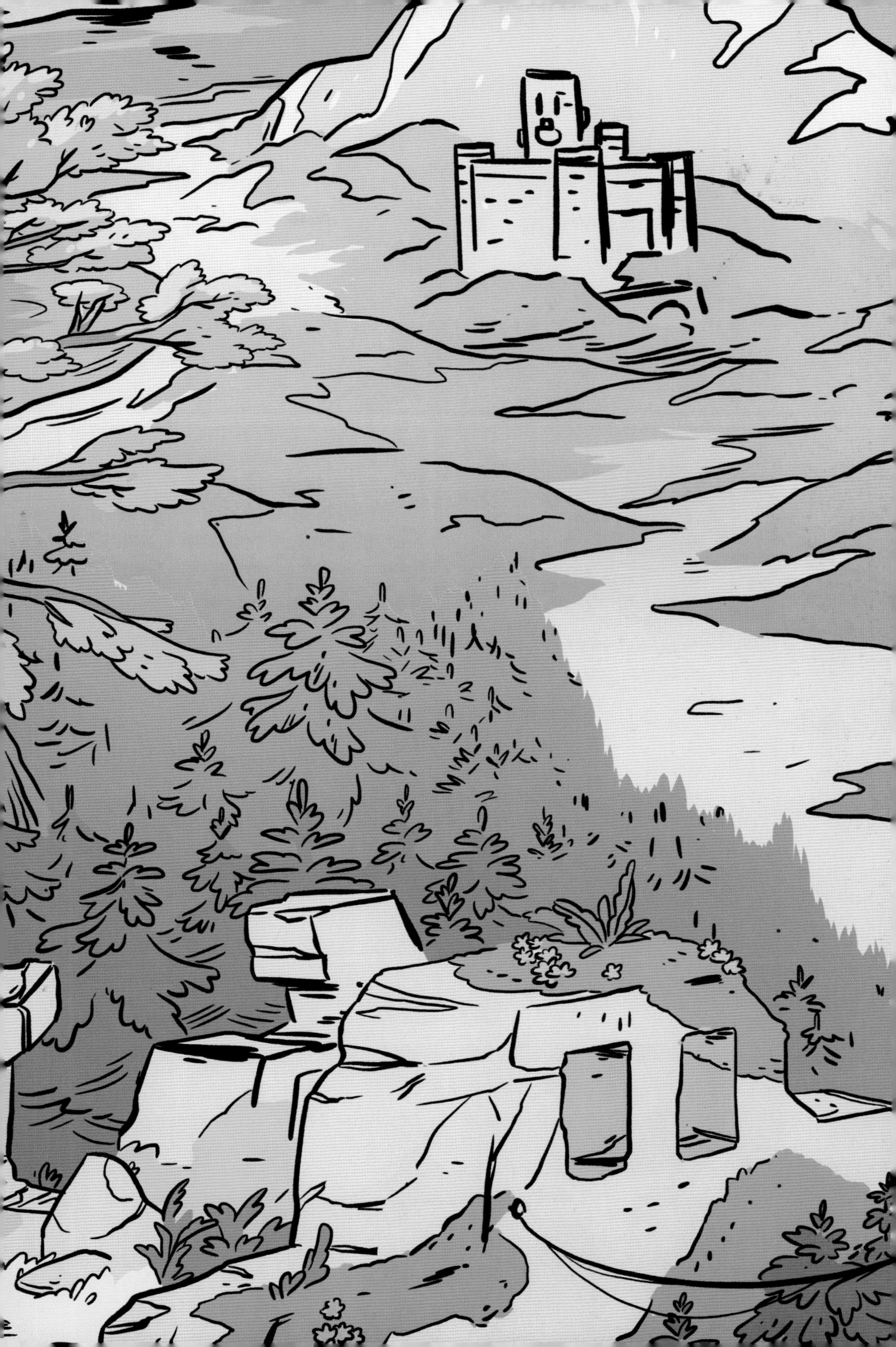

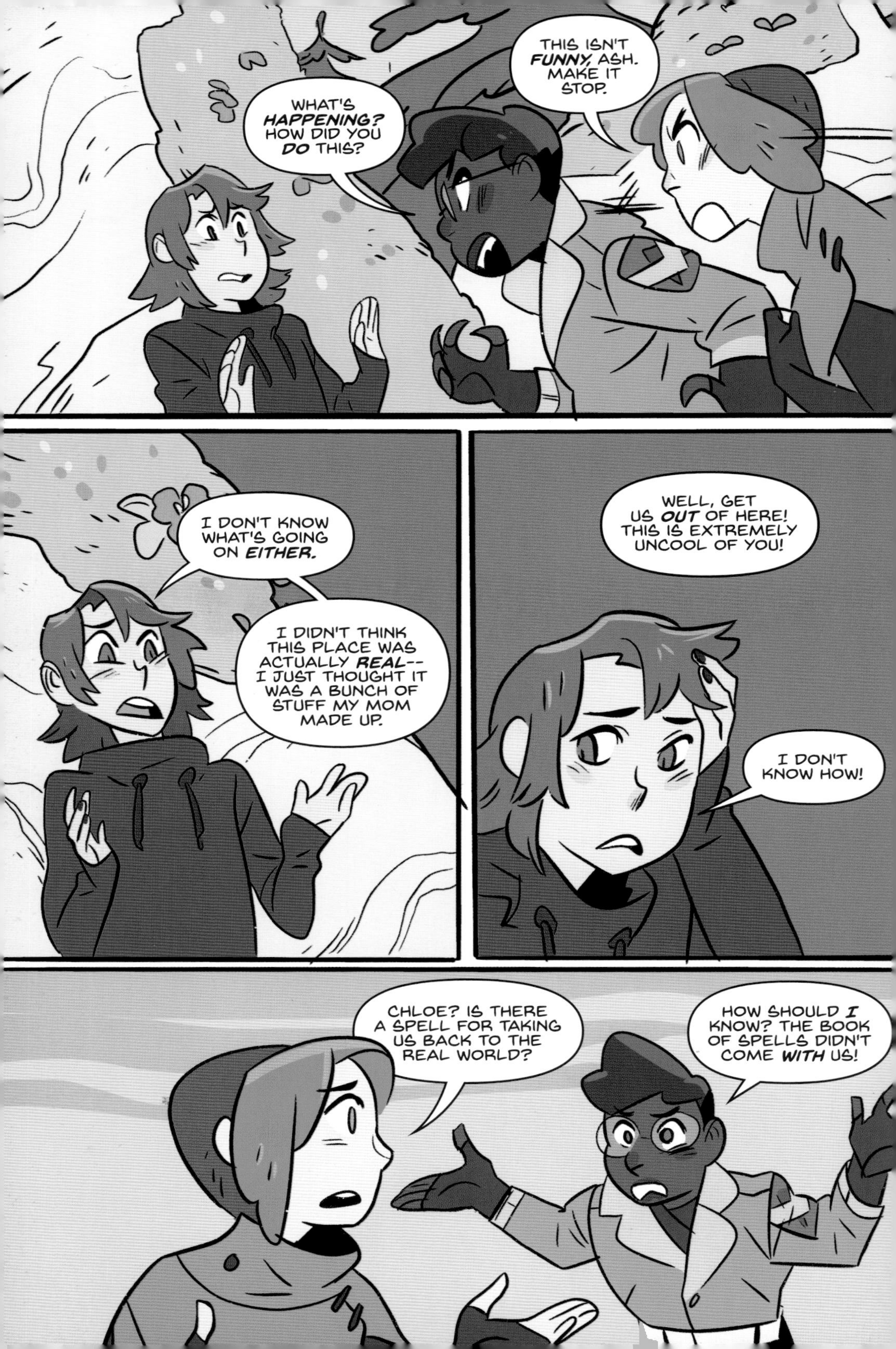
WHAT'S HAPPENING? HOW DID YOU DO THIS?
THIS ISN'T FUNNY, ASH. MAKE IT STOP.
I DON'T KNOW WHAT'S GOING ON EITHER.
I DIDN'T THINK THIS PLACE WAS ACTUALLY REAL-- I JUST THOUGHT IT WAS A BUNCH OF STUFF MY MOM MADE UP.
WELL, GET US OUT OF HERE! THIS IS EXTREMELY UNCOOL OF YOU!
I DON'T KNOW HOW!
CHLOE? IS THERE A SPELL FOR TAKING US BACK TO THE REAL WORLD?
HOW SHOULD I KNOW? THE BOOK OF SPELLS DIDN'T COME WITH US!

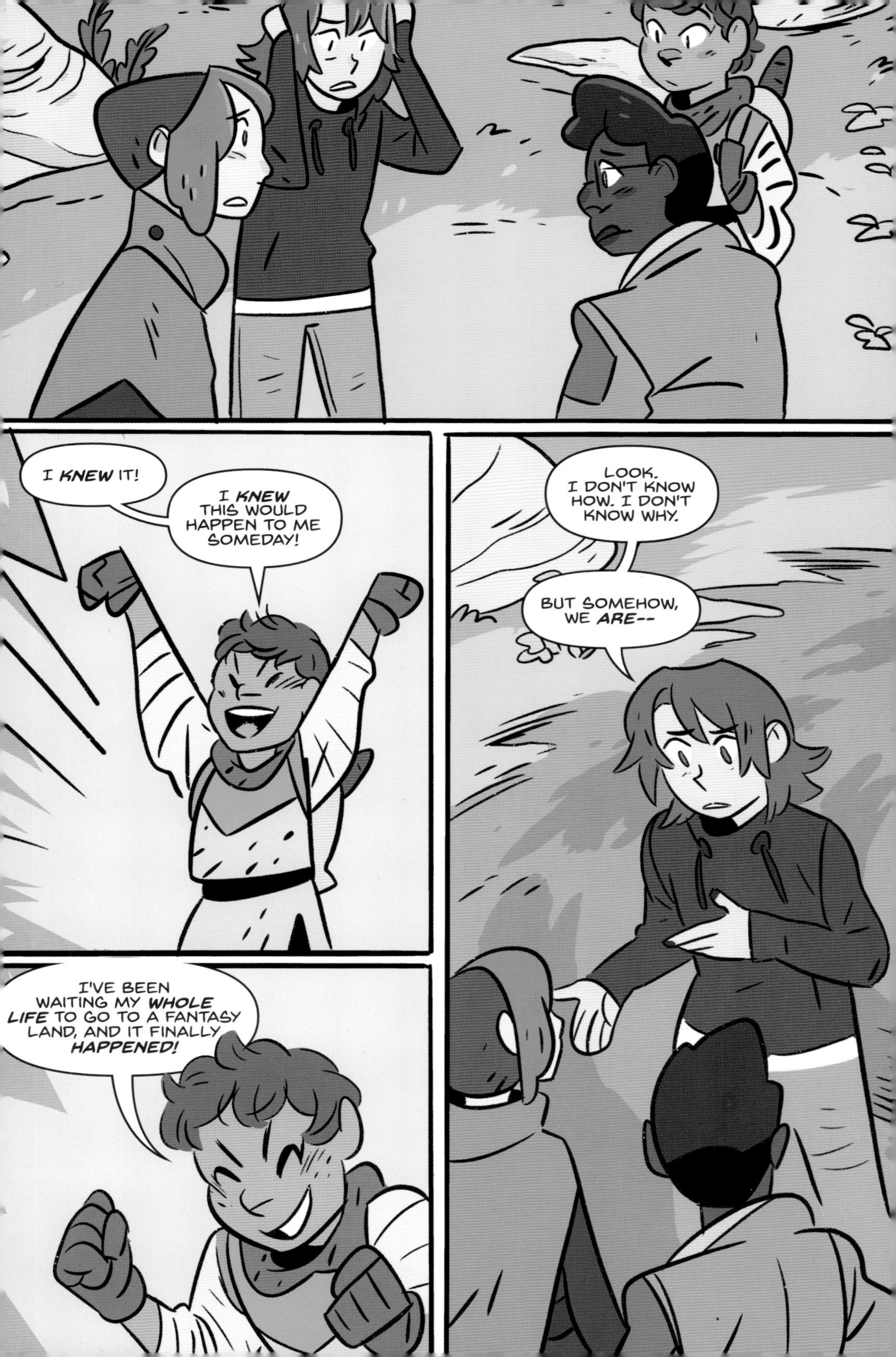
I KNEW IT!
I KNEW THIS WOULD HAPPEN TO ME SOMEDAY!
I'VE BEEN WAITING MY WHOLE LIFE TO GO TO A FANTASY LAND, AND IT FINALLY HAPPENED!
LOOK. I DON'T KNOW HOW. I DON'T KNOW WHY.
BUT SOMEHOW, WE ARE--

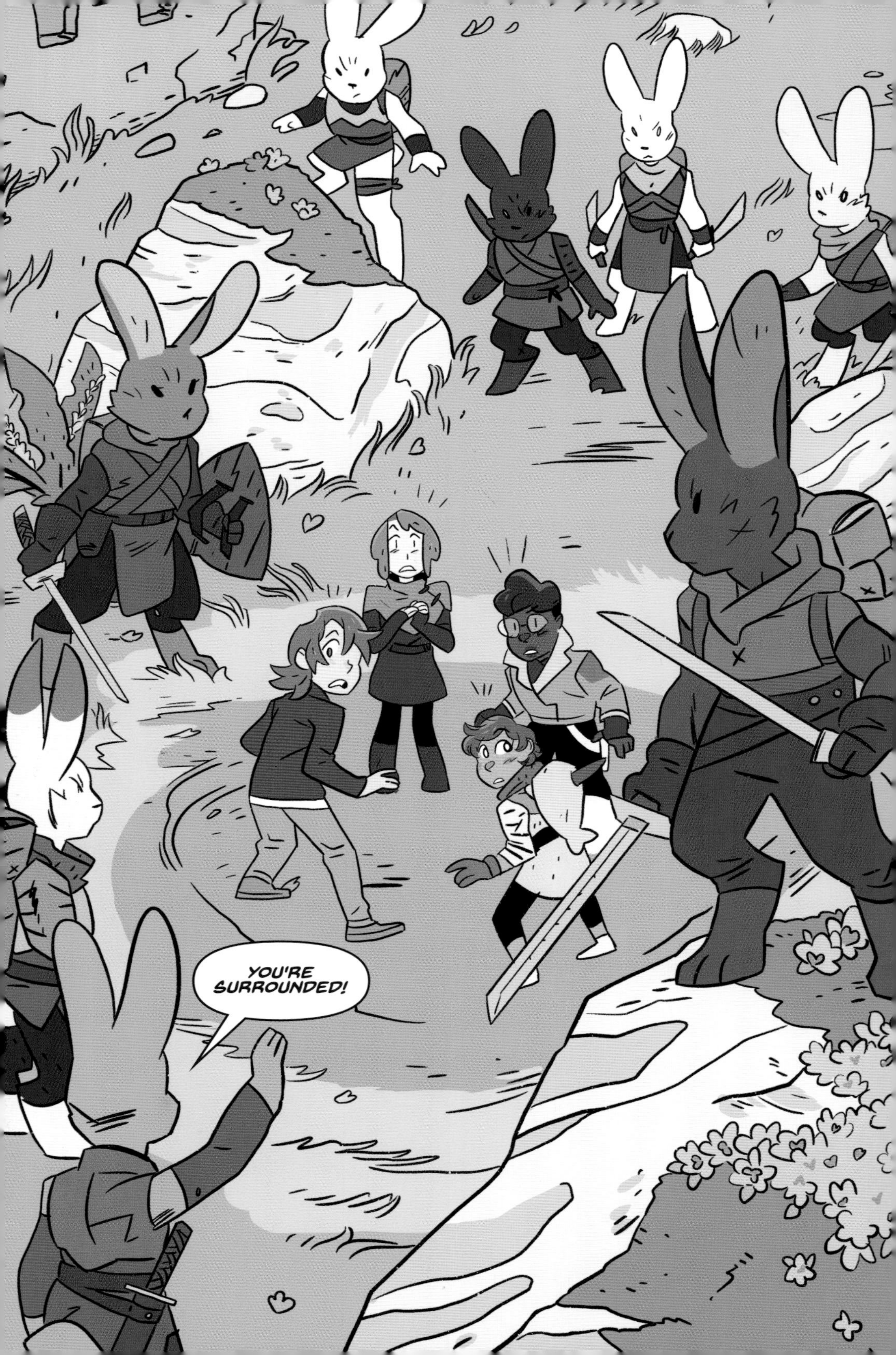
YOU'RE SURROUNDED!

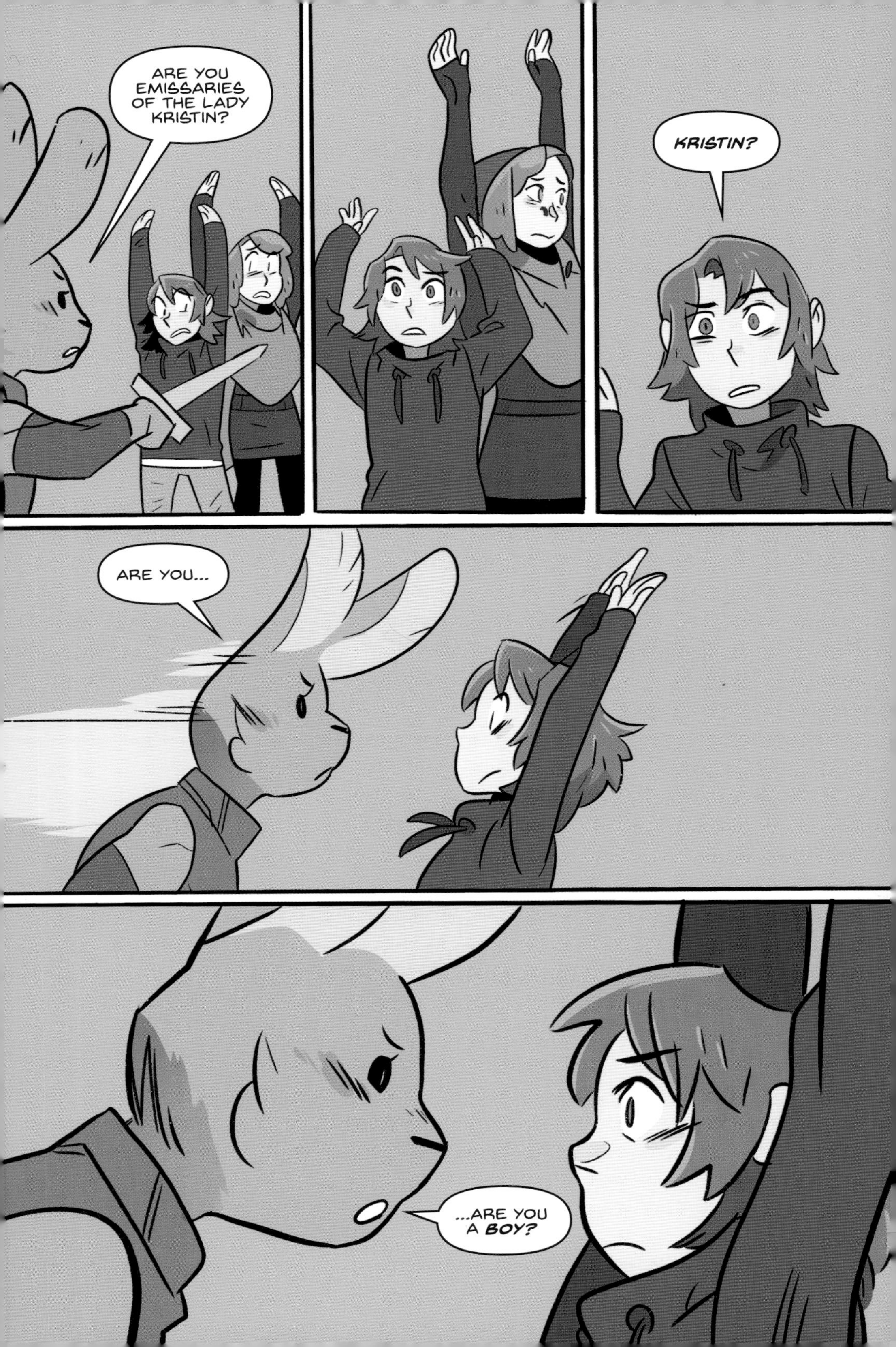
ARE YOU EMISSARIES OF THE LADY KRISTIN?
KRISTIN?
ARE YOU...
...ARE YOU A BOY?

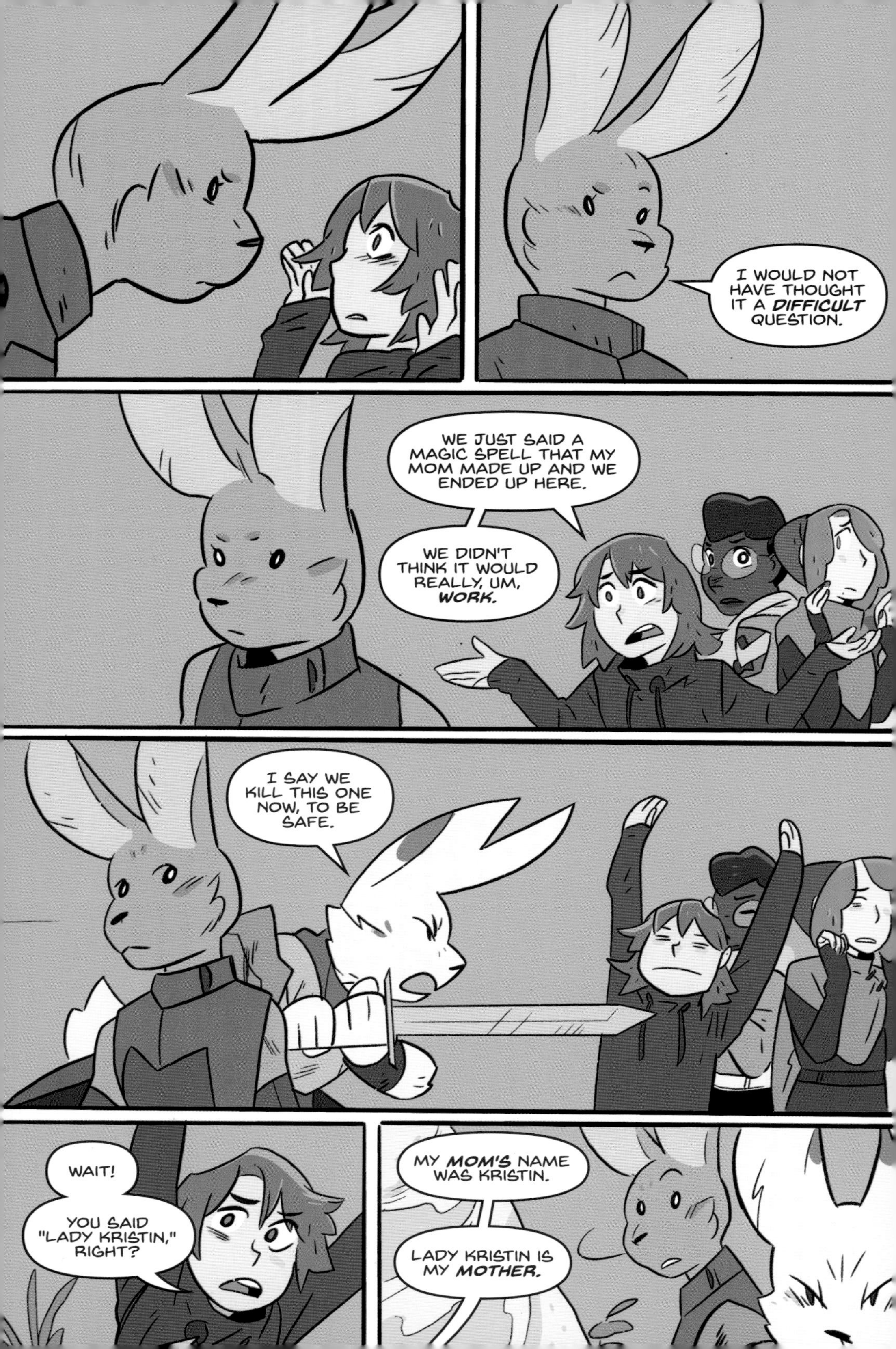
I WOULD NOT HAVE THOUGHT IT A DIFFICULT QUESTION.
WE JUST SAID A MAGIC SPELL THAT MY MOM MADE UP AND WE ENDED UP HERE.
WE DIDN'T THINK IT WOULD REALLY, UM, WORK.
I SAY WE KILL THIS ONE NOW, TO BE SAFE.
WAIT!
YOU SAID "LADY KRISTIN," RIGHT?
MY MOM'S NAME WAS KRISTIN.
LADY KRISTIN IS MY MOTHER.

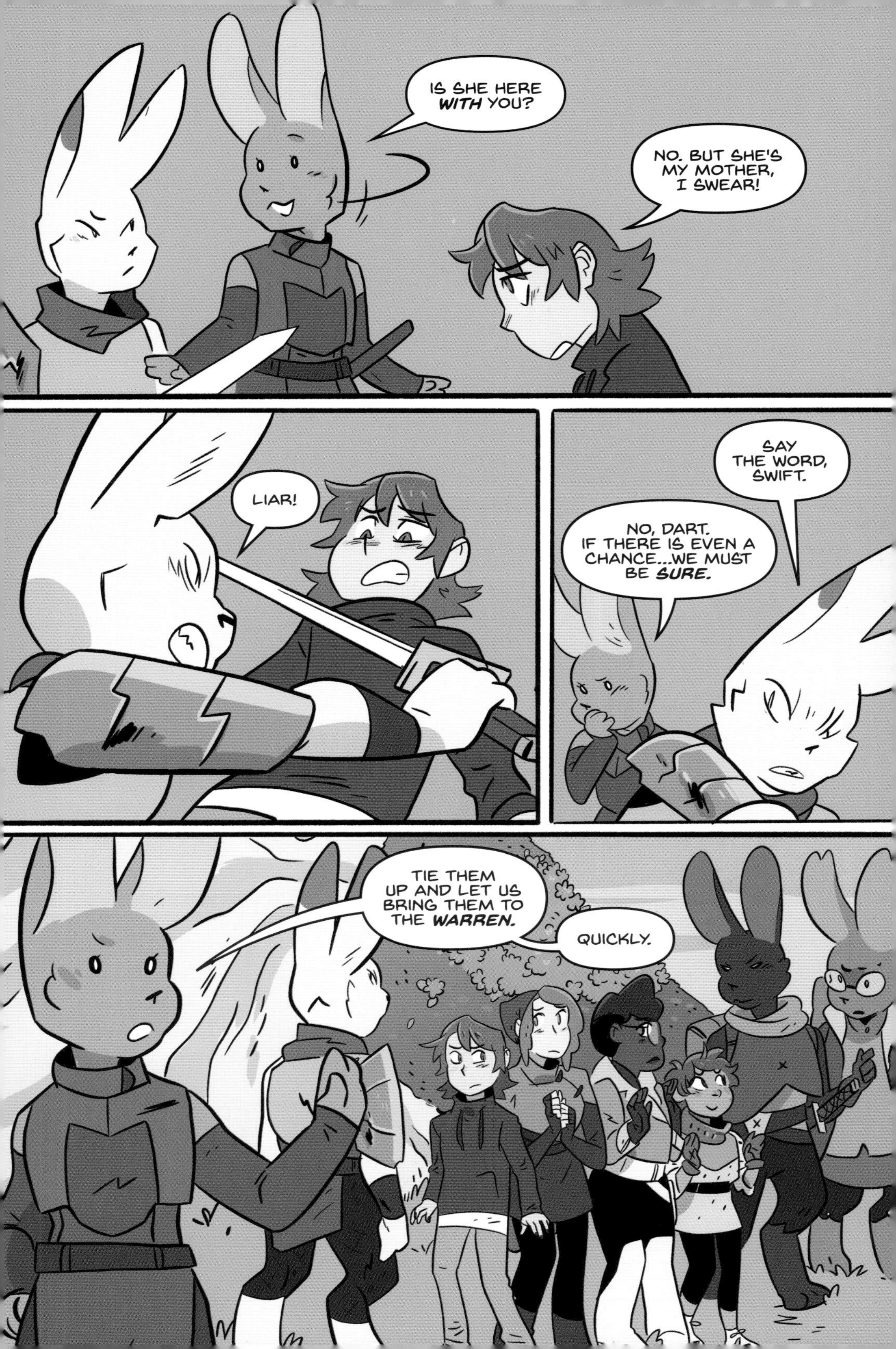
IS SHE HERE *WITH* YOU?
NO. BUT SHE'S MY MOTHER, I SWEAR!
LIAR!
SAY THE WORD, SWIFT.
NO, DART. IF THERE IS EVEN A CHANCE...WE MUST BE *SURE.*
TIE THEM UP AND LET US BRING THEM TO THE *WARREN.*
QUICKLY.

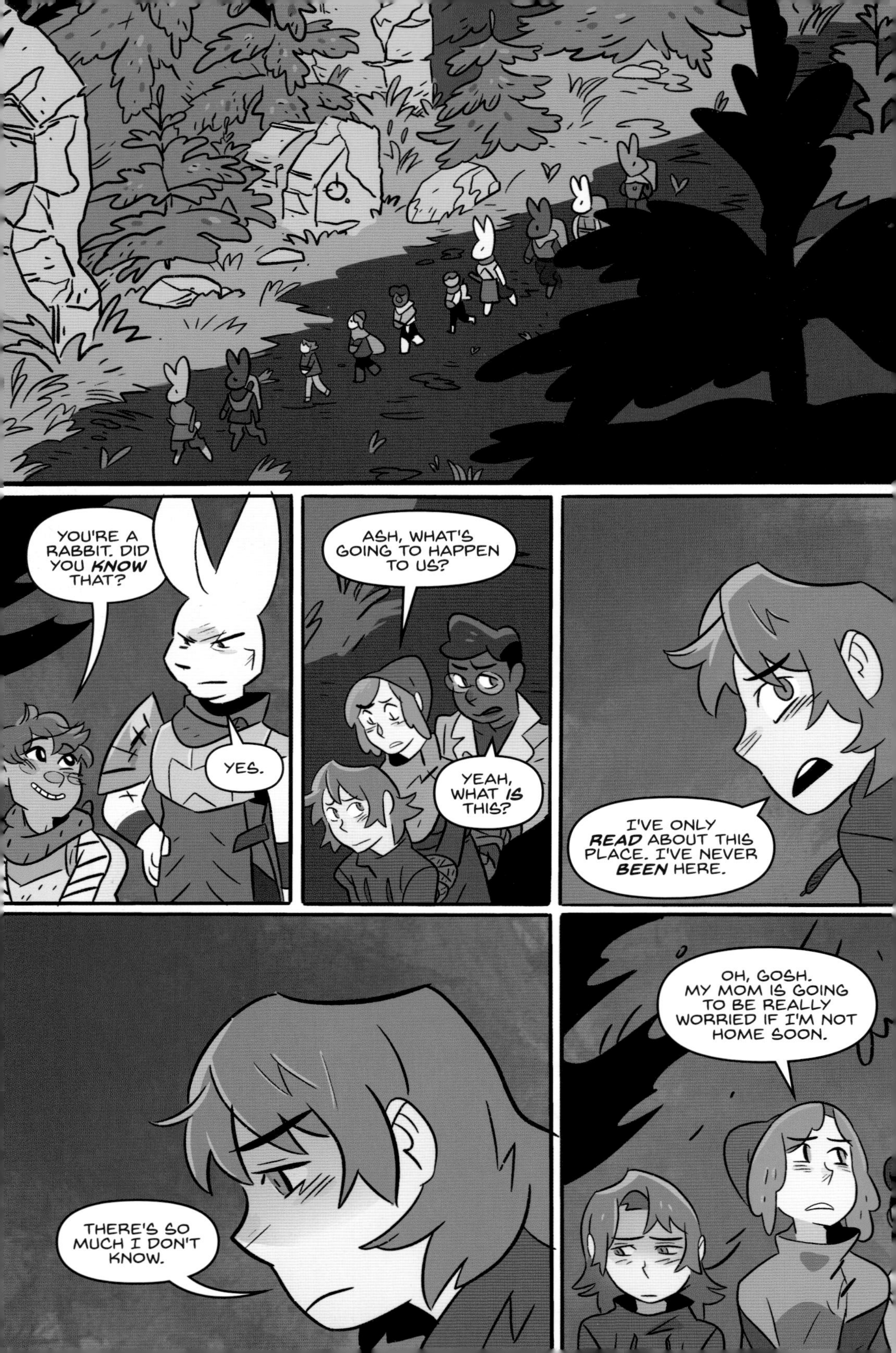
YOU'RE A RABBIT. DID YOU **KNOW** THAT?
YES.
ASH, WHAT'S GOING TO HAPPEN TO US?
YEAH, WHAT **IS** THIS?
I'VE ONLY **READ** ABOUT THIS PLACE. I'VE NEVER **BEEN** HERE.
THERE'S SO MUCH I DON'T KNOW.
OH, GOSH. MY MOM IS GOING TO BE REALLY WORRIED IF I'M NOT HOME SOON.

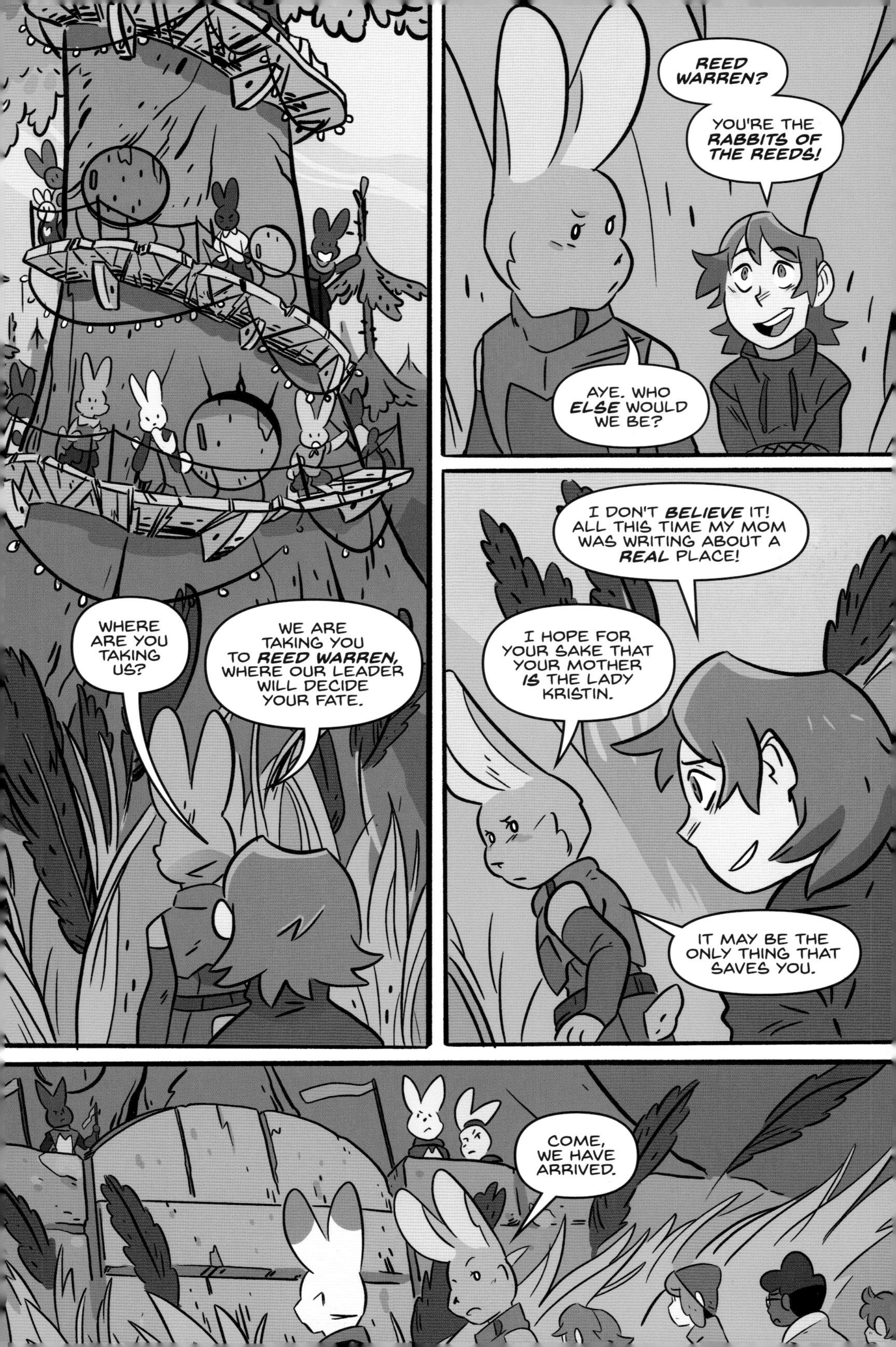

REED WARREN?
YOU'RE THE RABBITS OF THE REEDS!
AYE. WHO ELSE WOULD WE BE?
WHERE ARE YOU TAKING US?
WE ARE TAKING YOU TO REED WARREN, WHERE OUR LEADER WILL DECIDE YOUR FATE.
I DON'T BELIEVE IT! ALL THIS TIME MY MOM WAS WRITING ABOUT A REAL PLACE!
I HOPE FOR YOUR SAKE THAT YOUR MOTHER IS THE LADY KRISTIN.
IT MAY BE THE ONLY THING THAT SAVES YOU.
COME, WE HAVE ARRIVED.

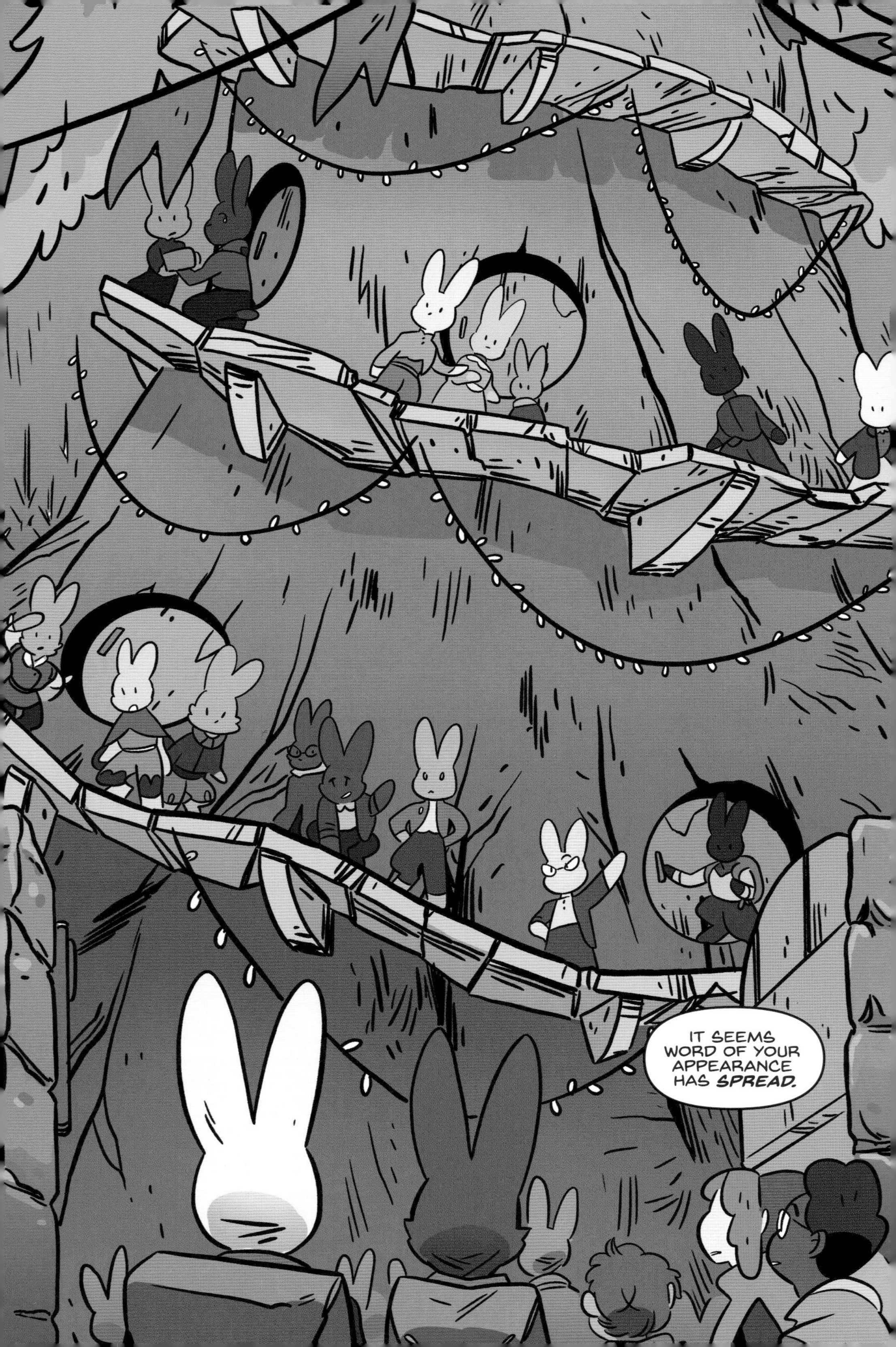
IT SEEMS WORD OF YOUR APPEARANCE HAS SPREAD.

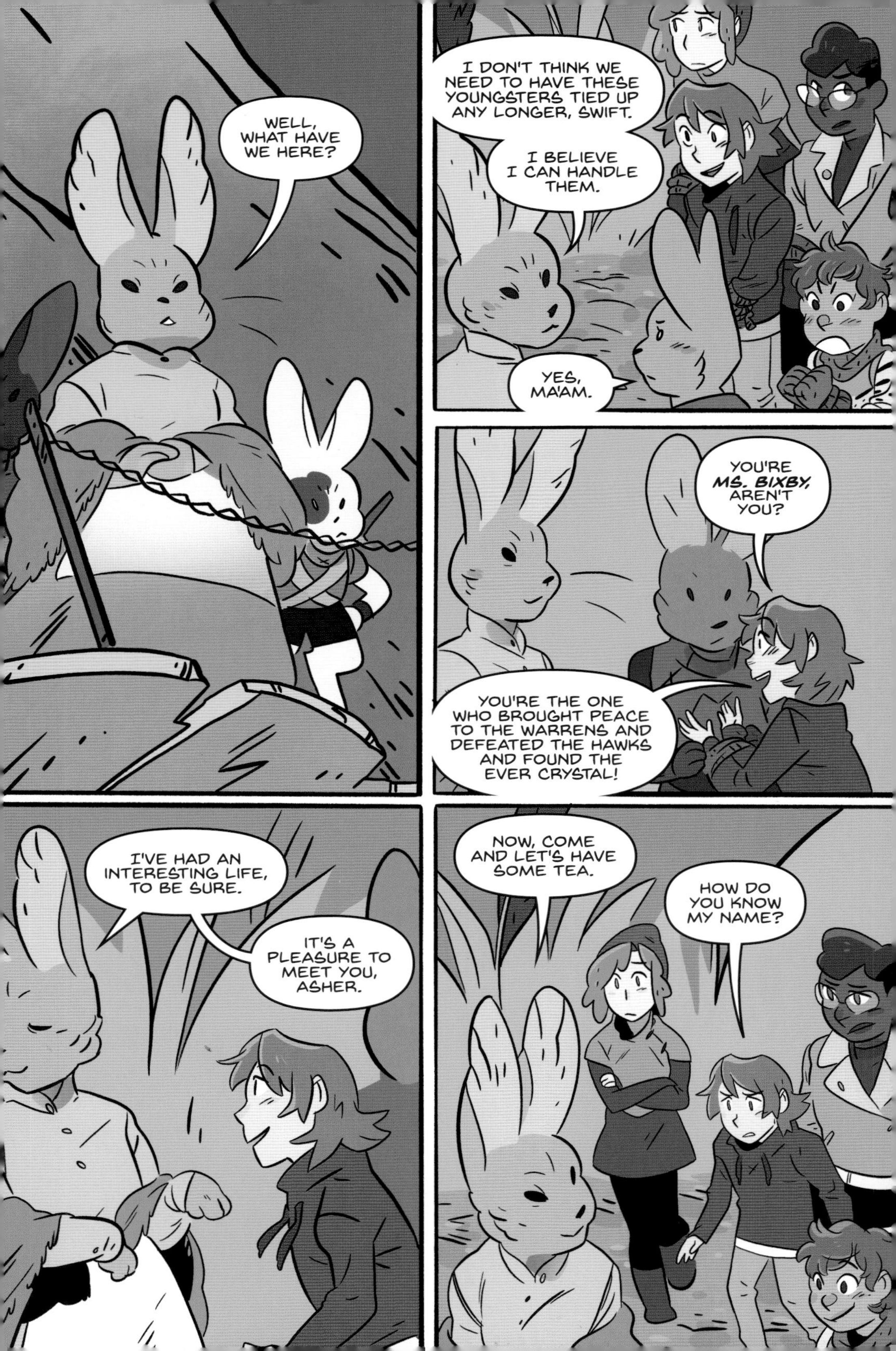
WELL, WHAT HAVE WE HERE?
I DON'T THINK WE NEED TO HAVE THESE YOUNGSTERS TIED UP ANY LONGER, SWIFT.
I BELIEVE I CAN HANDLE THEM.
YES, MA'AM.
YOU'RE MS. BIXBY, AREN'T YOU?
YOU'RE THE ONE WHO BROUGHT PEACE TO THE WARRENS AND DEFEATED THE HAWKS AND FOUND THE EVER CRYSTAL!
I'VE HAD AN INTERESTING LIFE, TO BE SURE.
IT'S A PLEASURE TO MEET YOU, ASHER.
NOW, COME AND LET'S HAVE SOME TEA.
HOW DO YOU KNOW MY NAME?

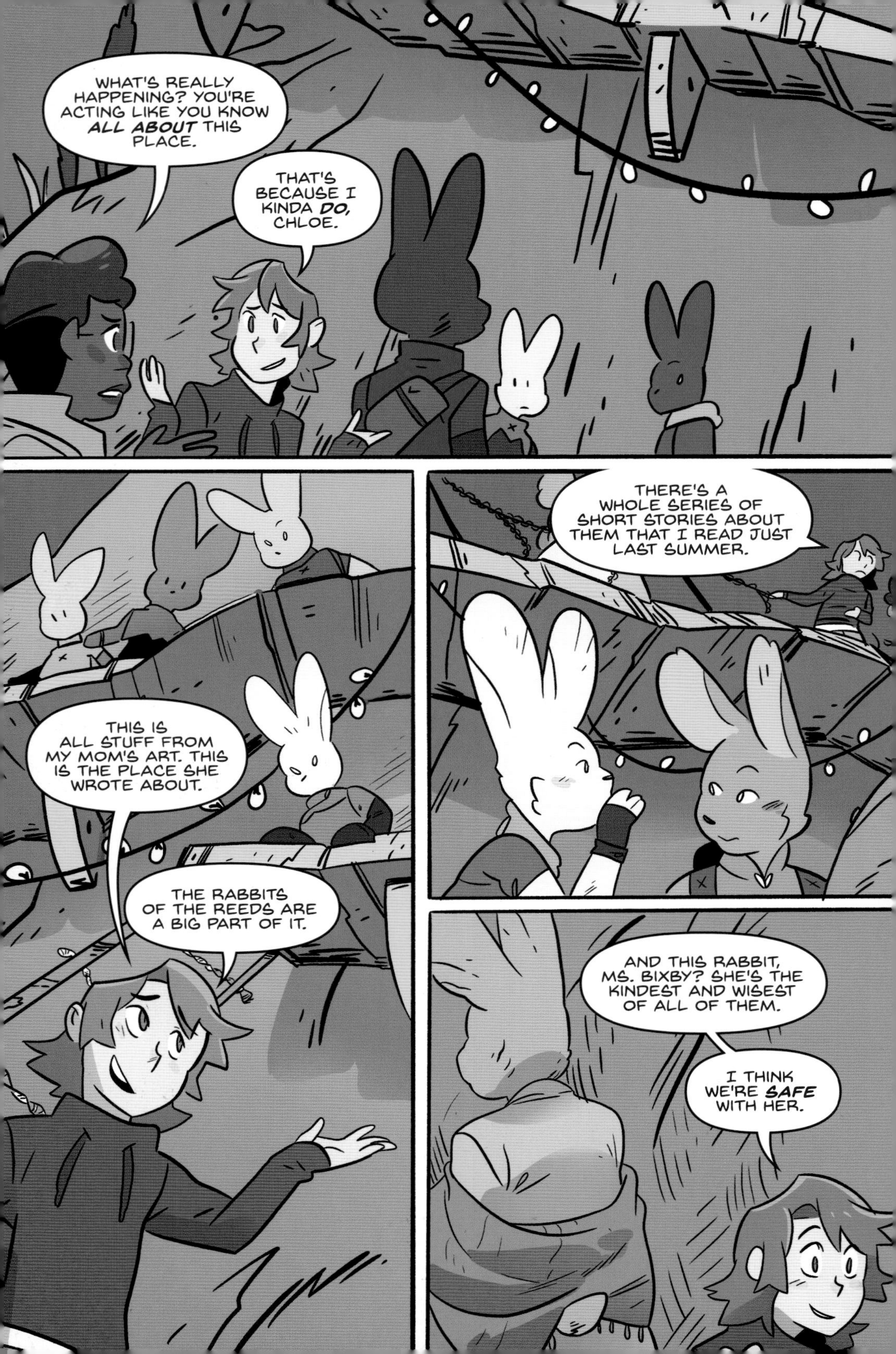
WHAT'S REALLY HAPPENING? YOU'RE ACTING LIKE YOU KNOW ALL ABOUT THIS PLACE.
THAT'S BECAUSE I KINDA DO, CHLOE.
THIS IS ALL STUFF FROM MY MOM'S ART. THIS IS THE PLACE SHE WROTE ABOUT.
THE RABBITS OF THE REEDS ARE A BIG PART OF IT.
THERE'S A WHOLE SERIES OF SHORT STORIES ABOUT THEM THAT I READ JUST LAST SUMMER.
AND THIS RABBIT, MS. BIXBY? SHE'S THE KINDEST AND WISEST OF ALL OF THEM.
I THINK WE'RE SAFE WITH HER.

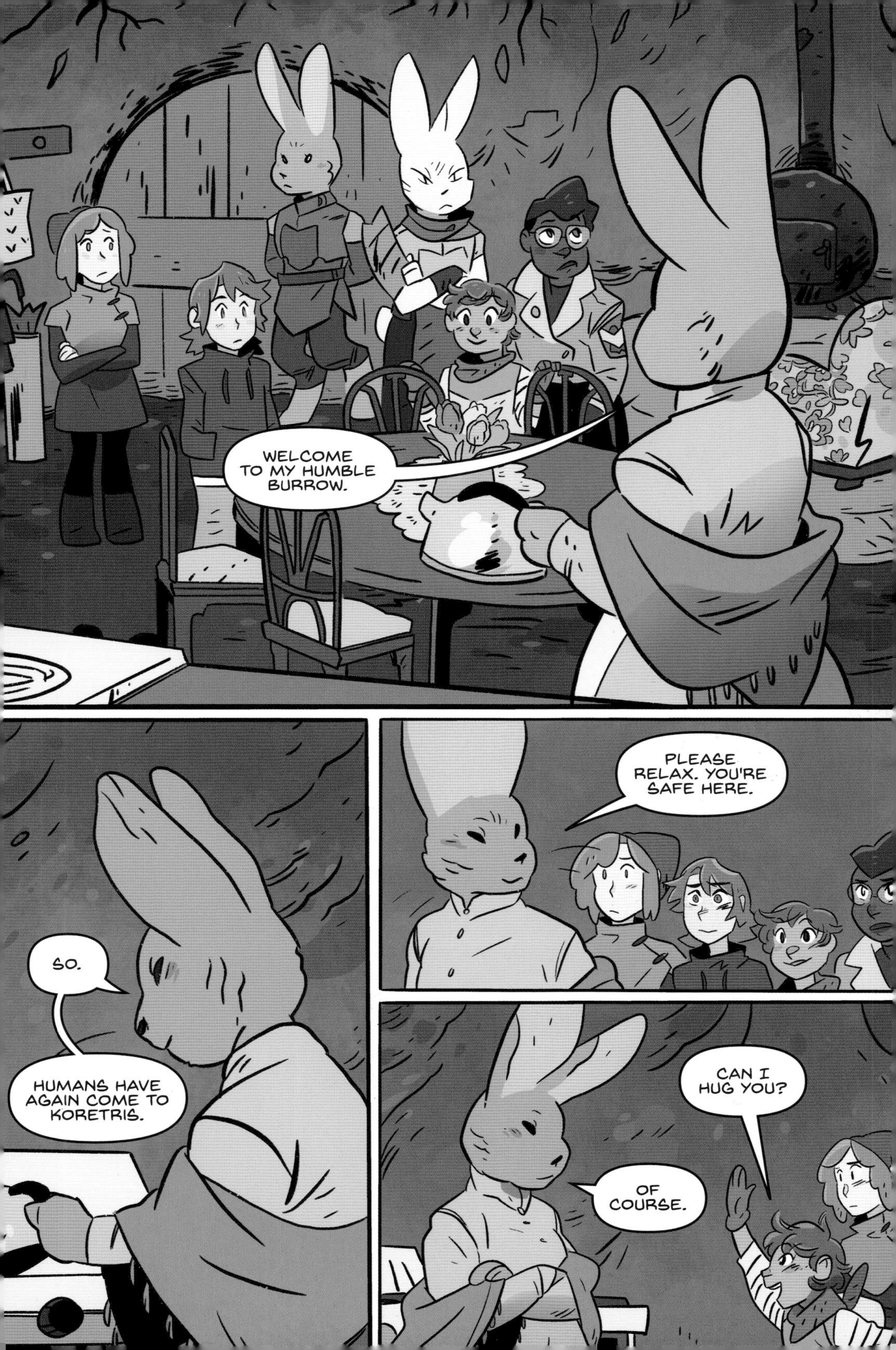
WELCOME TO MY HUMBLE BURROW.
SO.
HUMANS HAVE AGAIN COME TO KORETRIS.
PLEASE RELAX. YOU'RE SAFE HERE.
CAN I HUG YOU?
OF COURSE.

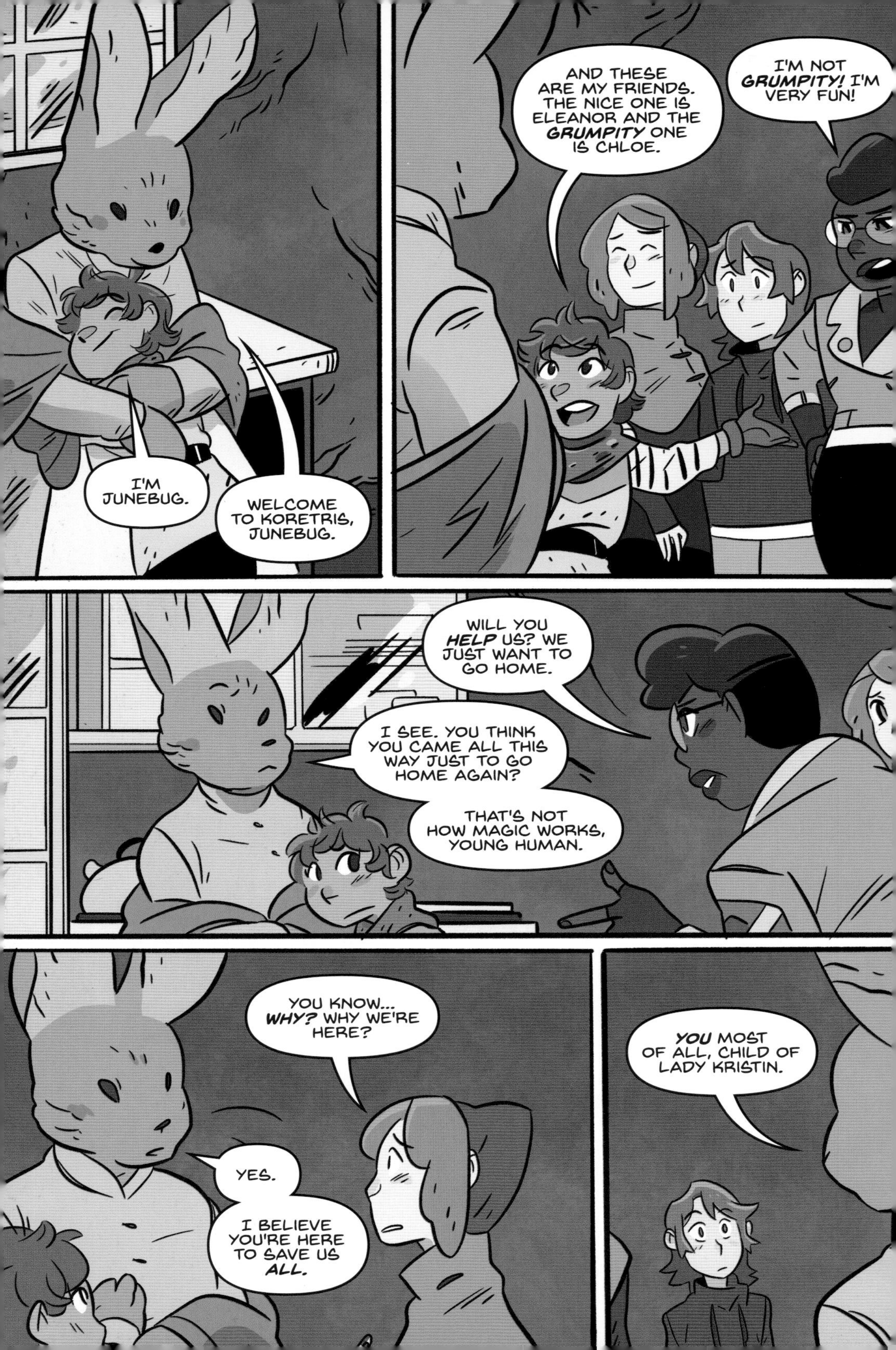
I'M JUNEBUG.
WELCOME TO KORETRIS, JUNEBUG.
AND THESE ARE MY FRIENDS. THE NICE ONE IS ELEANOR AND THE GRUMPITY ONE IS CHLOE.
I'M NOT GRUMPITY! I'M VERY FUN!
WILL YOU HELP US? WE JUST WANT TO GO HOME.
I SEE. YOU THINK YOU CAME ALL THIS WAY JUST TO GO HOME AGAIN?
THAT'S NOT HOW MAGIC WORKS, YOUNG HUMAN.
YOU KNOW... WHY? WHY WE'RE HERE?
YES.
I BELIEVE YOU'RE HERE TO SAVE US ALL.
YOU MOST OF ALL, CHILD OF LADY KRISTIN.

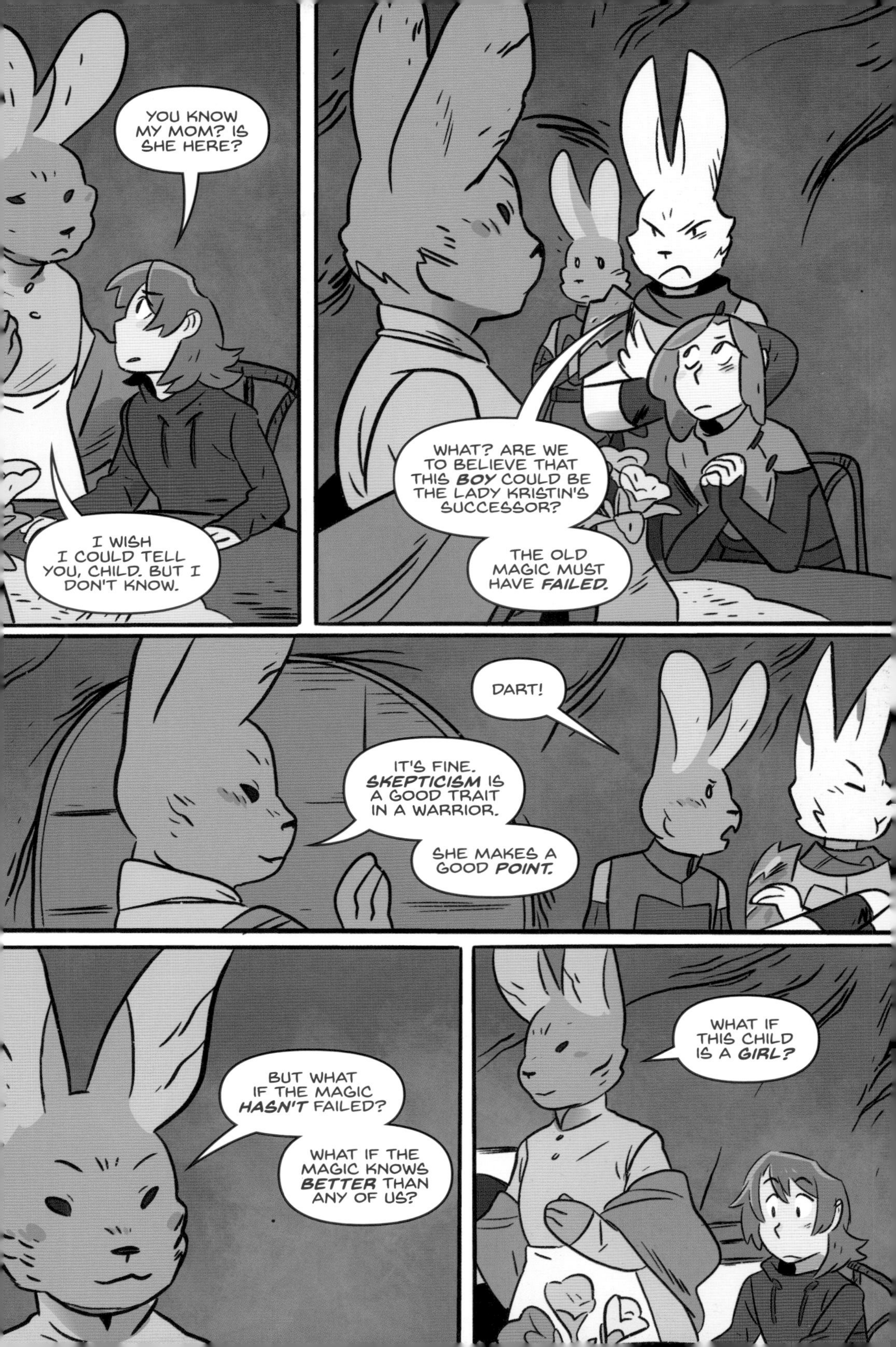
YOU KNOW MY MOM? IS SHE HERE?
I WISH I COULD TELL YOU, CHILD. BUT I DON'T KNOW.
WHAT? ARE WE TO BELIEVE THAT THIS *BOY* COULD BE THE LADY KRISTIN'S SUCCESSOR?
THE OLD MAGIC MUST HAVE *FAILED.*
DART!
IT'S FINE. *SKEPTICISM* IS A GOOD TRAIT IN A WARRIOR.
SHE MAKES A GOOD *POINT.*
BUT WHAT IF THE MAGIC *HASN'T* FAILED?
WHAT IF THE MAGIC KNOWS *BETTER* THAN ANY OF US?
WHAT IF THIS CHILD IS A *GIRL?*

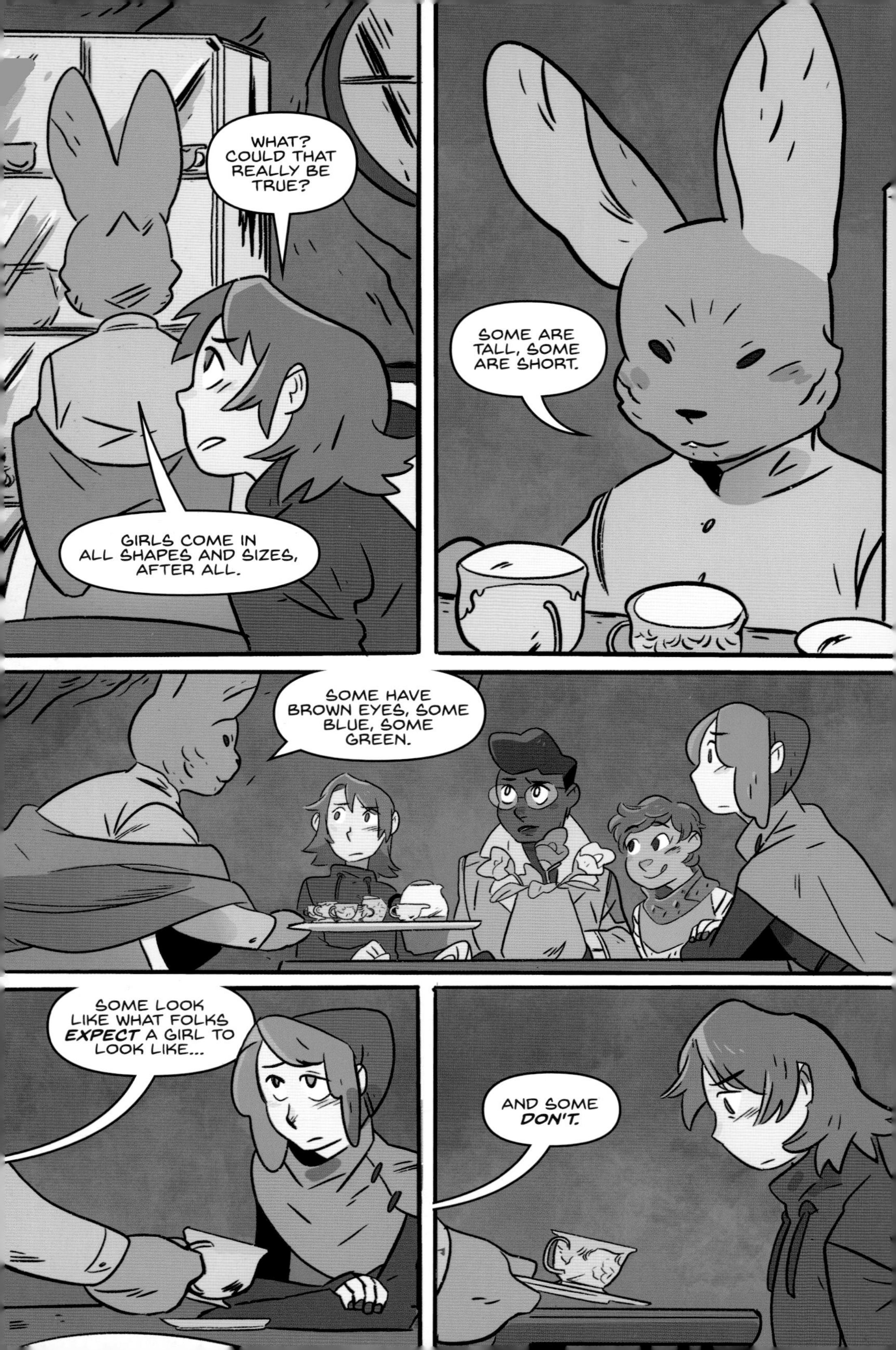
WHAT? COULD THAT REALLY BE TRUE?
GIRLS COME IN ALL SHAPES AND SIZES, AFTER ALL.
SOME ARE TALL, SOME ARE SHORT.
SOME HAVE BROWN EYES, SOME BLUE, SOME GREEN.
SOME LOOK LIKE WHAT FOLKS ***EXPECT*** A GIRL TO LOOK LIKE...
AND SOME ***DON'T.***

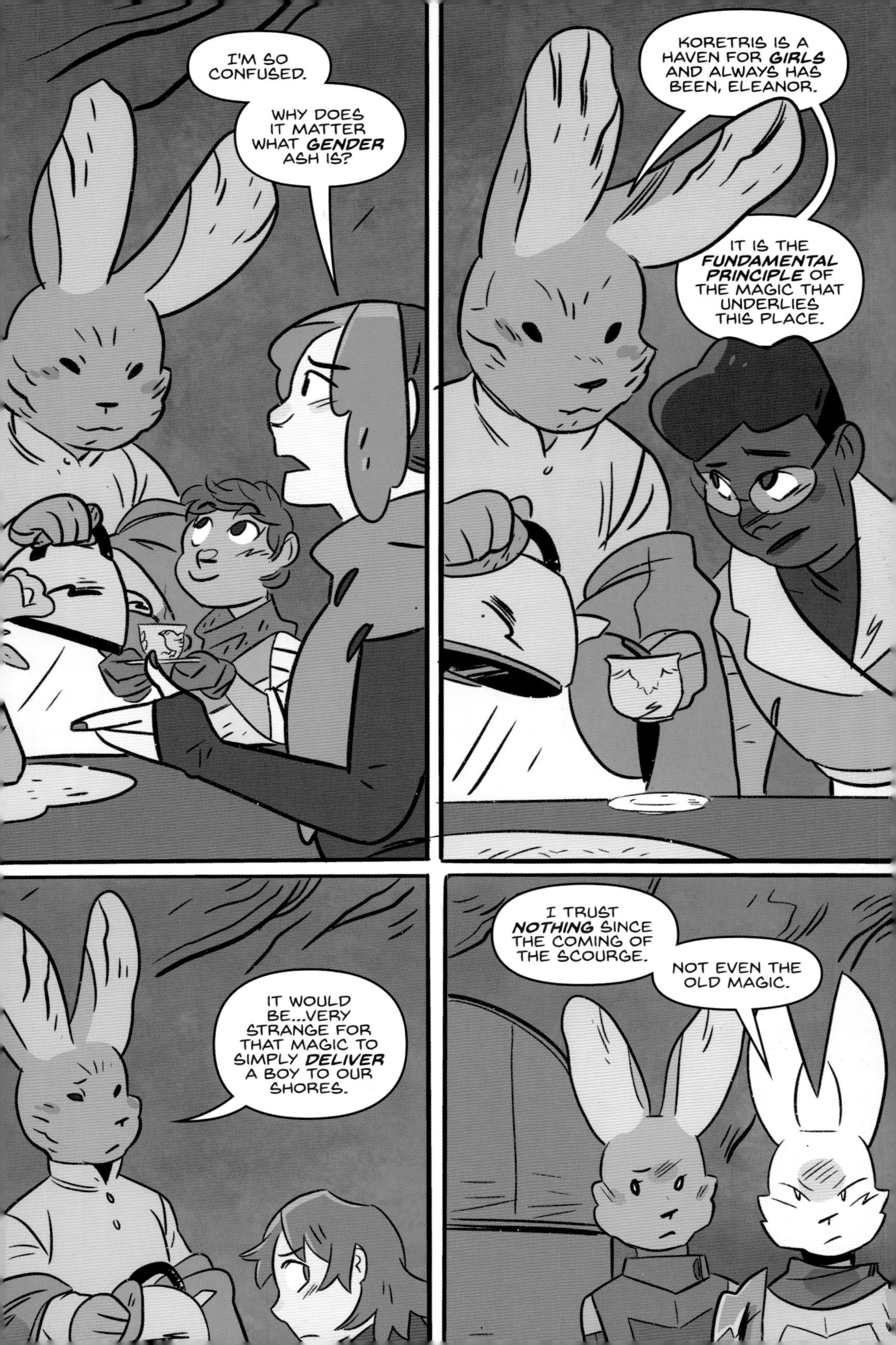
I'M SO CONFUSED.
WHY DOES IT MATTER WHAT GENDER ASH IS?
KORETRIS IS A HAVEN FOR GIRLS AND ALWAYS HAS BEEN, ELEANOR.
IT IS THE FUNDAMENTAL PRINCIPLE OF THE MAGIC THAT UNDERLIES THIS PLACE.
IT WOULD BE...VERY STRANGE FOR THAT MAGIC TO SIMPLY DELIVER A BOY TO OUR SHORES.
I TRUST NOTHING SINCE THE COMING OF THE SCOURGE.
NOT EVEN THE OLD MAGIC.

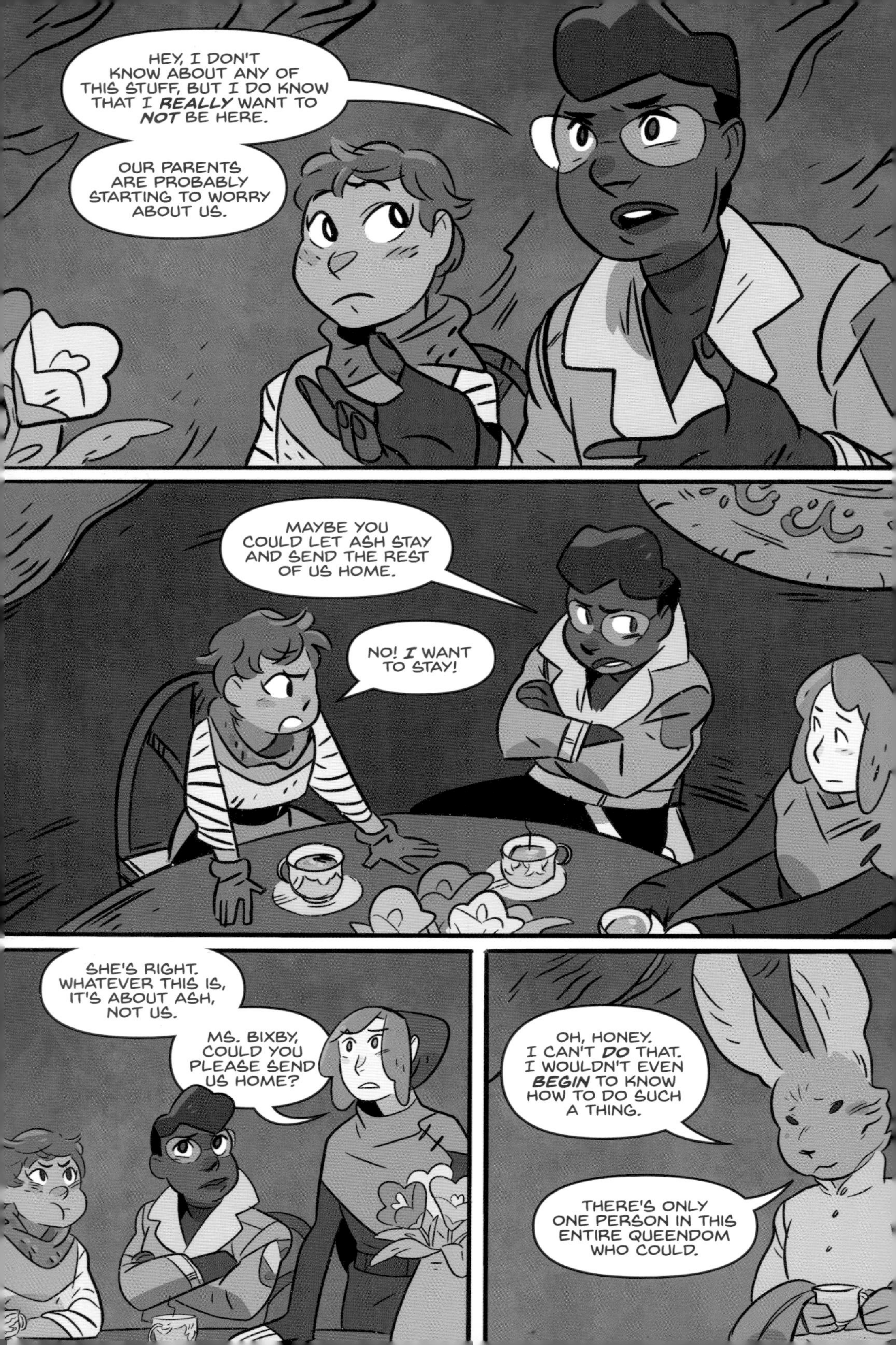
HEY, I DON'T KNOW ABOUT ANY OF THIS STUFF, BUT I DO KNOW THAT I REALLY WANT TO NOT BE HERE.
OUR PARENTS ARE PROBABLY STARTING TO WORRY ABOUT US.
MAYBE YOU COULD LET ASH STAY AND SEND THE REST OF US HOME.
NO! I WANT TO STAY!
SHE'S RIGHT. WHATEVER THIS IS, IT'S ABOUT ASH, NOT US.
MS. BIXBY, COULD YOU PLEASE SEND US HOME?
OH, HONEY. I CAN'T DO THAT. I WOULDN'T EVEN BEGIN TO KNOW HOW TO DO SUCH A THING.
THERE'S ONLY ONE PERSON IN THIS ENTIRE QUEENDOM WHO COULD.

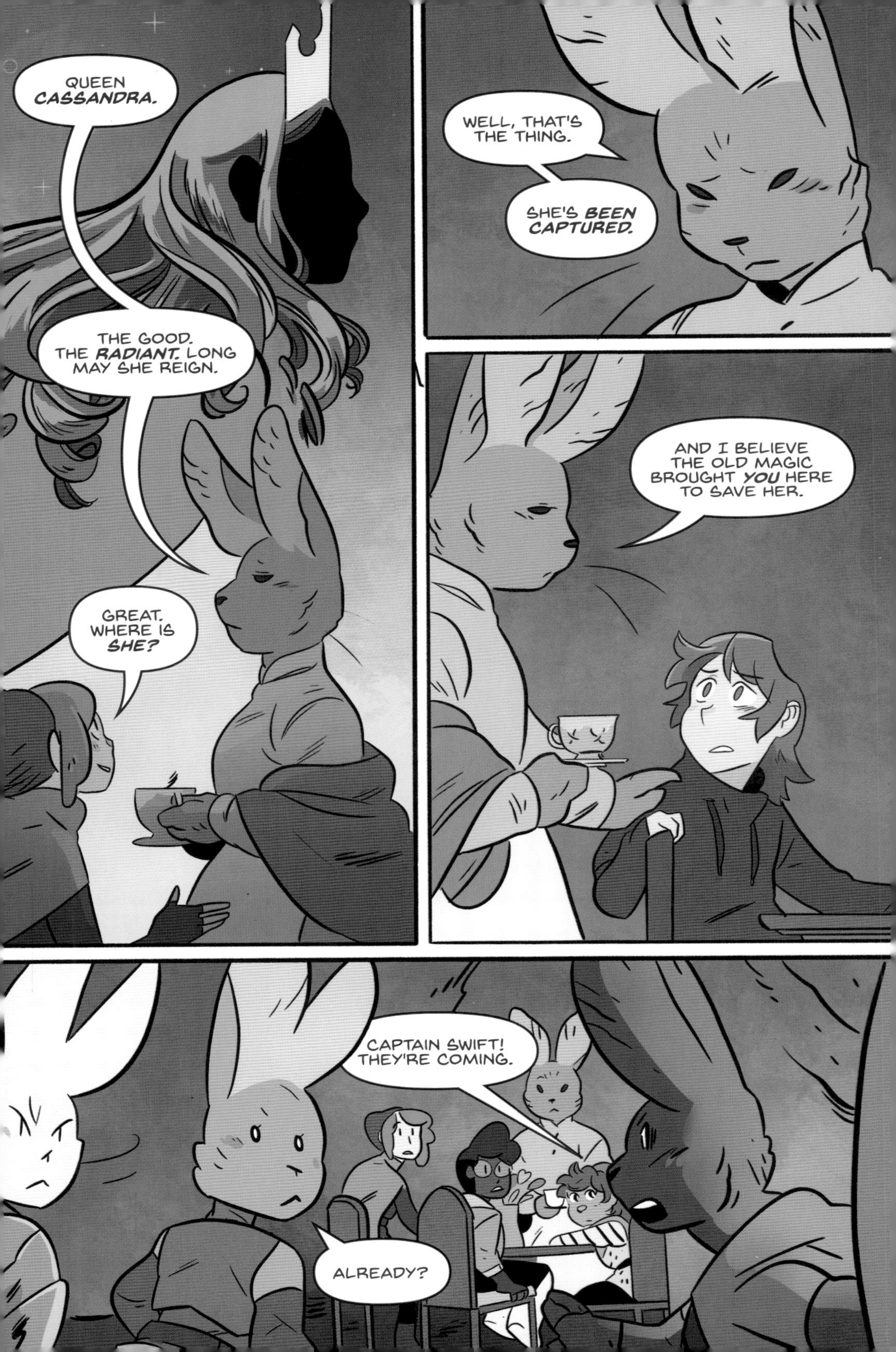
QUEEN *CASSANDRA.*
THE GOOD. THE *RADIANT.* LONG MAY SHE REIGN.
GREAT. WHERE IS *SHE?*
WELL, THAT'S THE THING.
SHE'S *BEEN CAPTURED.*
AND I BELIEVE THE OLD MAGIC BROUGHT *YOU* HERE TO SAVE HER.
CAPTAIN SWIFT! THEY'RE COMING.
ALREADY?

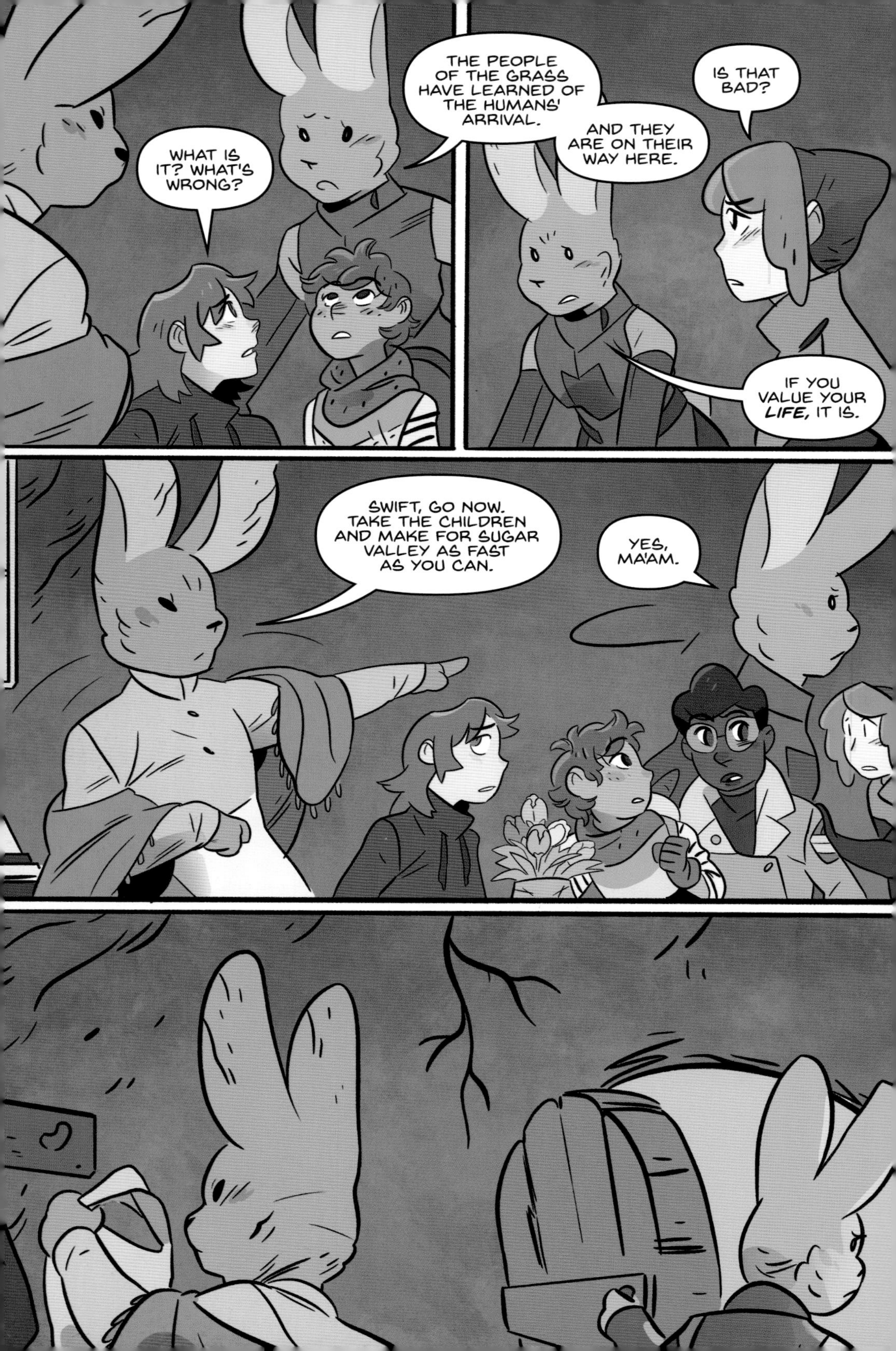
WHAT IS IT? WHAT'S WRONG?
THE PEOPLE OF THE GRASS HAVE LEARNED OF THE HUMANS' ARRIVAL.
AND THEY ARE ON THEIR WAY HERE.
IS THAT BAD?
IF YOU VALUE YOUR *LIFE,* IT IS.
SWIFT, GO NOW. TAKE THE CHILDREN AND MAKE FOR SUGAR VALLEY AS FAST AS YOU CAN.
YES, MA'AM.

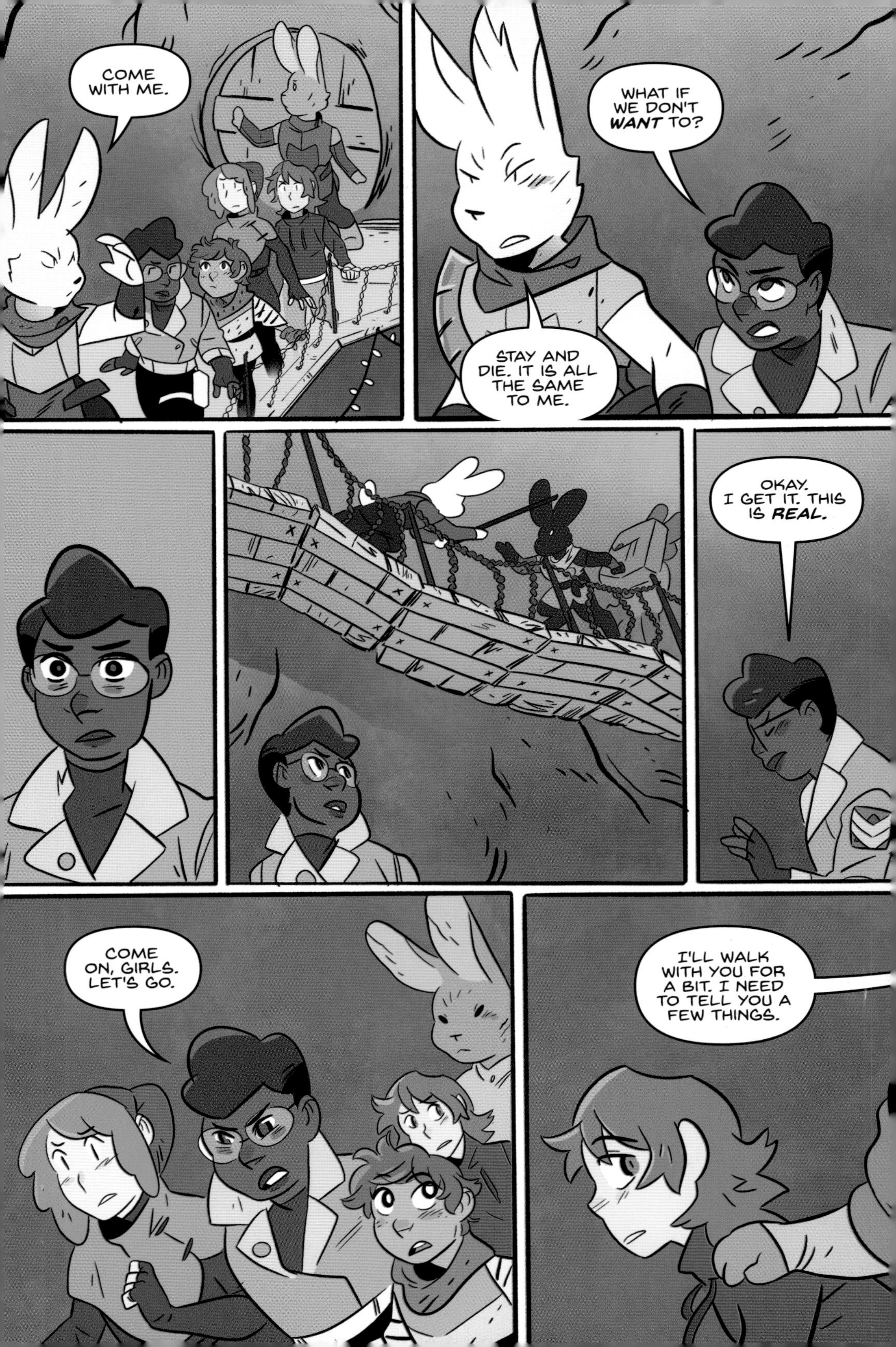
COME WITH ME.
WHAT IF WE DON'T *WANT* TO?
STAY AND DIE. IT IS ALL THE SAME TO ME.
OKAY. I GET IT. THIS IS *REAL.*
COME ON, GIRLS. LET'S GO.
I'LL WALK WITH YOU FOR A BIT. I NEED TO TELL YOU A FEW THINGS.

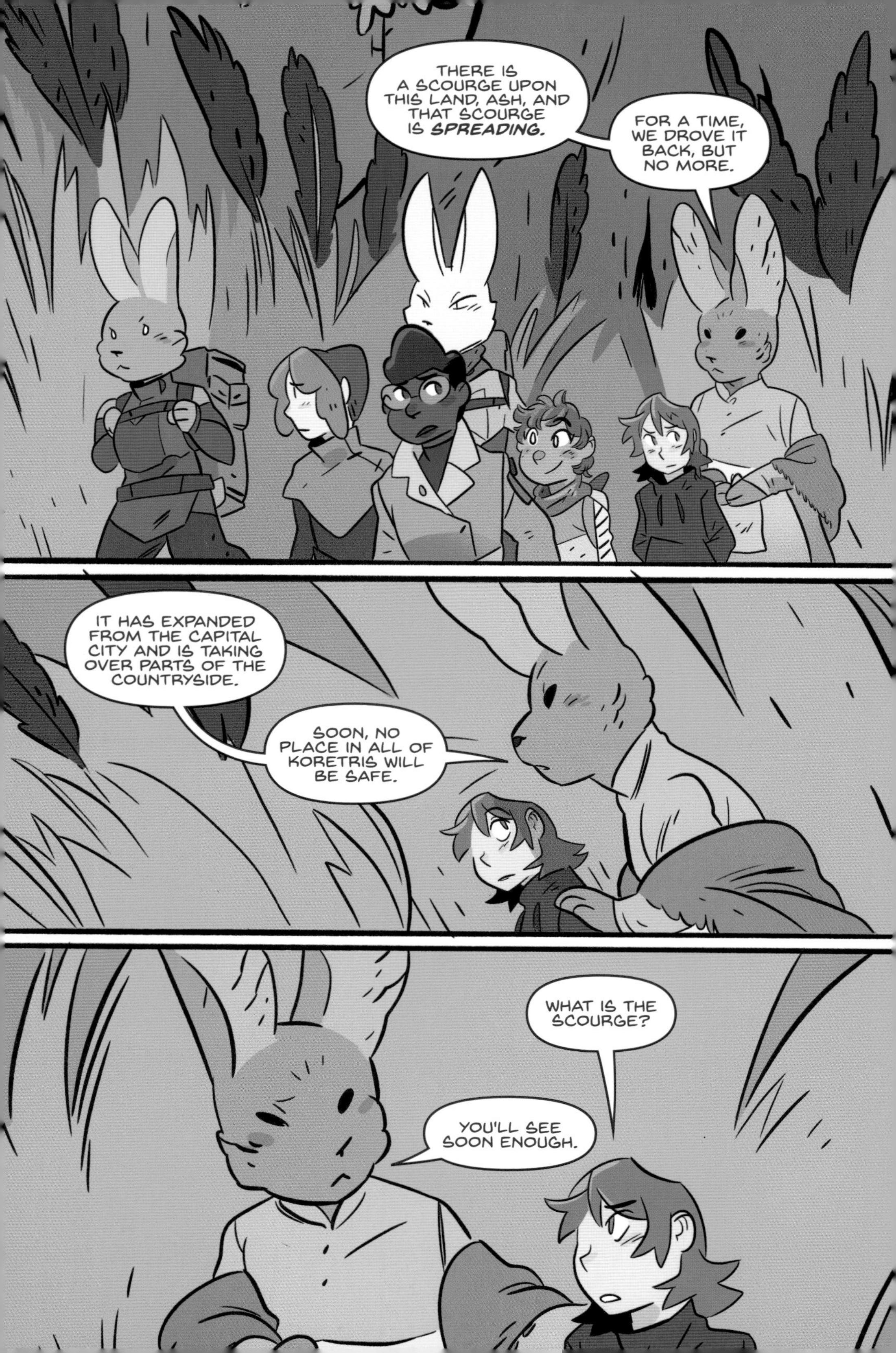
THERE IS A SCOURGE UPON THIS LAND, ASH, AND THAT SCOURGE IS *SPREADING.*
FOR A TIME, WE DROVE IT BACK, BUT NO MORE.
IT HAS EXPANDED FROM THE CAPITAL CITY AND IS TAKING OVER PARTS OF THE COUNTRYSIDE.
SOON, NO PLACE IN ALL OF KORETRIS WILL BE SAFE.
WHAT IS THE SCOURGE?
YOU'LL SEE SOON ENOUGH.

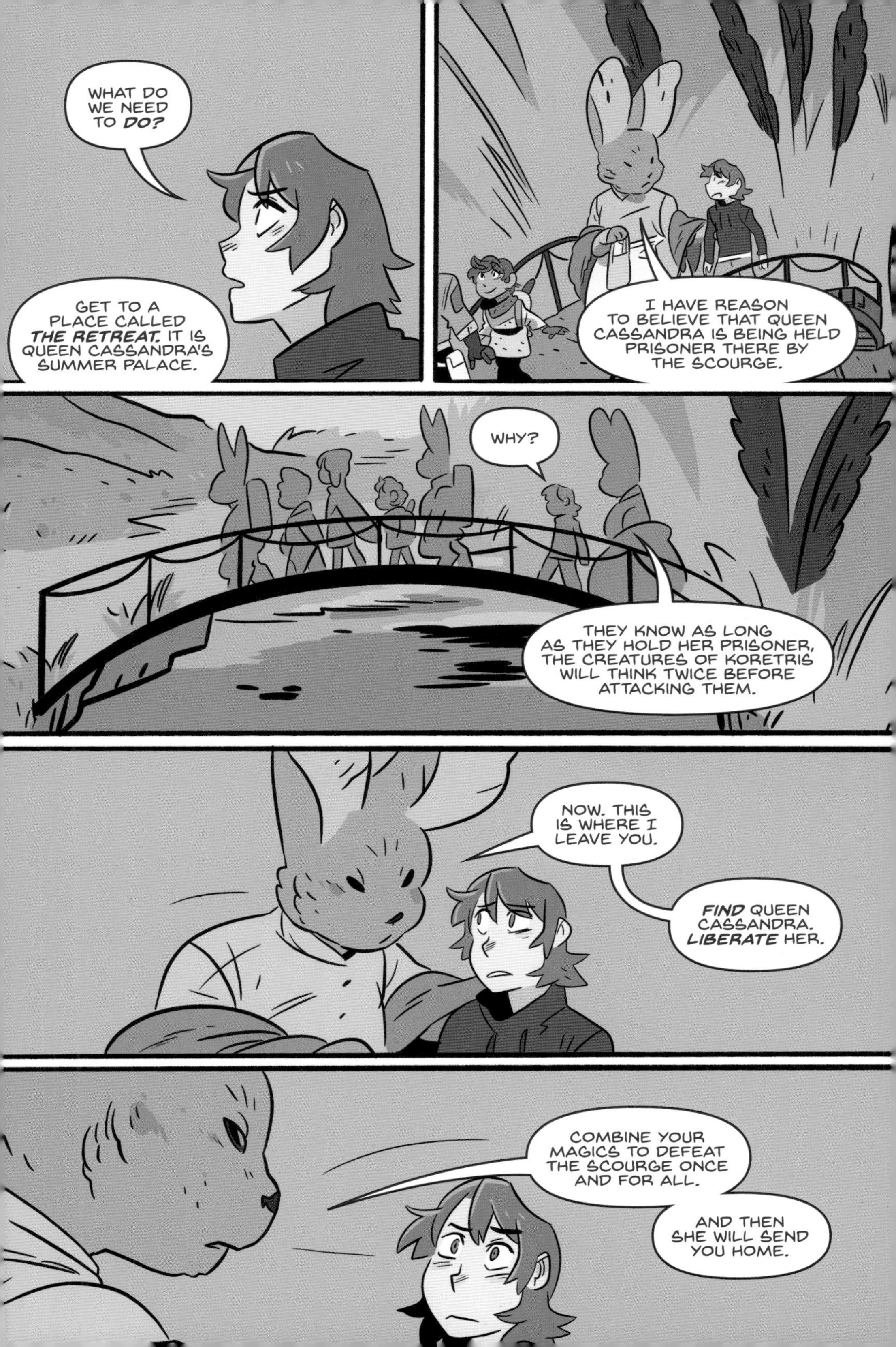
WHAT DO WE NEED TO *DO?*
GET TO A PLACE CALLED ***THE RETREAT.*** IT IS QUEEN CASSANDRA'S SUMMER PALACE.
I HAVE REASON TO BELIEVE THAT QUEEN CASSANDRA IS BEING HELD PRISONER THERE BY THE SCOURGE.
WHY?
THEY KNOW AS LONG AS THEY HOLD HER PRISONER, THE CREATURES OF KORETRIS WILL THINK TWICE BEFORE ATTACKING THEM.
NOW. THIS IS WHERE I LEAVE YOU.
FIND QUEEN CASSANDRA. ***LIBERATE*** HER.
COMBINE YOUR MAGICS TO DEFEAT THE SCOURGE ONCE AND FOR ALL.
AND THEN SHE WILL SEND YOU HOME.

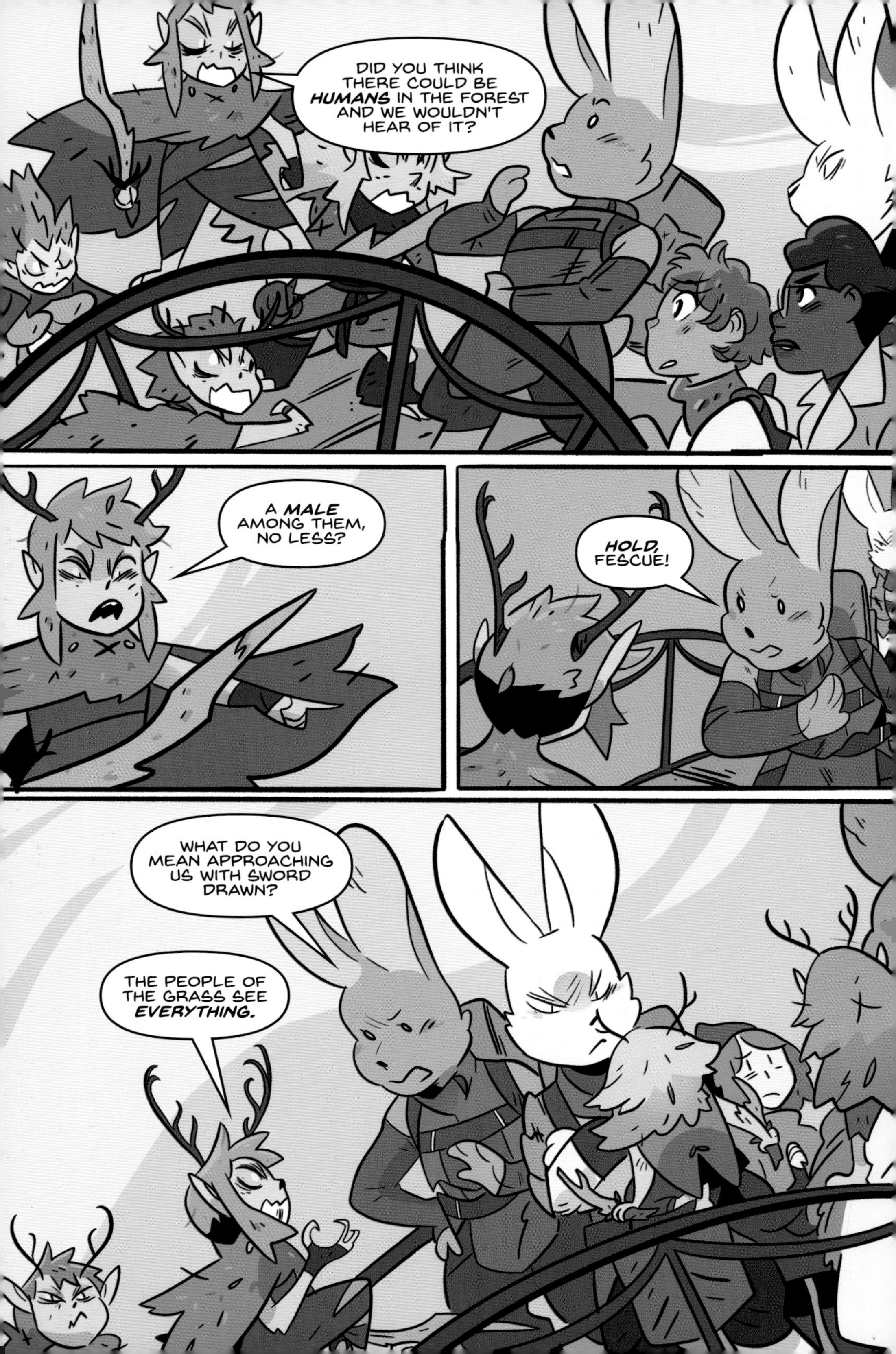
DID YOU THINK THERE COULD BE **HUMANS** IN THE FOREST AND WE WOULDN'T HEAR OF IT?
A **MALE** AMONG THEM, NO LESS?
HOLD, FESCUE!
WHAT DO YOU MEAN APPROACHING US WITH SWORD DRAWN?
THE PEOPLE OF THE GRASS SEE **EVERYTHING.**

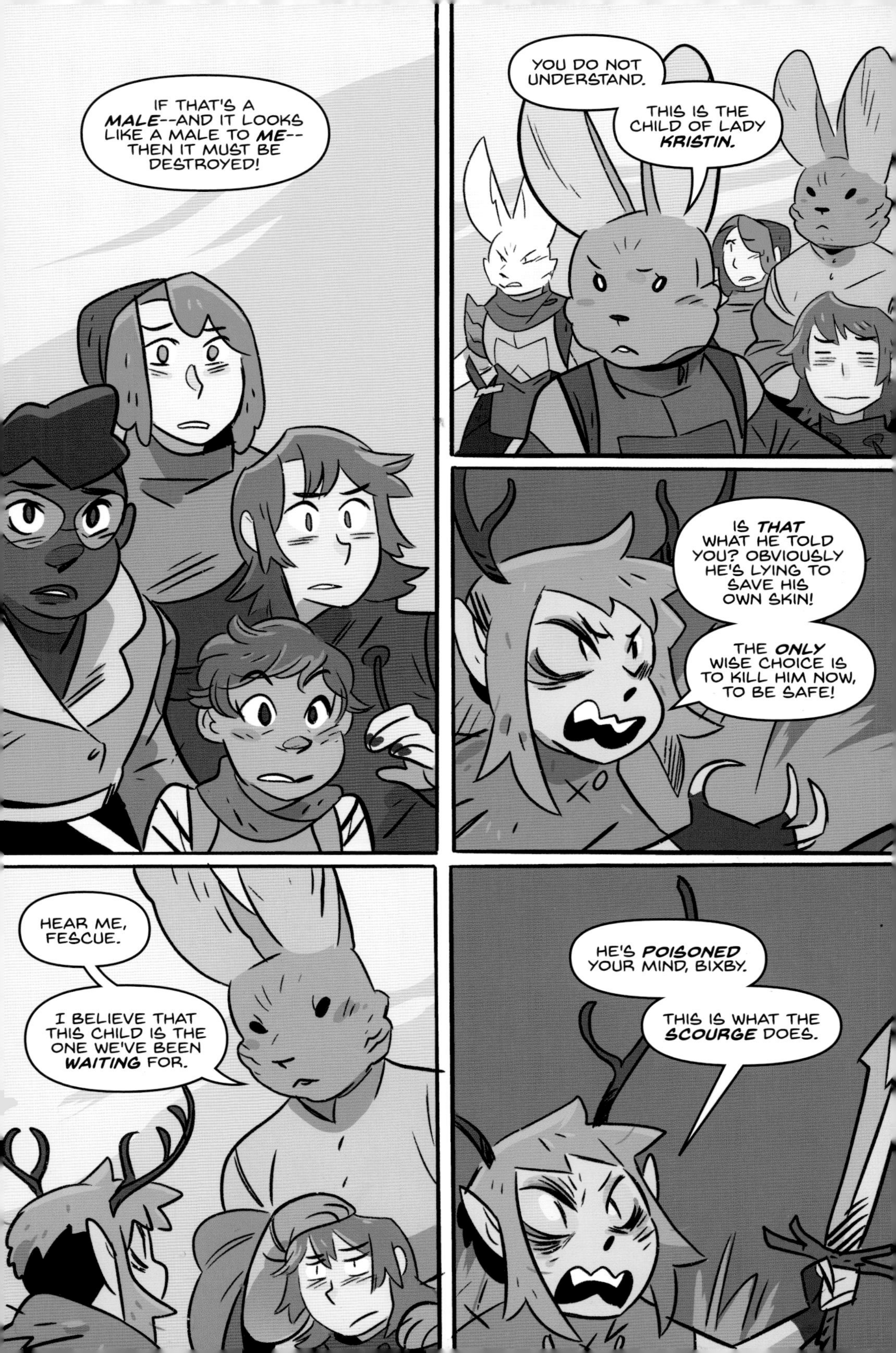

IF THAT'S A MALE--AND IT LOOKS LIKE A MALE TO ME--THEN IT MUST BE DESTROYED!
YOU DO NOT UNDERSTAND.
THIS IS THE CHILD OF LADY KRISTIN.
IS THAT WHAT HE TOLD YOU? OBVIOUSLY HE'S LYING TO SAVE HIS OWN SKIN!
THE ONLY WISE CHOICE IS TO KILL HIM NOW, TO BE SAFE!
HEAR ME, FESCUE.
I BELIEVE THAT THIS CHILD IS THE ONE WE'VE BEEN WAITING FOR.
HE'S POISONED YOUR MIND, BIXBY.
THIS IS WHAT THE SCOURGE DOES.

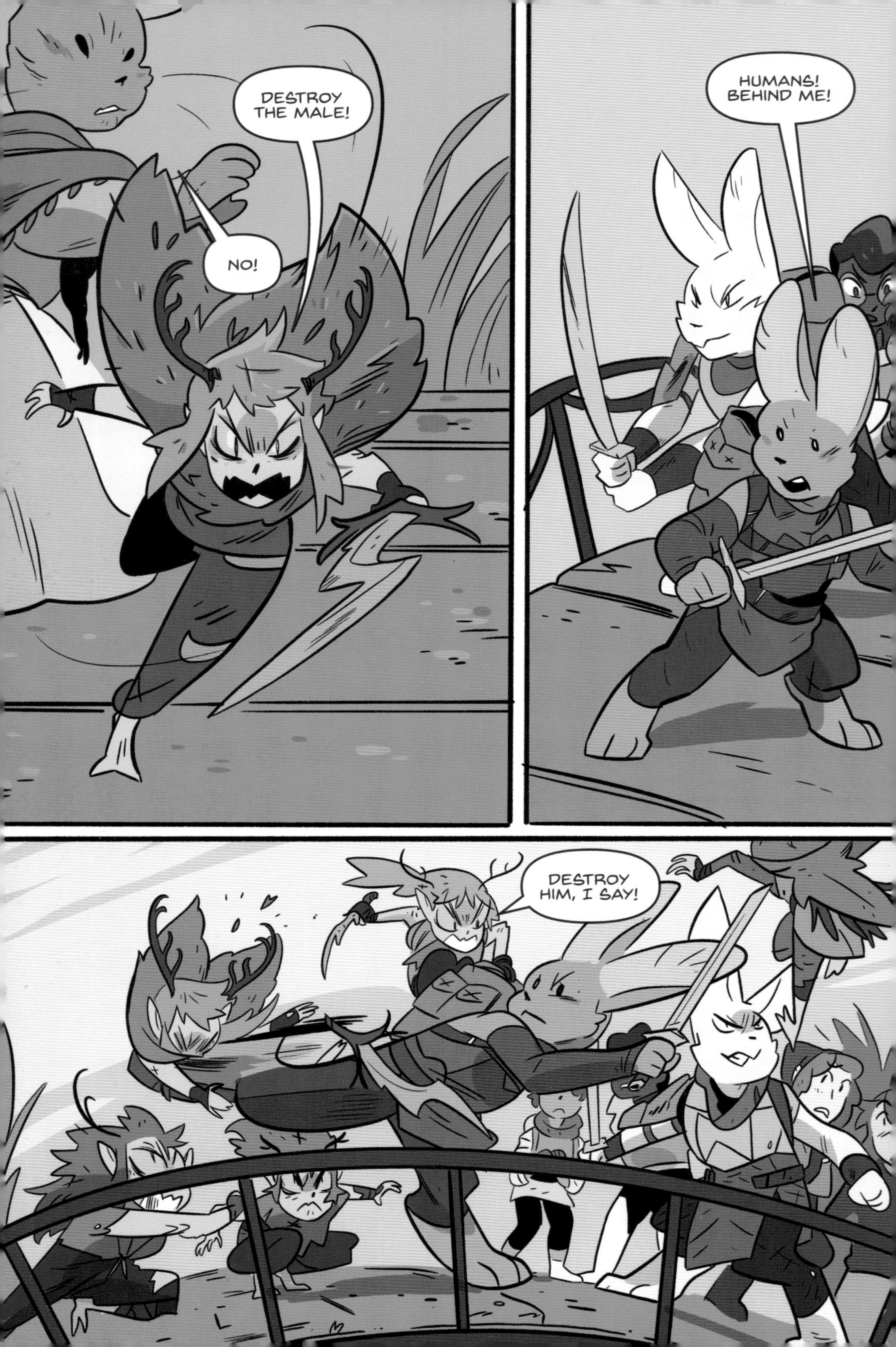
DESTROY THE MALE!
NO!
HUMANS! BEHIND ME!
DESTROY HIM, I SAY!

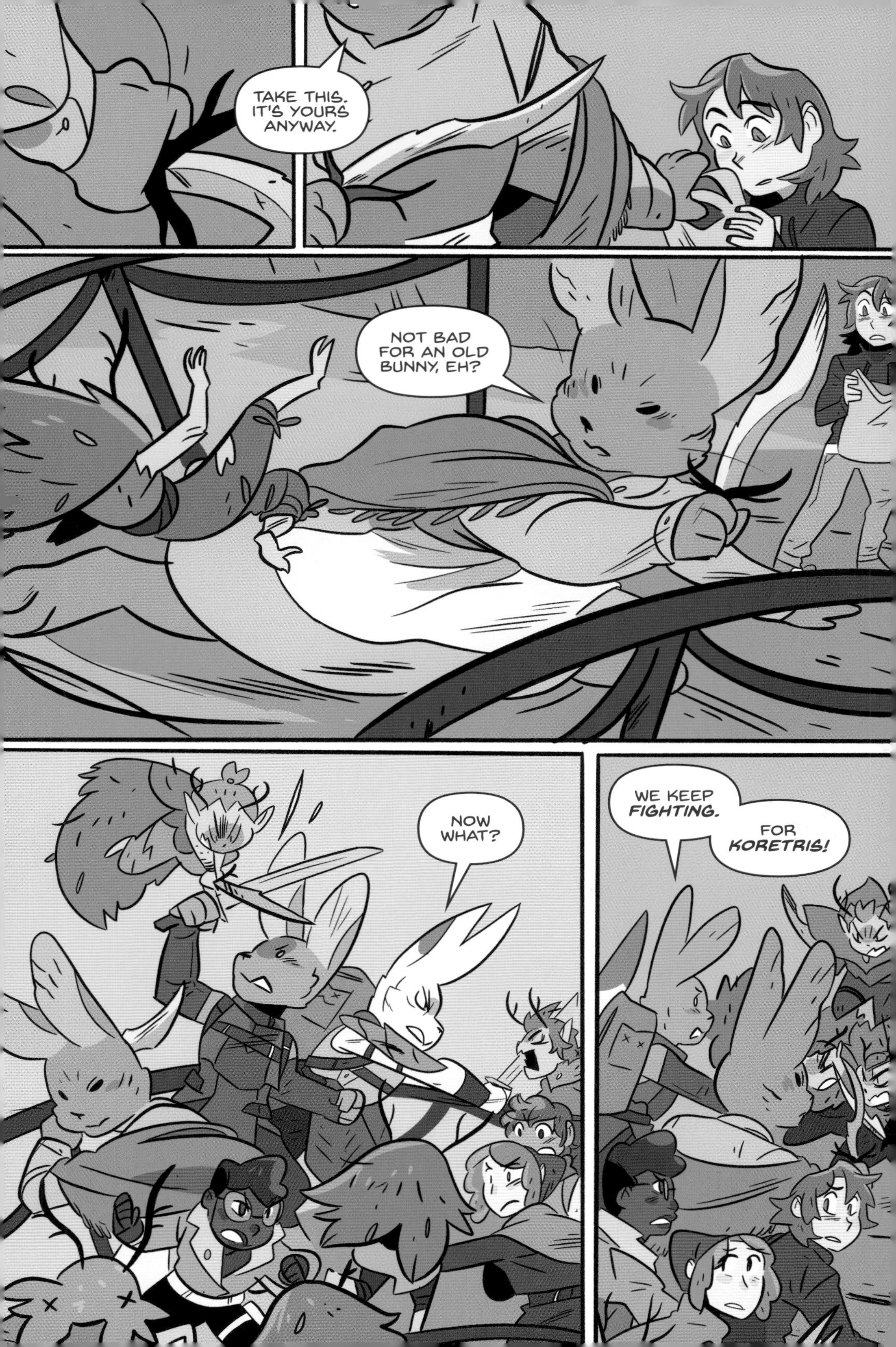
TAKE THIS. IT'S YOURS ANYWAY.
NOT BAD FOR AN OLD BUNNY, EH?
NOW WHAT?
WE KEEP *FIGHTING.*
FOR *KORETRIS!*

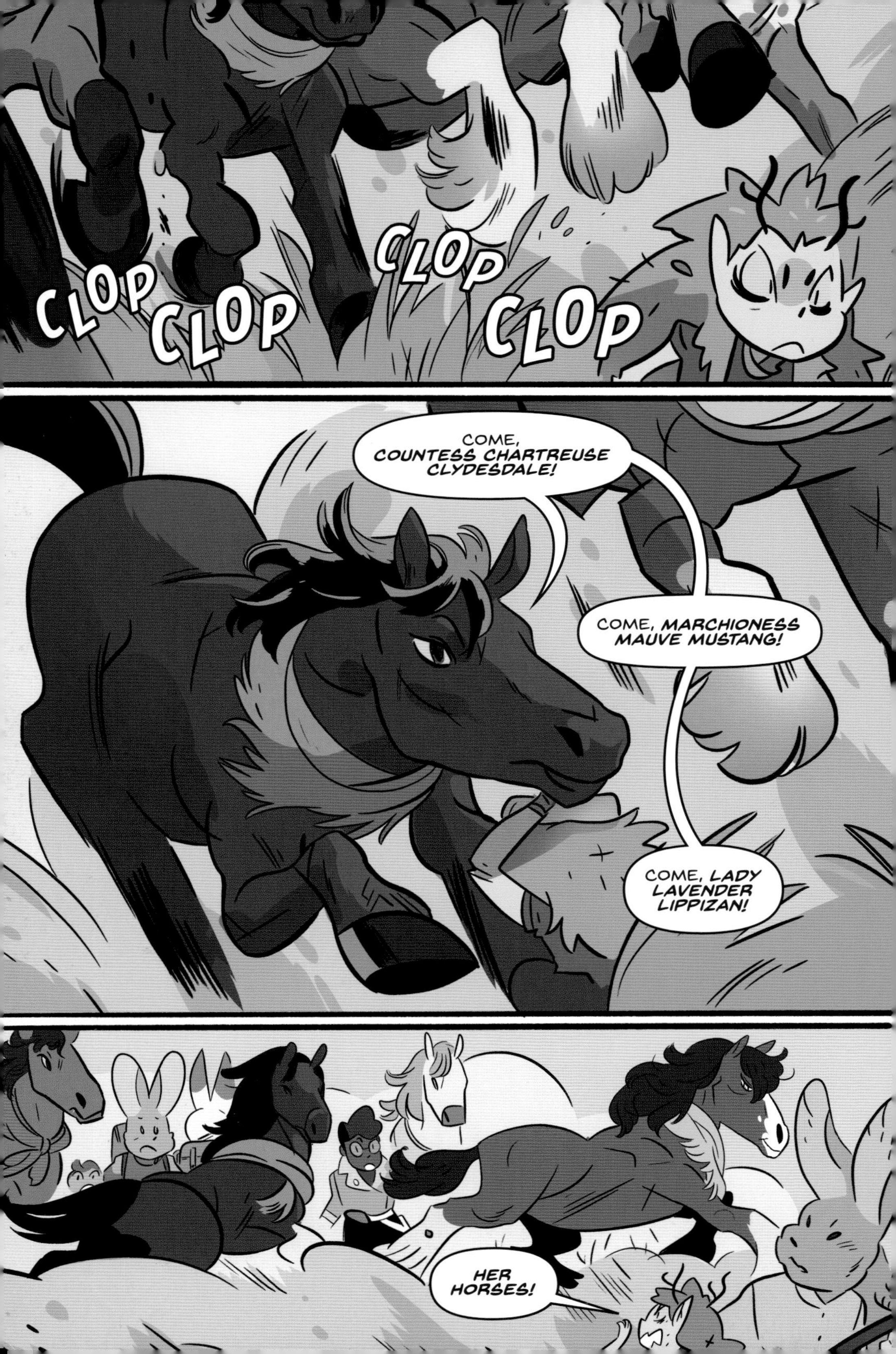
CLOP
CLOP
CLOP
CLOP
COME, COUNTESS CHARTREUSE CLYDESDALE!
COME, MARCHIONESS MAUVE MUSTANG!
COME, LADY LAVENDER LIPPIZAN!
HER HORSES!

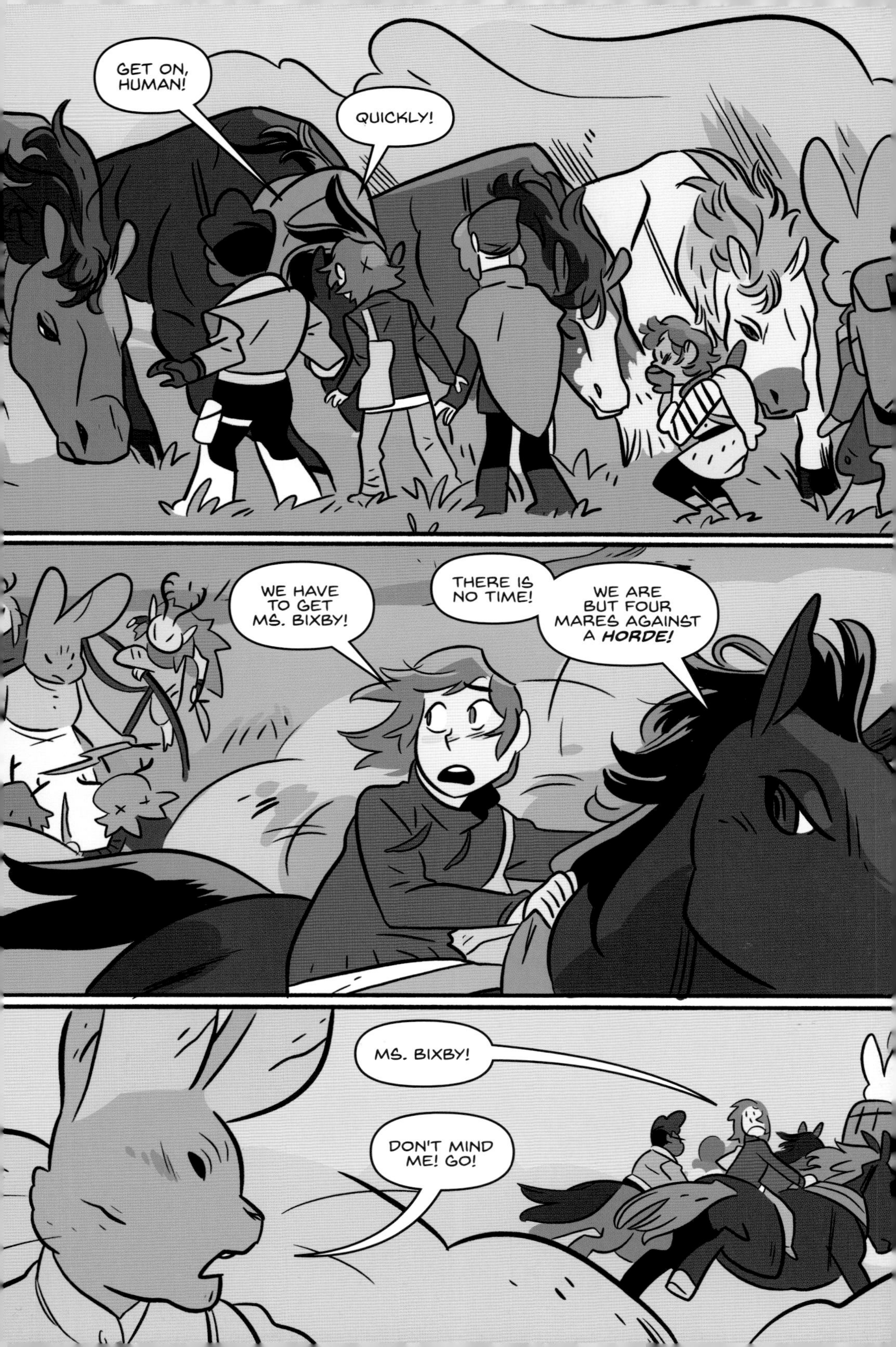
GET ON, HUMAN!
QUICKLY!
WE HAVE TO GET MS. BIXBY!
THERE IS NO TIME!
WE ARE BUT FOUR MARES AGAINST A *HORDE!*
MS. BIXBY!
DON'T MIND ME! GO!

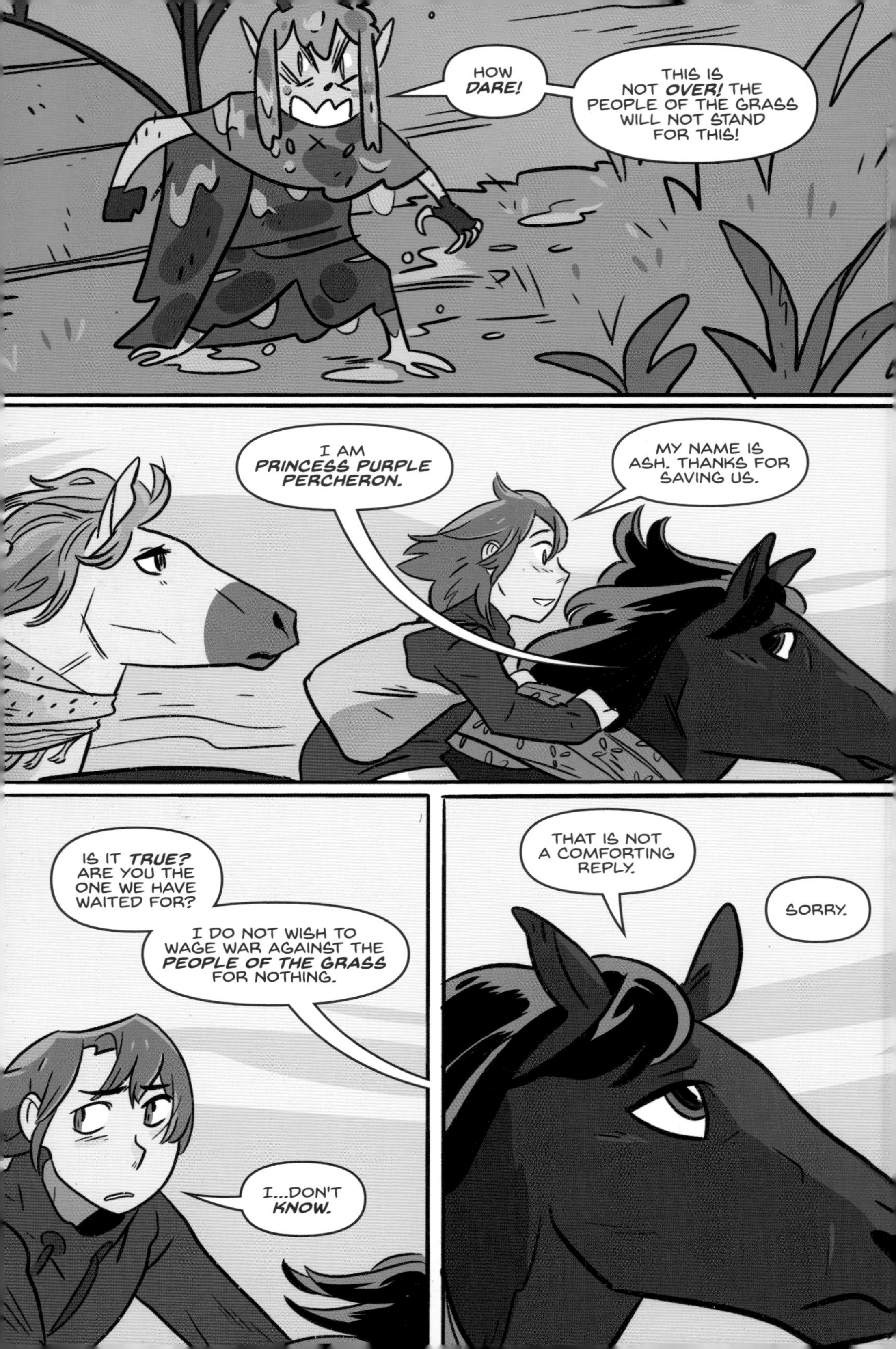
HOW DARE!
THIS IS NOT OVER! THE PEOPLE OF THE GRASS WILL NOT STAND FOR THIS!
I AM PRINCESS PURPLE PERCHERON.
MY NAME IS ASH. THANKS FOR SAVING US.
IS IT TRUE? ARE YOU THE ONE WE HAVE WAITED FOR?
I DO NOT WISH TO WAGE WAR AGAINST THE PEOPLE OF THE GRASS FOR NOTHING.
I...DON'T KNOW.
THAT IS NOT A COMFORTING REPLY.
SORRY.

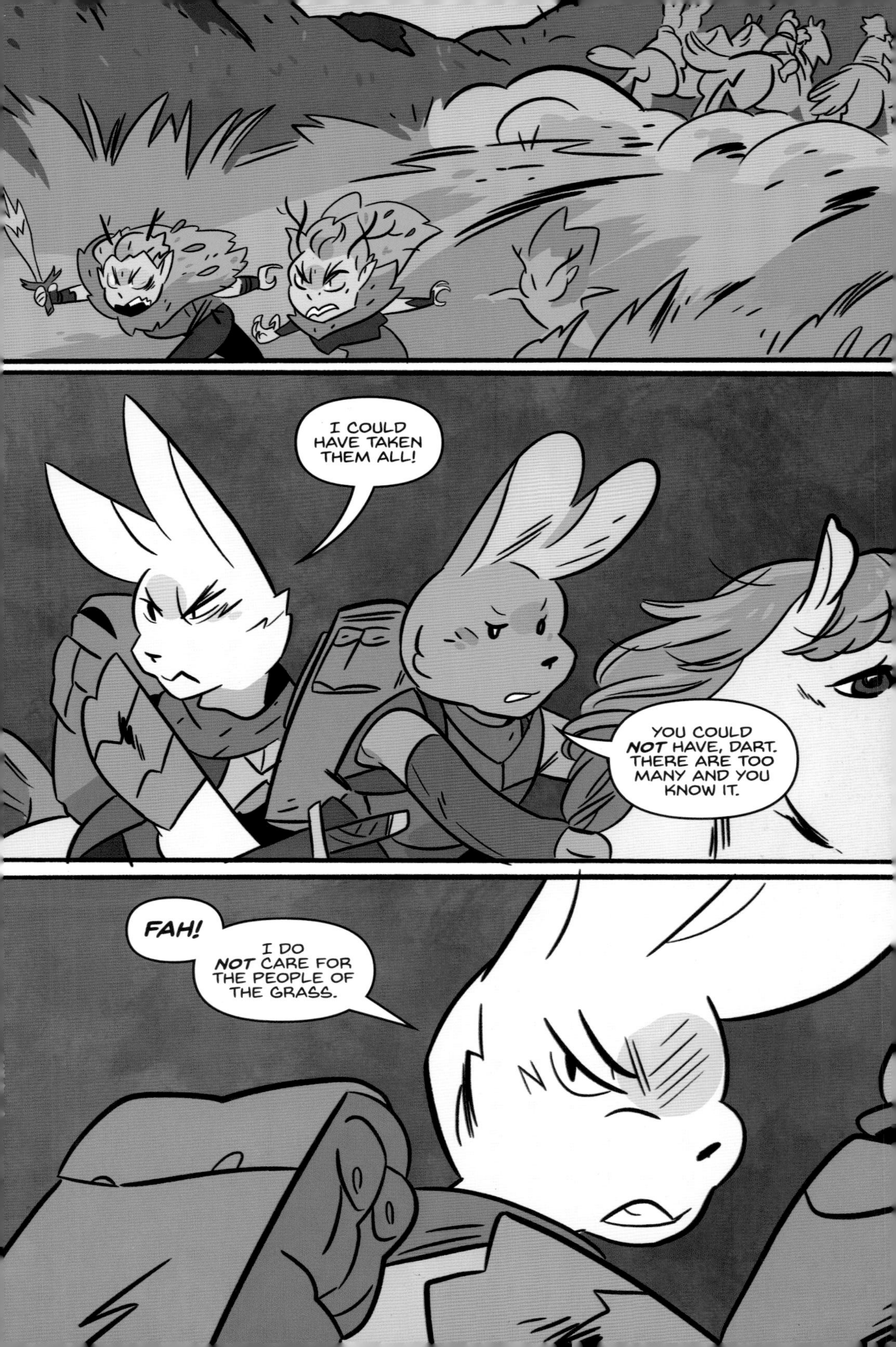
I COULD HAVE TAKEN THEM ALL!
YOU COULD NOT HAVE, DART. THERE ARE TOO MANY AND YOU KNOW IT.
FAH!
I DO NOT CARE FOR THE PEOPLE OF THE GRASS.

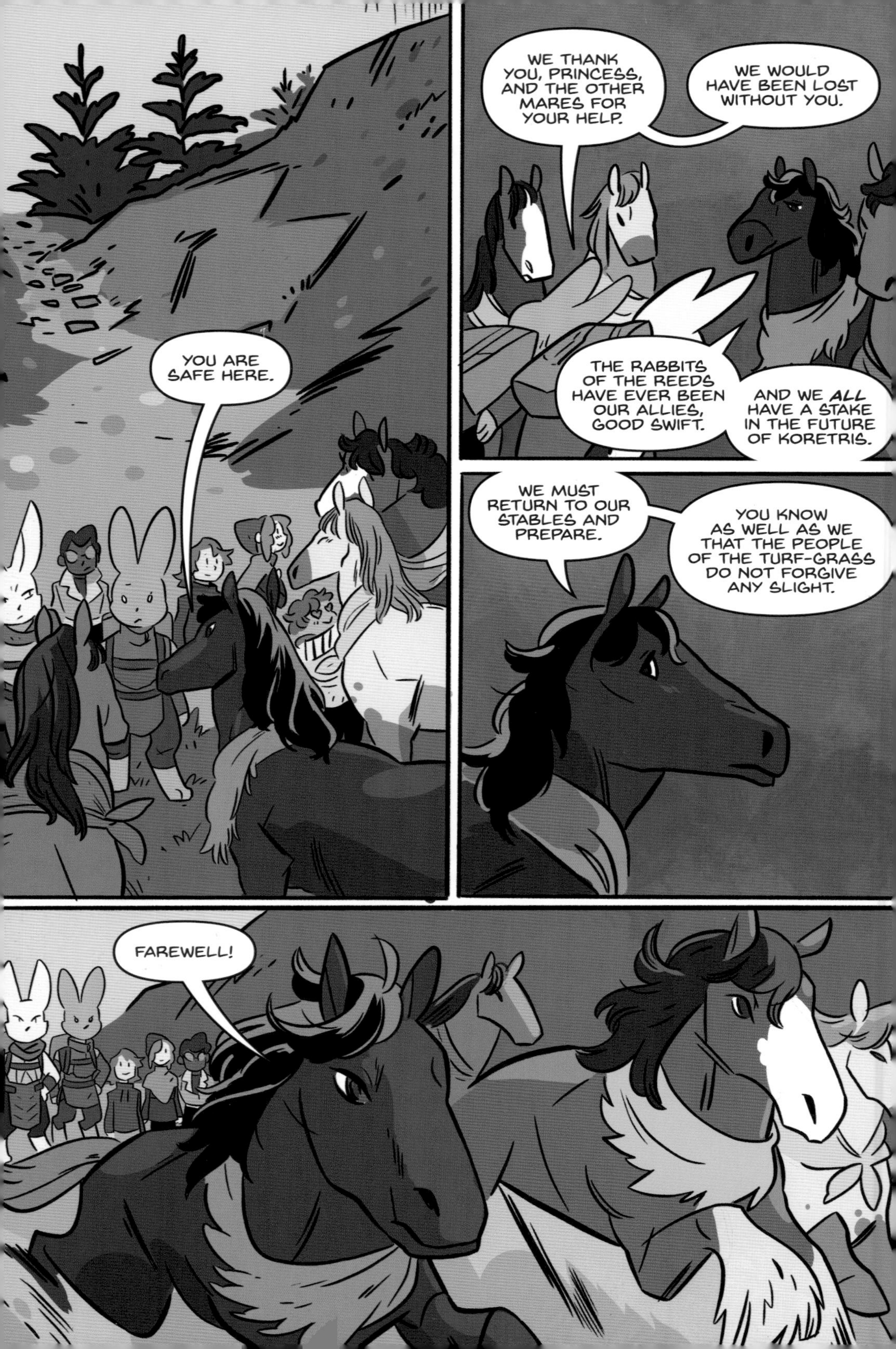
YOU ARE SAFE HERE.
WE THANK YOU, PRINCESS, AND THE OTHER MARES FOR YOUR HELP.
WE WOULD HAVE BEEN LOST WITHOUT YOU.
THE RABBITS OF THE REEDS HAVE EVER BEEN OUR ALLIES, GOOD SWIFT.
AND WE ALL HAVE A STAKE IN THE FUTURE OF KORETRIS.
WE MUST RETURN TO OUR STABLES AND PREPARE.
YOU KNOW AS WELL AS WE THAT THE PEOPLE OF THE TURF-GRASS DO NOT FORGIVE ANY SLIGHT.
FAREWELL!

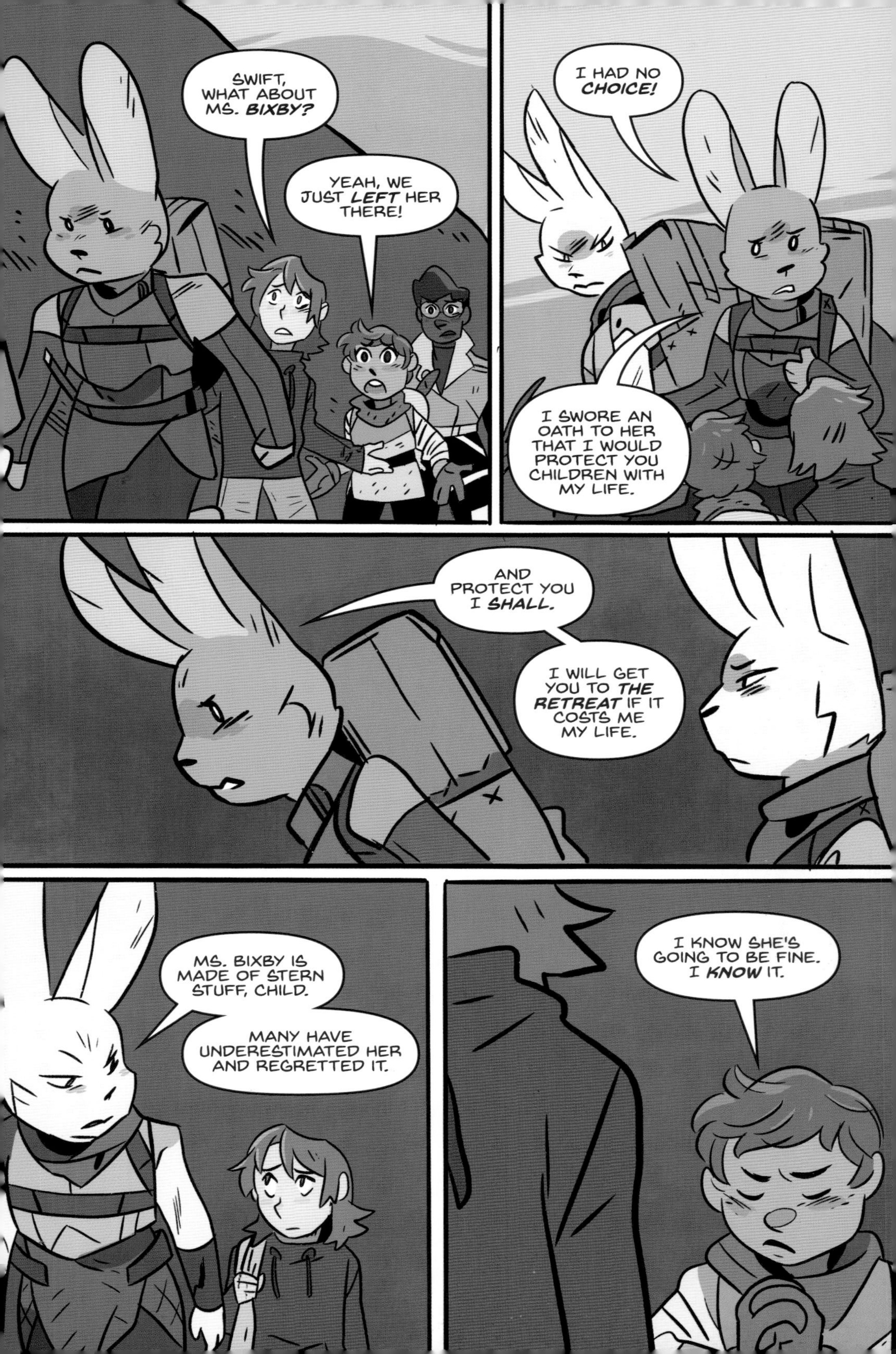
SWIFT, WHAT ABOUT MS. BIXBY?
YEAH, WE JUST LEFT HER THERE!
I HAD NO CHOICE!
I SWORE AN OATH TO HER THAT I WOULD PROTECT YOU CHILDREN WITH MY LIFE.
AND PROTECT YOU I SHALL.
I WILL GET YOU TO THE RETREAT IF IT COSTS ME MY LIFE.
MS. BIXBY IS MADE OF STERN STUFF, CHILD.
MANY HAVE UNDERESTIMATED HER AND REGRETTED IT.
I KNOW SHE'S GOING TO BE FINE. I KNOW IT.

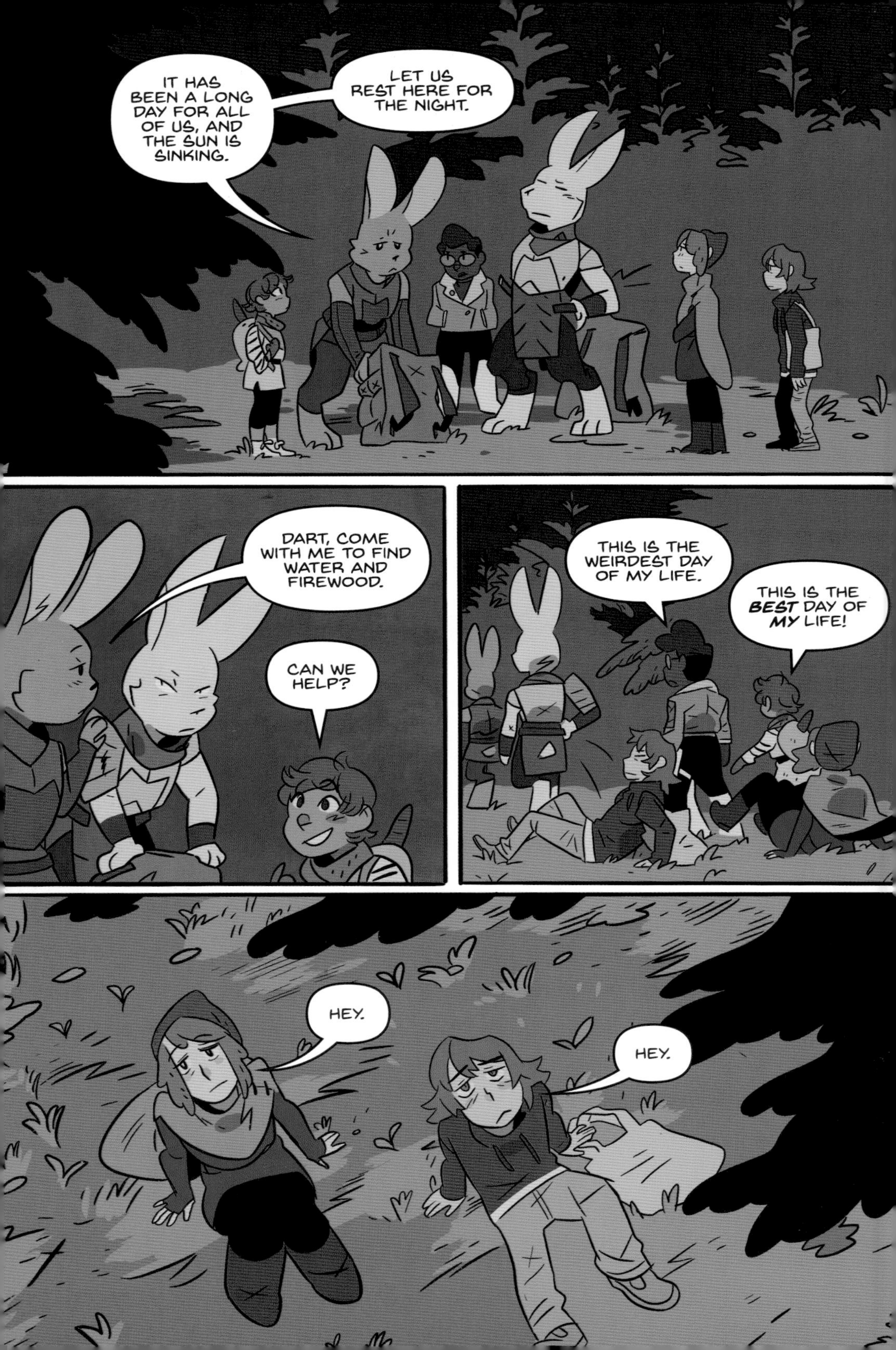
IT HAS BEEN A LONG DAY FOR ALL OF US, AND THE SUN IS SINKING.
LET US REST HERE FOR THE NIGHT.
DART, COME WITH ME TO FIND WATER AND FIREWOOD.
CAN WE HELP?
THIS IS THE WEIRDEST DAY OF MY LIFE.
THIS IS THE **BEST** DAY OF ***MY*** LIFE!
HEY.
HEY.

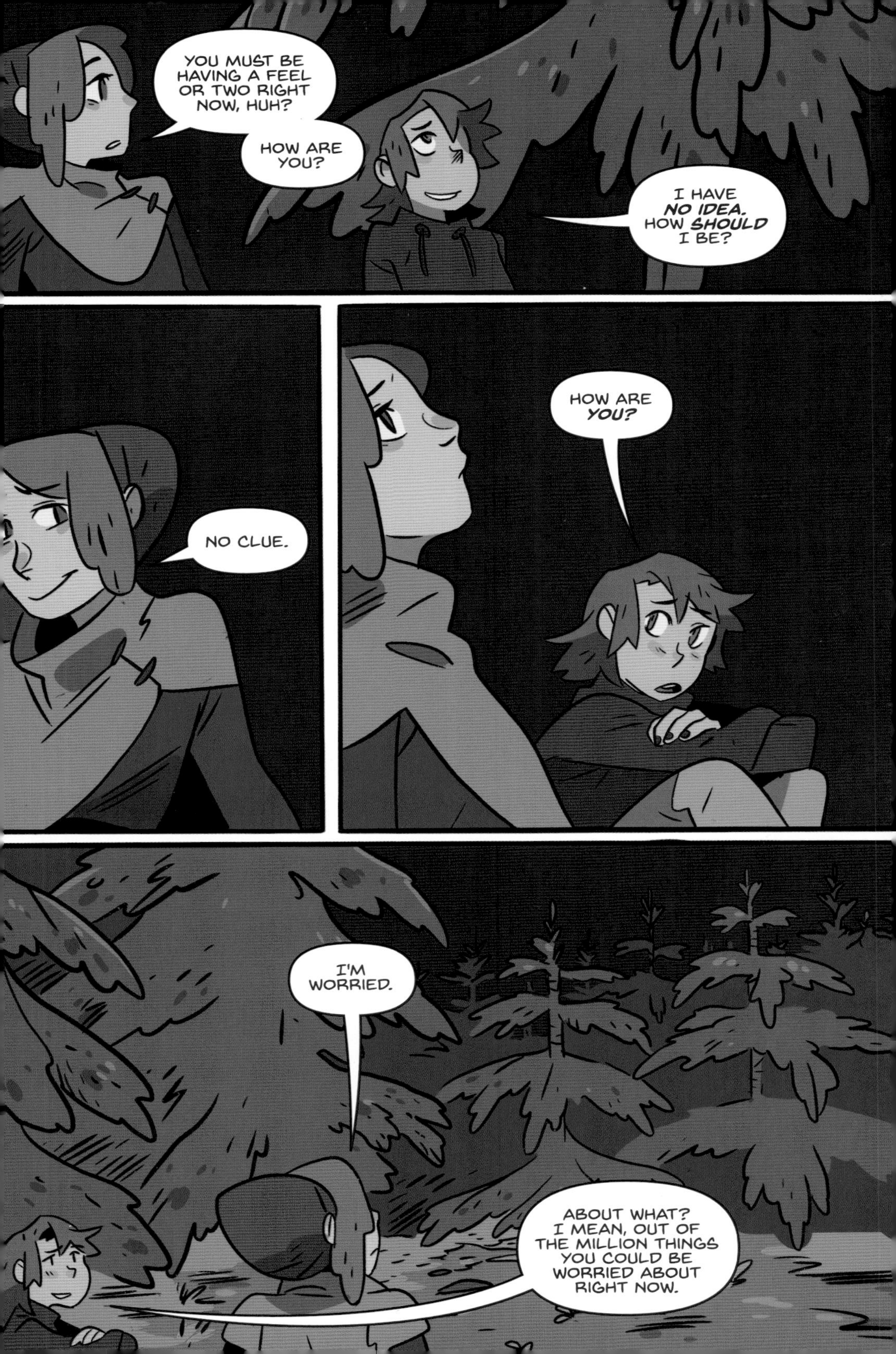
YOU MUST BE HAVING A FEEL OR TWO RIGHT NOW, HUH?
HOW ARE YOU?
I HAVE *NO IDEA.* HOW *SHOULD* I BE?
NO CLUE.
HOW ARE *YOU?*
I'M WORRIED.
ABOUT WHAT? I MEAN, OUT OF THE MILLION THINGS YOU COULD BE WORRIED ABOUT RIGHT NOW.

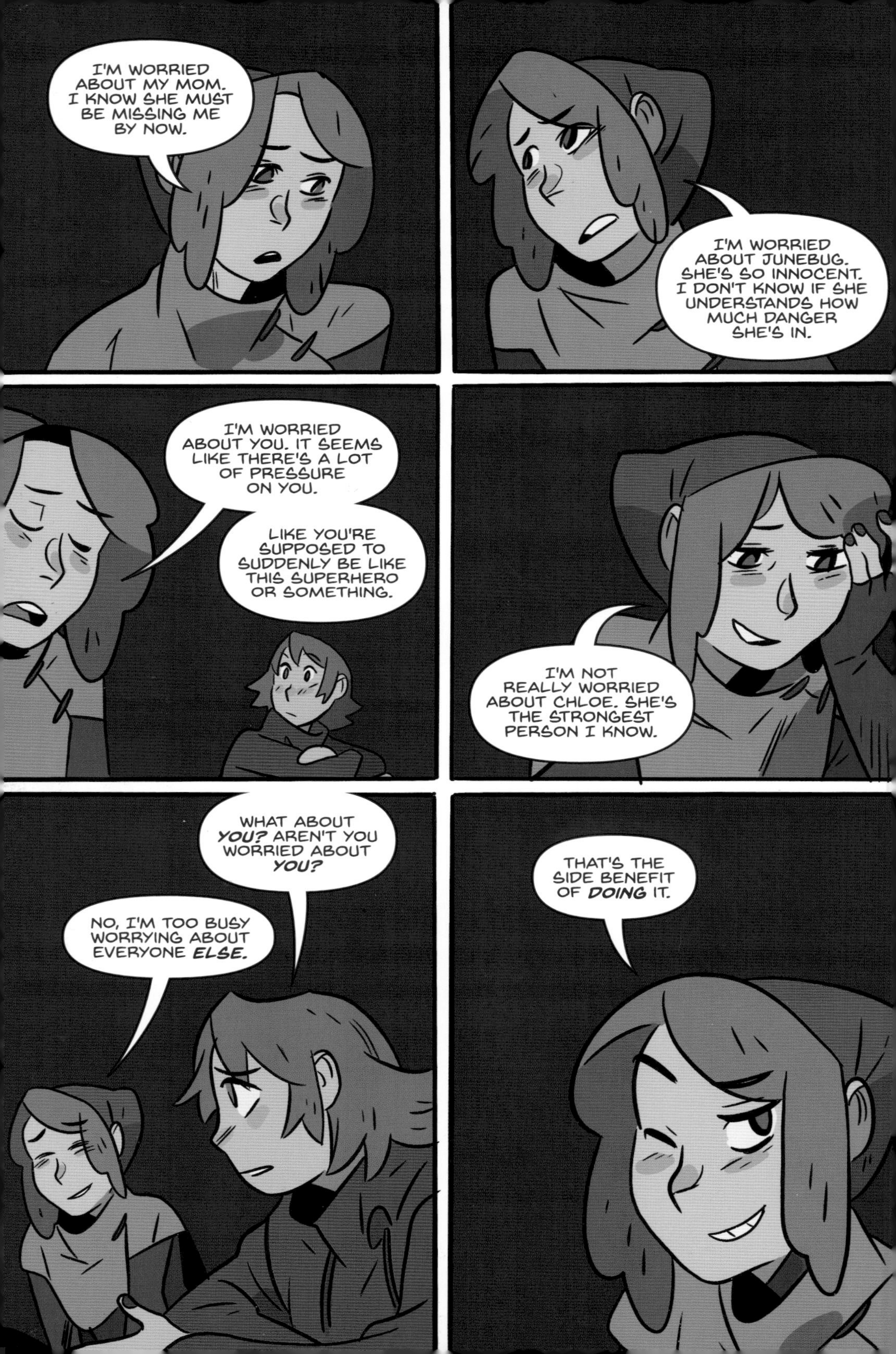
I'M WORRIED ABOUT MY MOM. I KNOW SHE MUST BE MISSING ME BY NOW.
I'M WORRIED ABOUT JUNEBUG. SHE'S SO INNOCENT. I DON'T KNOW IF SHE UNDERSTANDS HOW MUCH DANGER SHE'S IN.
I'M WORRIED ABOUT YOU. IT SEEMS LIKE THERE'S A LOT OF PRESSURE ON YOU.
LIKE YOU'RE SUPPOSED TO SUDDENLY BE LIKE THIS SUPERHERO OR SOMETHING.
I'M NOT REALLY WORRIED ABOUT CHLOE. SHE'S THE STRONGEST PERSON I KNOW.
WHAT ABOUT *YOU?* AREN'T YOU WORRIED ABOUT *YOU?*
NO, I'M TOO BUSY WORRYING ABOUT EVERYONE *ELSE.*
THAT'S THE SIDE BENEFIT OF *DOING* IT.

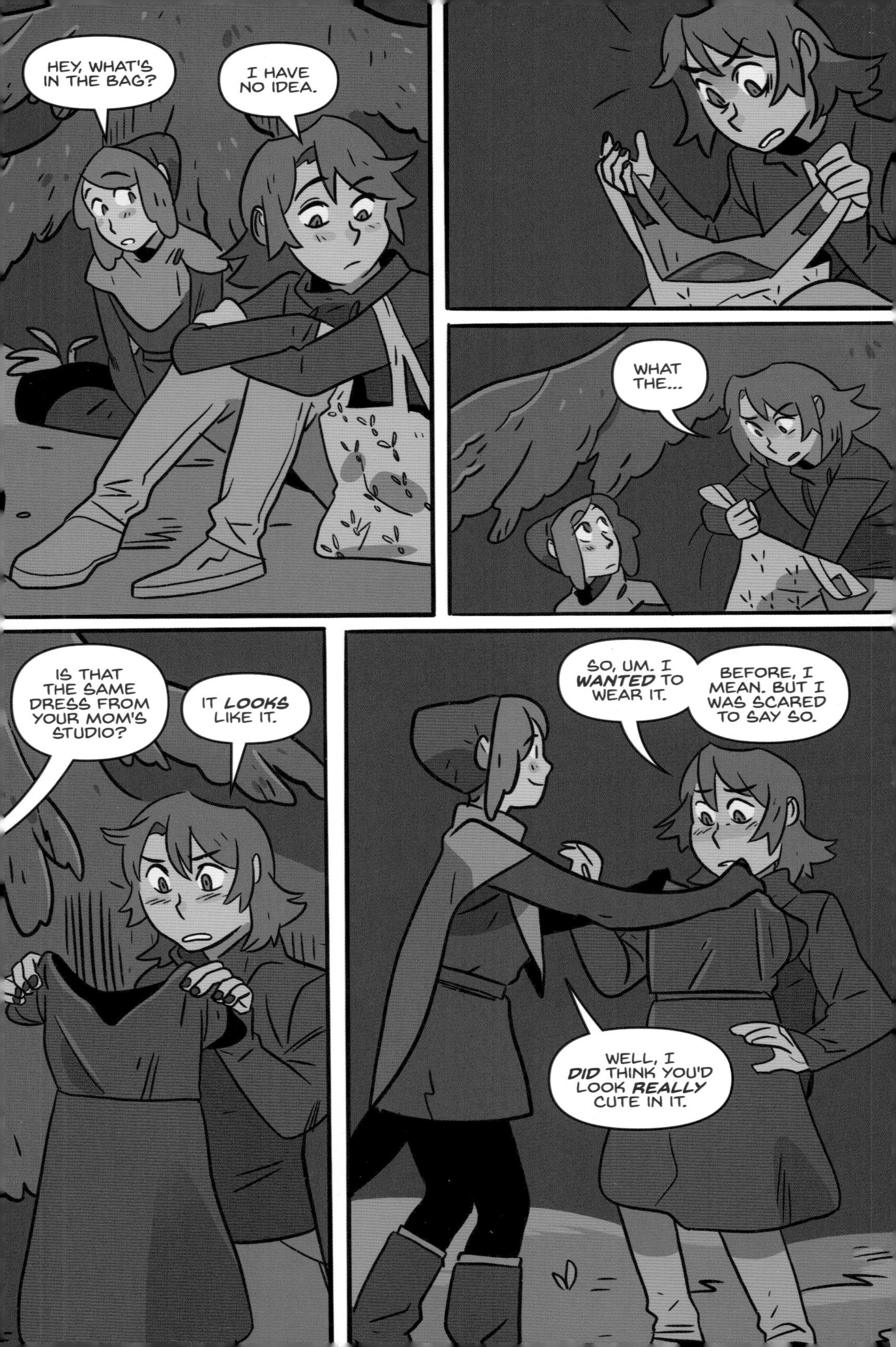
HEY, WHAT'S IN THE BAG?
I HAVE NO IDEA.
WHAT THE...
IS THAT THE SAME DRESS FROM YOUR MOM'S STUDIO?
IT LOOKS LIKE IT.
SO, UM. I WANTED TO WEAR IT.
BEFORE, I MEAN. BUT I WAS SCARED TO SAY SO.
WELL, I DID THINK YOU'D LOOK REALLY CUTE IN IT.

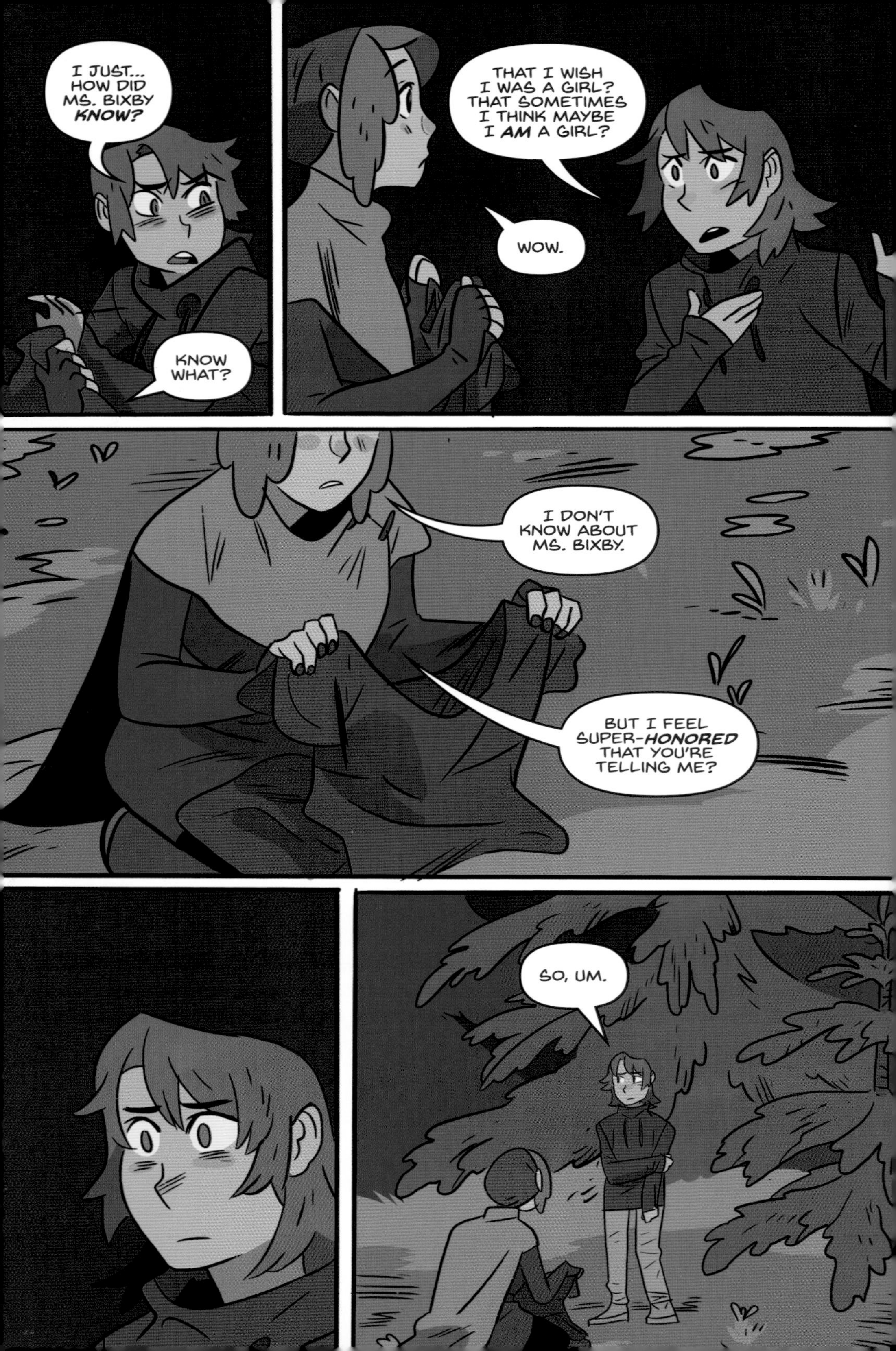
I JUST... HOW DID MS. BIXBY *KNOW?*
KNOW WHAT?
THAT I WISH I WAS A GIRL? THAT SOMETIMES I THINK MAYBE I *AM* A GIRL?
WOW.
I DON'T KNOW ABOUT MS. BIXBY.
BUT I FEEL SUPER-*HONORED* THAT YOU'RE TELLING ME?
SO, UM.

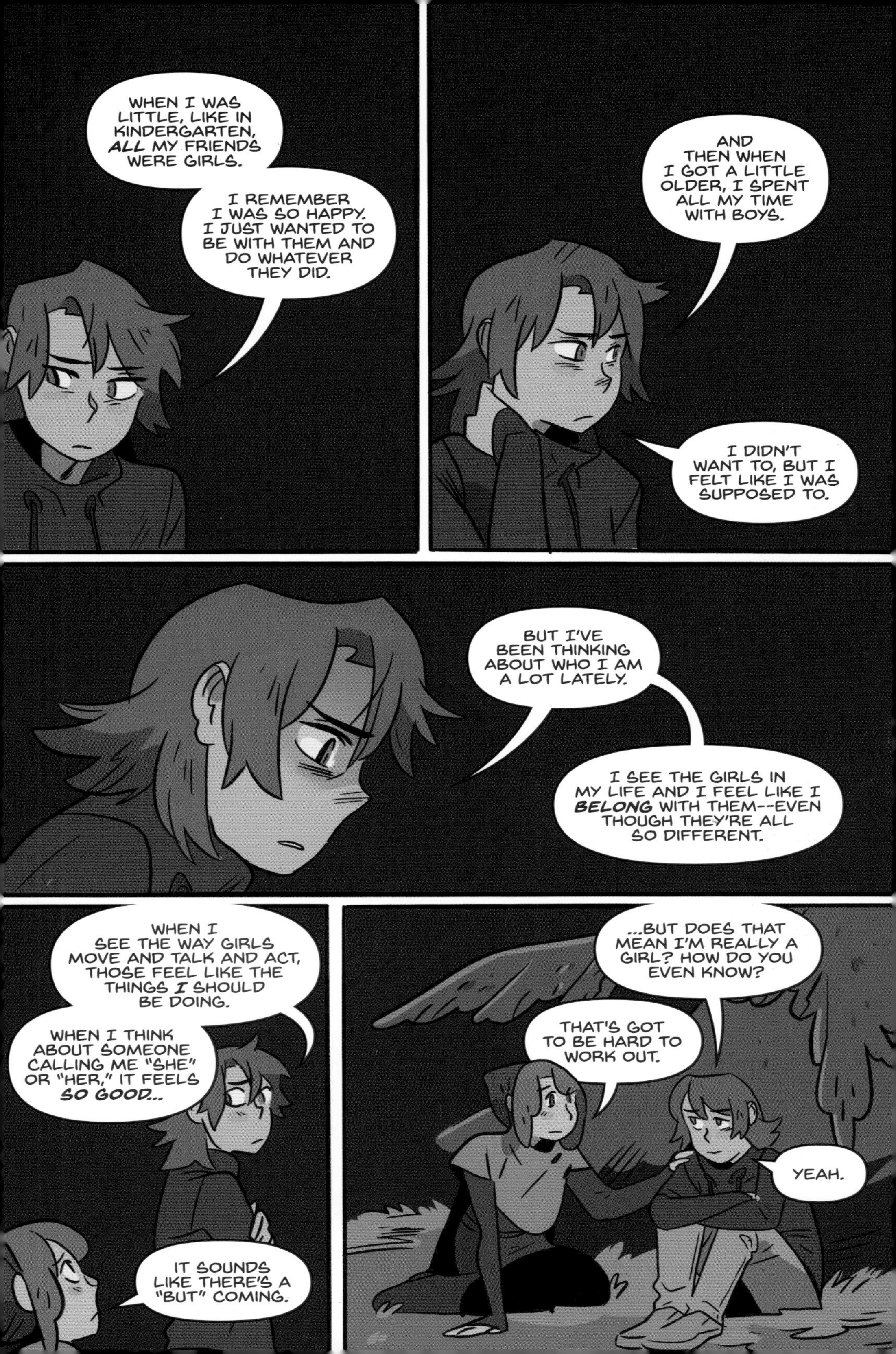
WHEN I WAS LITTLE, LIKE IN KINDERGARTEN, ***ALL*** MY FRIENDS WERE GIRLS.
I REMEMBER I WAS SO HAPPY. I JUST WANTED TO BE WITH THEM AND DO WHATEVER THEY DID.
AND THEN WHEN I GOT A LITTLE OLDER, I SPENT ALL MY TIME WITH BOYS.
I DIDN'T WANT TO, BUT I FELT LIKE I WAS SUPPOSED TO.
BUT I'VE BEEN THINKING ABOUT WHO I AM A LOT LATELY.
I SEE THE GIRLS IN MY LIFE AND I FEEL LIKE I ***BELONG*** WITH THEM--EVEN THOUGH THEY'RE ALL SO DIFFERENT.
WHEN I SEE THE WAY GIRLS MOVE AND TALK AND ACT, THOSE FEEL LIKE THE THINGS *I* SHOULD BE DOING.
WHEN I THINK ABOUT SOMEONE CALLING ME "SHE" OR "HER," IT FEELS ***SO GOOD...***
IT SOUNDS LIKE THERE'S A "BUT" COMING.
...BUT DOES THAT MEAN I'M REALLY A GIRL? HOW DO YOU EVEN KNOW?
THAT'S GOT TO BE HARD TO WORK OUT.
YEAH.

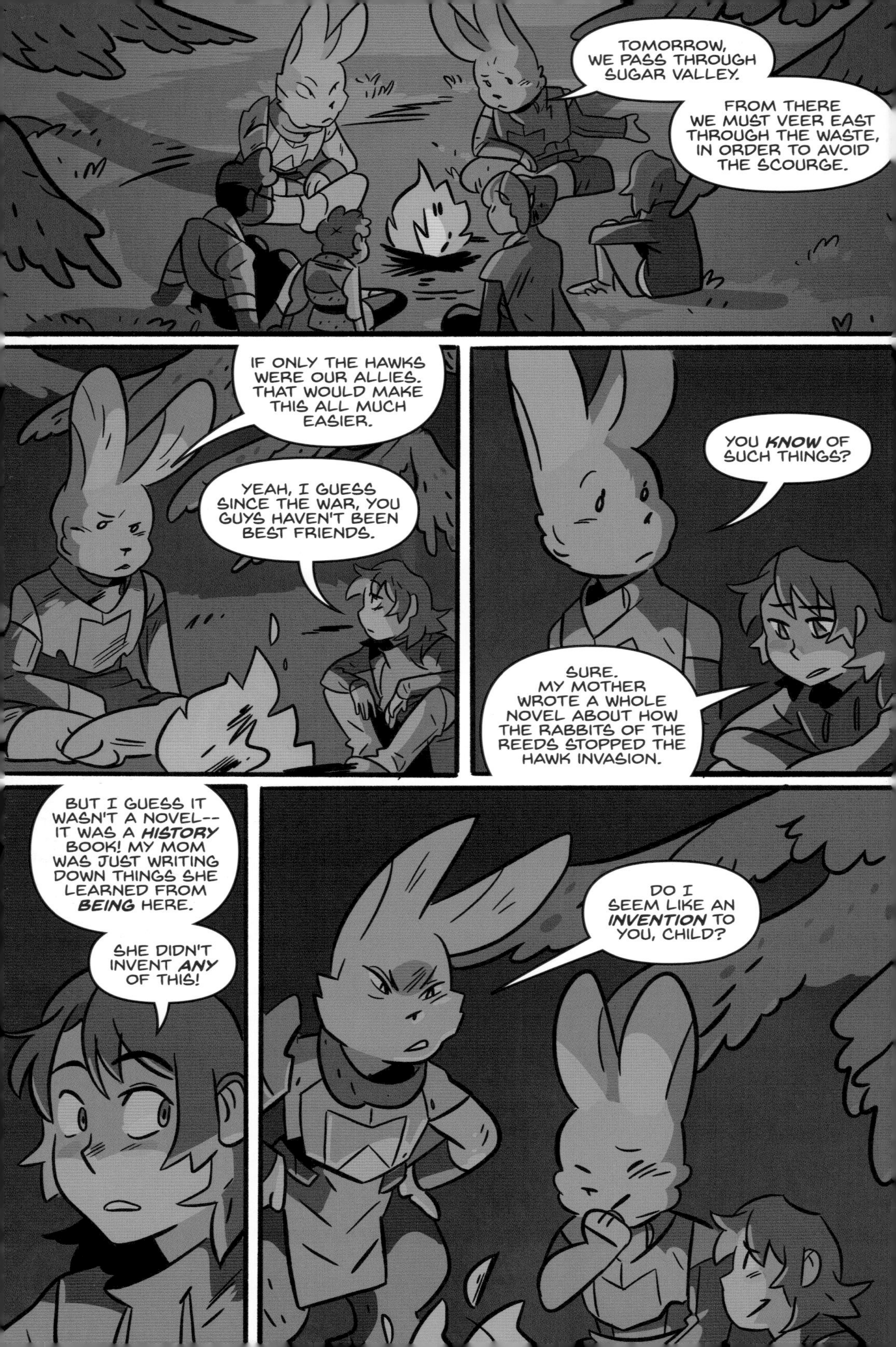
TOMORROW, WE PASS THROUGH SUGAR VALLEY.
FROM THERE WE MUST VEER EAST THROUGH THE WASTE, IN ORDER TO AVOID THE SCOURGE.
IF ONLY THE HAWKS WERE OUR ALLIES. THAT WOULD MAKE THIS ALL MUCH EASIER.
YEAH, I GUESS SINCE THE WAR, YOU GUYS HAVEN'T BEEN BEST FRIENDS.
YOU *KNOW* OF SUCH THINGS?
SURE. MY MOTHER WROTE A WHOLE NOVEL ABOUT HOW THE RABBITS OF THE REEDS STOPPED THE HAWK INVASION.
BUT I GUESS IT WASN'T A NOVEL-- IT WAS A *HISTORY* BOOK! MY MOM WAS JUST WRITING DOWN THINGS SHE LEARNED FROM *BEING* HERE.
SHE DIDN'T INVENT *ANY* OF THIS!
DO I SEEM LIKE AN *INVENTION* TO YOU, CHILD?

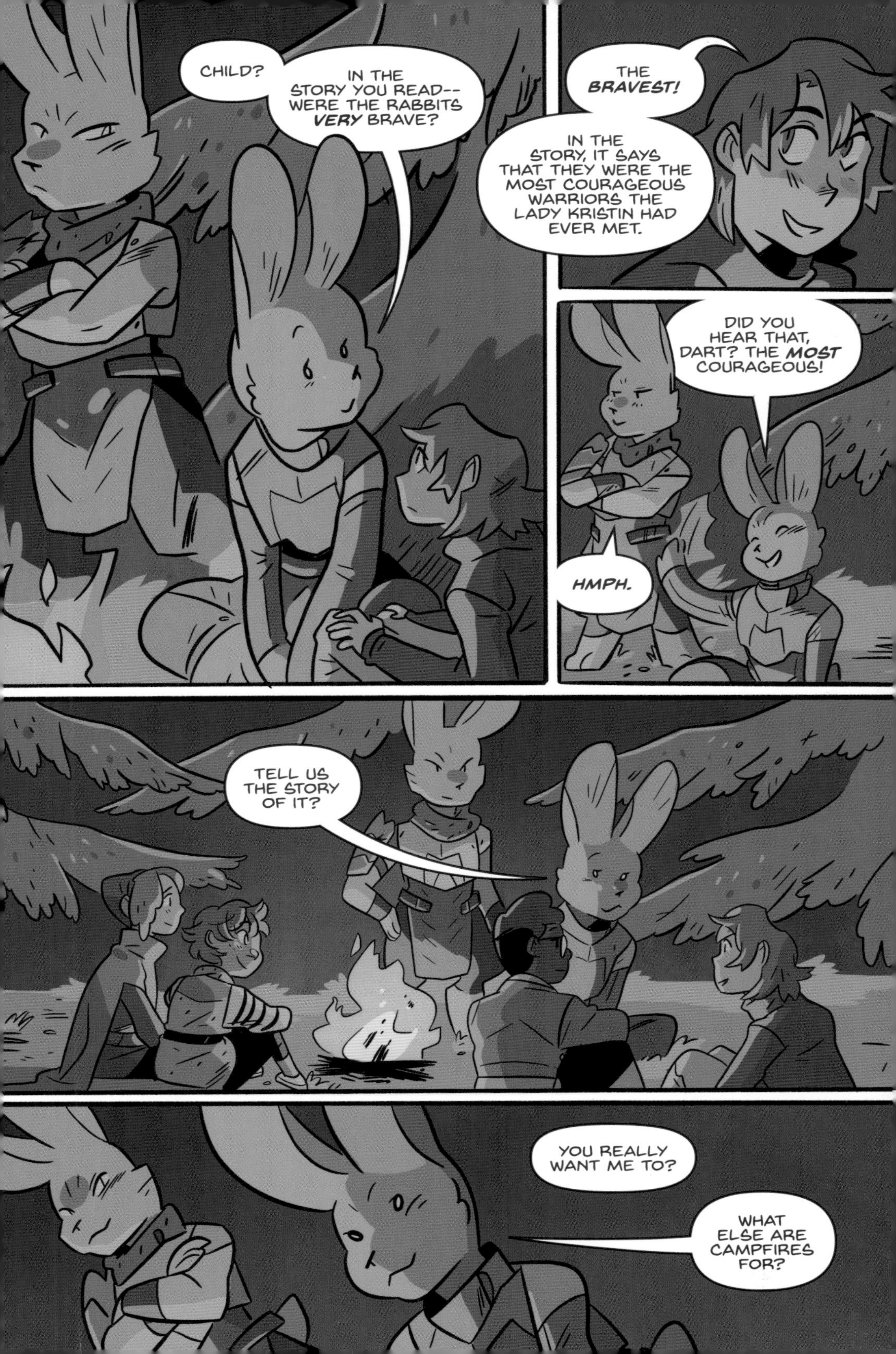
CHILD?
IN THE STORY YOU READ-- WERE THE RABBITS *VERY* BRAVE?
THE *BRAVEST!*
IN THE STORY, IT SAYS THAT THEY WERE THE MOST COURAGEOUS WARRIORS THE LADY KRISTIN HAD EVER MET.
DID YOU HEAR THAT, DART? THE *MOST* COURAGEOUS!
HMPH.
TELL US THE STORY OF IT?
YOU REALLY WANT ME TO?
WHAT ELSE ARE CAMPFIRES FOR?

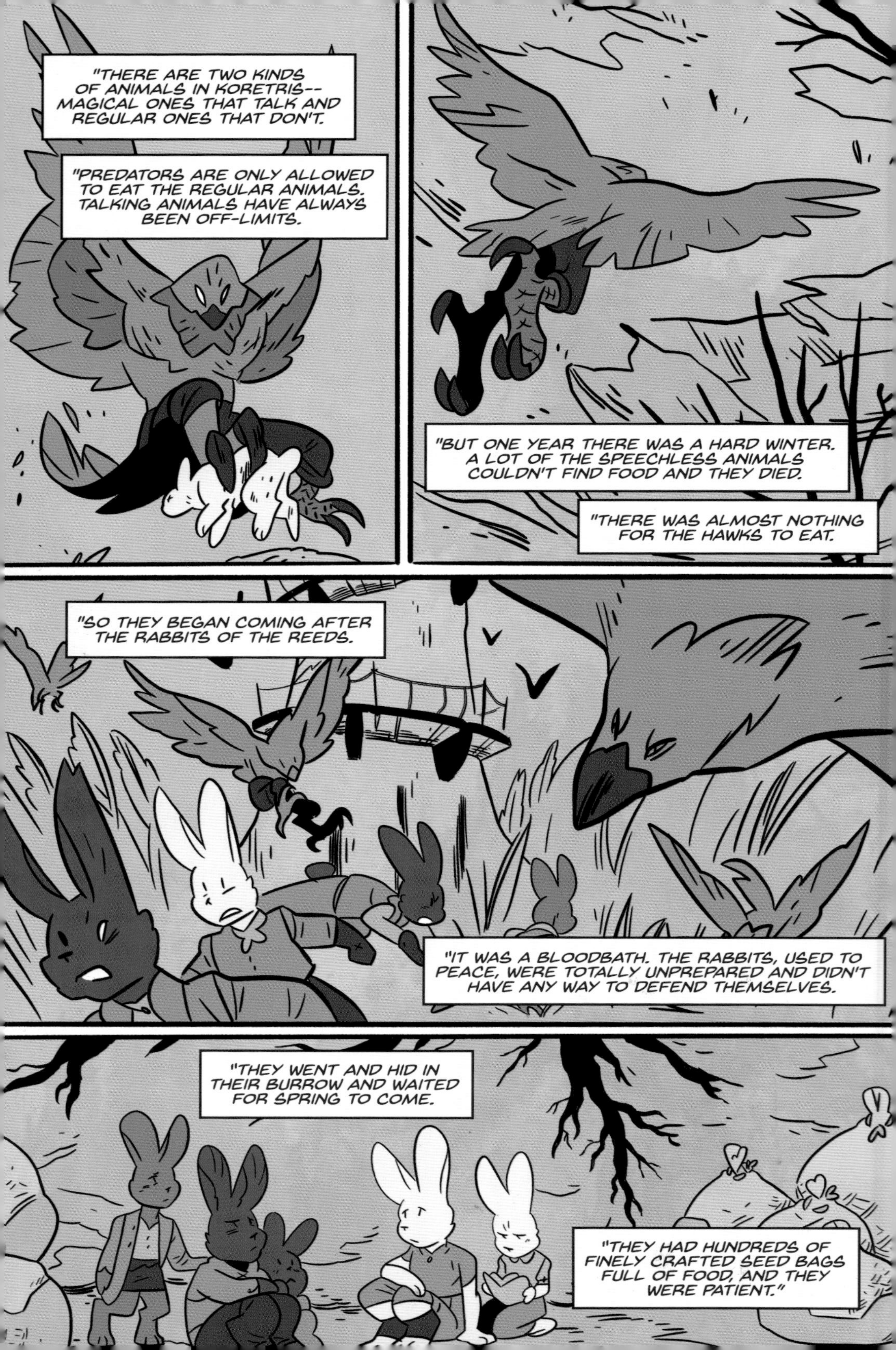
"THERE ARE TWO KINDS OF ANIMALS IN KORETRIS-- MAGICAL ONES THAT TALK AND REGULAR ONES THAT DON'T.
"PREDATORS ARE ONLY ALLOWED TO EAT THE REGULAR ANIMALS. TALKING ANIMALS HAVE ALWAYS BEEN OFF-LIMITS.
"BUT ONE YEAR THERE WAS A HARD WINTER. A LOT OF THE SPEECHLESS ANIMALS COULDN'T FIND FOOD AND THEY DIED.
"THERE WAS ALMOST NOTHING FOR THE HAWKS TO EAT.
"SO THEY BEGAN COMING AFTER THE RABBITS OF THE REEDS.
"IT WAS A BLOODBATH. THE RABBITS, USED TO PEACE, WERE TOTALLY UNPREPARED AND DIDN'T HAVE ANY WAY TO DEFEND THEMSELVES.
"THEY WENT AND HID IN THEIR BURROW AND WAITED FOR SPRING TO COME.
"THEY HAD HUNDREDS OF FINELY CRAFTED SEED BAGS FULL OF FOOD, AND THEY WERE PATIENT."

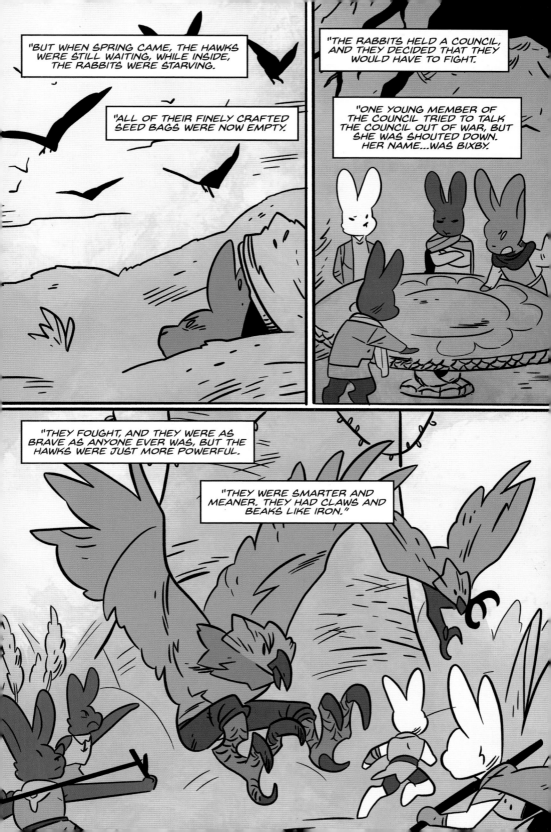

"BUT WHEN SPRING CAME, THE HAWKS WERE STILL WAITING, WHILE INSIDE, THE RABBITS WERE STARVING.

"ALL OF THEIR FINELY CRAFTED SEED BAGS WERE NOW EMPTY.

"THE RABBITS HELD A COUNCIL, AND THEY DECIDED THAT THEY WOULD HAVE TO FIGHT.

"ONE YOUNG MEMBER OF THE COUNCIL TRIED TO TALK THE COUNCIL OUT OF WAR, BUT SHE WAS SHOUTED DOWN. HER NAME...WAS BIXBY.

"THEY FOUGHT, AND THEY WERE AS BRAVE AS ANYONE EVER WAS, BUT THE HAWKS WERE JUST MORE POWERFUL.

"THEY WERE SMARTER AND MEANER. THEY HAD CLAWS AND BEAKS LIKE IRON."

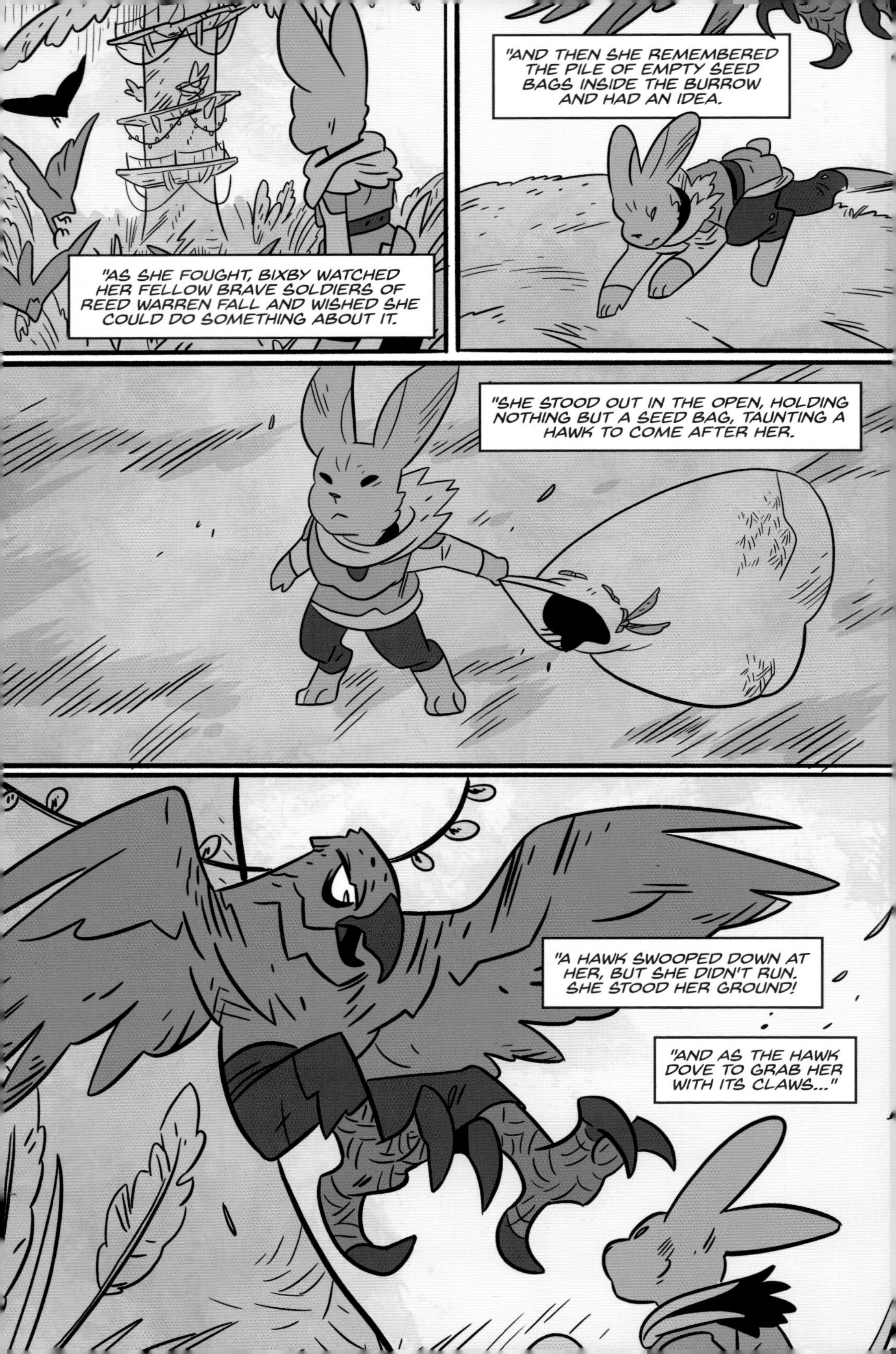
"AS SHE FOUGHT, BIXBY WATCHED HER FELLOW BRAVE SOLDIERS OF REED WARREN FALL AND WISHED SHE COULD DO SOMETHING ABOUT IT.
"AND THEN SHE REMEMBERED THE PILE OF EMPTY SEED BAGS INSIDE THE BURROW AND HAD AN IDEA.
"SHE STOOD OUT IN THE OPEN, HOLDING NOTHING BUT A SEED BAG, TAUNTING A HAWK TO COME AFTER HER.
"A HAWK SWOOPED DOWN AT HER, BUT SHE DIDN'T RUN. SHE STOOD HER GROUND!
"AND AS THE HAWK DOVE TO GRAB HER WITH ITS CLAWS..."

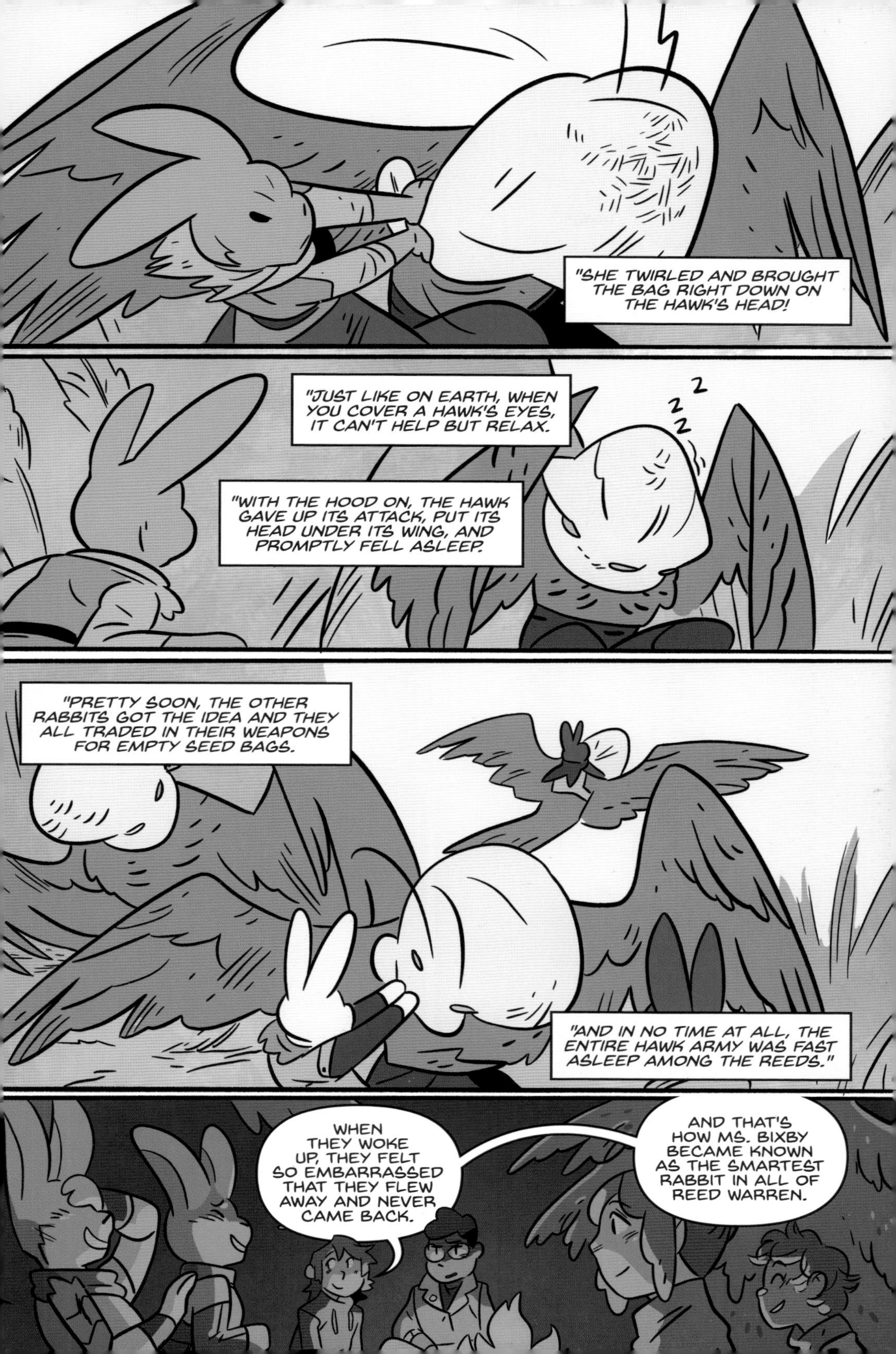
"SHE TWIRLED AND BROUGHT THE BAG RIGHT DOWN ON THE HAWK'S HEAD!
"JUST LIKE ON EARTH, WHEN YOU COVER A HAWK'S EYES, IT CAN'T HELP BUT RELAX.
Z Z Z
"WITH THE HOOD ON, THE HAWK GAVE UP ITS ATTACK, PUT ITS HEAD UNDER ITS WING, AND PROMPTLY FELL ASLEEP.
"PRETTY SOON, THE OTHER RABBITS GOT THE IDEA AND THEY ALL TRADED IN THEIR WEAPONS FOR EMPTY SEED BAGS.
"AND IN NO TIME AT ALL, THE ENTIRE HAWK ARMY WAS FAST ASLEEP AMONG THE REEDS."
WHEN THEY WOKE UP, THEY FELT SO EMBARRASSED THAT THEY FLEW AWAY AND NEVER CAME BACK.
AND THAT'S HOW MS. BIXBY BECAME KNOWN AS THE SMARTEST RABBIT IN ALL OF REED WARREN.

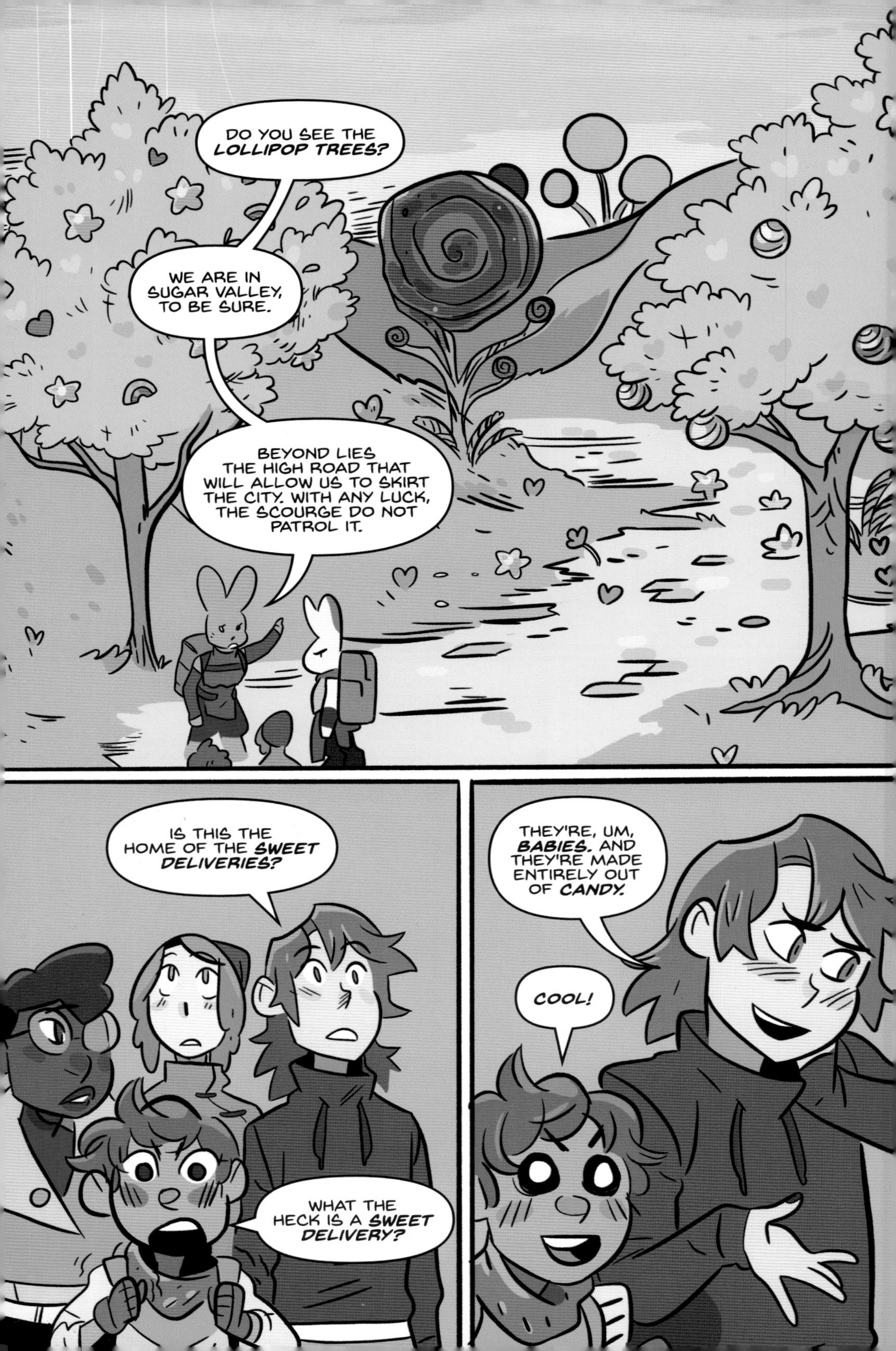
DO YOU SEE THE LOLLIPOP TREES?
WE ARE IN SUGAR VALLEY, TO BE SURE.
BEYOND LIES THE HIGH ROAD THAT WILL ALLOW US TO SKIRT THE CITY. WITH ANY LUCK, THE SCOURGE DO NOT PATROL IT.
IS THIS THE HOME OF THE SWEET DELIVERIES?
WHAT THE HECK IS A SWEET DELIVERY?
THEY'RE, UM, BABIES. AND THEY'RE MADE ENTIRELY OUT OF CANDY.
COOL!

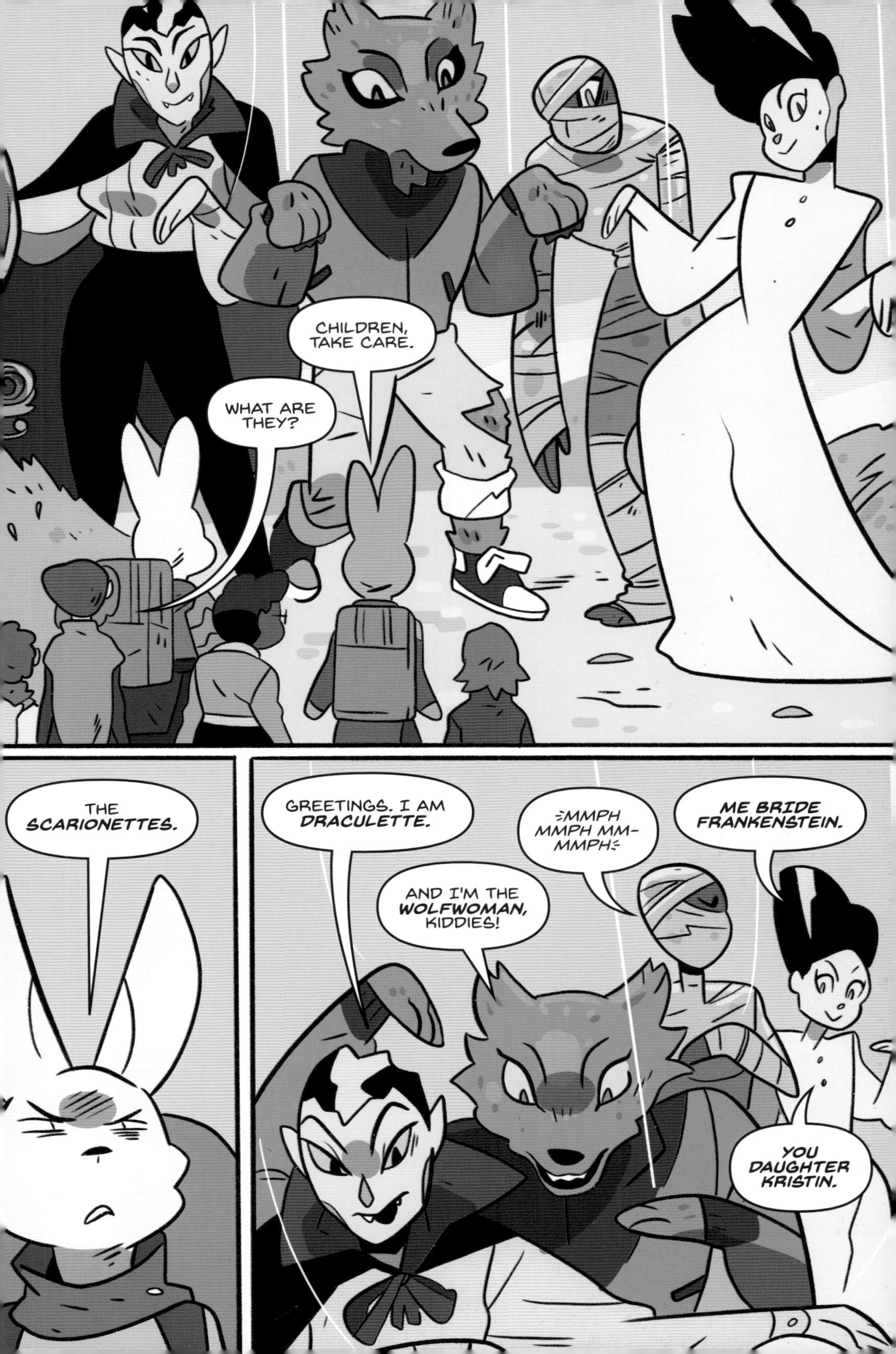
CHILDREN, TAKE CARE.
WHAT ARE THEY?
THE SCARIONETTES.
GREETINGS. I AM DRACULETTE.
AND I'M THE WOLFWOMAN, KIDDIES!
MMPH MMPH MM-MMPH
ME BRIDE FRANKENSTEIN.
YOU DAUGHTER KRISTIN.

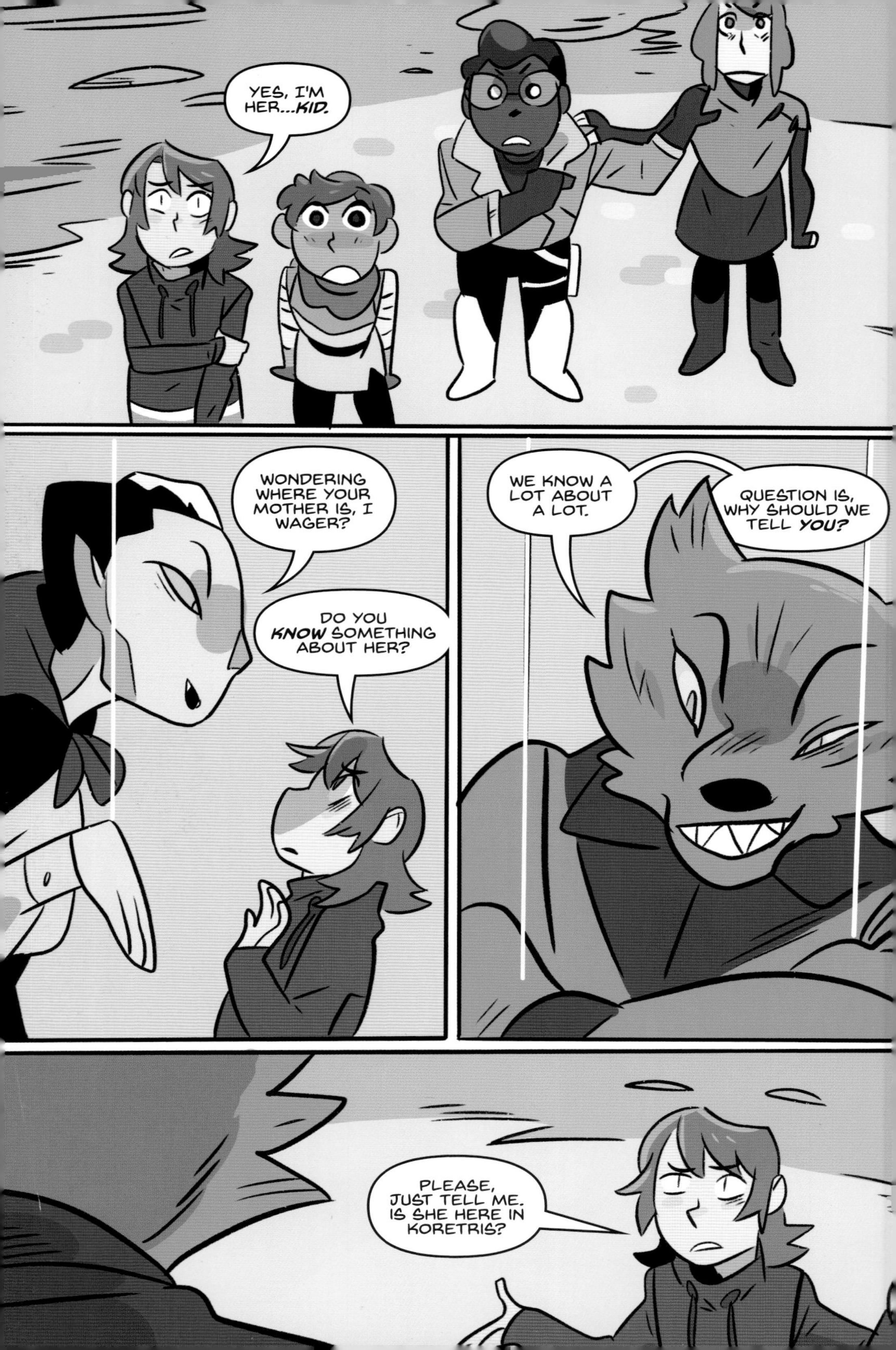
YES, I'M HER...KID.
WONDERING WHERE YOUR MOTHER IS, I WAGER?
DO YOU KNOW SOMETHING ABOUT HER?
WE KNOW A LOT ABOUT A LOT.
QUESTION IS, WHY SHOULD WE TELL YOU?
PLEASE, JUST TELL ME. IS SHE HERE IN KORETRIS?

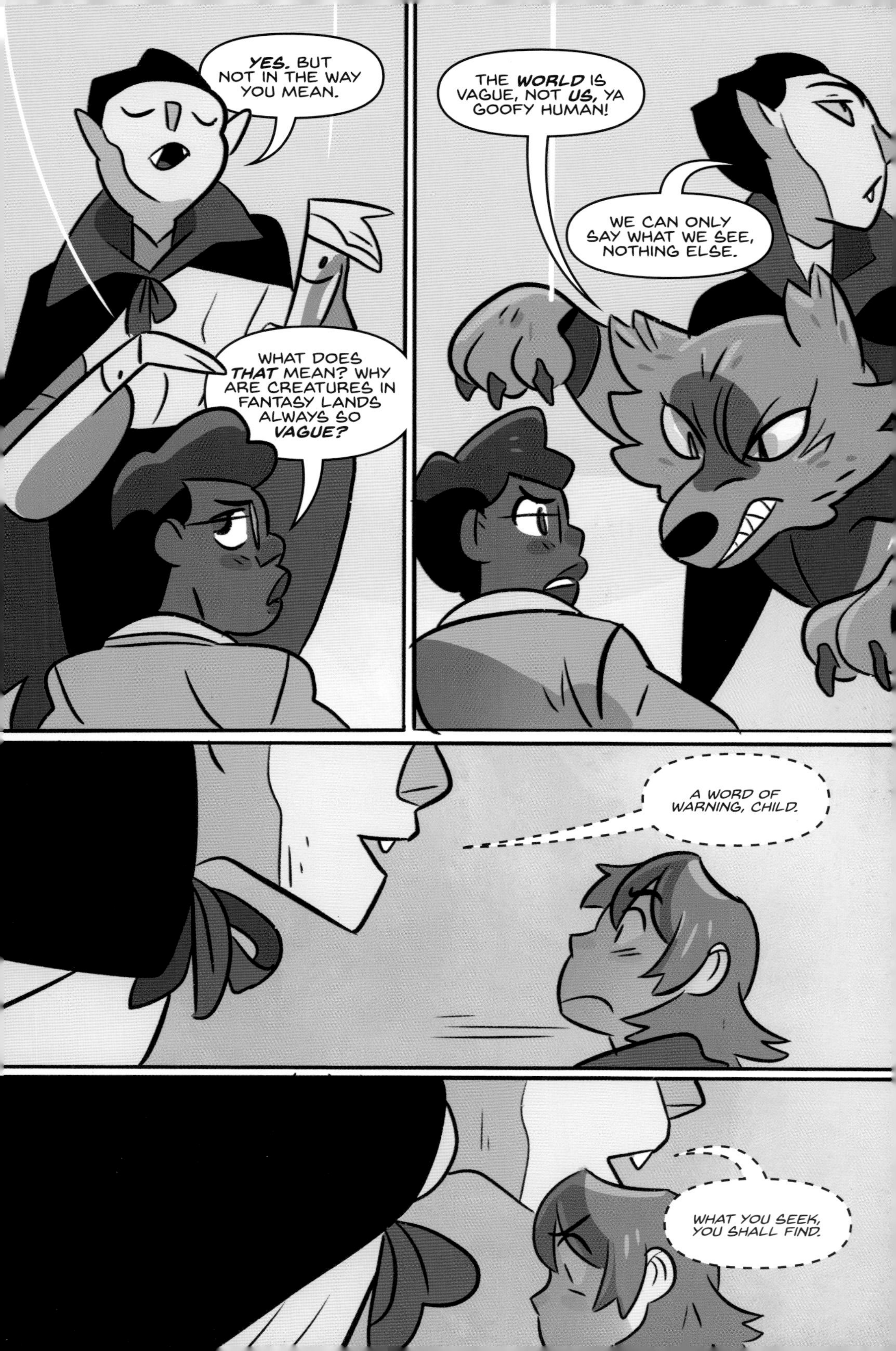
YES. BUT NOT IN THE WAY YOU MEAN.
WHAT DOES THAT MEAN? WHY ARE CREATURES IN FANTASY LANDS ALWAYS SO VAGUE?
THE WORLD IS VAGUE, NOT US, YA GOOFY HUMAN!
WE CAN ONLY SAY WHAT WE SEE, NOTHING ELSE.
A WORD OF WARNING, CHILD.
WHAT YOU SEEK, YOU SHALL FIND.

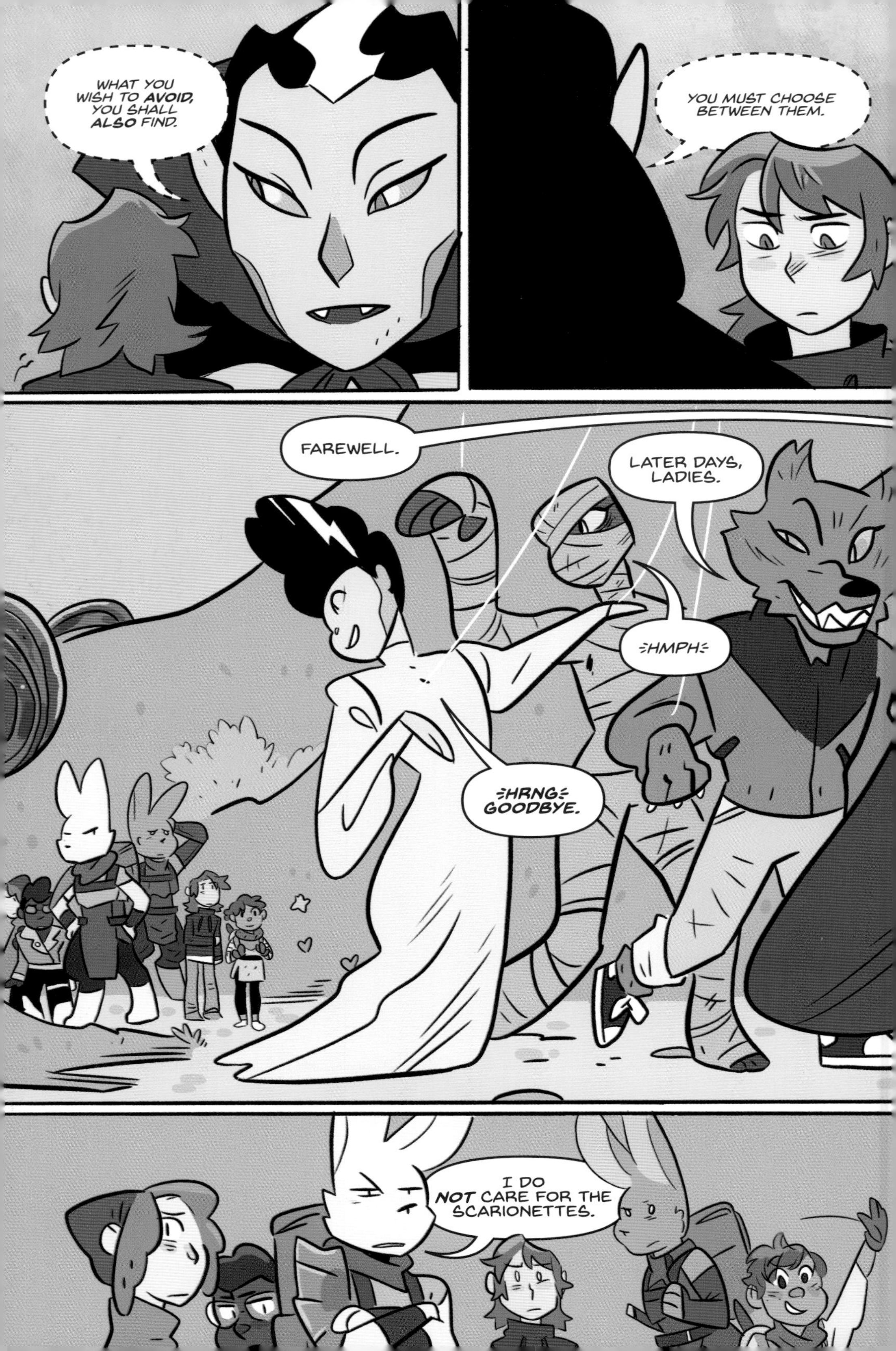
WHAT YOU WISH TO AVOID, YOU SHALL ALSO FIND.
YOU MUST CHOOSE BETWEEN THEM.
FAREWELL.
LATER DAYS, LADIES.
HMPH
HRNG GOODBYE.
I DO NOT CARE FOR THE SCARIONETTES.

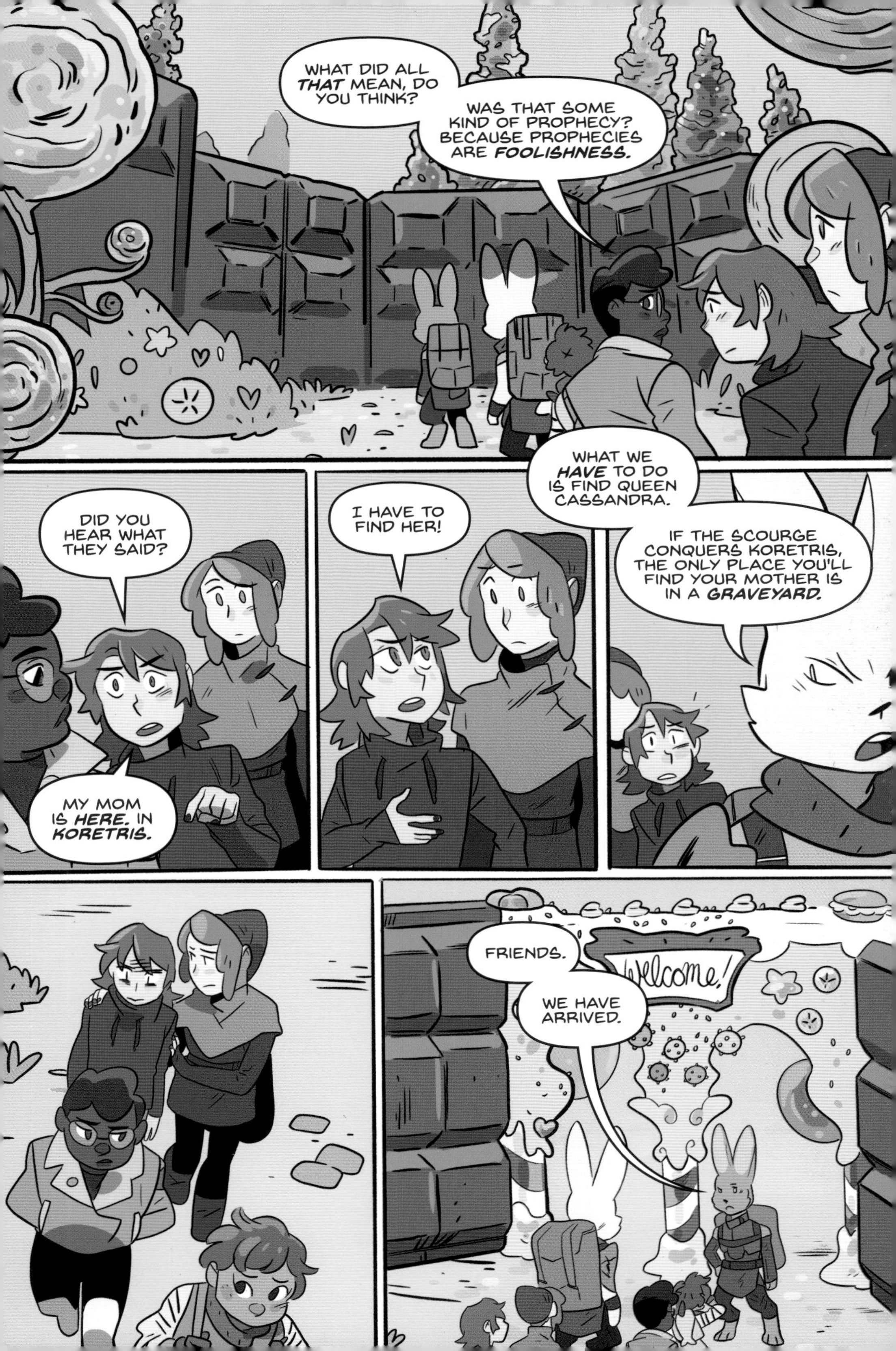
WHAT DID ALL THAT MEAN, DO YOU THINK?
WAS THAT SOME KIND OF PROPHECY? BECAUSE PROPHECIES ARE FOOLISHNESS.
DID YOU HEAR WHAT THEY SAID?
MY MOM IS HERE. IN KORETRIS.
I HAVE TO FIND HER!
WHAT WE HAVE TO DO IS FIND QUEEN CASSANDRA.
IF THE SCOURGE CONQUERS KORETRIS, THE ONLY PLACE YOU'LL FIND YOUR MOTHER IS IN A GRAVEYARD.
FRIENDS.
WE HAVE ARRIVED.
Welcome!

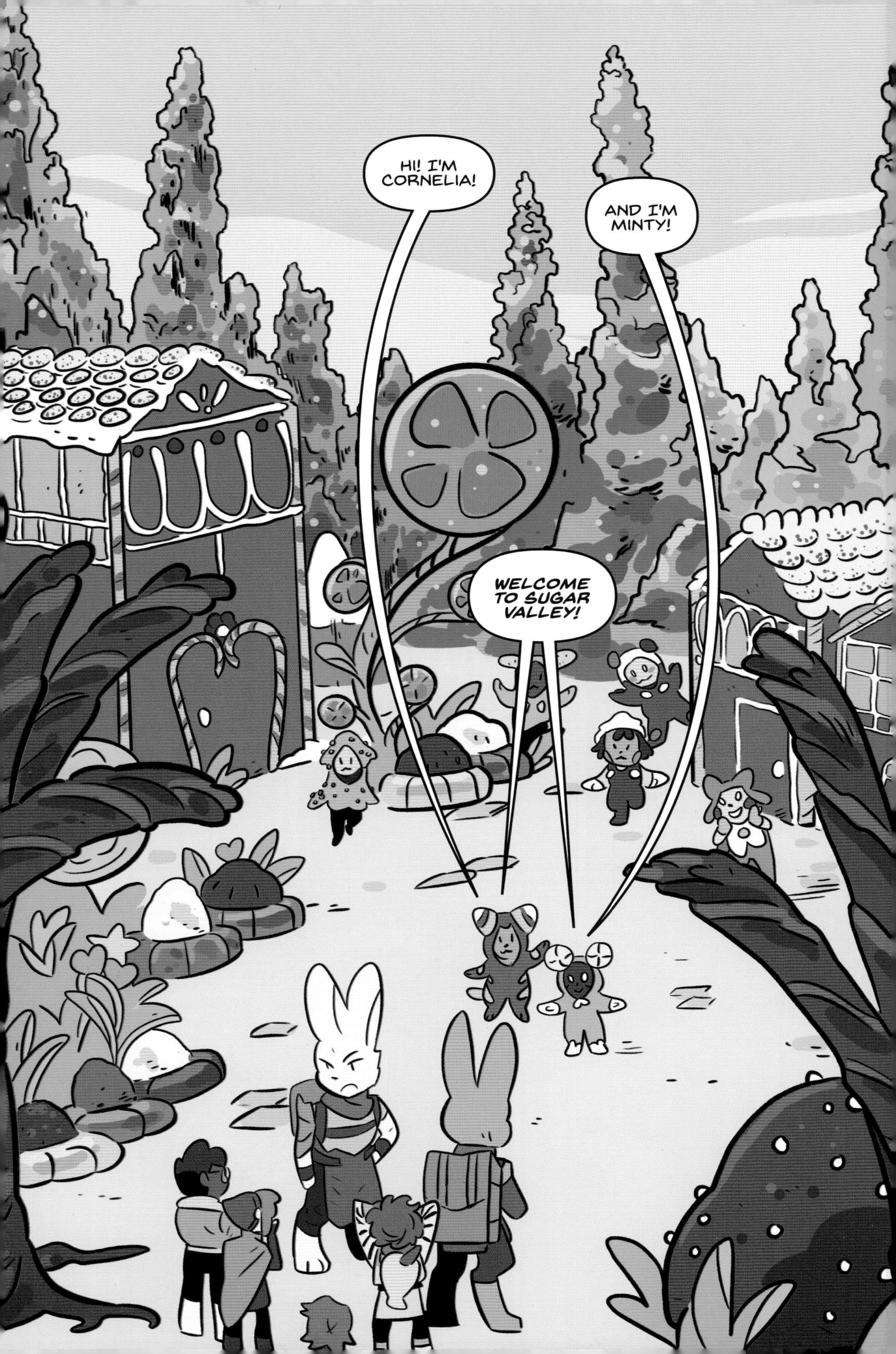
HI! I'M CORNELIA!
AND I'M MINTY!
WELCOME TO SUGAR VALLEY!

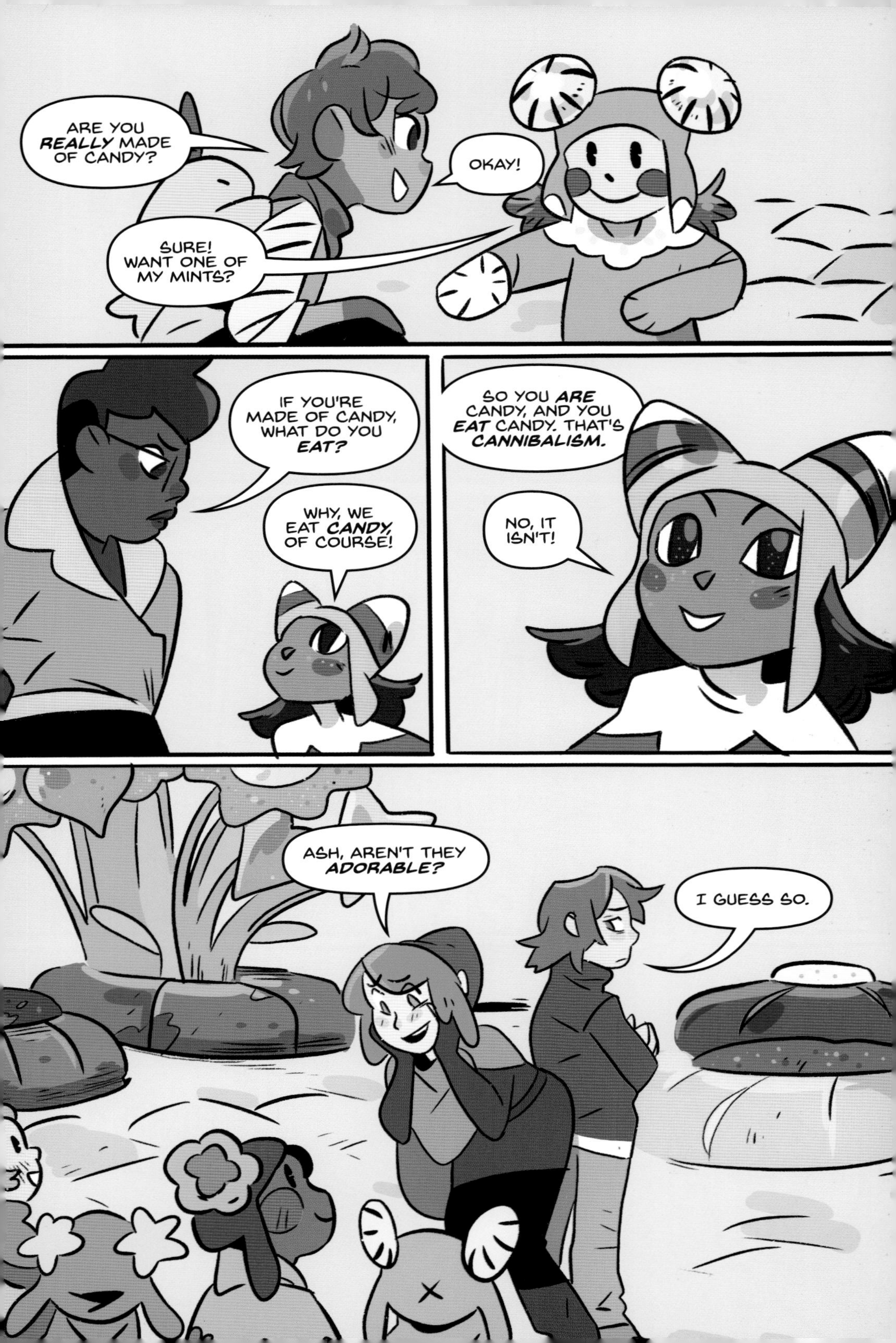
ARE YOU REALLY MADE OF CANDY?
OKAY!
SURE! WANT ONE OF MY MINTS?
IF YOU'RE MADE OF CANDY, WHAT DO YOU EAT?
WHY, WE EAT CANDY, OF COURSE!
SO YOU ARE CANDY, AND YOU EAT CANDY. THAT'S CANNIBALISM.
NO, IT ISN'T!
ASH, AREN'T THEY ADORABLE?
I GUESS SO.

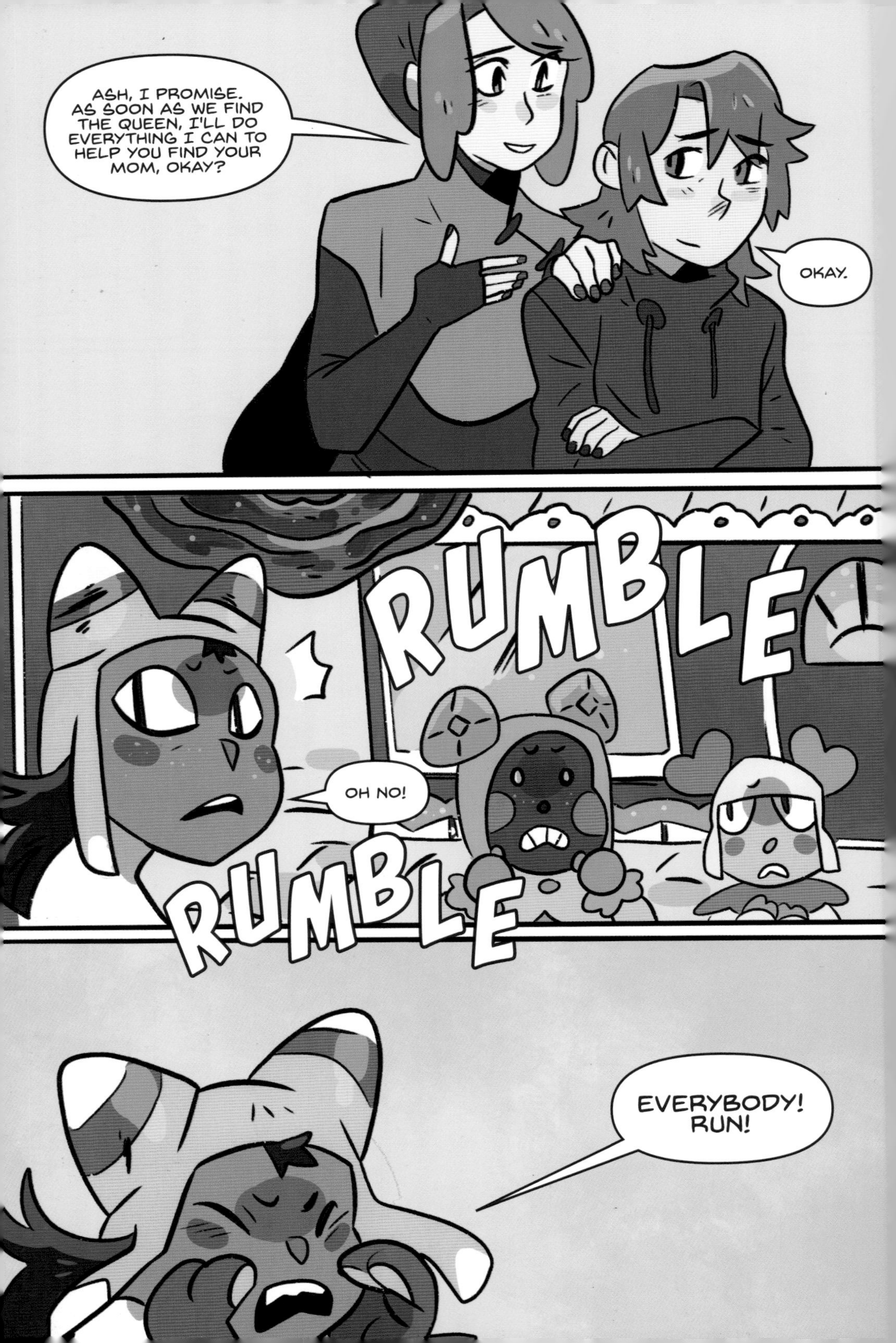
ASH, I PROMISE. AS SOON AS WE FIND THE QUEEN, I'LL DO EVERYTHING I CAN TO HELP YOU FIND YOUR MOM, OKAY?
OKAY.
RUMBLE
OH NO!
RUMBLE
EVERYBODY! RUN!

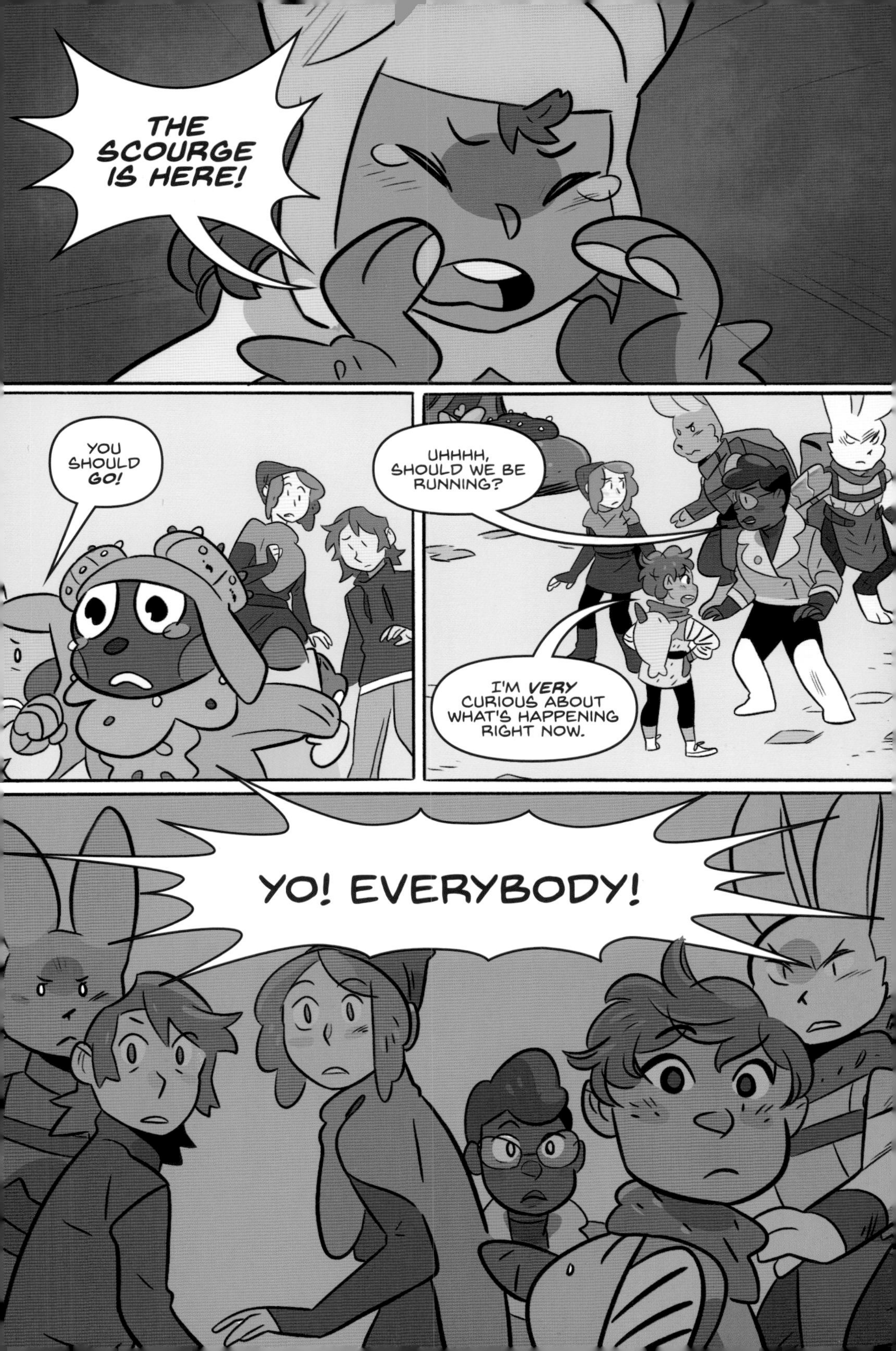
THE SCOURGE IS HERE!
YOU SHOULD *GO!*
UHHHH, SHOULD WE BE RUNNING?
I'M *VERY* CURIOUS ABOUT WHAT'S HAPPENING RIGHT NOW.
YO! EVERYBODY!

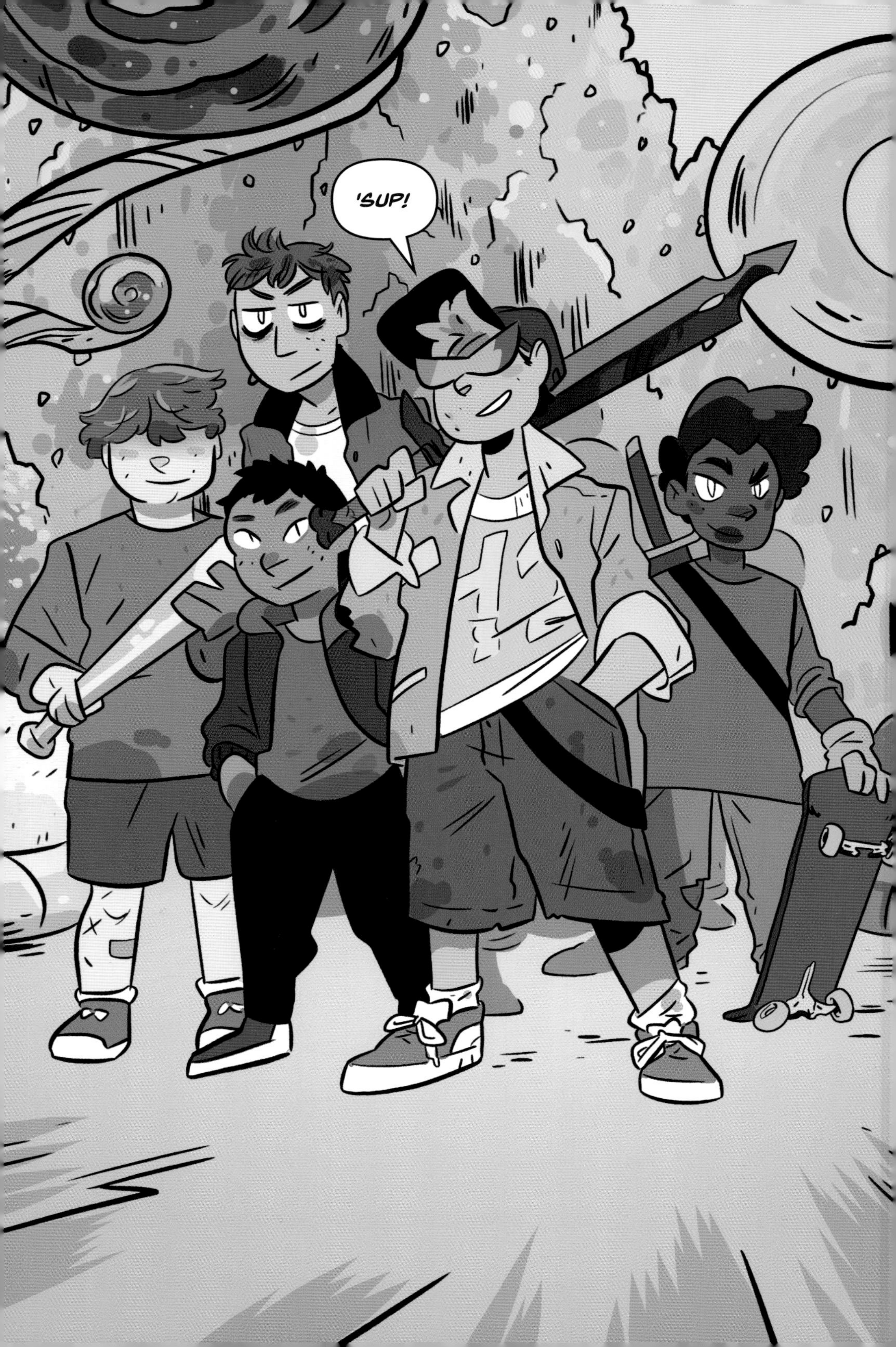
'SUP!

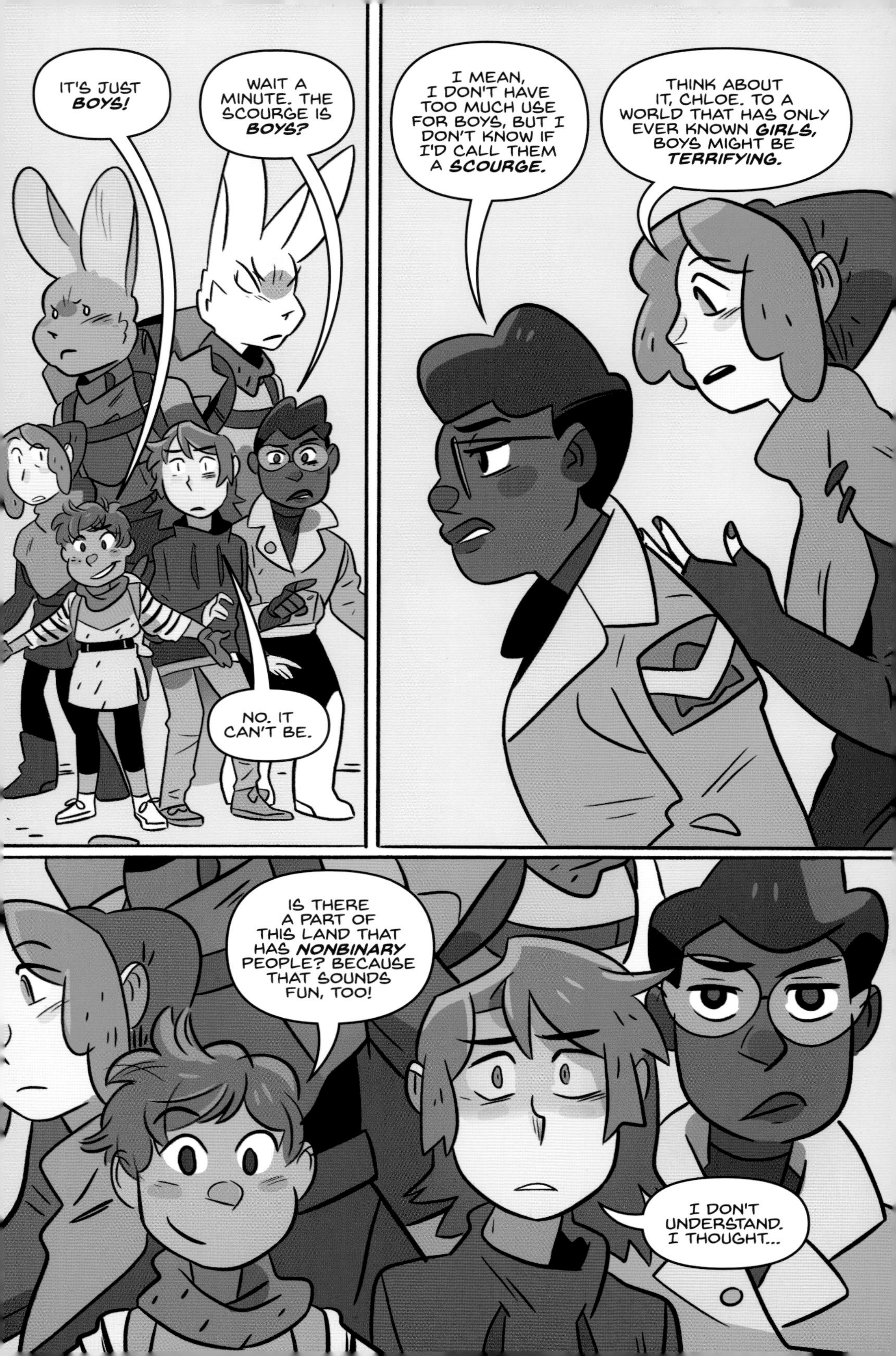
IT'S JUST **BOYS!**
WAIT A MINUTE. THE SCOURGE IS **BOYS?**
NO. IT CAN'T BE.
I MEAN, I DON'T HAVE TOO MUCH USE FOR BOYS, BUT I DON'T KNOW IF I'D CALL THEM A **SCOURGE.**
THINK ABOUT IT, CHLOE. TO A WORLD THAT HAS ONLY EVER KNOWN **GIRLS,** BOYS MIGHT BE **TERRIFYING.**
IS THERE A PART OF THIS LAND THAT HAS **NONBINARY** PEOPLE? BECAUSE THAT SOUNDS FUN, TOO!
I DON'T UNDERSTAND. I THOUGHT...

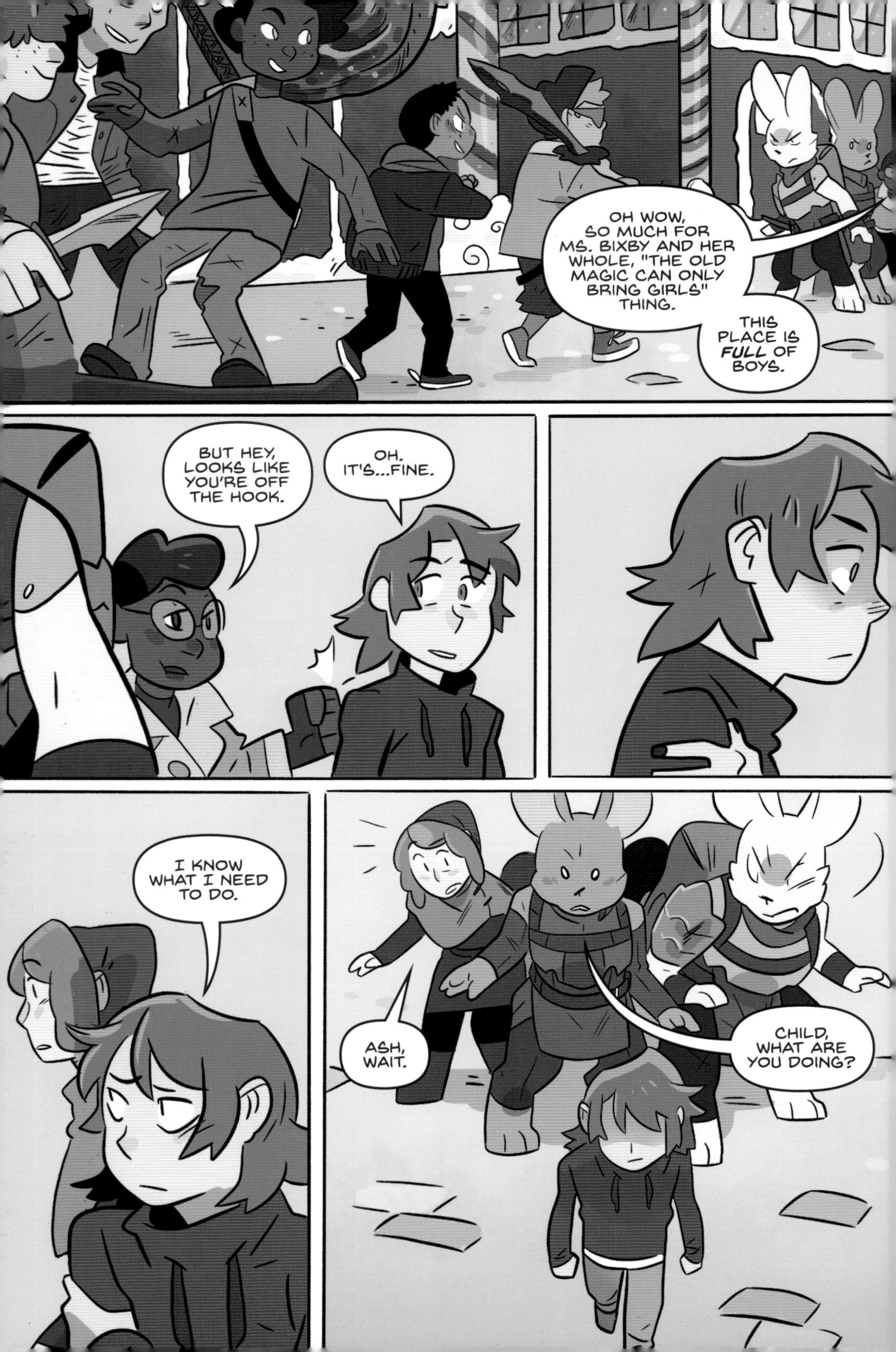
OH WOW, SO MUCH FOR MS. BIXBY AND HER WHOLE, "THE OLD MAGIC CAN ONLY BRING GIRLS" THING.
THIS PLACE IS *FULL* OF BOYS.
BUT HEY, LOOKS LIKE YOU'RE OFF THE HOOK.
OH. IT'S...FINE.
I KNOW WHAT I NEED TO DO.
ASH, WAIT.
CHILD, WHAT ARE YOU DOING?

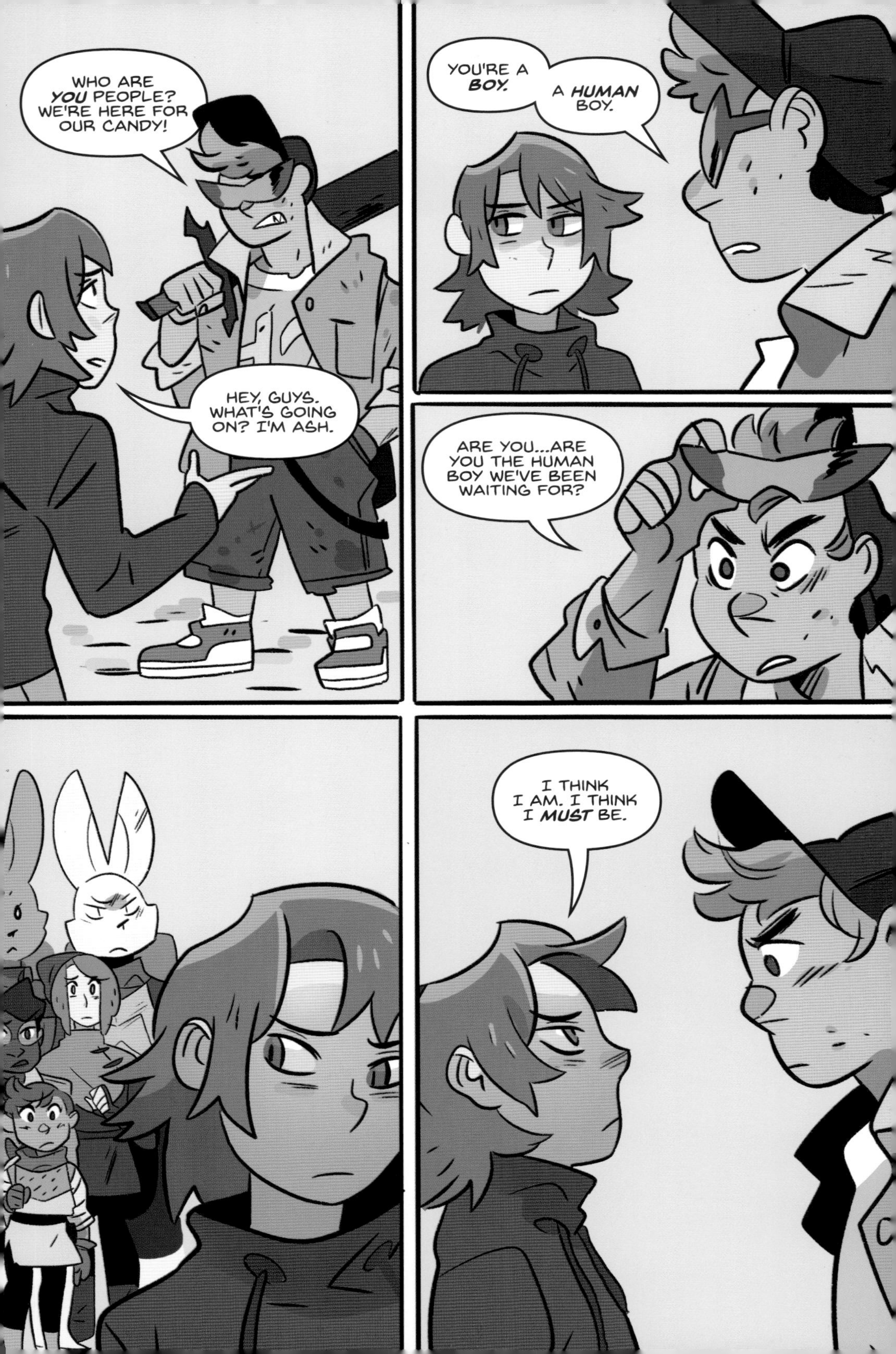
WHO ARE YOU PEOPLE? WE'RE HERE FOR OUR CANDY!
HEY, GUYS. WHAT'S GOING ON? I'M ASH.
YOU'RE A BOY.
A HUMAN BOY.
ARE YOU...ARE YOU THE HUMAN BOY WE'VE BEEN WAITING FOR?
I THINK I AM. I THINK I MUST BE.

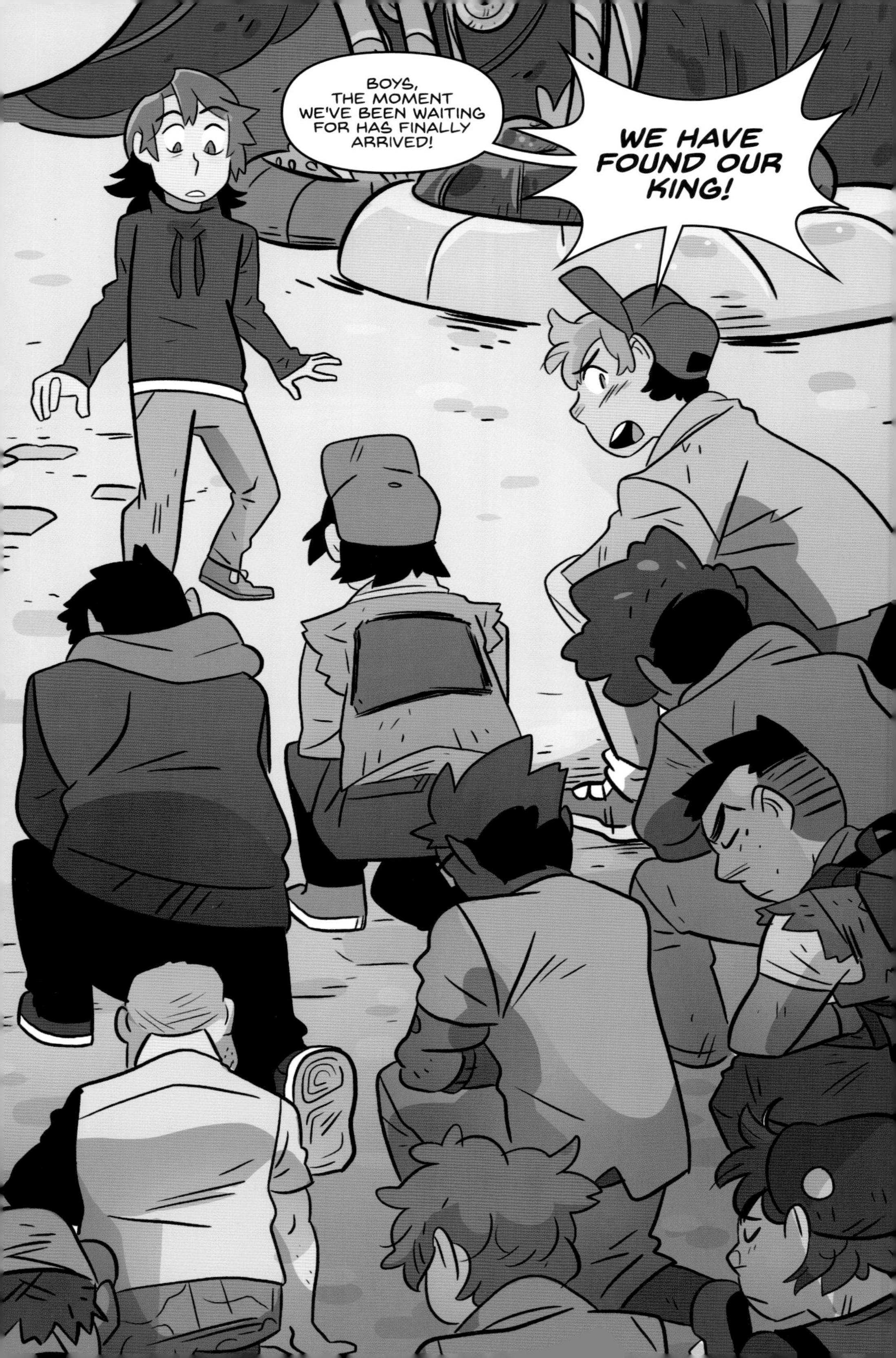
BOYS, THE MOMENT WE'VE BEEN WAITING FOR HAS FINALLY ARRIVED!
WE HAVE FOUND OUR KING!

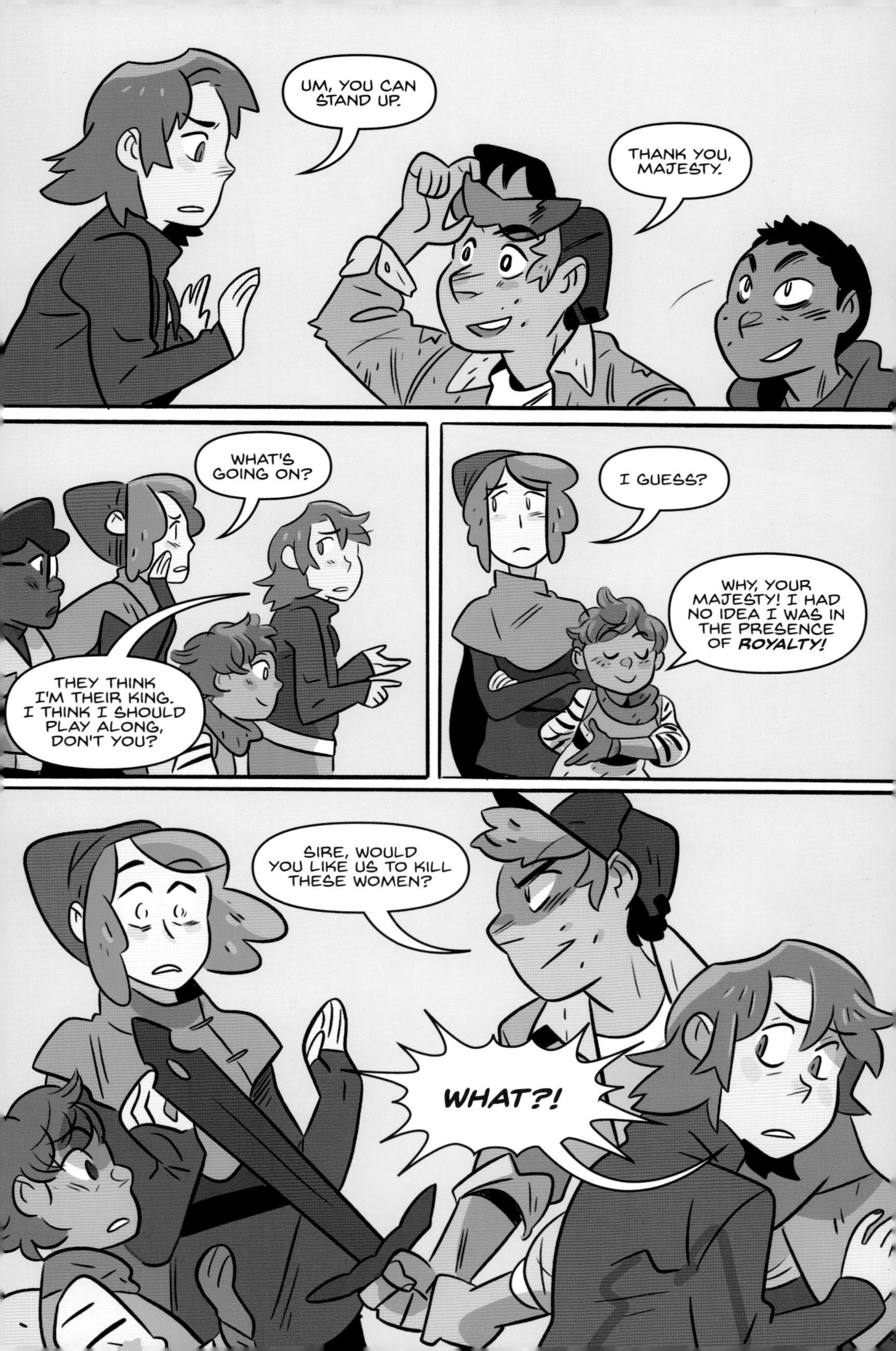
UM, YOU CAN STAND UP.
THANK YOU, MAJESTY.
WHAT'S GOING ON?
THEY THINK I'M THEIR KING. I THINK I SHOULD PLAY ALONG, DON'T YOU?
I GUESS?
WHY, YOUR MAJESTY! I HAD NO IDEA I WAS IN THE PRESENCE OF *ROYALTY!*
SIRE, WOULD YOU LIKE US TO KILL THESE WOMEN?
WHAT?!

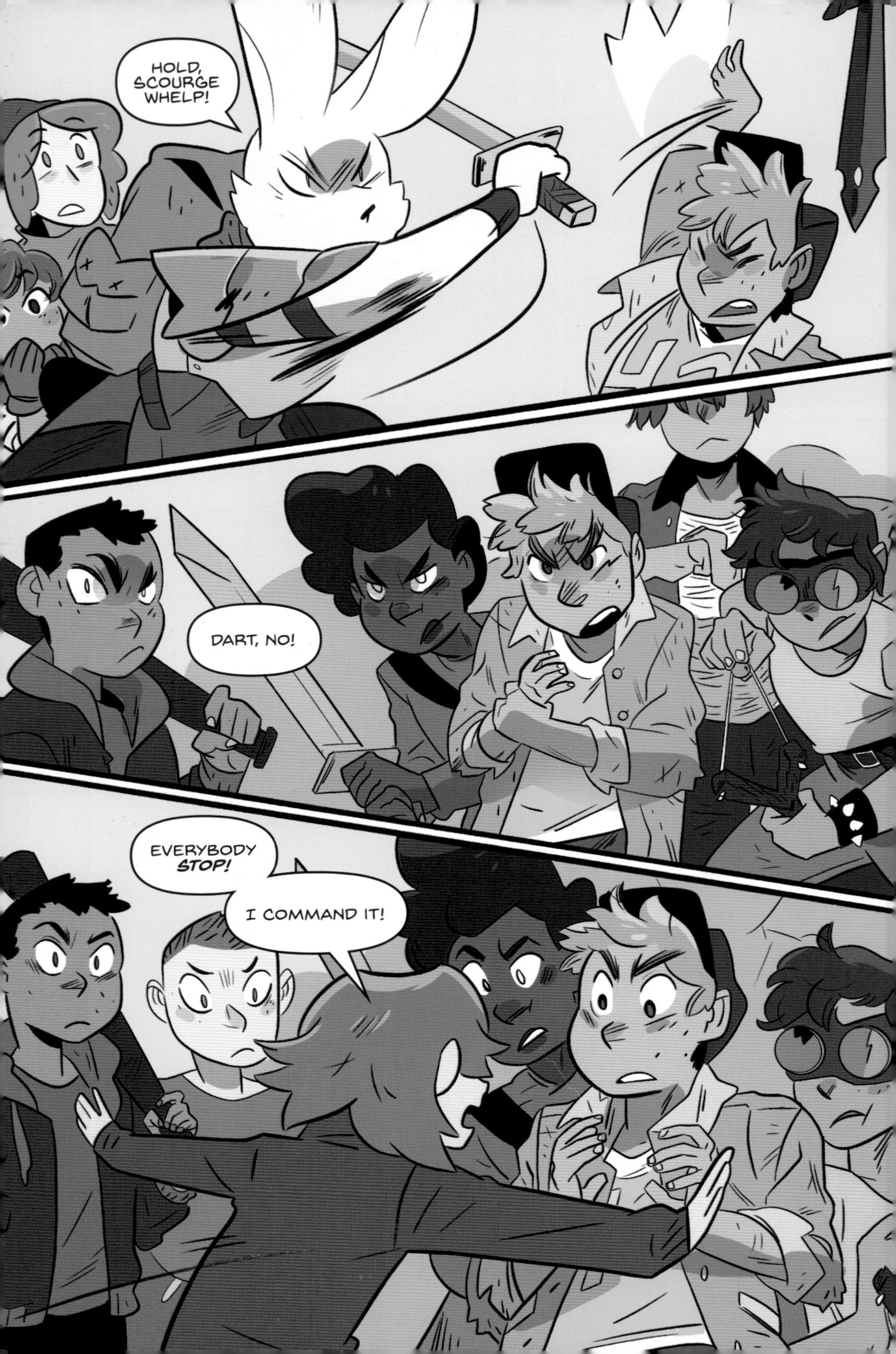
HOLD, SCOURGE WHELP!
DART, NO!
EVERYBODY *STOP!*
I COMMAND IT!

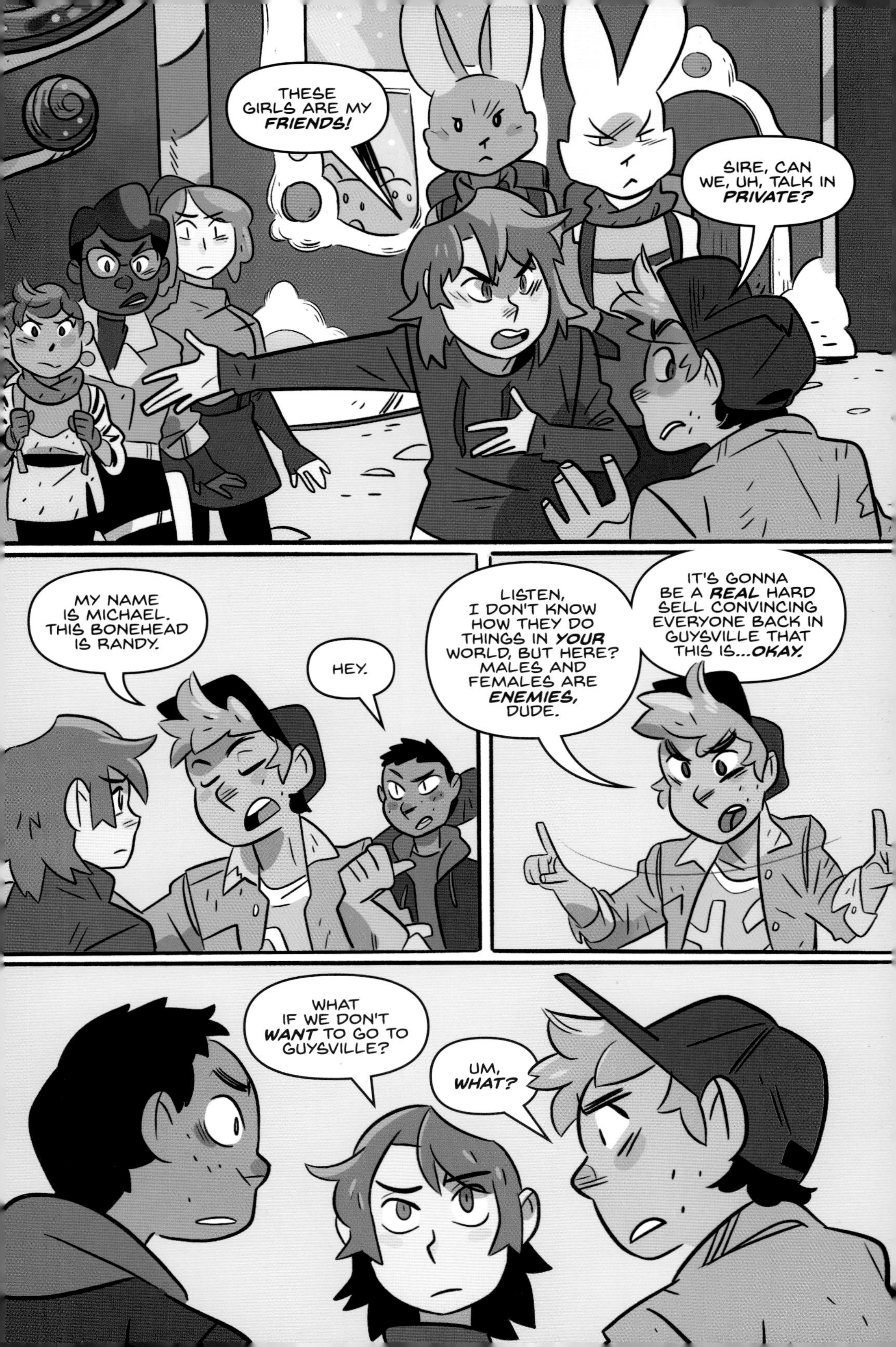
THESE GIRLS ARE MY FRIENDS!
SIRE, CAN WE, UH, TALK IN PRIVATE?
MY NAME IS MICHAEL. THIS BONEHEAD IS RANDY.
HEY.
LISTEN, I DON'T KNOW HOW THEY DO THINGS IN YOUR WORLD, BUT HERE? MALES AND FEMALES ARE ENEMIES, DUDE.
IT'S GONNA BE A REAL HARD SELL CONVINCING EVERYONE BACK IN GUYSVILLE THAT THIS IS...OKAY.
WHAT IF WE DON'T WANT TO GO TO GUYSVILLE?
UM, WHAT?

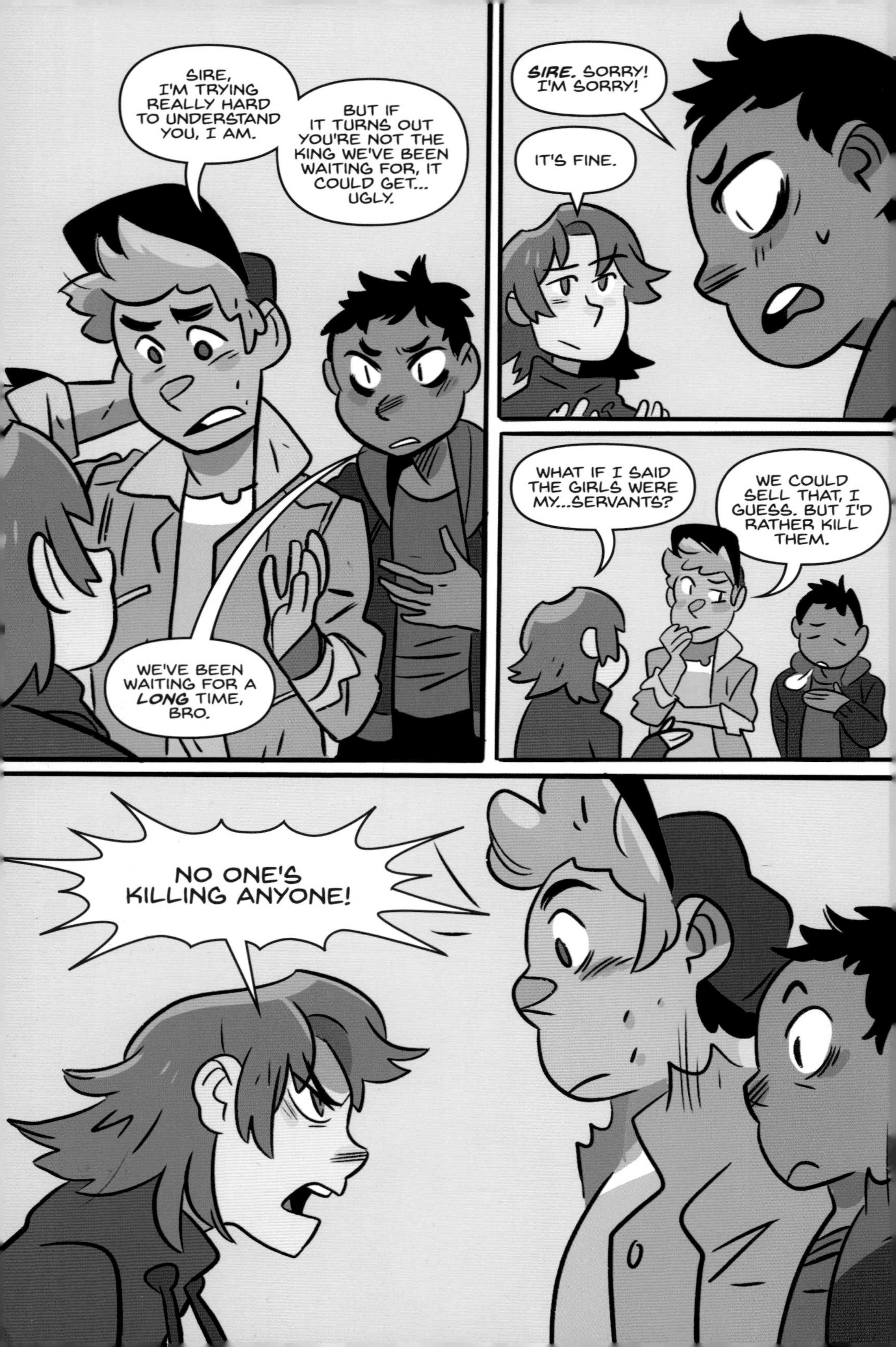
SIRE, I'M TRYING REALLY HARD TO UNDERSTAND YOU, I AM.
BUT IF IT TURNS OUT YOU'RE NOT THE KING WE'VE BEEN WAITING FOR, IT COULD GET... UGLY.
WE'VE BEEN WAITING FOR A LONG TIME, BRO.
SIRE. SORRY! I'M SORRY!
IT'S FINE.
WHAT IF I SAID THE GIRLS WERE MY...SERVANTS?
WE COULD SELL THAT, I GUESS. BUT I'D RATHER KILL THEM.
NO ONE'S KILLING ANYONE!

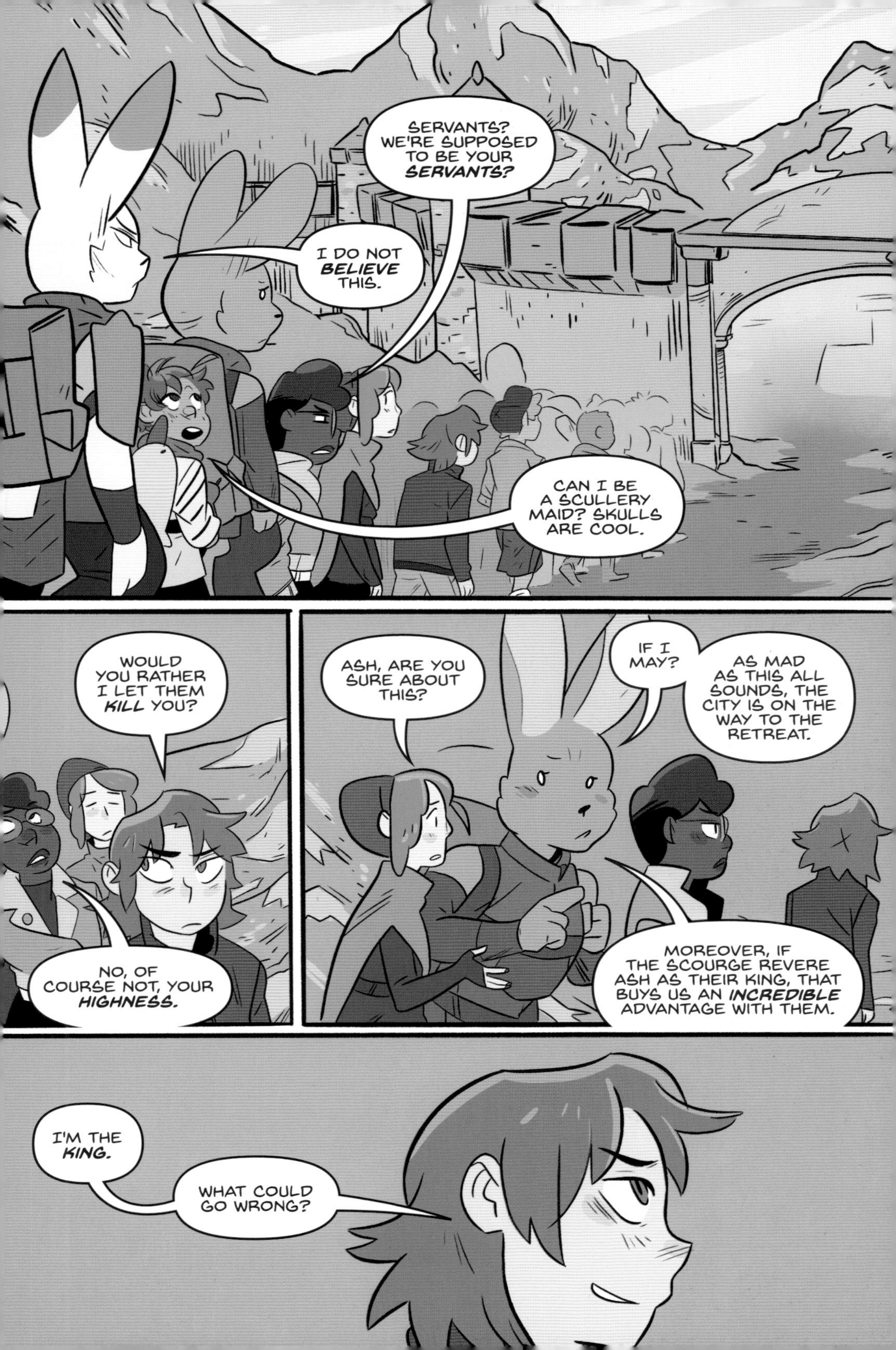
SERVANTS? WE'RE SUPPOSED TO BE YOUR SERVANTS?
I DO NOT BELIEVE THIS.
CAN I BE A SCULLERY MAID? SKULLS ARE COOL.
WOULD YOU RATHER I LET THEM KILL YOU?
NO, OF COURSE NOT, YOUR HIGHNESS.
ASH, ARE YOU SURE ABOUT THIS?
IF I MAY?
AS MAD AS THIS ALL SOUNDS, THE CITY IS ON THE WAY TO THE RETREAT.
MOREOVER, IF THE SCOURGE REVERE ASH AS THEIR KING, THAT BUYS US AN INCREDIBLE ADVANTAGE WITH THEM.
I'M THE KING.
WHAT COULD GO WRONG?

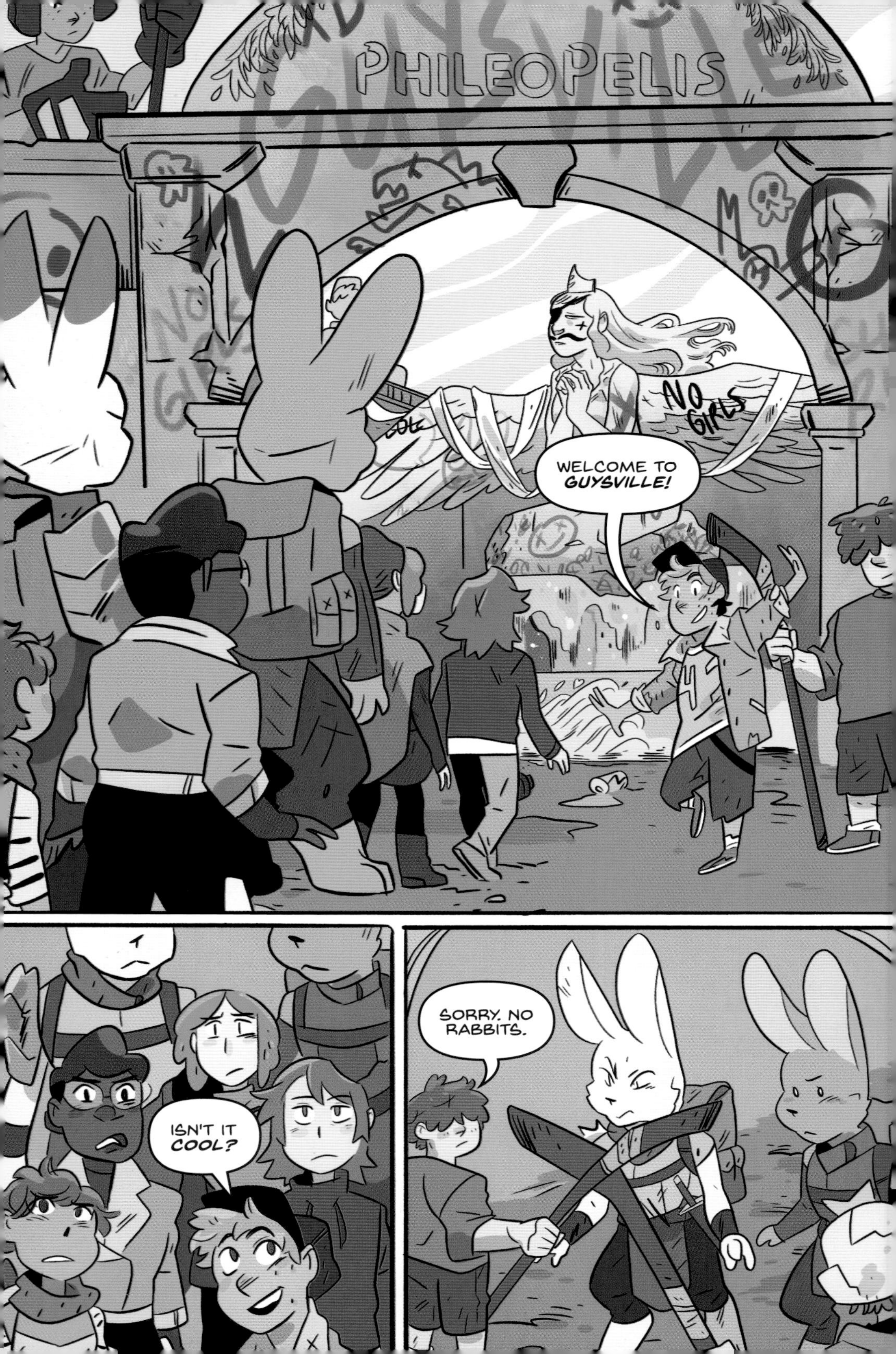
PHILEOPELIS
GUYSVILLE
NO GIRLS
WELCOME TO GUYSVILLE!
ISN'T IT COOL?
SORRY. NO RABBITS.

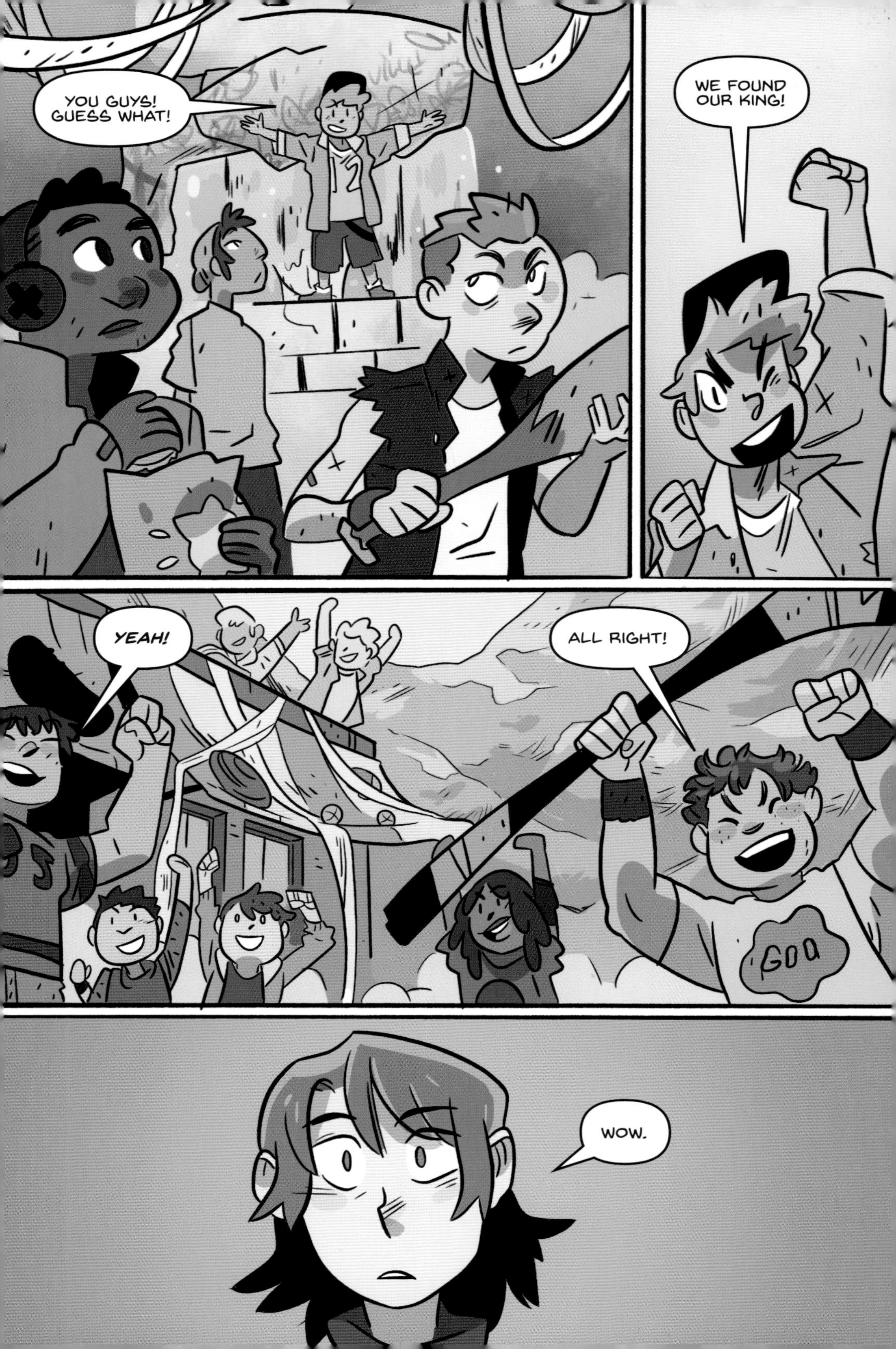

YOU GUYS! GUESS WHAT!
WE FOUND OUR KING!
YEAH!
ALL RIGHT!
GOA
WOW.

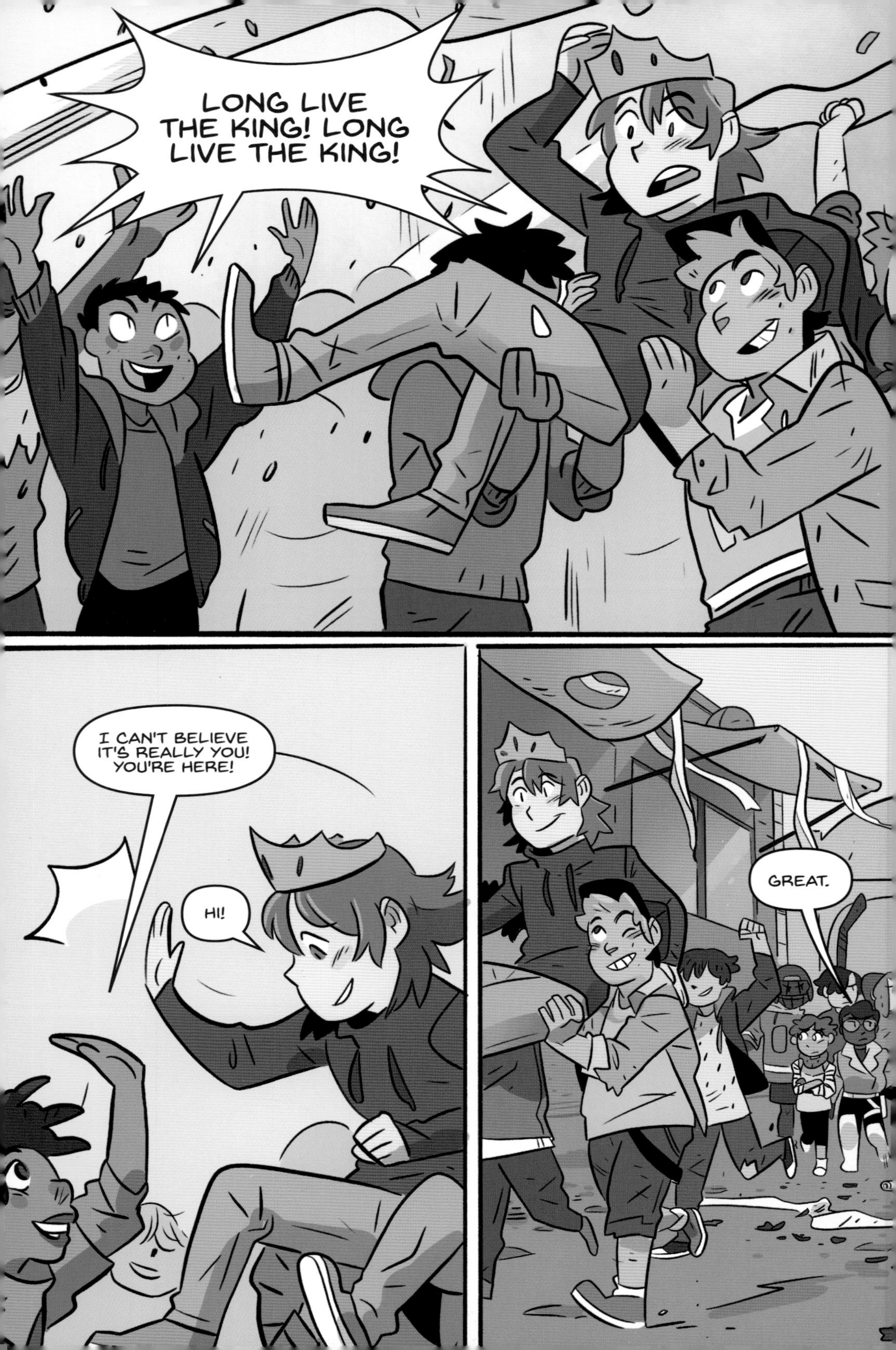
LONG LIVE THE KING! LONG LIVE THE KING!
I CAN'T BELIEVE IT'S REALLY YOU! YOU'RE HERE!
HI!
GREAT.

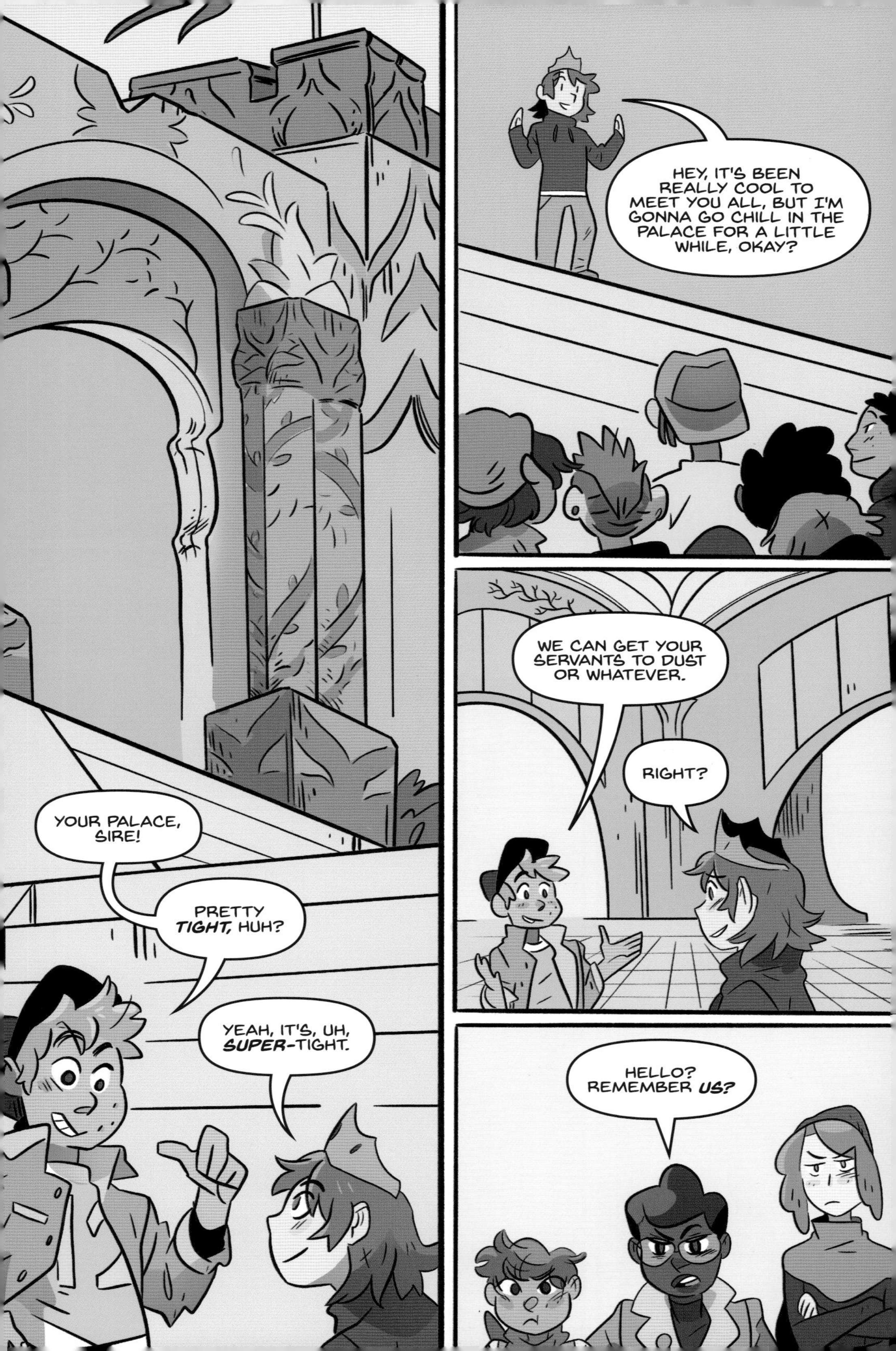
YOUR PALACE, SIRE!
PRETTY TIGHT, HUH?
YEAH, IT'S, UH, SUPER-TIGHT.
HEY, IT'S BEEN REALLY COOL TO MEET YOU ALL, BUT I'M GONNA GO CHILL IN THE PALACE FOR A LITTLE WHILE, OKAY?
WE CAN GET YOUR SERVANTS TO DUST OR WHATEVER.
RIGHT?
HELLO? REMEMBER US?

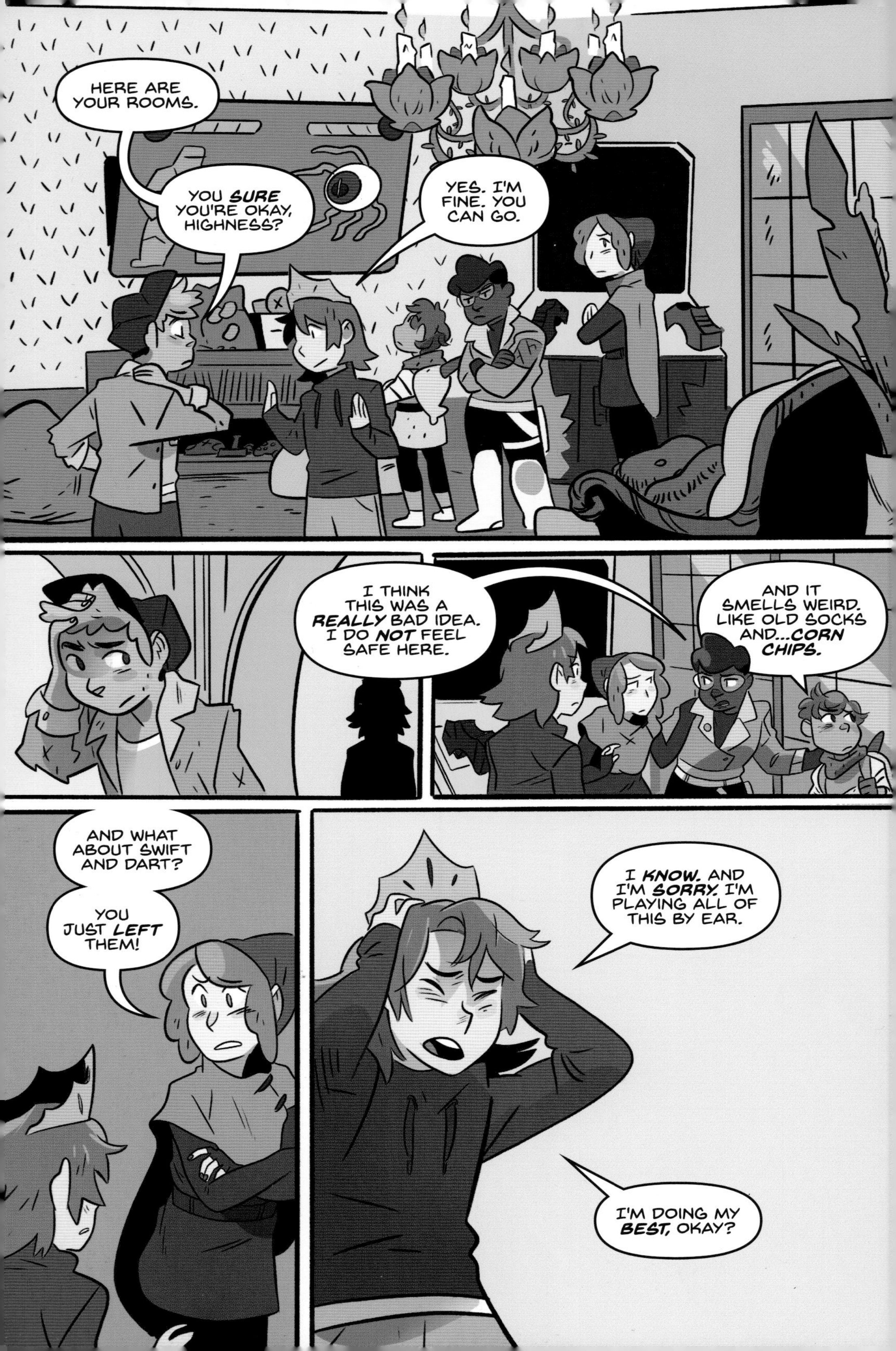
HERE ARE YOUR ROOMS.
YOU SURE YOU'RE OKAY, HIGHNESS?
YES. I'M FINE. YOU CAN GO.
I THINK THIS WAS A REALLY BAD IDEA. I DO NOT FEEL SAFE HERE.
AND IT SMELLS WEIRD. LIKE OLD SOCKS AND...CORN CHIPS.
AND WHAT ABOUT SWIFT AND DART?
YOU JUST LEFT THEM!
I KNOW. AND I'M SORRY. I'M PLAYING ALL OF THIS BY EAR.
I'M DOING MY BEST, OKAY?

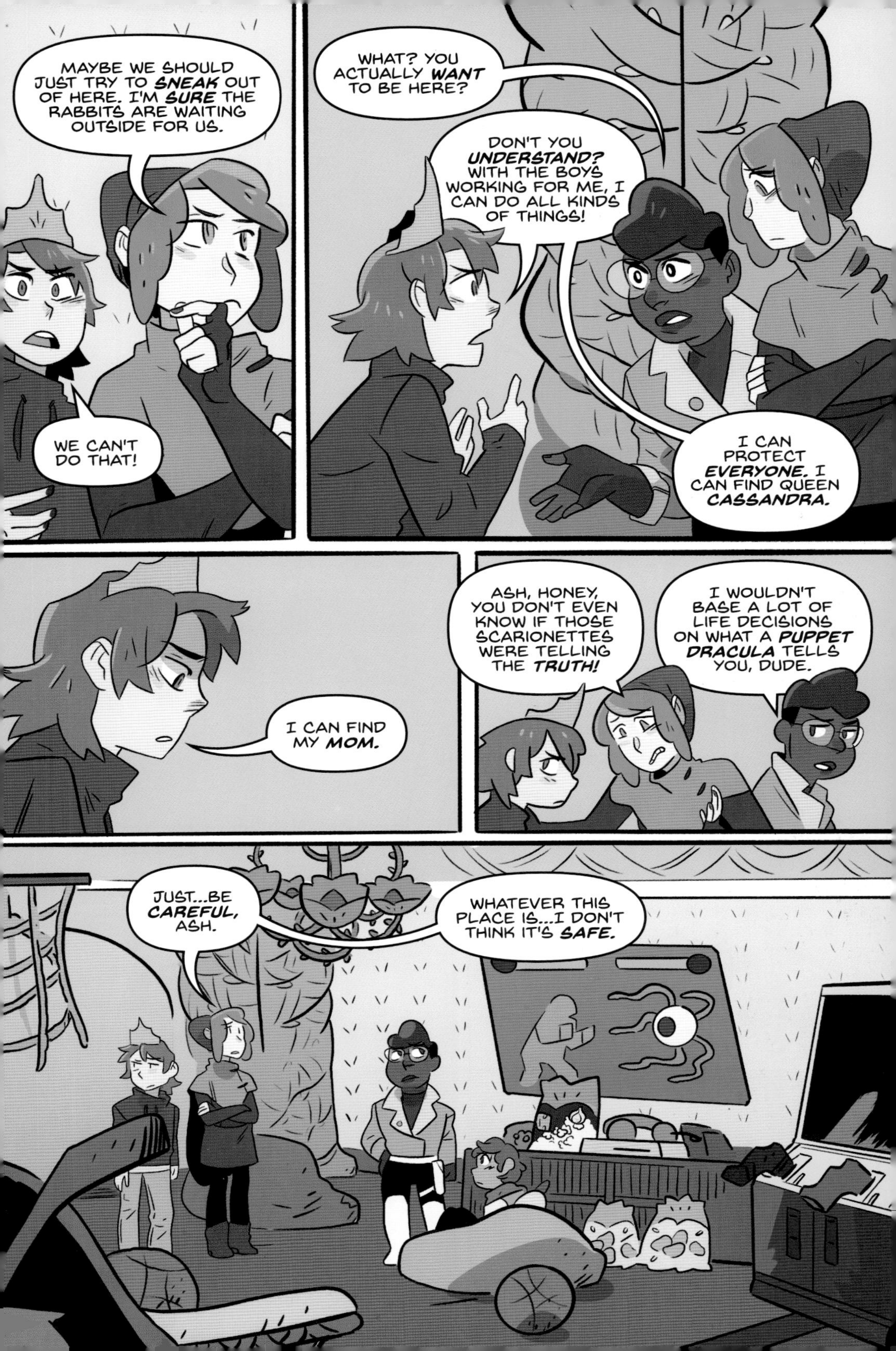
MAYBE WE SHOULD JUST TRY TO SNEAK OUT OF HERE. I'M SURE THE RABBITS ARE WAITING OUTSIDE FOR US.
WE CAN'T DO THAT!
WHAT? YOU ACTUALLY WANT TO BE HERE?
DON'T YOU UNDERSTAND? WITH THE BOYS WORKING FOR ME, I CAN DO ALL KINDS OF THINGS!
I CAN PROTECT EVERYONE. I CAN FIND QUEEN CASSANDRA.
I CAN FIND MY MOM.
ASH, HONEY, YOU DON'T EVEN KNOW IF THOSE SCARIONETTES WERE TELLING THE TRUTH!
I WOULDN'T BASE A LOT OF LIFE DECISIONS ON WHAT A PUPPET DRACULA TELLS YOU, DUDE.
JUST...BE CAREFUL, ASH.
WHATEVER THIS PLACE IS...I DON'T THINK IT'S SAFE.

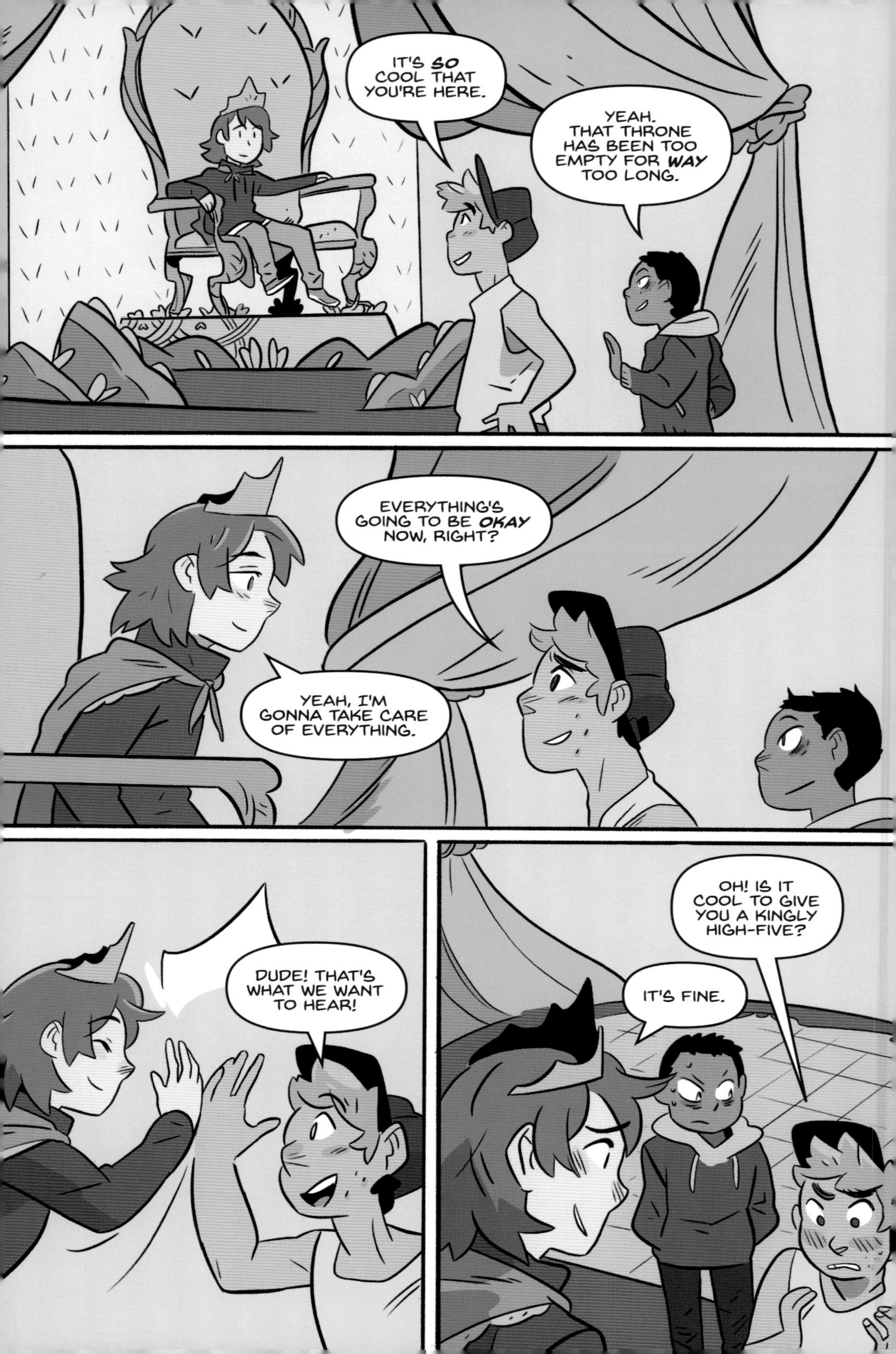
IT'S SO COOL THAT YOU'RE HERE.
YEAH. THAT THRONE HAS BEEN TOO EMPTY FOR WAY TOO LONG.
EVERYTHING'S GOING TO BE OKAY NOW, RIGHT?
YEAH, I'M GONNA TAKE CARE OF EVERYTHING.
DUDE! THAT'S WHAT WE WANT TO HEAR!
OH! IS IT COOL TO GIVE YOU A KINGLY HIGH-FIVE?
IT'S FINE.

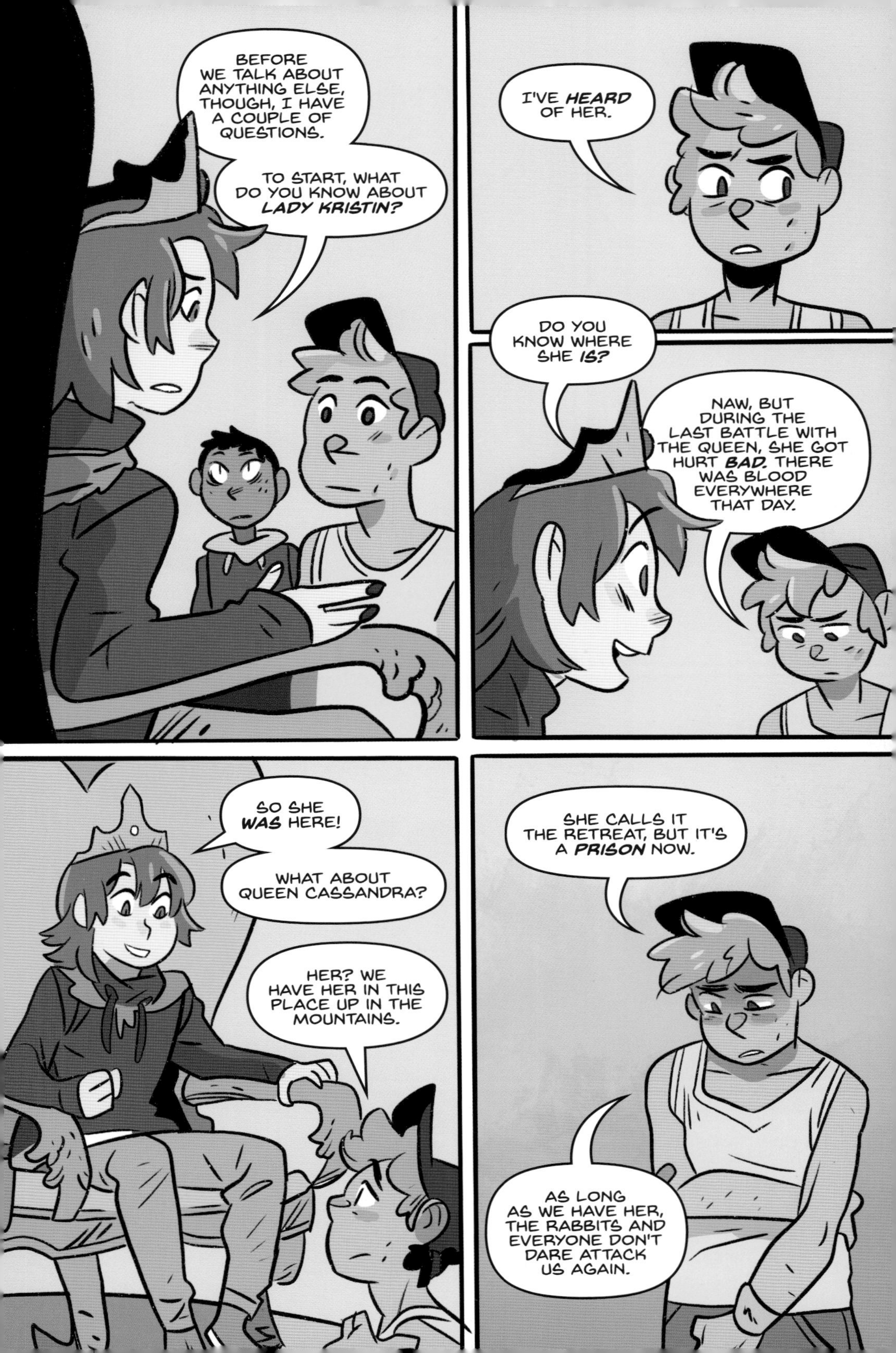
BEFORE WE TALK ABOUT ANYTHING ELSE, THOUGH, I HAVE A COUPLE OF QUESTIONS.
TO START, WHAT DO YOU KNOW ABOUT LADY KRISTIN?
I'VE HEARD OF HER.
DO YOU KNOW WHERE SHE IS?
NAW, BUT DURING THE LAST BATTLE WITH THE QUEEN, SHE GOT HURT BAD. THERE WAS BLOOD EVERYWHERE THAT DAY.
SO SHE WAS HERE!
WHAT ABOUT QUEEN CASSANDRA?
HER? WE HAVE HER IN THIS PLACE UP IN THE MOUNTAINS.
SHE CALLS IT THE RETREAT, BUT IT'S A PRISON NOW.
AS LONG AS WE HAVE HER, THE RABBITS AND EVERYONE DON'T DARE ATTACK US AGAIN.

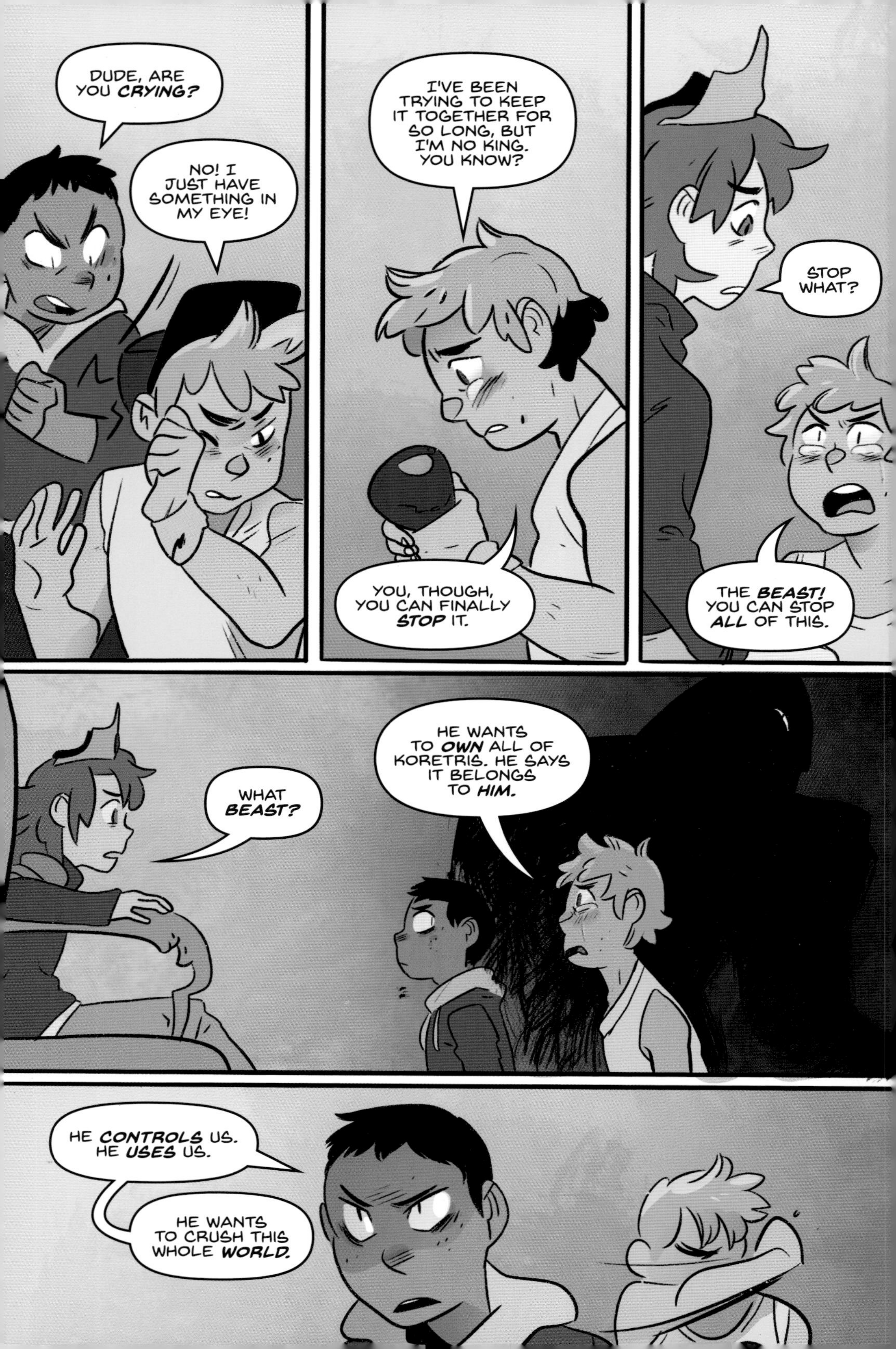
DUDE, ARE YOU *CRYING?*
NO! I JUST HAVE SOMETHING IN MY EYE!
I'VE BEEN TRYING TO KEEP IT TOGETHER FOR SO LONG, BUT I'M NO KING. YOU KNOW?
YOU, THOUGH, YOU CAN FINALLY *STOP* IT.
STOP WHAT?
THE *BEAST!* YOU CAN STOP *ALL* OF THIS.
WHAT *BEAST?*
HE WANTS TO *OWN* ALL OF KORETRIS. HE SAYS IT BELONGS TO *HIM.*
HE *CONTROLS* US. HE *USES* US.
HE WANTS TO CRUSH THIS WHOLE *WORLD.*

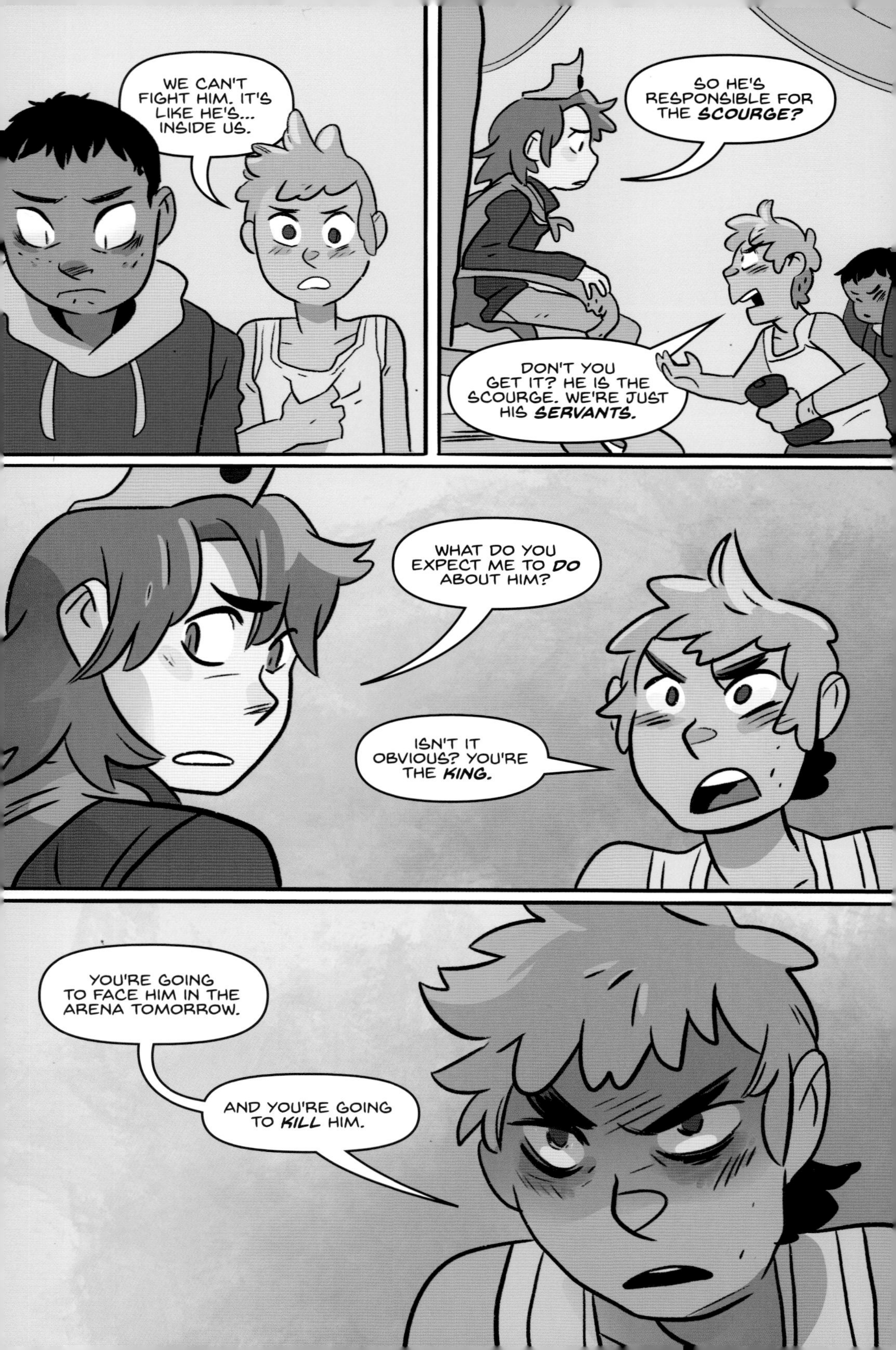
WE CAN'T FIGHT HIM. IT'S LIKE HE'S... INSIDE US.
SO HE'S RESPONSIBLE FOR THE SCOURGE?
DON'T YOU GET IT? HE IS THE SCOURGE. WE'RE JUST HIS SERVANTS.
WHAT DO YOU EXPECT ME TO DO ABOUT HIM?
ISN'T IT OBVIOUS? YOU'RE THE KING.
YOU'RE GOING TO FACE HIM IN THE ARENA TOMORROW.
AND YOU'RE GOING TO KILL HIM.

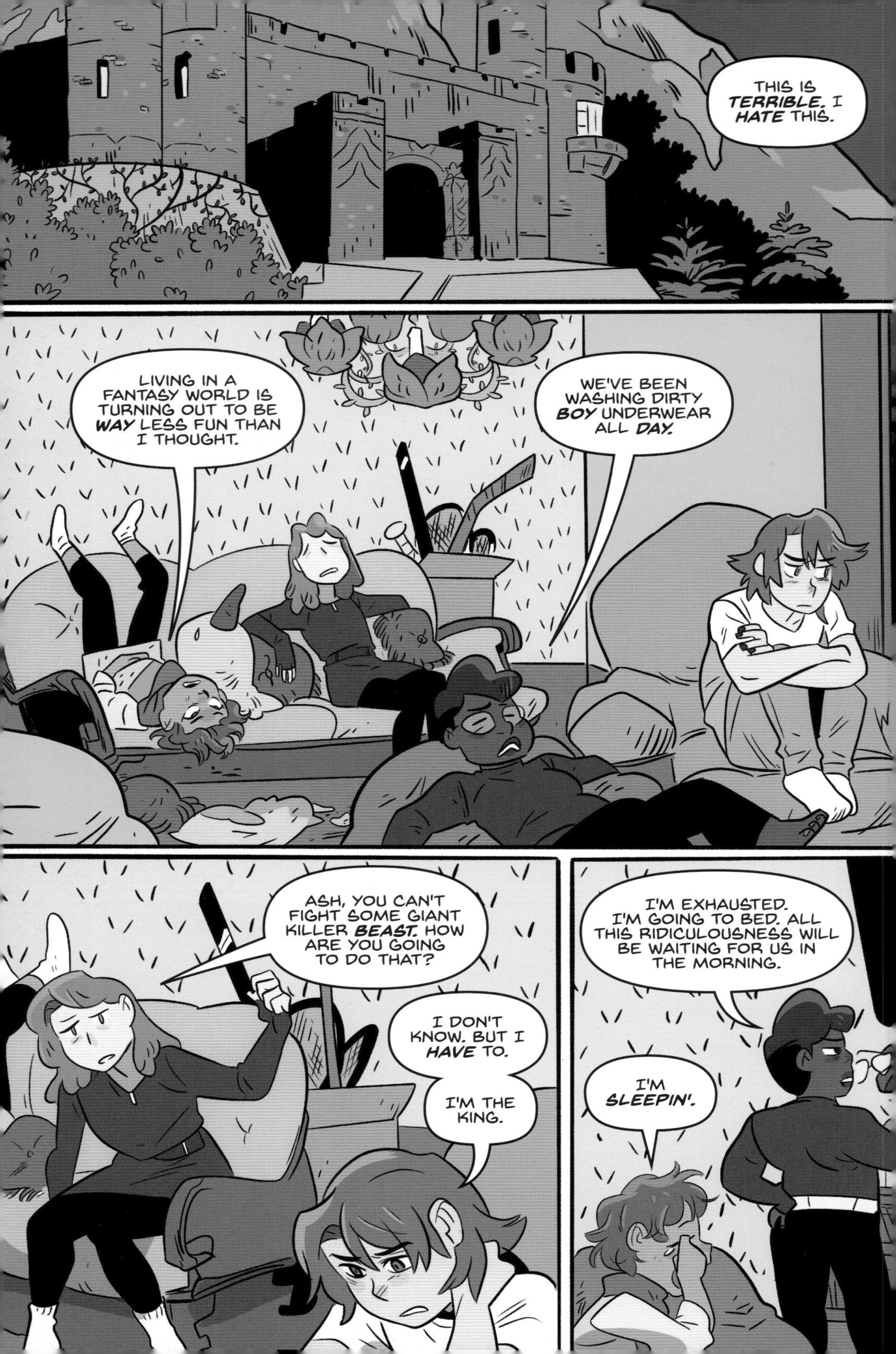
THIS IS *TERRIBLE.* I *HATE* THIS.
LIVING IN A FANTASY WORLD IS TURNING OUT TO BE *WAY* LESS FUN THAN I THOUGHT.
WE'VE BEEN WASHING DIRTY *BOY* UNDERWEAR ALL *DAY.*
ASH, YOU CAN'T FIGHT SOME GIANT KILLER *BEAST.* HOW ARE YOU GOING TO DO THAT?
I DON'T KNOW. BUT I *HAVE* TO.
I'M THE KING.
I'M EXHAUSTED. I'M GOING TO BED. ALL THIS RIDICULOUSNESS WILL BE WAITING FOR US IN THE MORNING.
I'M *SLEEPIN'.*

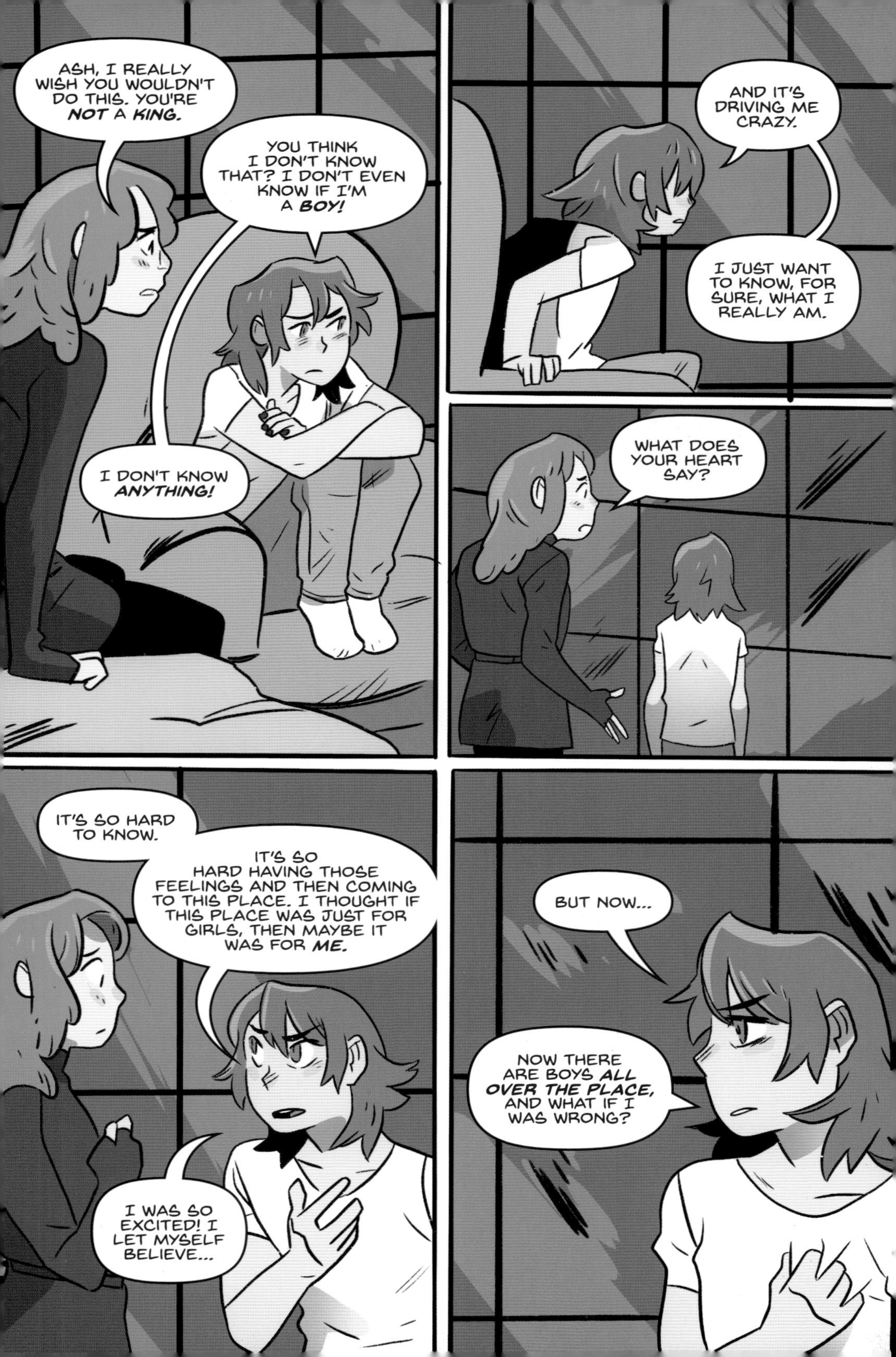
ASH, I REALLY WISH YOU WOULDN'T DO THIS. YOU'RE *NOT* A *KING.*
YOU THINK I DON'T KNOW THAT? I DON'T EVEN KNOW IF I'M A *BOY!*
I DON'T KNOW *ANYTHING!*
AND IT'S DRIVING ME CRAZY.
I JUST WANT TO KNOW, FOR SURE, WHAT I REALLY AM.
WHAT DOES YOUR HEART SAY?
IT'S SO HARD TO KNOW.
IT'S SO HARD HAVING THOSE FEELINGS AND THEN COMING TO THIS PLACE. I THOUGHT IF THIS PLACE WAS JUST FOR GIRLS, THEN MAYBE IT WAS FOR *ME.*
I WAS SO EXCITED! I LET MYSELF BELIEVE...
BUT NOW...
NOW THERE ARE BOYS *ALL OVER THE PLACE,* AND WHAT IF I WAS WRONG?

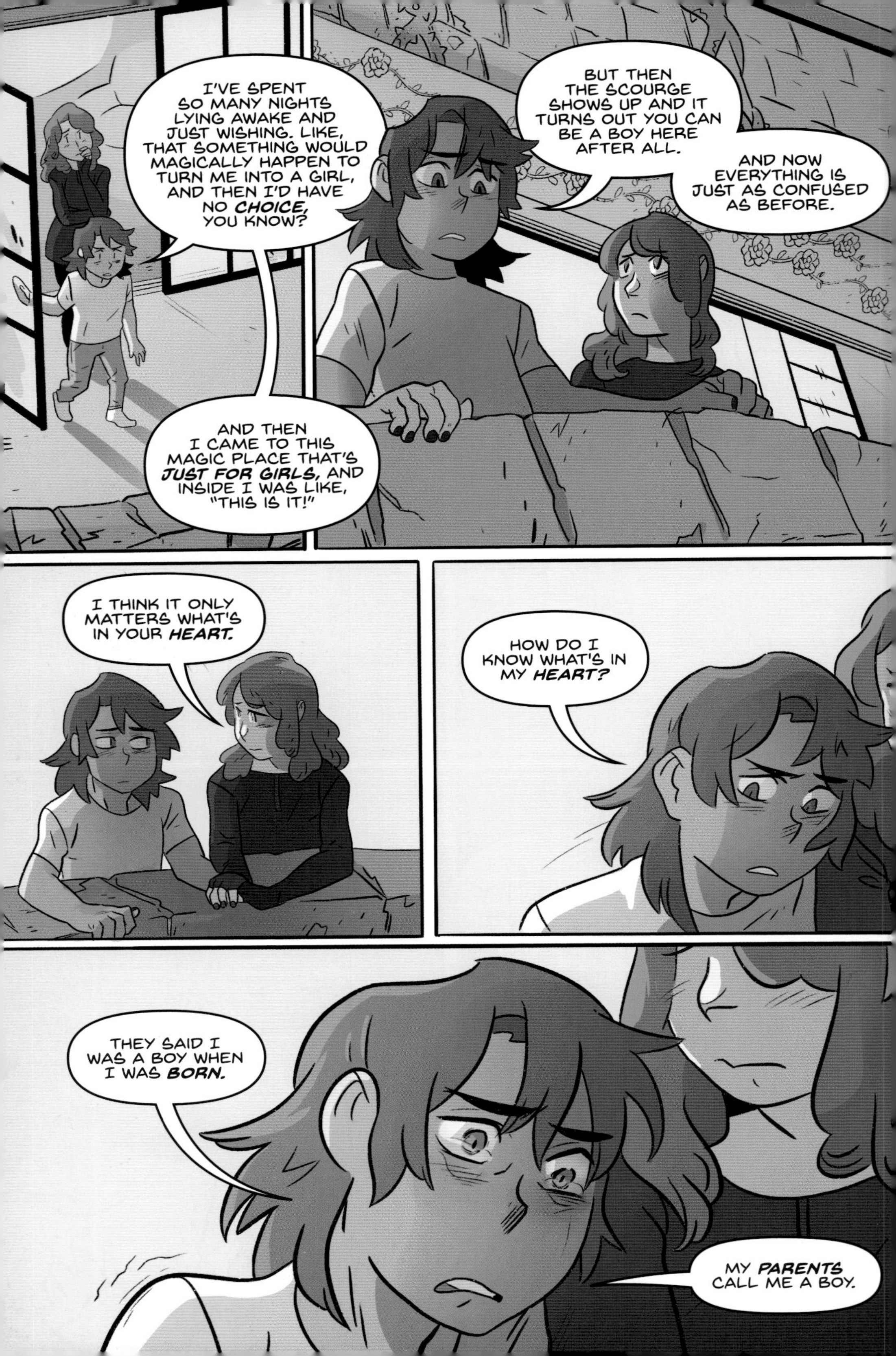
I'VE SPENT SO MANY NIGHTS LYING AWAKE AND JUST WISHING. LIKE, THAT SOMETHING WOULD MAGICALLY HAPPEN TO TURN ME INTO A GIRL, AND THEN I'D HAVE NO *CHOICE,* YOU KNOW?
AND THEN I CAME TO THIS MAGIC PLACE THAT'S *JUST FOR GIRLS,* AND INSIDE I WAS LIKE, "THIS IS IT!"
BUT THEN THE SCOURGE SHOWS UP AND IT TURNS OUT YOU CAN BE A BOY HERE AFTER ALL.
AND NOW EVERYTHING IS JUST AS CONFUSED AS BEFORE.
I THINK IT ONLY MATTERS WHAT'S IN YOUR *HEART.*
HOW DO I KNOW WHAT'S IN MY *HEART?*
THEY SAID I WAS A BOY WHEN I WAS *BORN.*
MY *PARENTS* CALL ME A BOY.

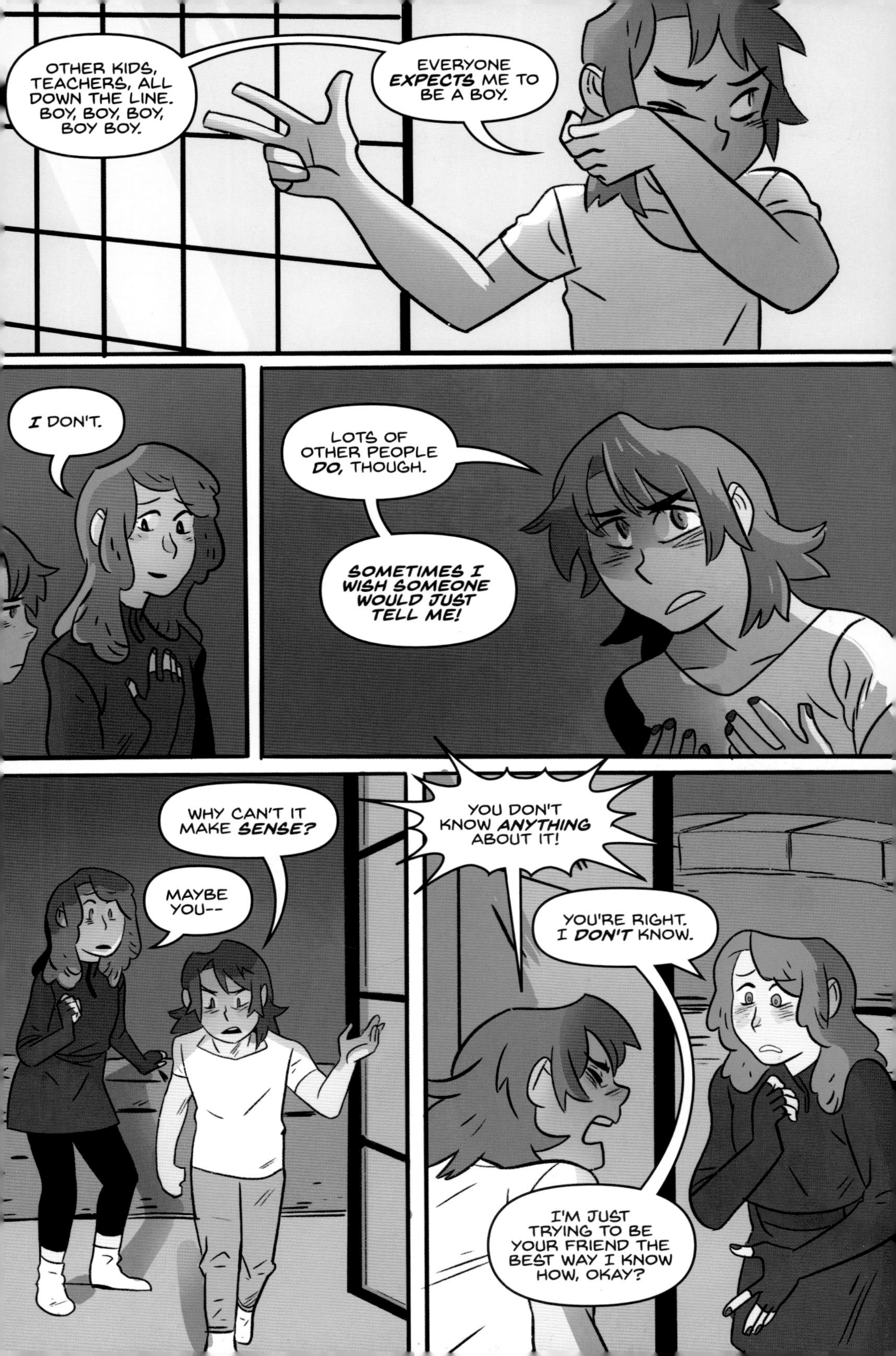
OTHER KIDS, TEACHERS, ALL DOWN THE LINE. BOY, BOY, BOY, BOY BOY.
EVERYONE EXPECTS ME TO BE A BOY.
I DON'T.
LOTS OF OTHER PEOPLE DO, THOUGH.
SOMETIMES I WISH SOMEONE WOULD JUST TELL ME!
WHY CAN'T IT MAKE SENSE?
MAYBE YOU--
YOU DON'T KNOW ANYTHING ABOUT IT!
YOU'RE RIGHT. I DON'T KNOW.
I'M JUST TRYING TO BE YOUR FRIEND THE BEST WAY I KNOW HOW, OKAY?

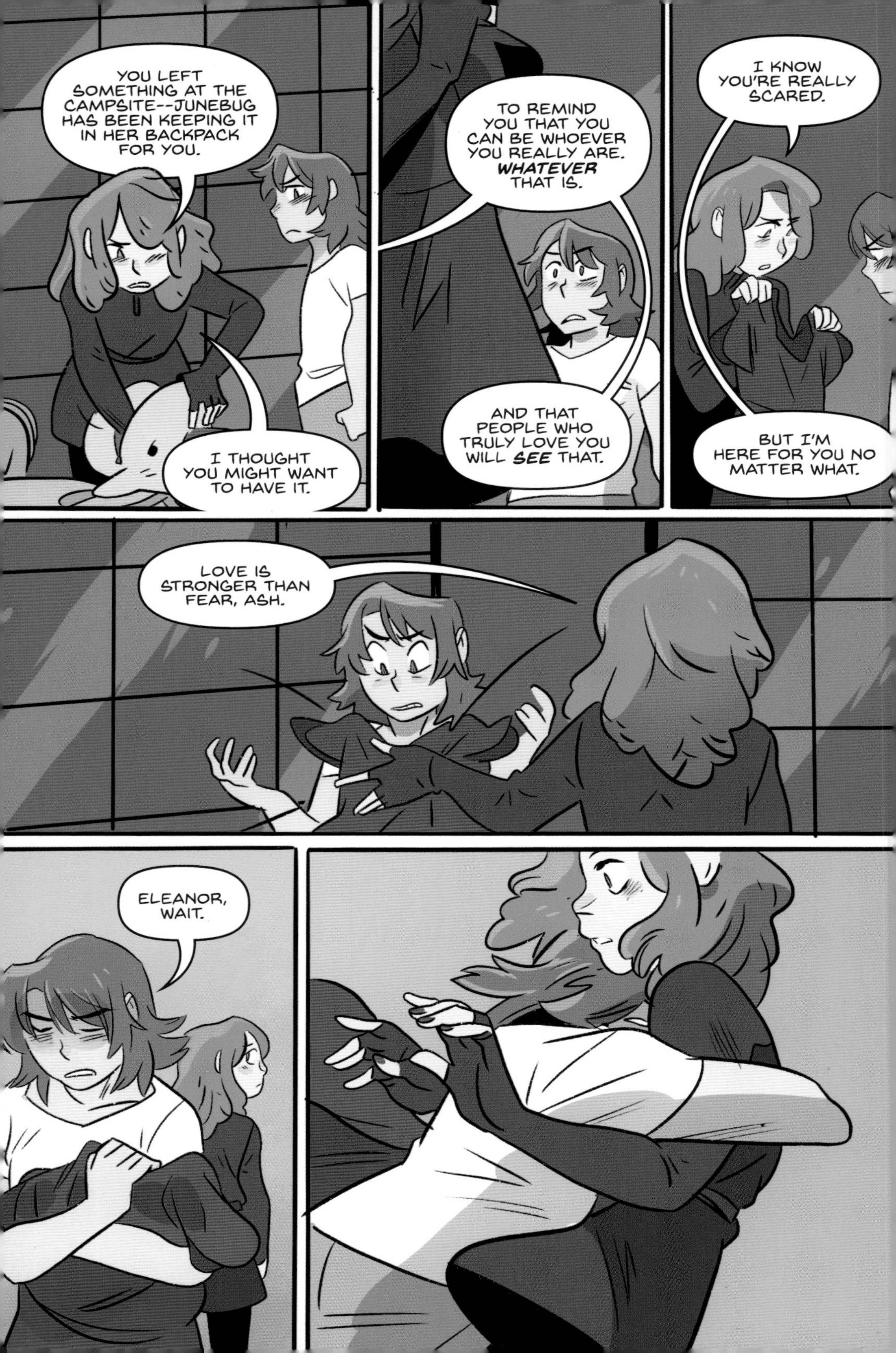
YOU LEFT SOMETHING AT THE CAMPSITE--JUNEBUG HAS BEEN KEEPING IT IN HER BACKPACK FOR YOU.
I THOUGHT YOU MIGHT WANT TO HAVE IT.
TO REMIND YOU THAT YOU CAN BE WHOEVER YOU REALLY ARE. ***WHATEVER*** THAT IS.
AND THAT PEOPLE WHO TRULY LOVE YOU WILL ***SEE*** THAT.
I KNOW YOU'RE REALLY SCARED.
BUT I'M HERE FOR YOU NO MATTER WHAT.
LOVE IS STRONGER THAN FEAR, ASH.
ELEANOR, WAIT.

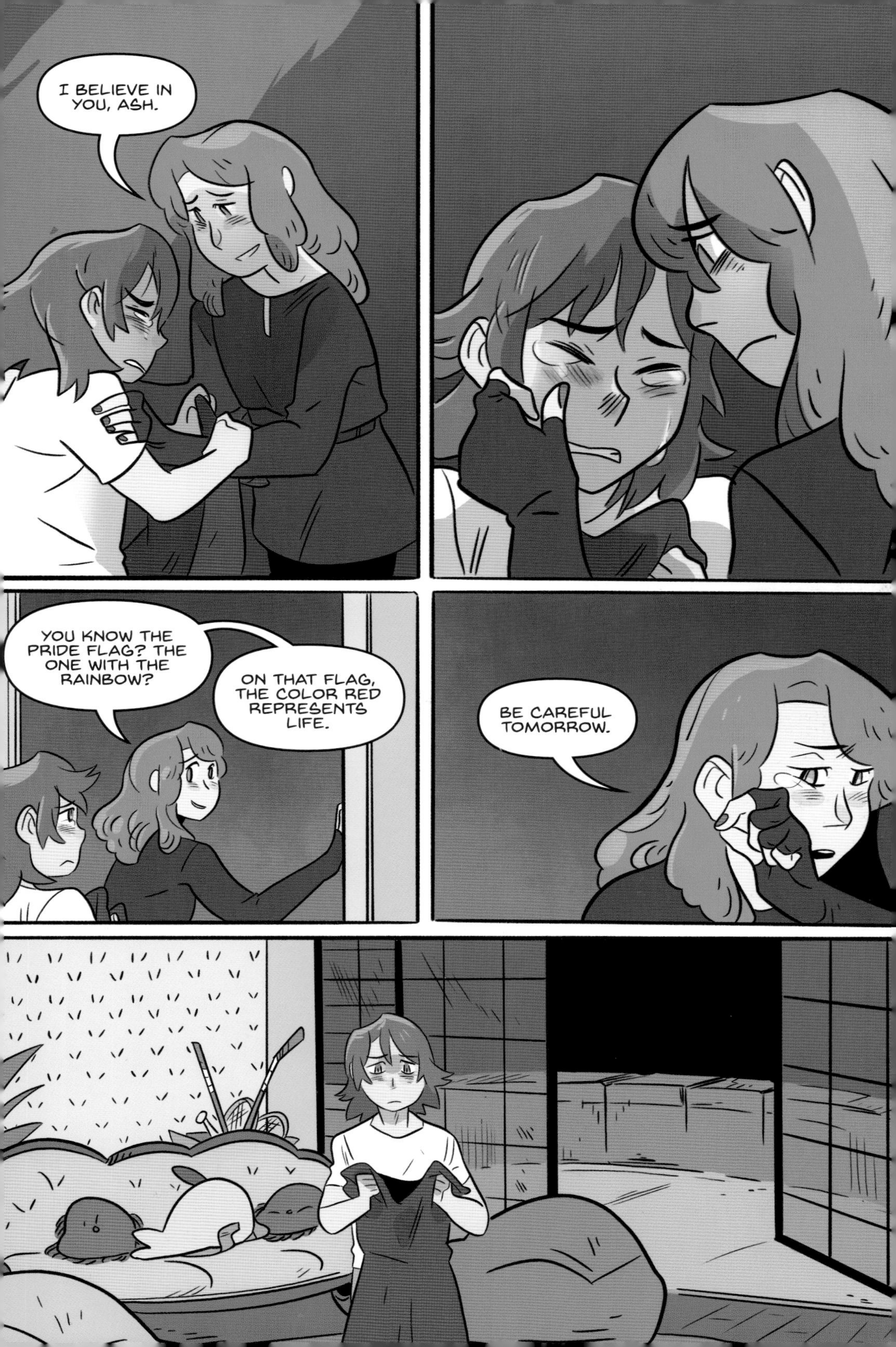
I BELIEVE IN YOU, ASH.
YOU KNOW THE PRIDE FLAG? THE ONE WITH THE RAINBOW?
ON THAT FLAG, THE COLOR RED REPRESENTS LIFE.
BE CAREFUL TOMORROW.

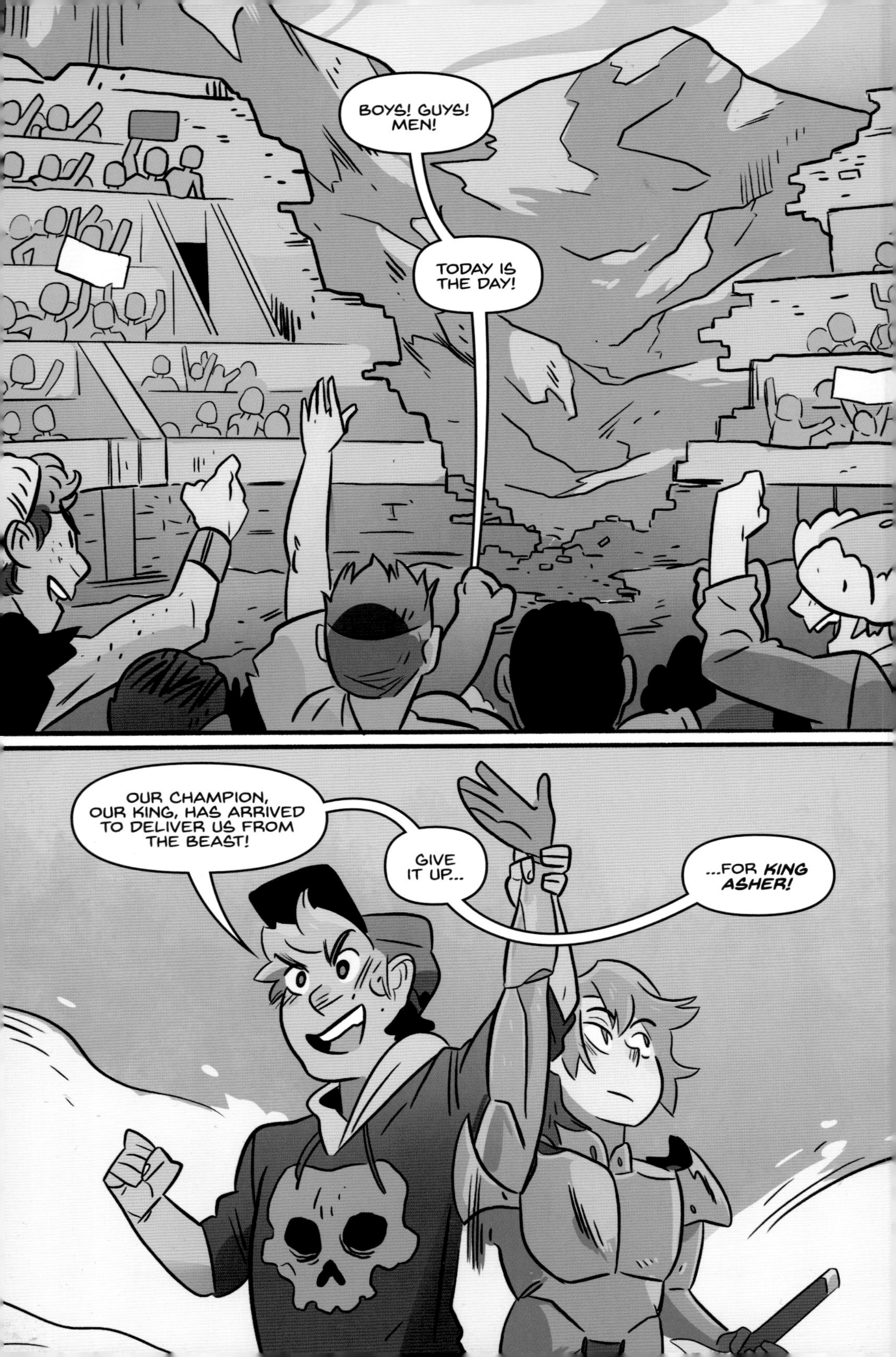
BOYS! GUYS! MEN!
TODAY IS THE DAY!
OUR CHAMPION, OUR KING, HAS ARRIVED TO DELIVER US FROM THE BEAST!
GIVE IT UP...
...FOR **KING ASHER!**

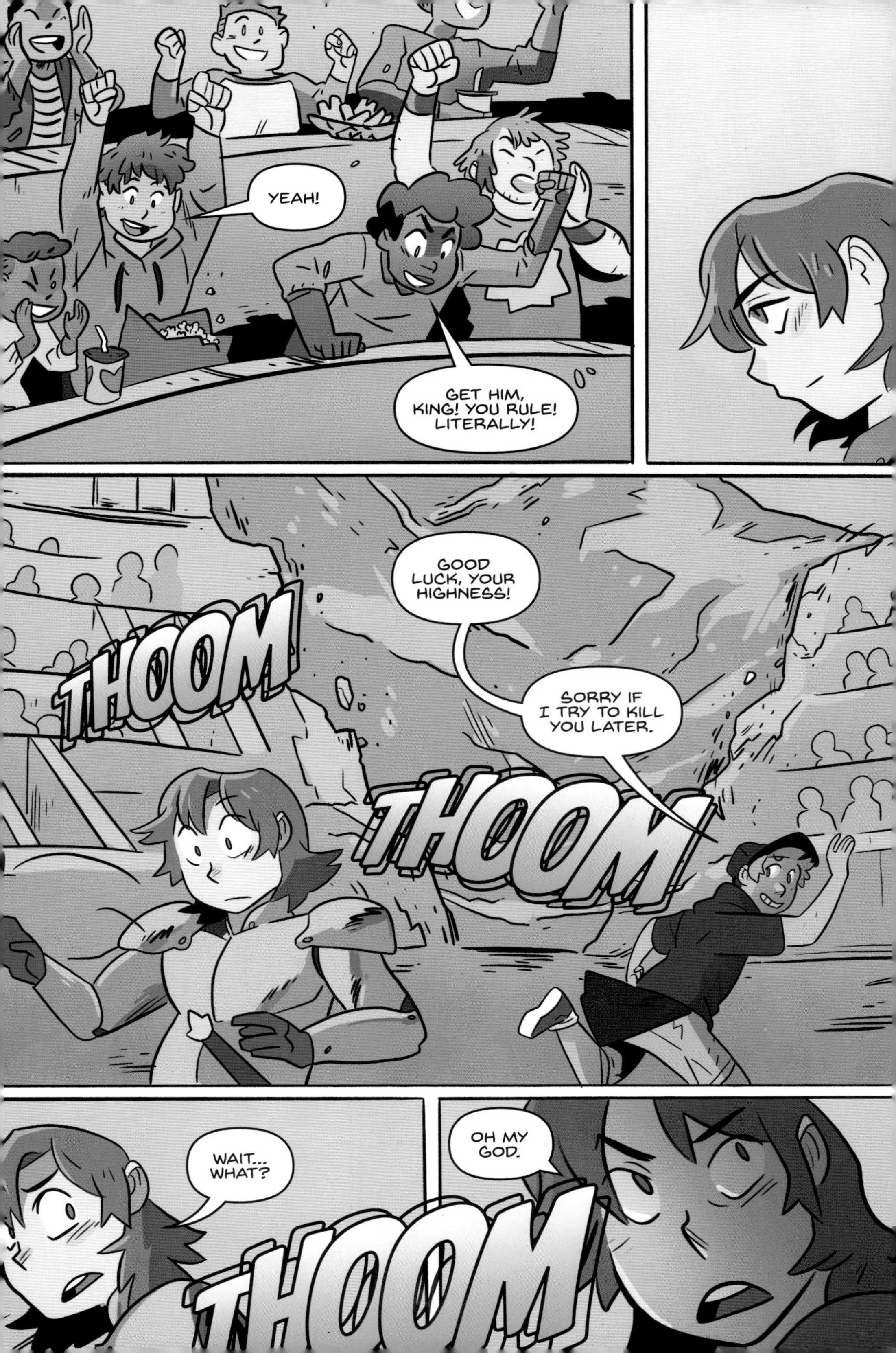
YEAH!
GET HIM, KING! YOU RULE! LITERALLY!
THOOM
GOOD LUCK, YOUR HIGHNESS!
SORRY IF I TRY TO KILL YOU LATER.
THOOM
WAIT... WHAT?
OH MY GOD.
THOOM

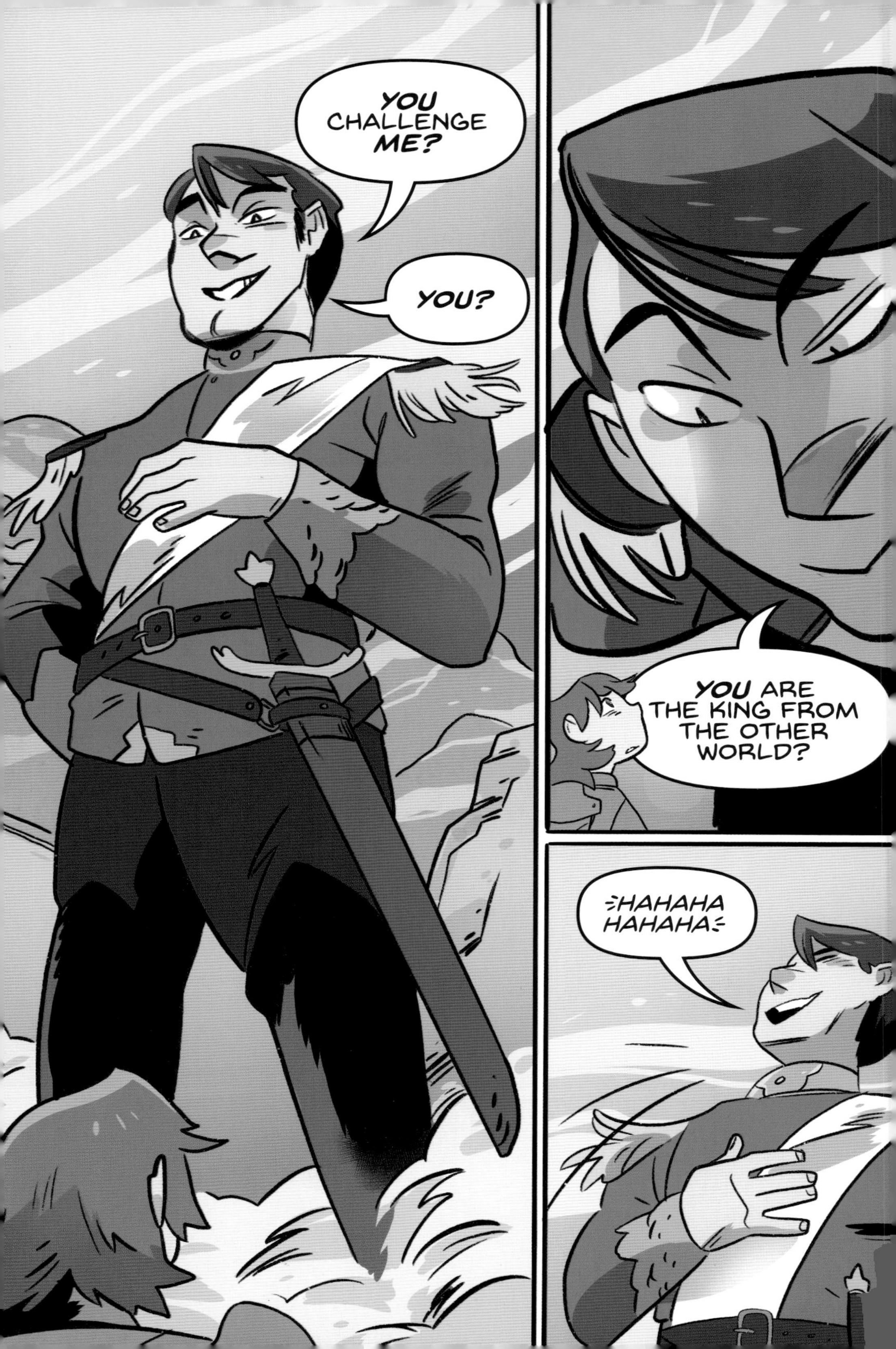
YOU CHALLENGE ME?
YOU?
YOU ARE THE KING FROM THE OTHER WORLD?
HAHAHA HAHAHA

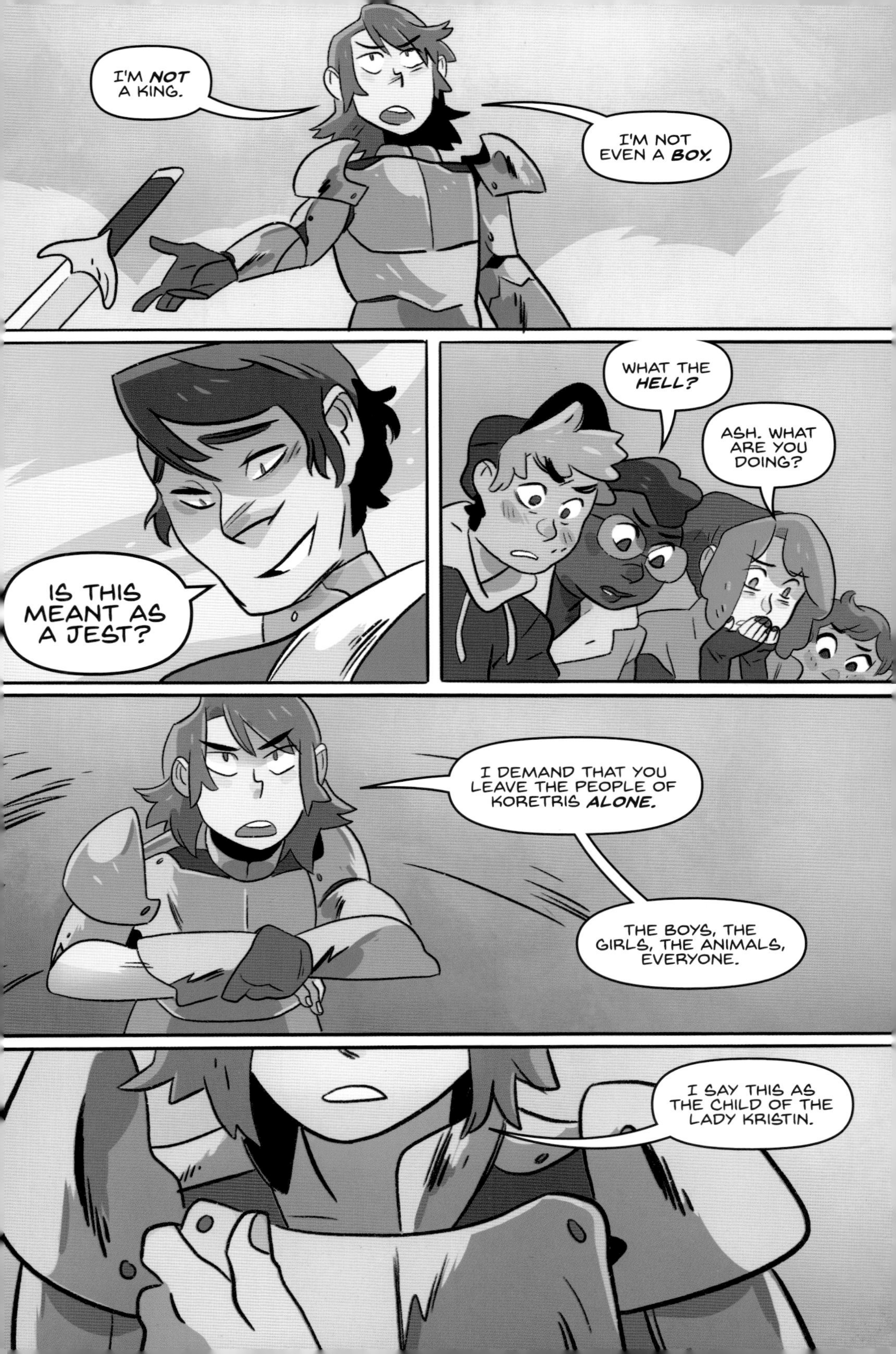
I'M NOT A KING.
I'M NOT EVEN A BOY.
IS THIS MEANT AS A JEST?
WHAT THE HELL?
ASH. WHAT ARE YOU DOING?
I DEMAND THAT YOU LEAVE THE PEOPLE OF KORETRIS ALONE.
THE BOYS, THE GIRLS, THE ANIMALS, EVERYONE.
I SAY THIS AS THE CHILD OF THE LADY KRISTIN.

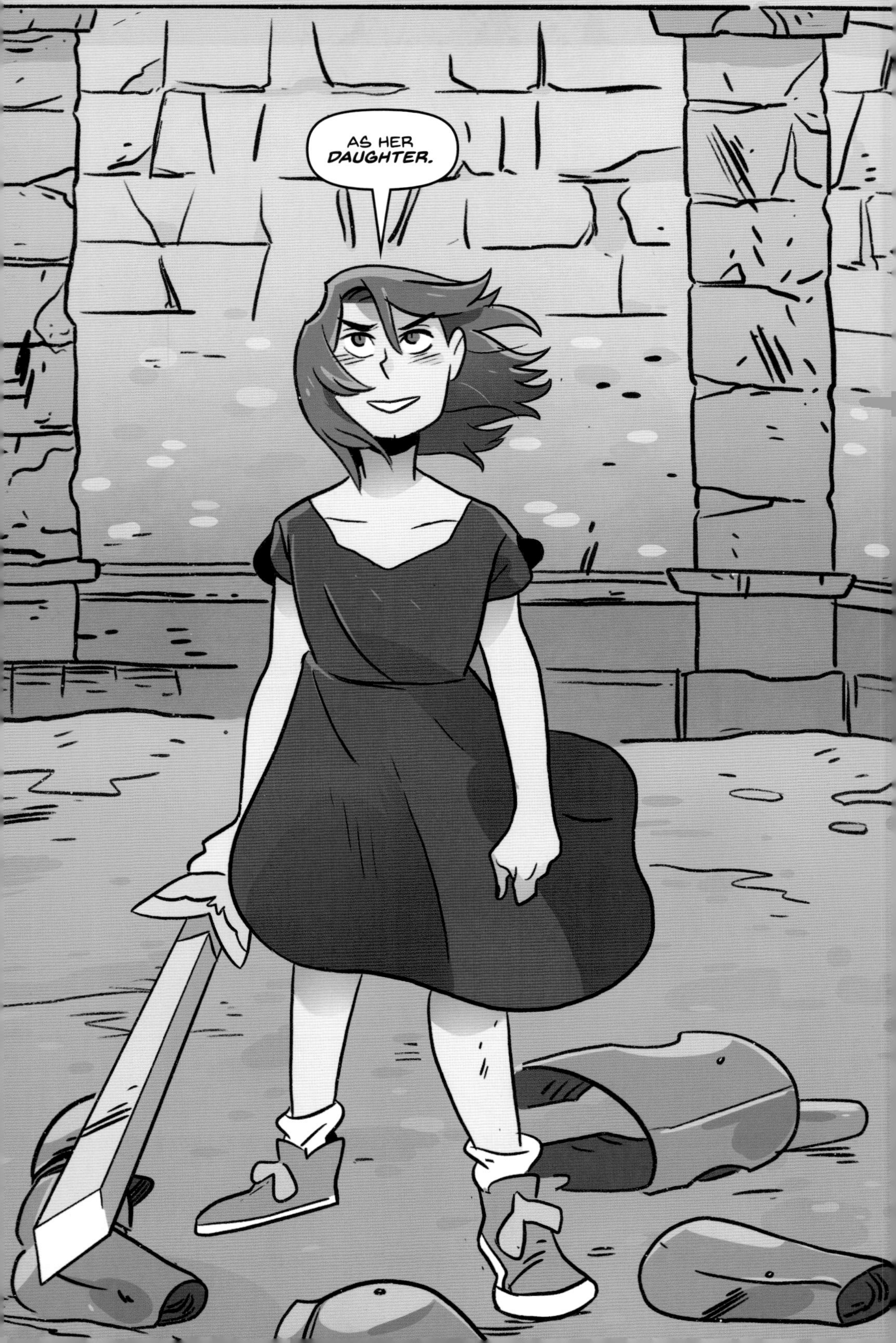
AS HER *DAUGHTER.*

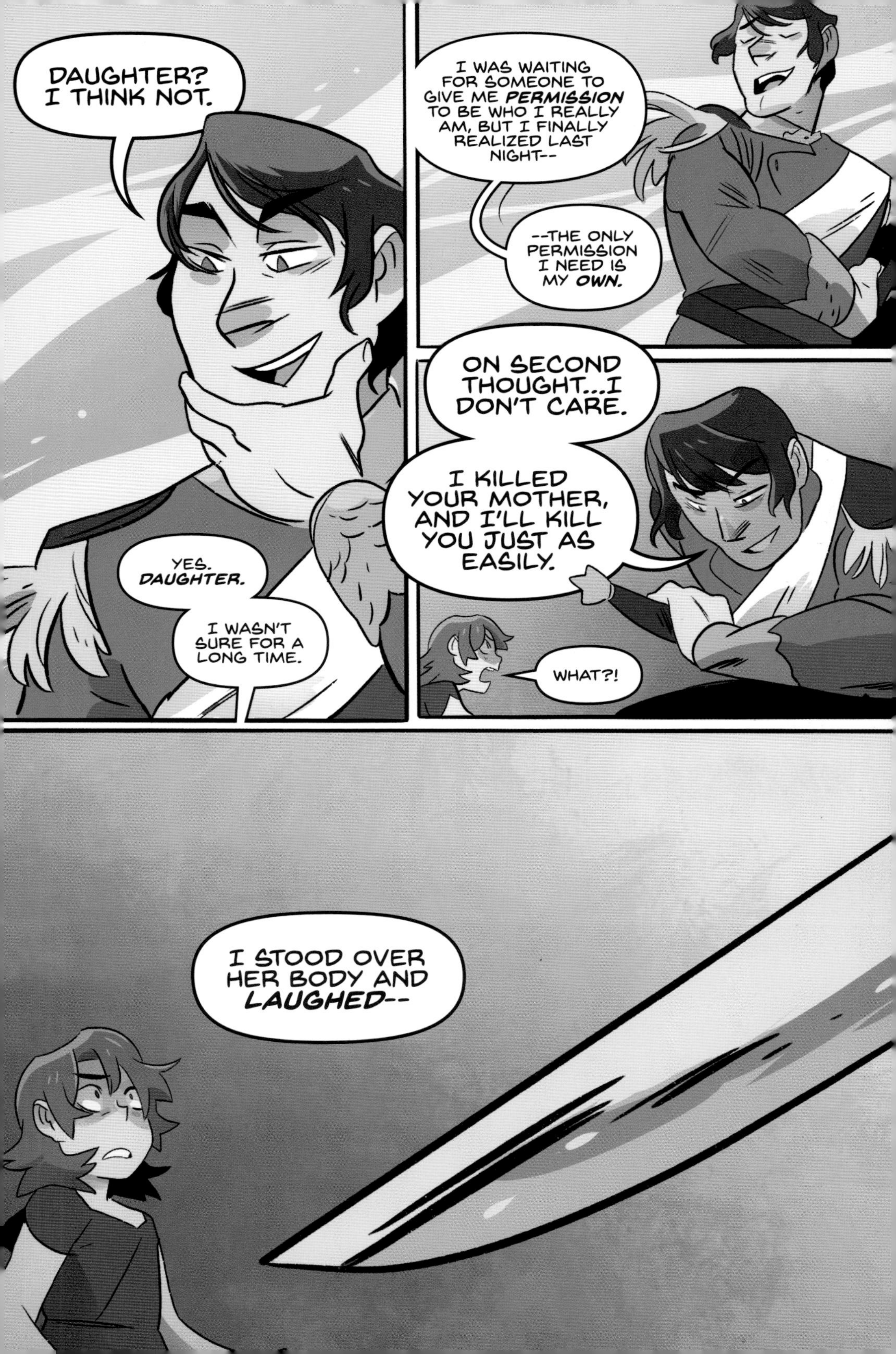
DAUGHTER? I THINK NOT.
YES. DAUGHTER.
I WASN'T SURE FOR A LONG TIME.
I WAS WAITING FOR SOMEONE TO GIVE ME PERMISSION TO BE WHO I REALLY AM, BUT I FINALLY REALIZED LAST NIGHT--
--THE ONLY PERMISSION I NEED IS MY OWN.
ON SECOND THOUGHT...I DON'T CARE.
I KILLED YOUR MOTHER, AND I'LL KILL YOU JUST AS EASILY.
WHAT?!
I STOOD OVER HER BODY AND LAUGHED--

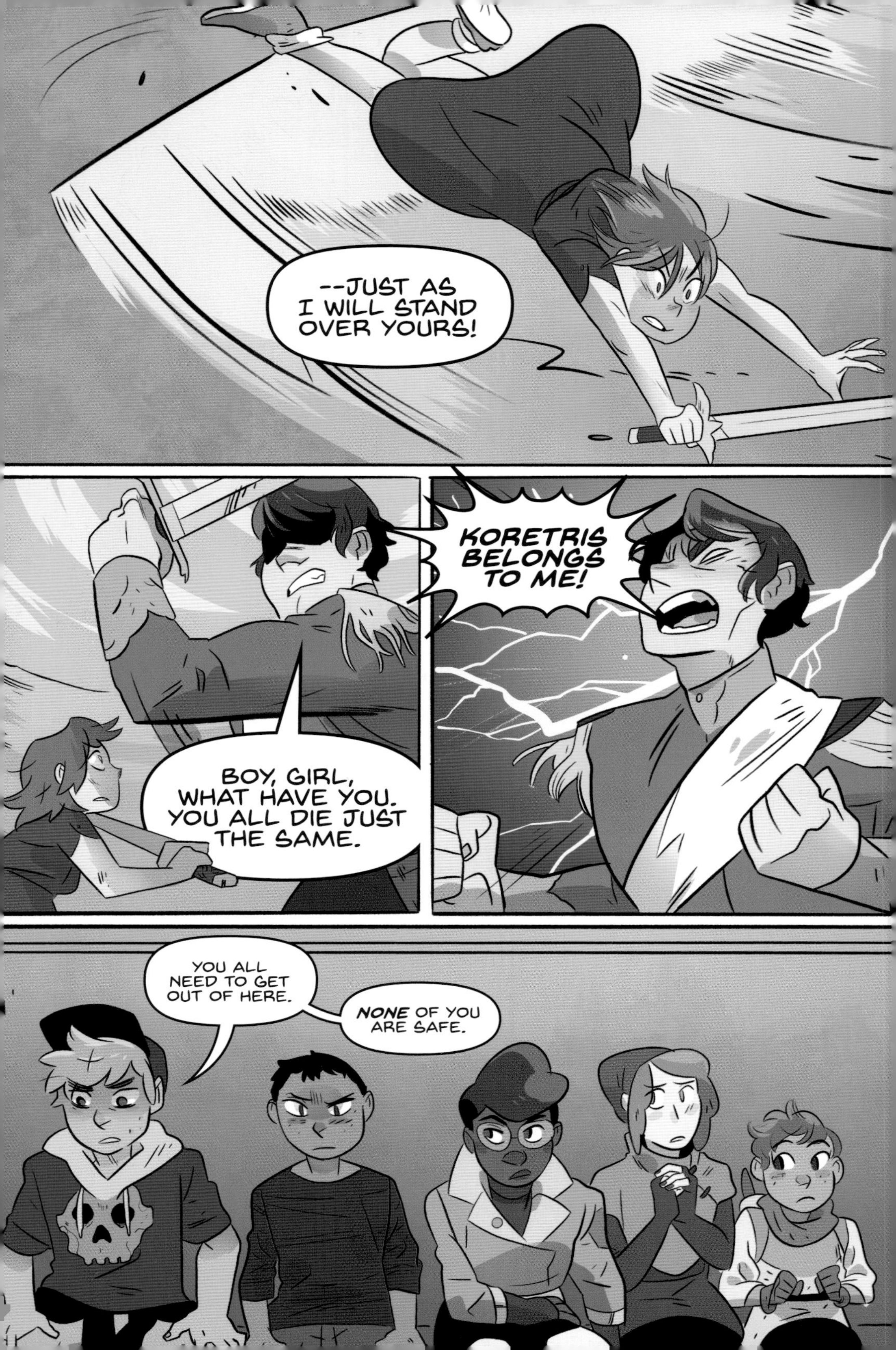
--JUST AS I WILL STAND OVER YOURS!
BOY, GIRL, WHAT HAVE YOU. YOU ALL DIE JUST THE SAME.
KORETRIS BELONGS TO ME!
YOU ALL NEED TO GET OUT OF HERE.
NONE OF YOU ARE SAFE.

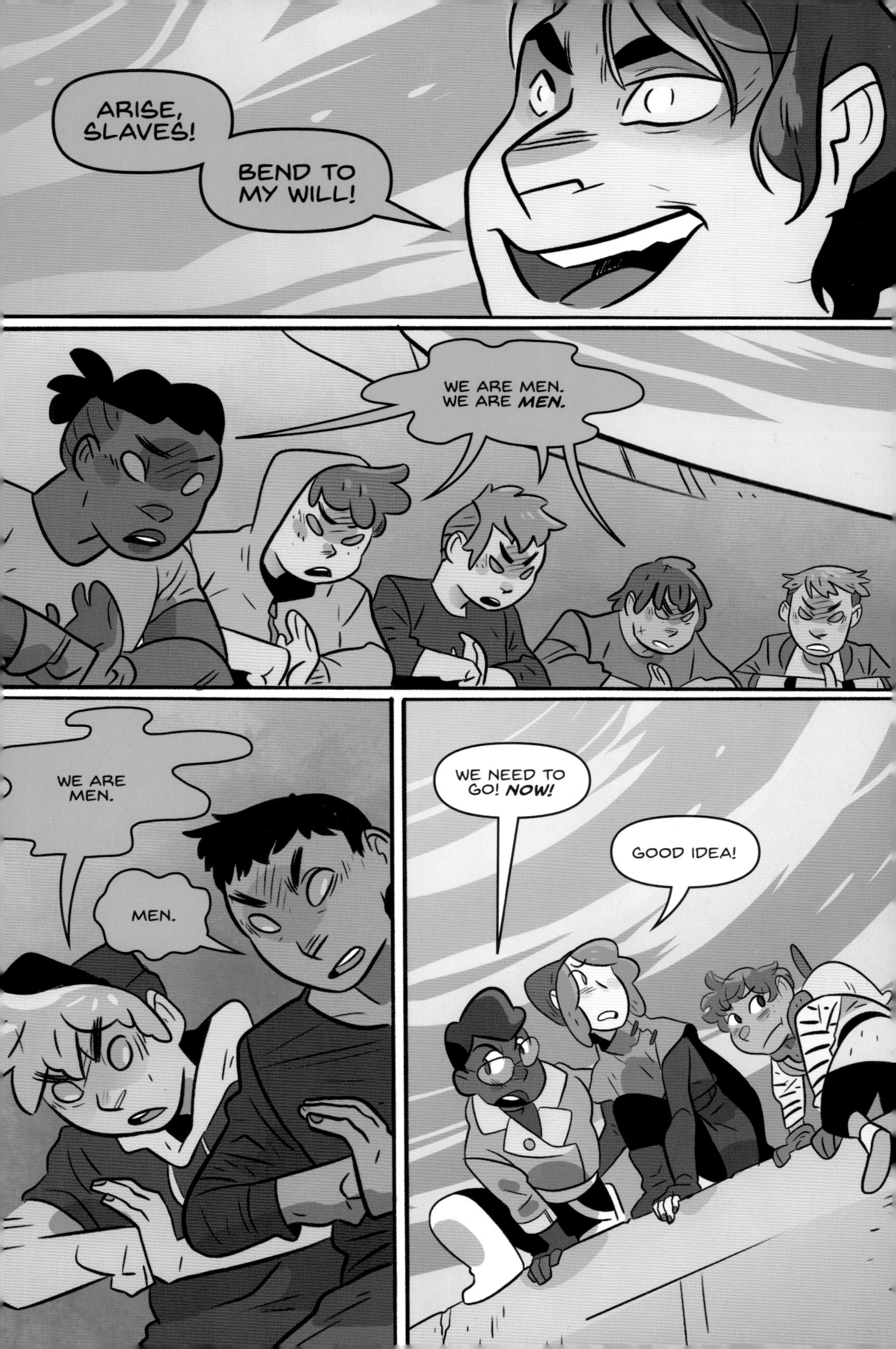
ARISE, SLAVES!
BEND TO MY WILL!
WE ARE MEN. WE ARE MEN.
WE ARE MEN.
MEN.
WE NEED TO GO! NOW!
GOOD IDEA!

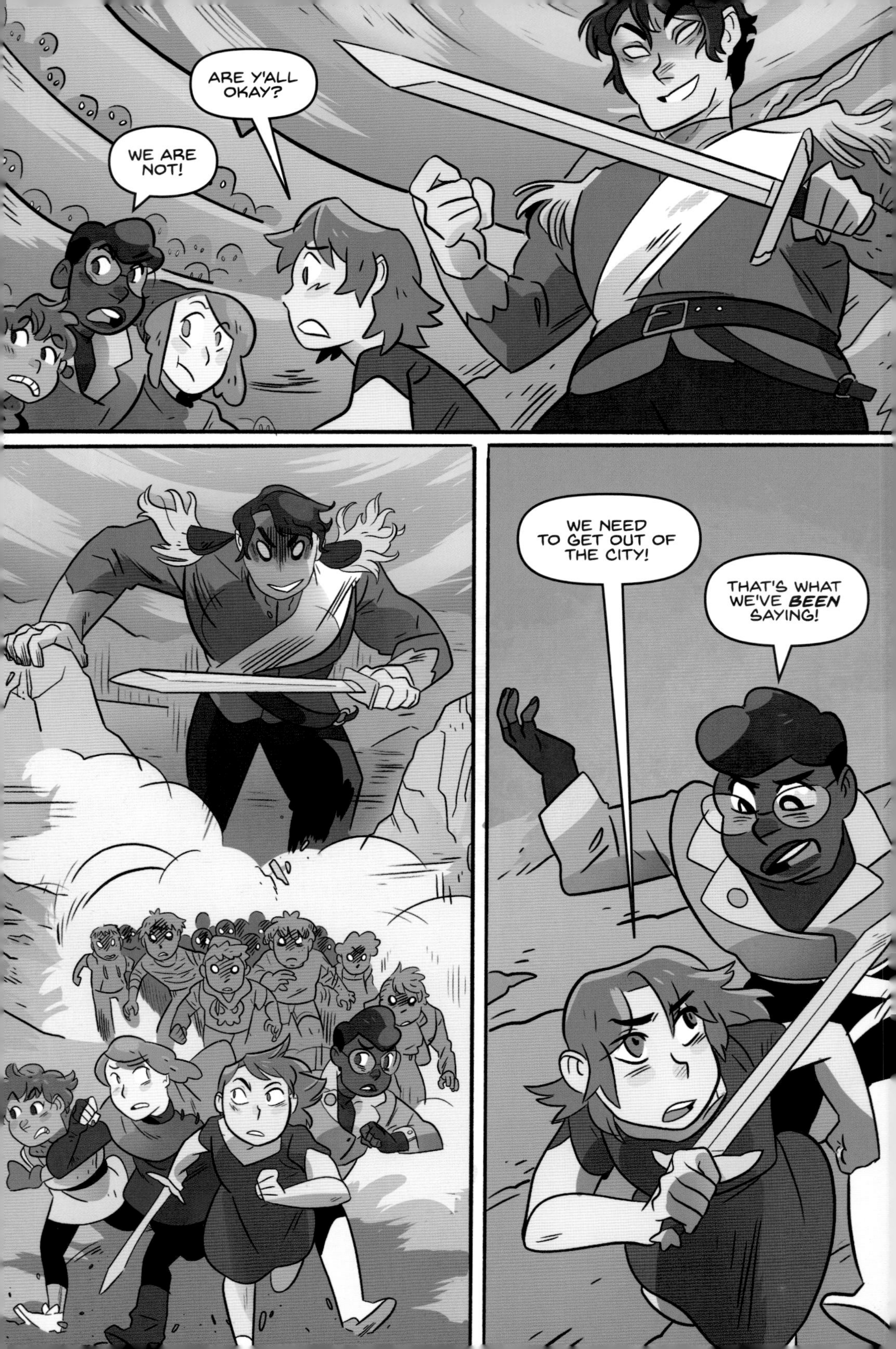
ARE Y'ALL OKAY?
WE ARE NOT!
WE NEED TO GET OUT OF THE CITY!
THAT'S WHAT WE'VE ***BEEN*** SAYING!

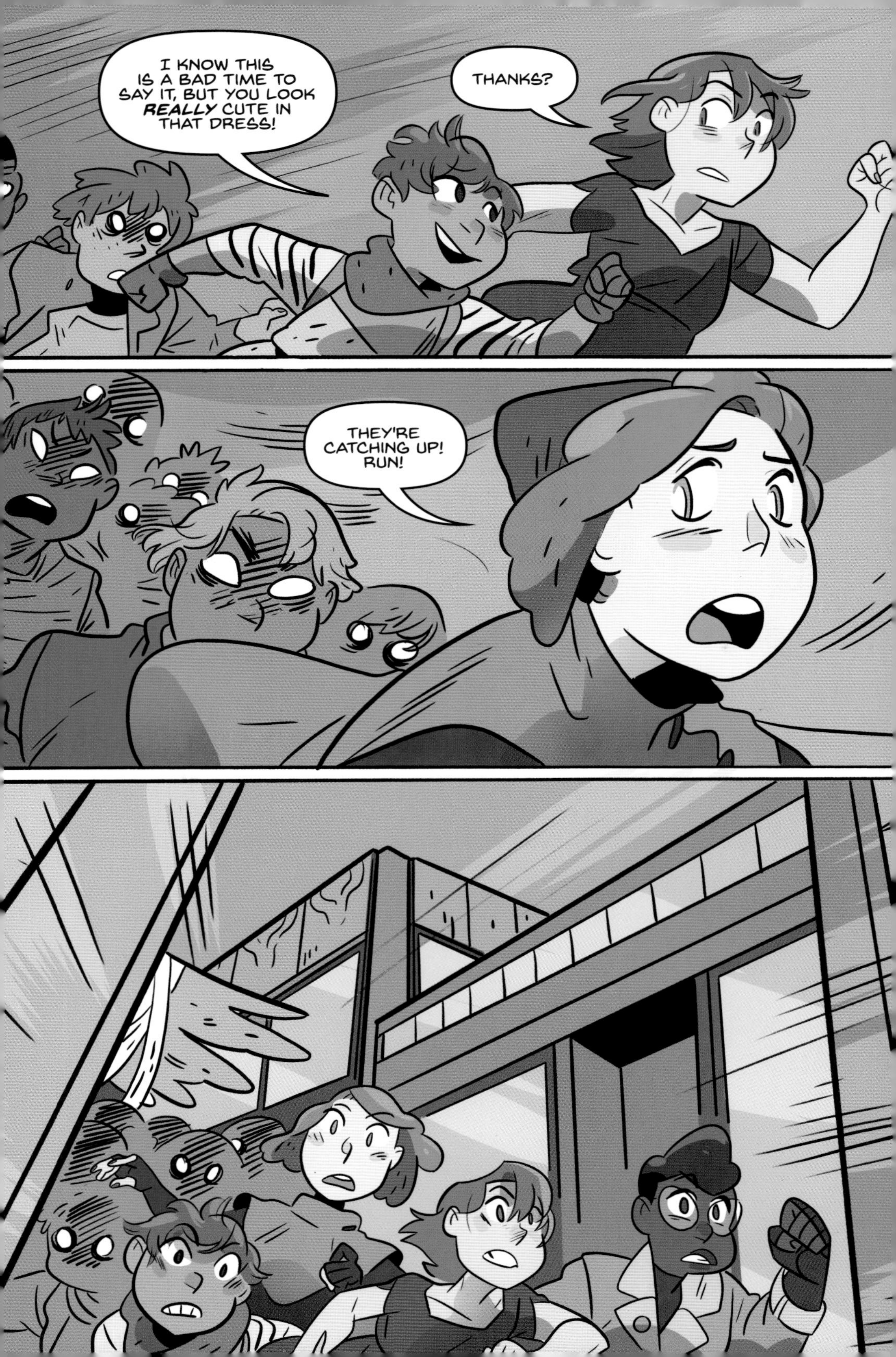
I KNOW THIS IS A BAD TIME TO SAY IT, BUT YOU LOOK *REALLY* CUTE IN THAT DRESS!
THANKS?
THEY'RE CATCHING UP! RUN!

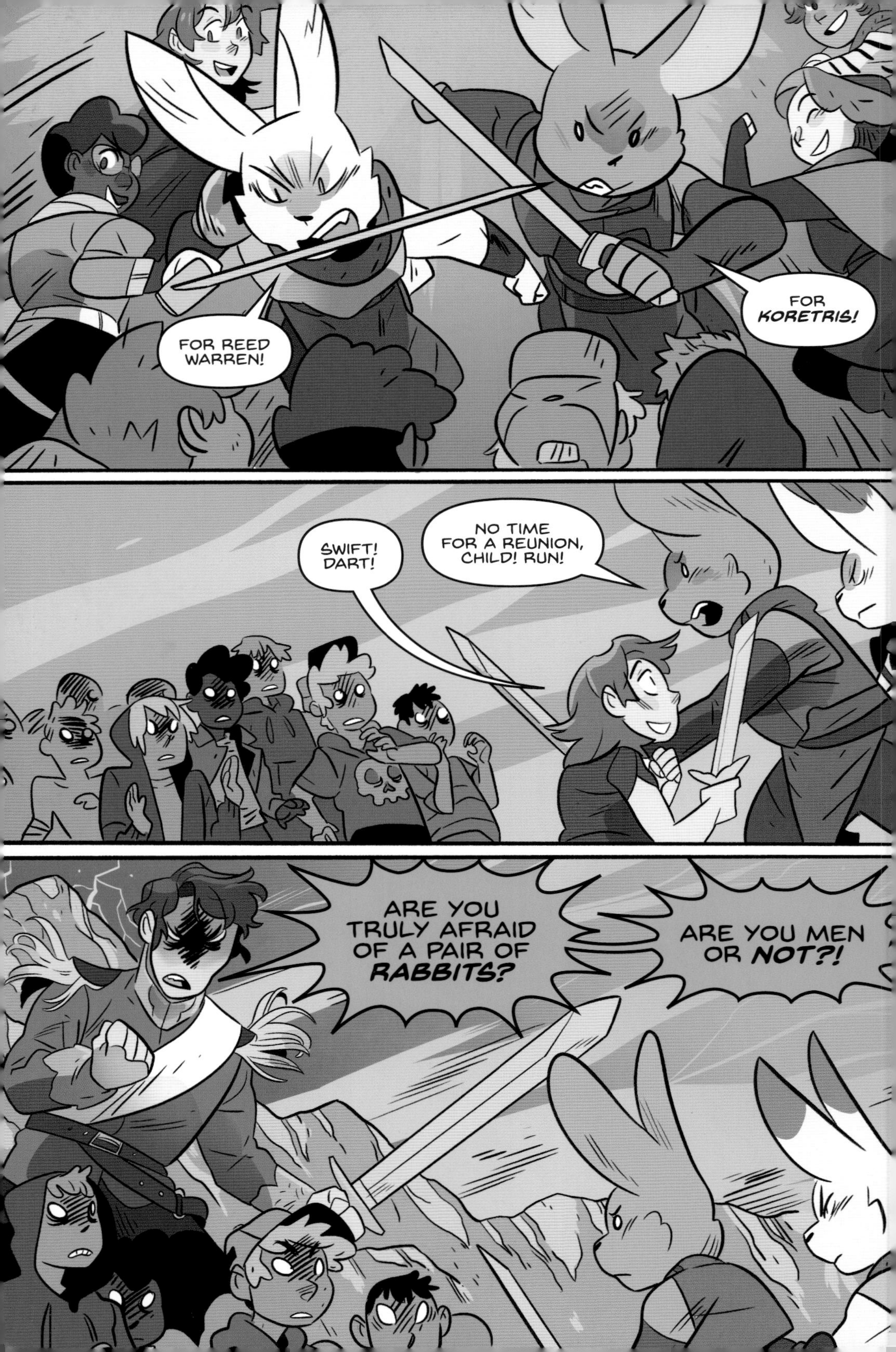
FOR REED WARREN!
FOR KORETRIS!
SWIFT! DART!
NO TIME FOR A REUNION, CHILD! RUN!
ARE YOU TRULY AFRAID OF A PAIR OF *RABBITS?*
ARE YOU MEN OR *NOT?!*

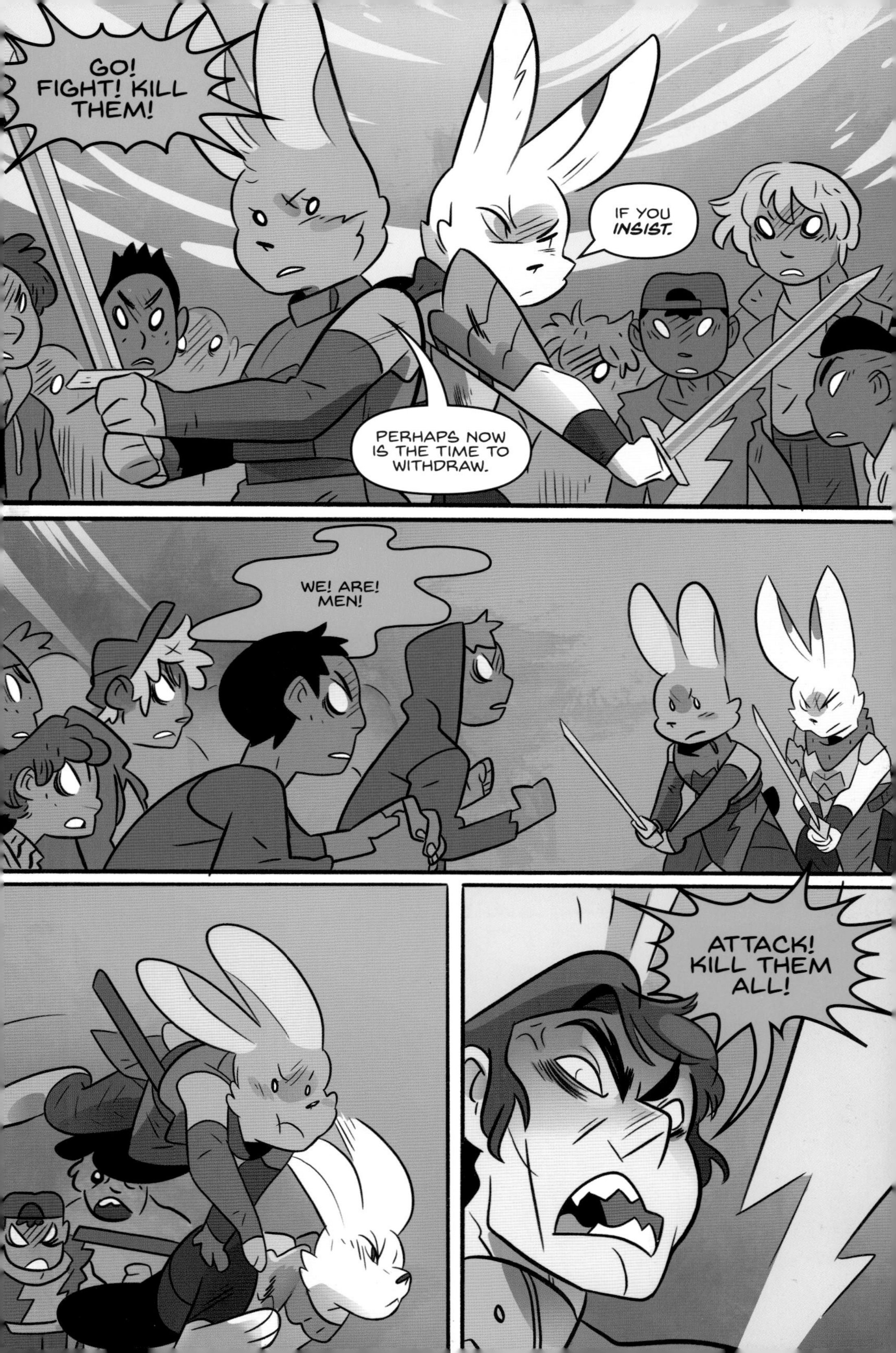
GO! FIGHT! KILL THEM!
IF YOU *INSIST.*
PERHAPS NOW IS THE TIME TO WITHDRAW.
WE! ARE! MEN!
ATTACK! KILL THEM ALL!

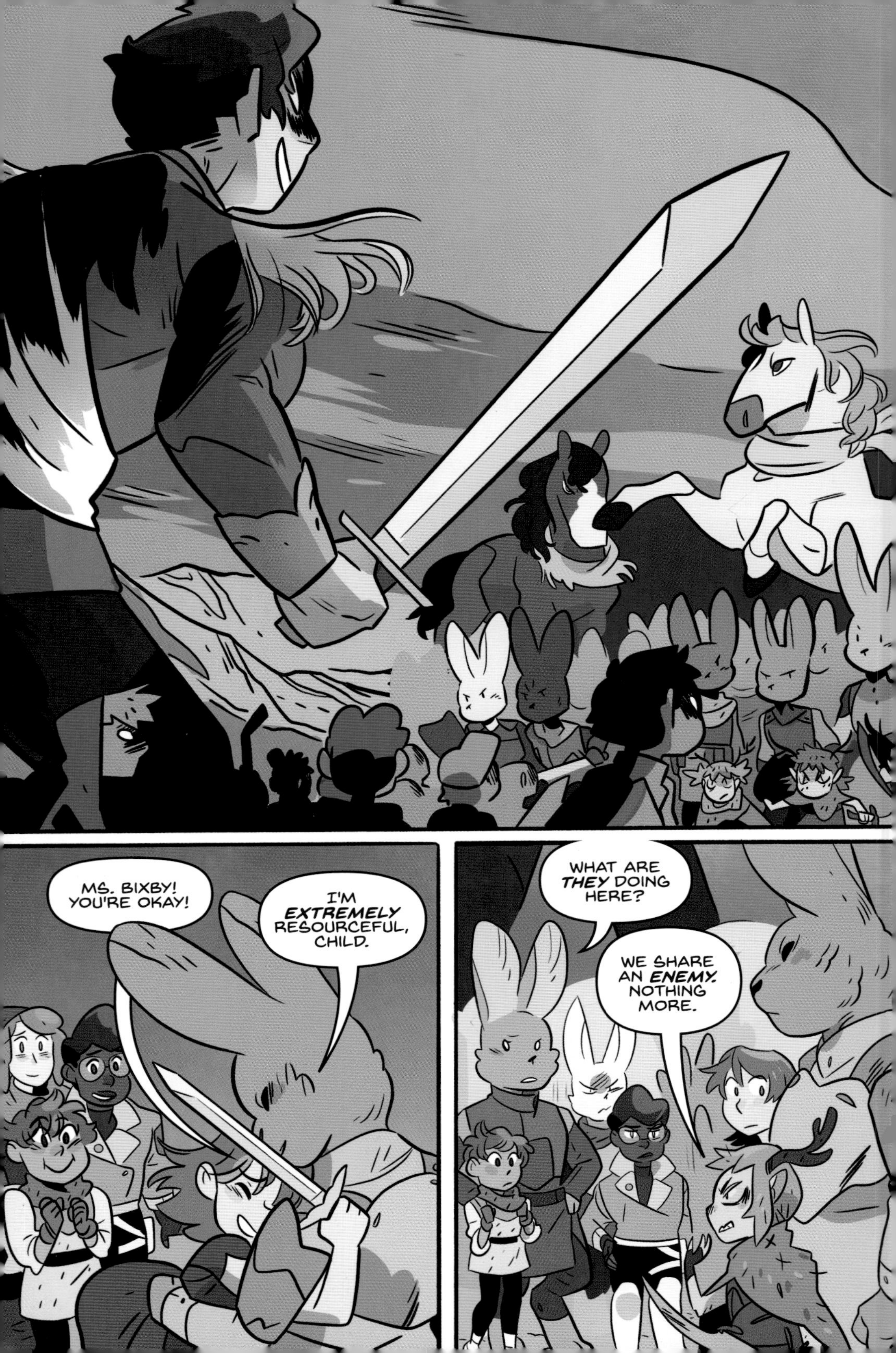
MS. BIXBY! YOU'RE OKAY!
I'M *EXTREMELY* RESOURCEFUL, CHILD.
WHAT ARE *THEY* DOING HERE?
WE SHARE AN *ENEMY.* NOTHING MORE.

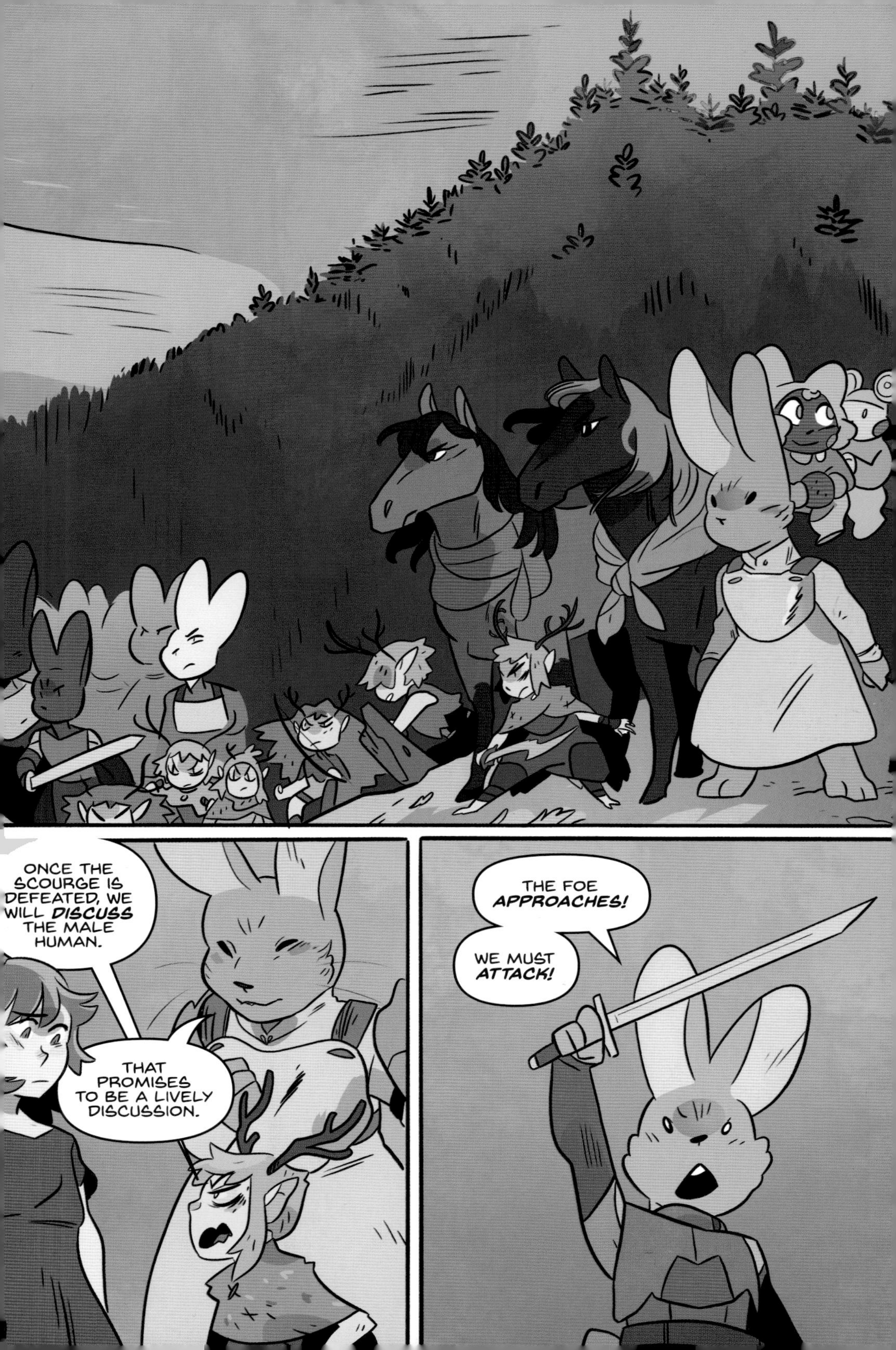
ONCE THE SCOURGE IS DEFEATED, WE WILL DISCUSS THE MALE HUMAN.
THAT PROMISES TO BE A LIVELY DISCUSSION.
THE FOE APPROACHES!
WE MUST ATTACK!

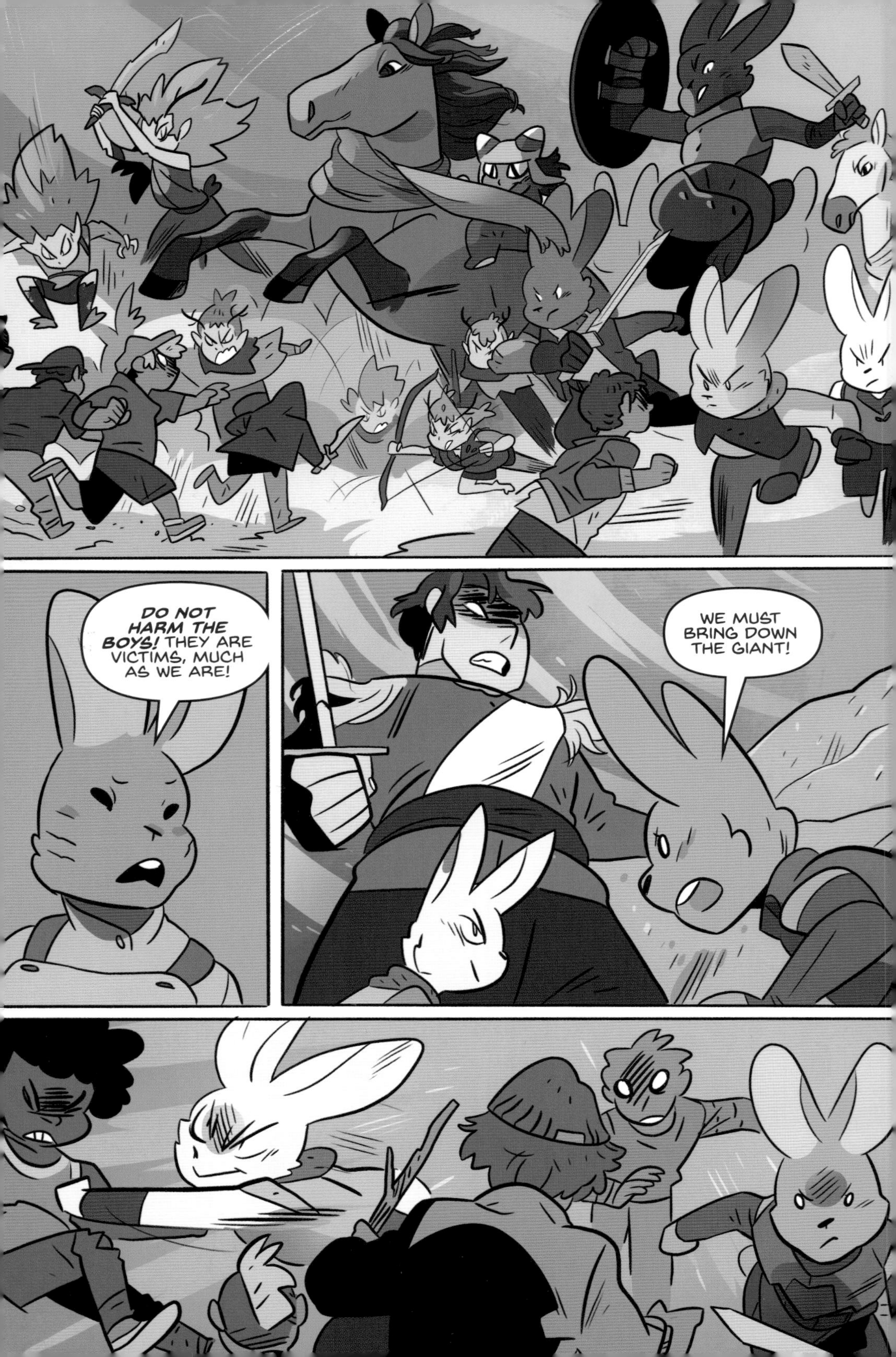
DO NOT HARM THE BOYS! THEY ARE VICTIMS, MUCH AS WE ARE!
WE MUST BRING DOWN THE GIANT!

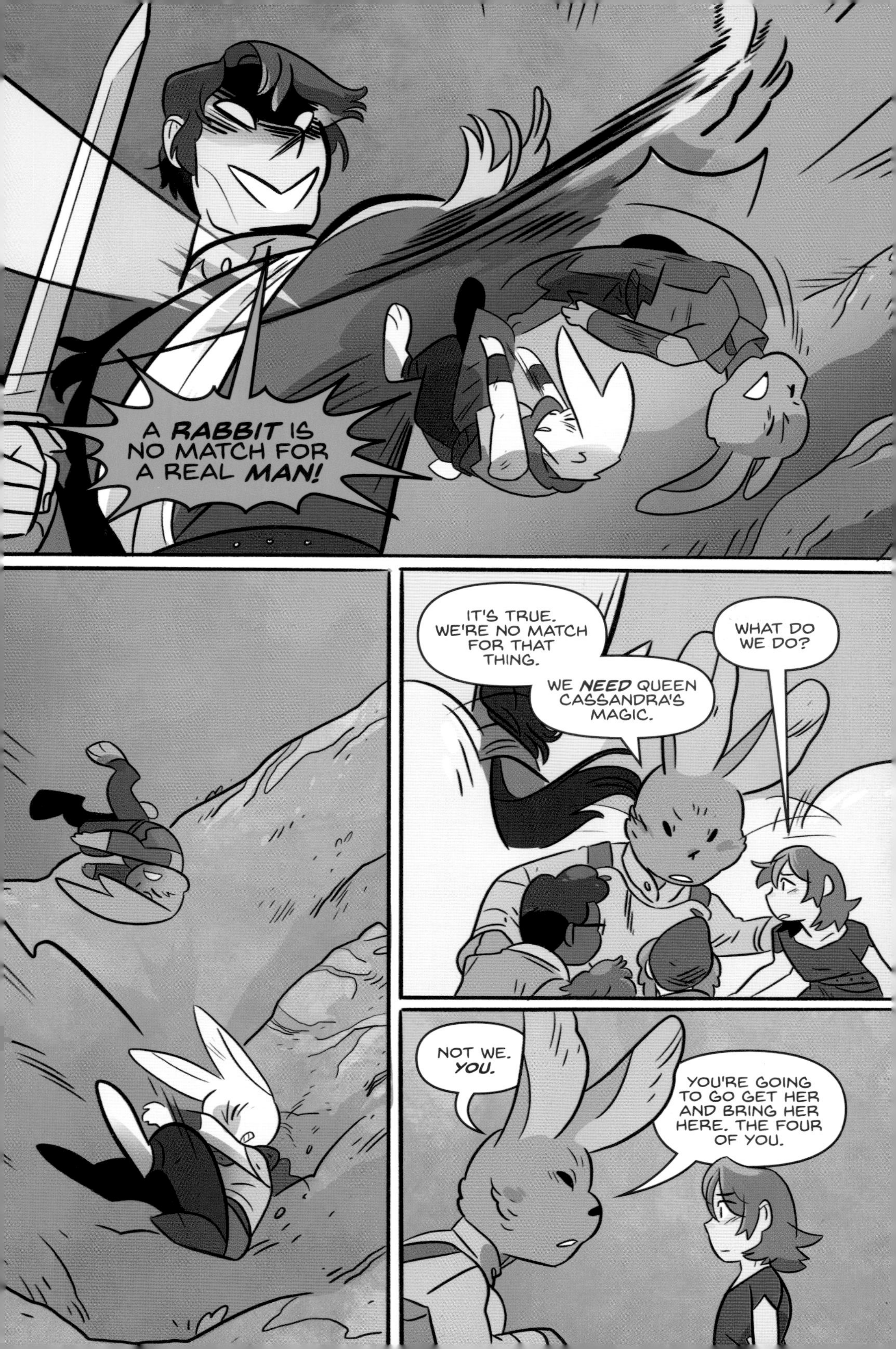
A **RABBIT** IS NO MATCH FOR A REAL **MAN!**
IT'S TRUE. WE'RE NO MATCH FOR THAT THING.
WE **NEED** QUEEN CASSANDRA'S MAGIC.
WHAT DO WE DO?
NOT WE. **YOU.**
YOU'RE GOING TO GO GET HER AND BRING HER HERE. THE FOUR OF YOU.

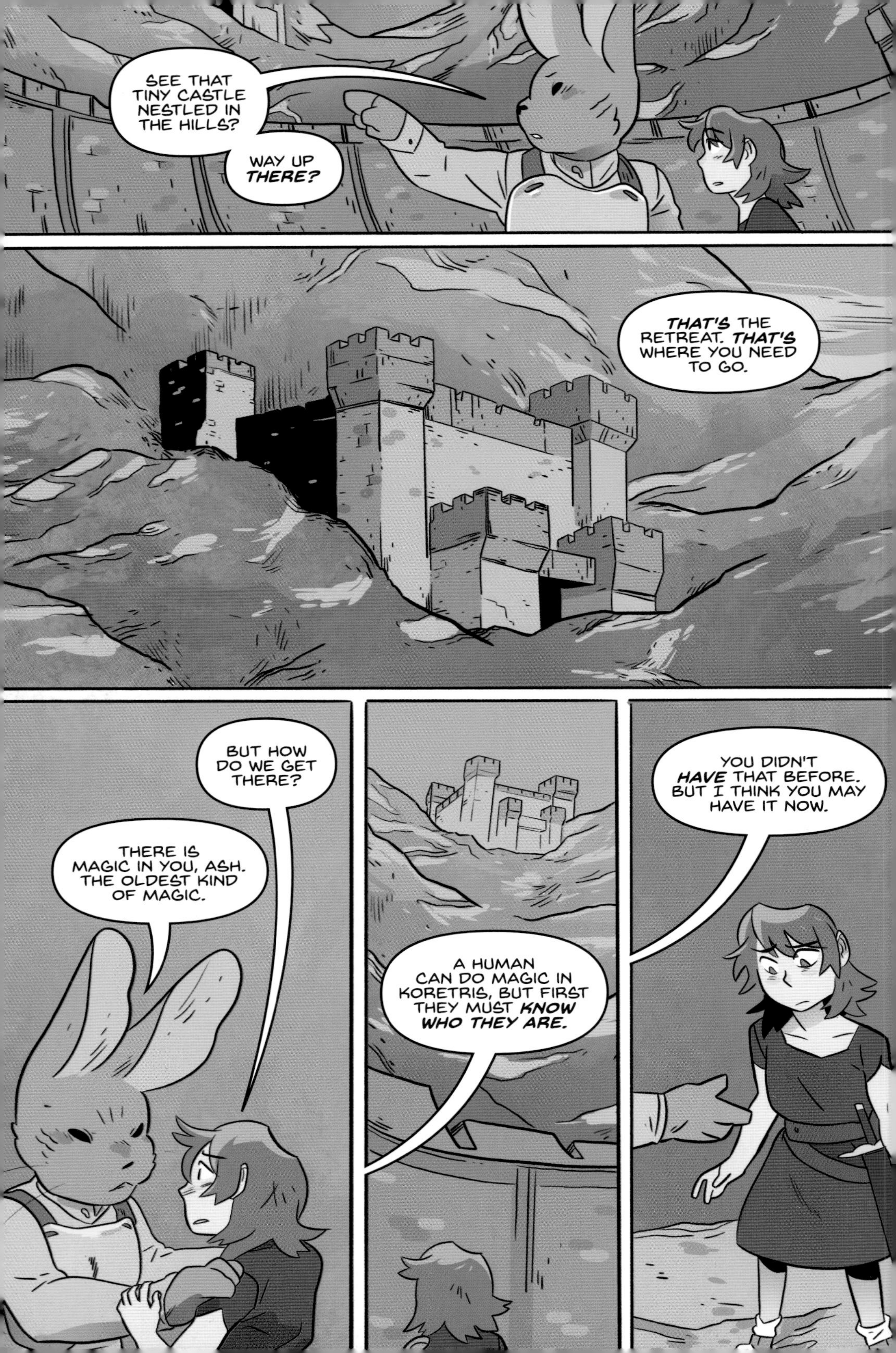
SEE THAT TINY CASTLE NESTLED IN THE HILLS?
WAY UP *THERE?*
THAT'S THE RETREAT. *THAT'S* WHERE YOU NEED TO GO.
BUT HOW DO WE GET THERE?
THERE IS MAGIC IN YOU, ASH. THE OLDEST KIND OF MAGIC.
A HUMAN CAN DO MAGIC IN KORETRIS, BUT FIRST THEY MUST *KNOW WHO THEY ARE.*
YOU DIDN'T *HAVE* THAT BEFORE. BUT I THINK YOU MAY HAVE IT NOW.

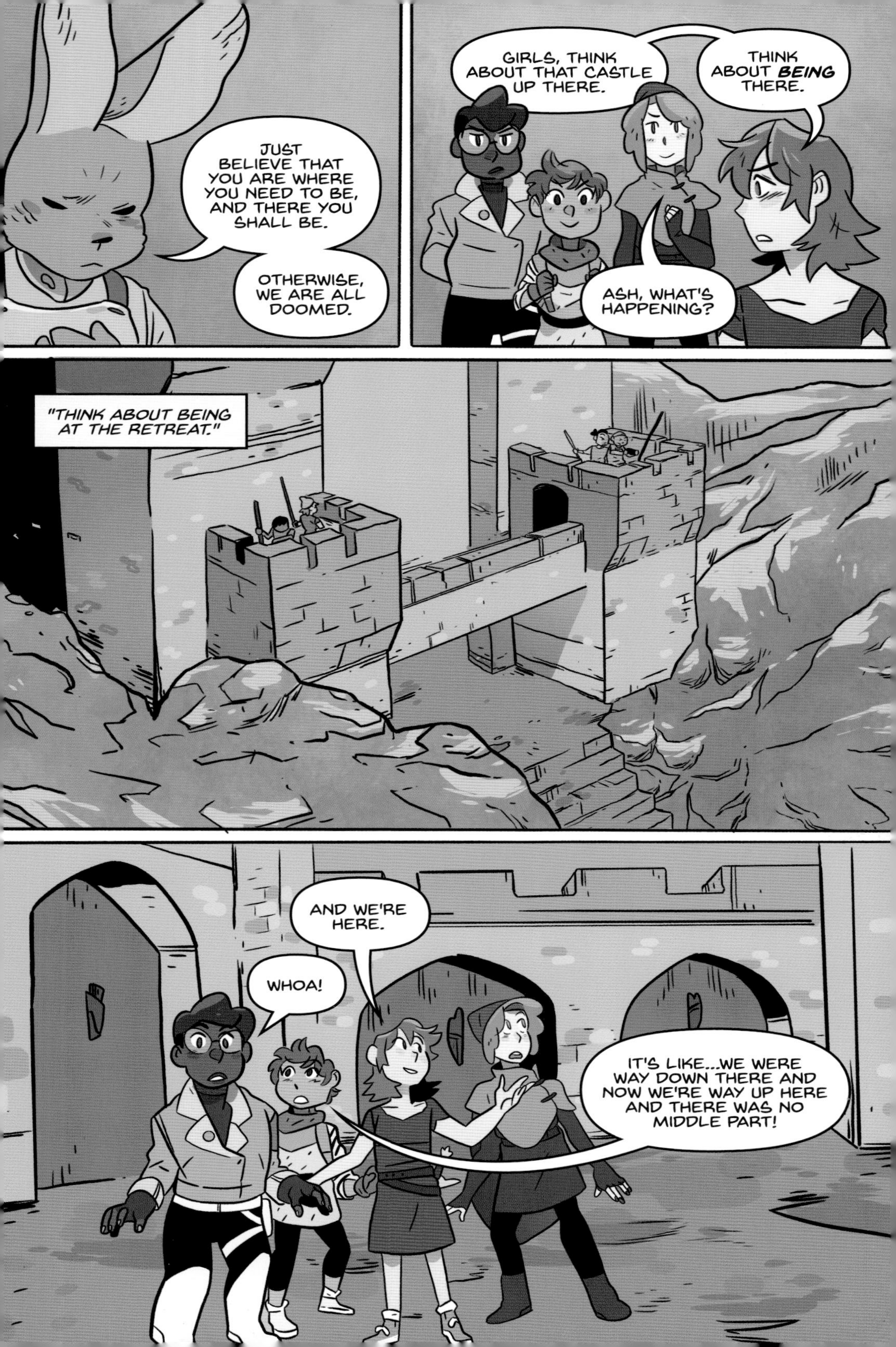
JUST BELIEVE THAT YOU ARE WHERE YOU NEED TO BE, AND THERE YOU SHALL BE.
OTHERWISE, WE ARE ALL DOOMED.
GIRLS, THINK ABOUT THAT CASTLE UP THERE.
THINK ABOUT BEING THERE.
ASH, WHAT'S HAPPENING?
"THINK ABOUT BEING AT THE RETREAT."
WHOA!
AND WE'RE HERE.
IT'S LIKE...WE WERE WAY DOWN THERE AND NOW WE'RE WAY UP HERE AND THERE WAS NO MIDDLE PART!

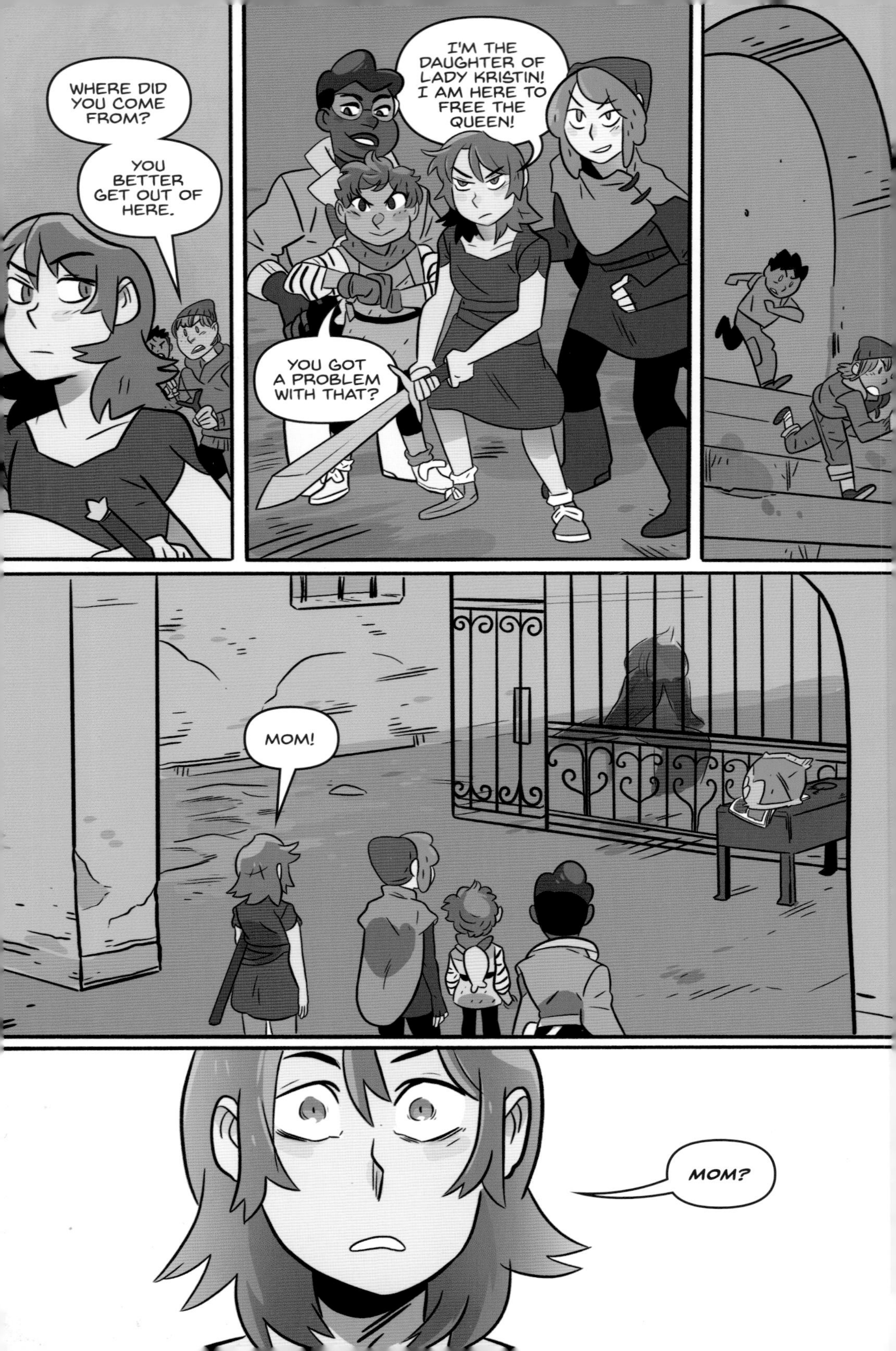
WHERE DID YOU COME FROM?
YOU BETTER GET OUT OF HERE.
I'M THE DAUGHTER OF LADY KRISTIN! I AM HERE TO FREE THE QUEEN!
YOU GOT A PROBLEM WITH THAT?
MOM!
MOM?

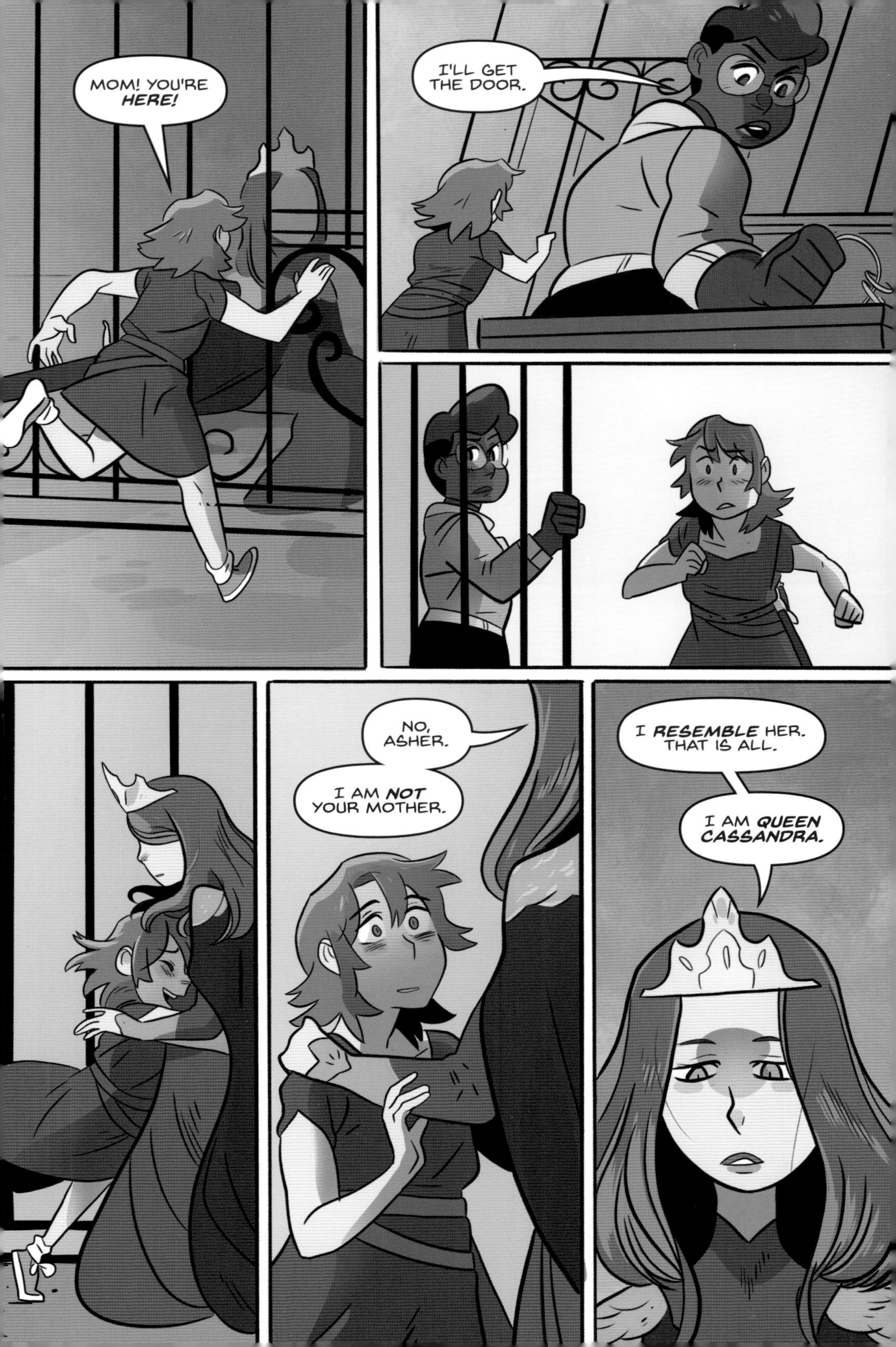
MOM! YOU'RE *HERE!*
I'LL GET THE DOOR.
NO, ASHER.
I AM *NOT* YOUR MOTHER.
I *RESEMBLE* HER. THAT IS ALL.
I AM *QUEEN CASSANDRA.*

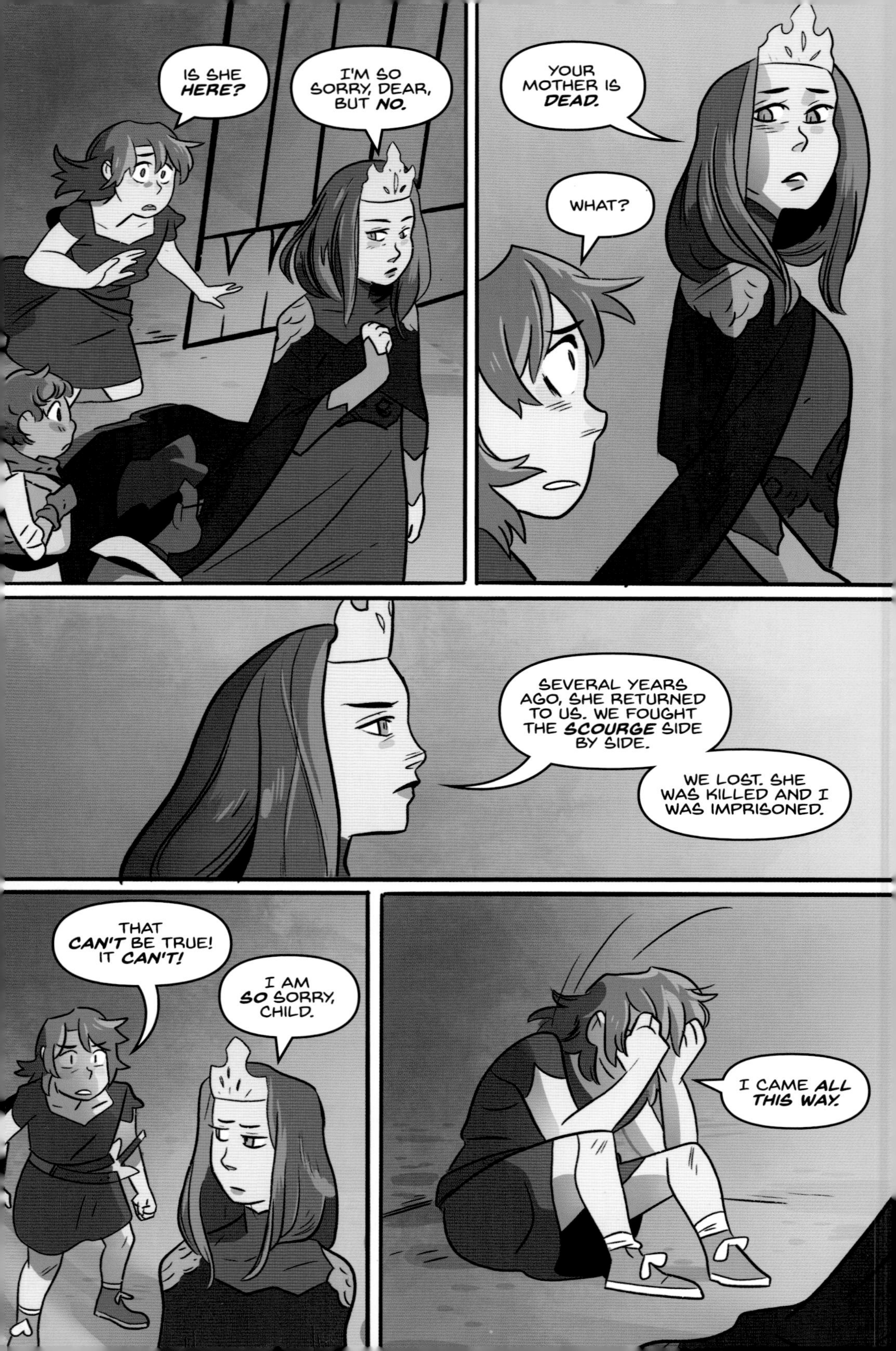
IS SHE *HERE?*
I'M SO SORRY, DEAR, BUT *NO.*
YOUR MOTHER IS *DEAD.*
WHAT?
SEVERAL YEARS AGO, SHE RETURNED TO US. WE FOUGHT THE *SCOURGE* SIDE BY SIDE.
WE LOST. SHE WAS KILLED AND I WAS IMPRISONED.
THAT *CAN'T* BE TRUE! IT *CAN'T!*
I AM *SO* SORRY, CHILD.
I CAME *ALL THIS WAY.*

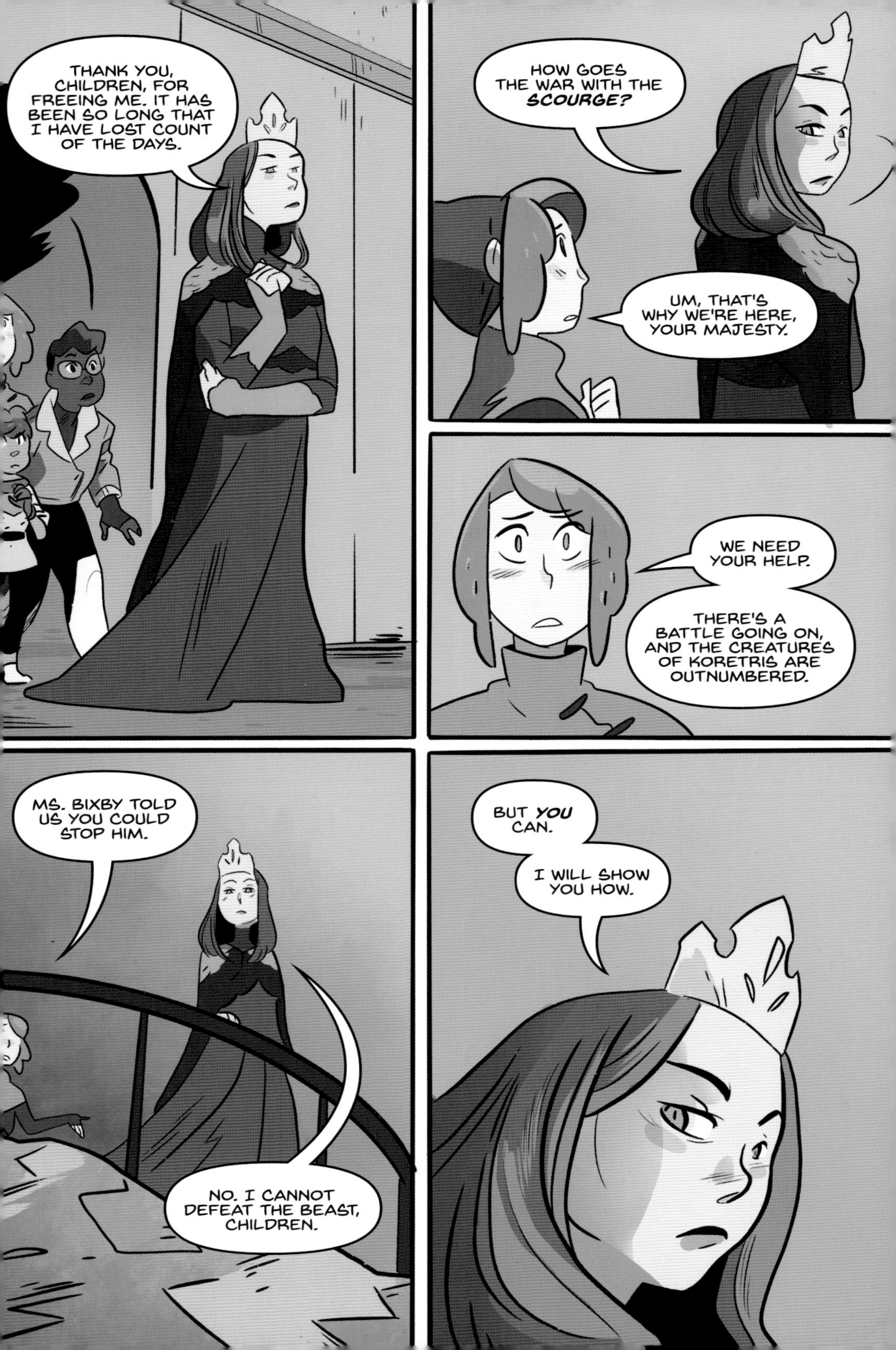
THANK YOU, CHILDREN, FOR FREEING ME. IT HAS BEEN SO LONG THAT I HAVE LOST COUNT OF THE DAYS.
HOW GOES THE WAR WITH THE *SCOURGE?*
UM, THAT'S WHY WE'RE HERE, YOUR MAJESTY.
WE NEED YOUR HELP.
THERE'S A BATTLE GOING ON, AND THE CREATURES OF KORETRIS ARE OUTNUMBERED.
MS. BIXBY TOLD US YOU COULD STOP HIM.
NO. I CANNOT DEFEAT THE BEAST, CHILDREN.
BUT *YOU* CAN.
I WILL SHOW YOU HOW.

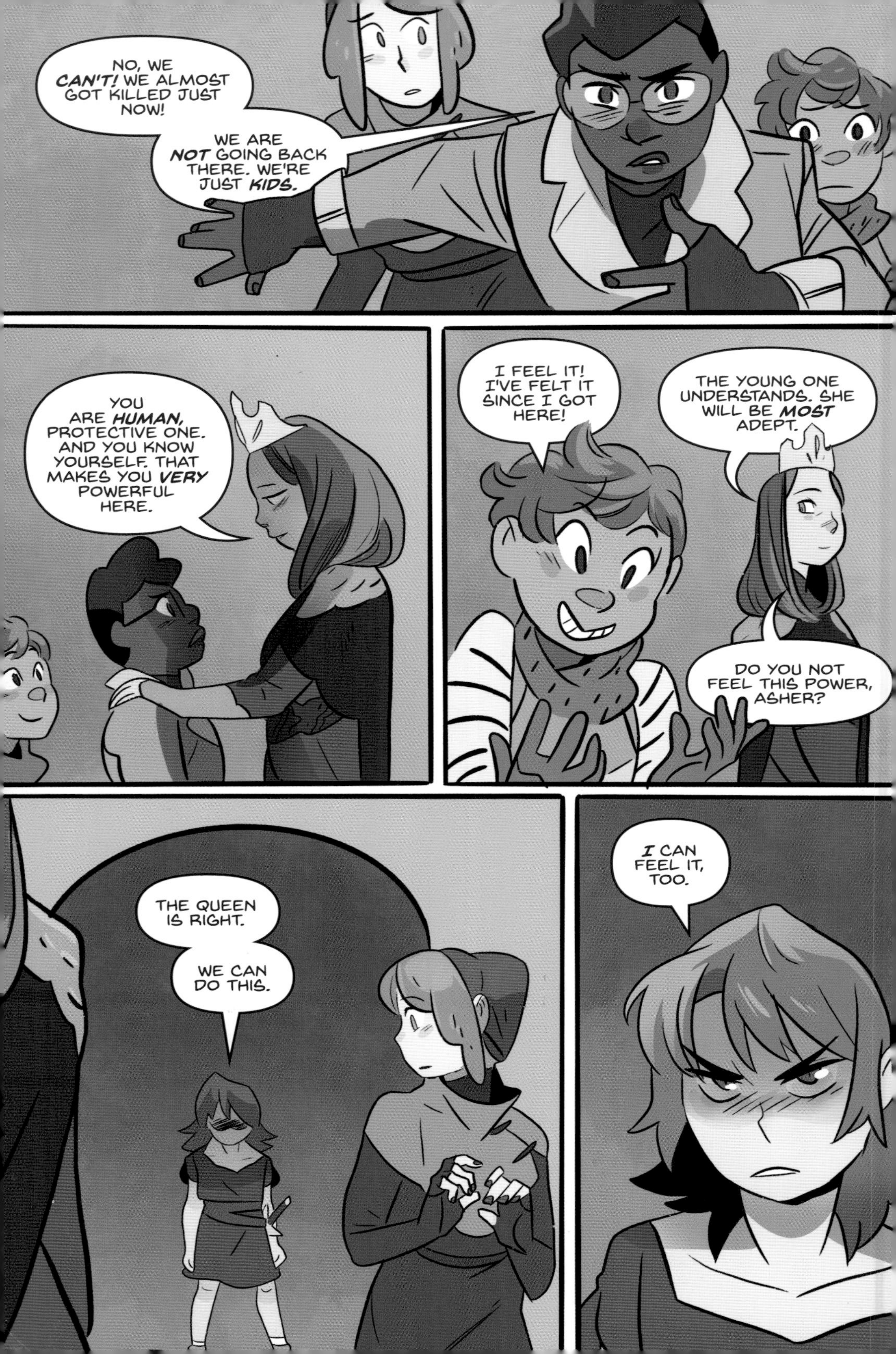
NO, WE **CAN'T!** WE ALMOST GOT KILLED JUST NOW!
WE ARE **NOT** GOING BACK THERE. WE'RE JUST **KIDS.**
YOU ARE **HUMAN,** PROTECTIVE ONE. AND YOU KNOW YOURSELF. THAT MAKES YOU **VERY** POWERFUL HERE.
I FEEL IT! I'VE FELT IT SINCE I GOT HERE!
THE YOUNG ONE UNDERSTANDS. SHE WILL BE **MOST** ADEPT.
DO YOU NOT FEEL THIS POWER, ASHER?
THE QUEEN IS RIGHT.
WE CAN DO THIS.
I CAN FEEL IT, TOO.

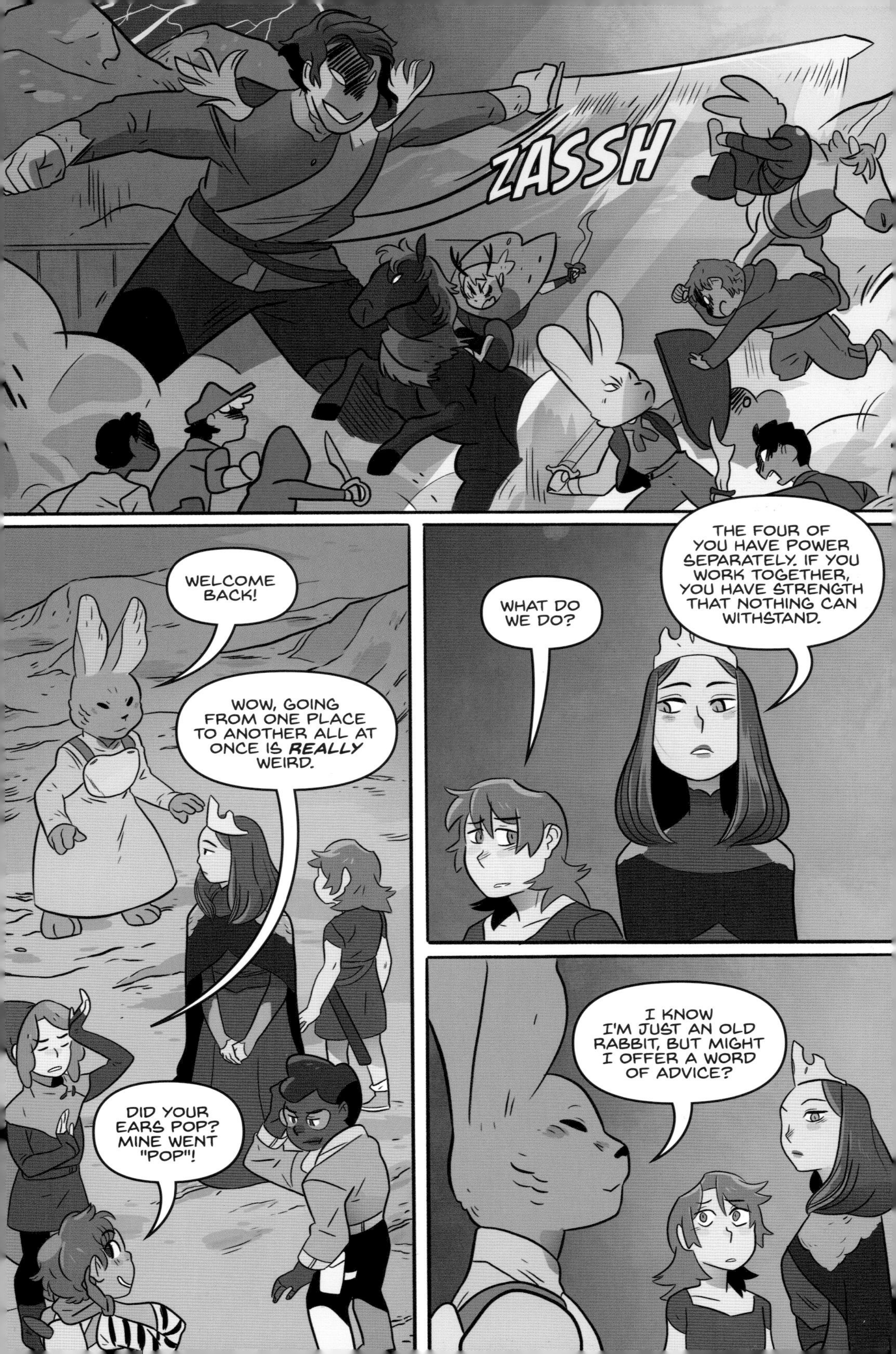
ZASSH
WELCOME BACK!
WOW, GOING FROM ONE PLACE TO ANOTHER ALL AT ONCE IS *REALLY* WEIRD.
DID YOUR EARS POP? MINE WENT "POP"!
WHAT DO WE DO?
THE FOUR OF YOU HAVE POWER SEPARATELY. IF YOU WORK TOGETHER, YOU HAVE STRENGTH THAT NOTHING CAN WITHSTAND.
I KNOW I'M JUST AN OLD RABBIT, BUT MIGHT I OFFER A WORD OF ADVICE?

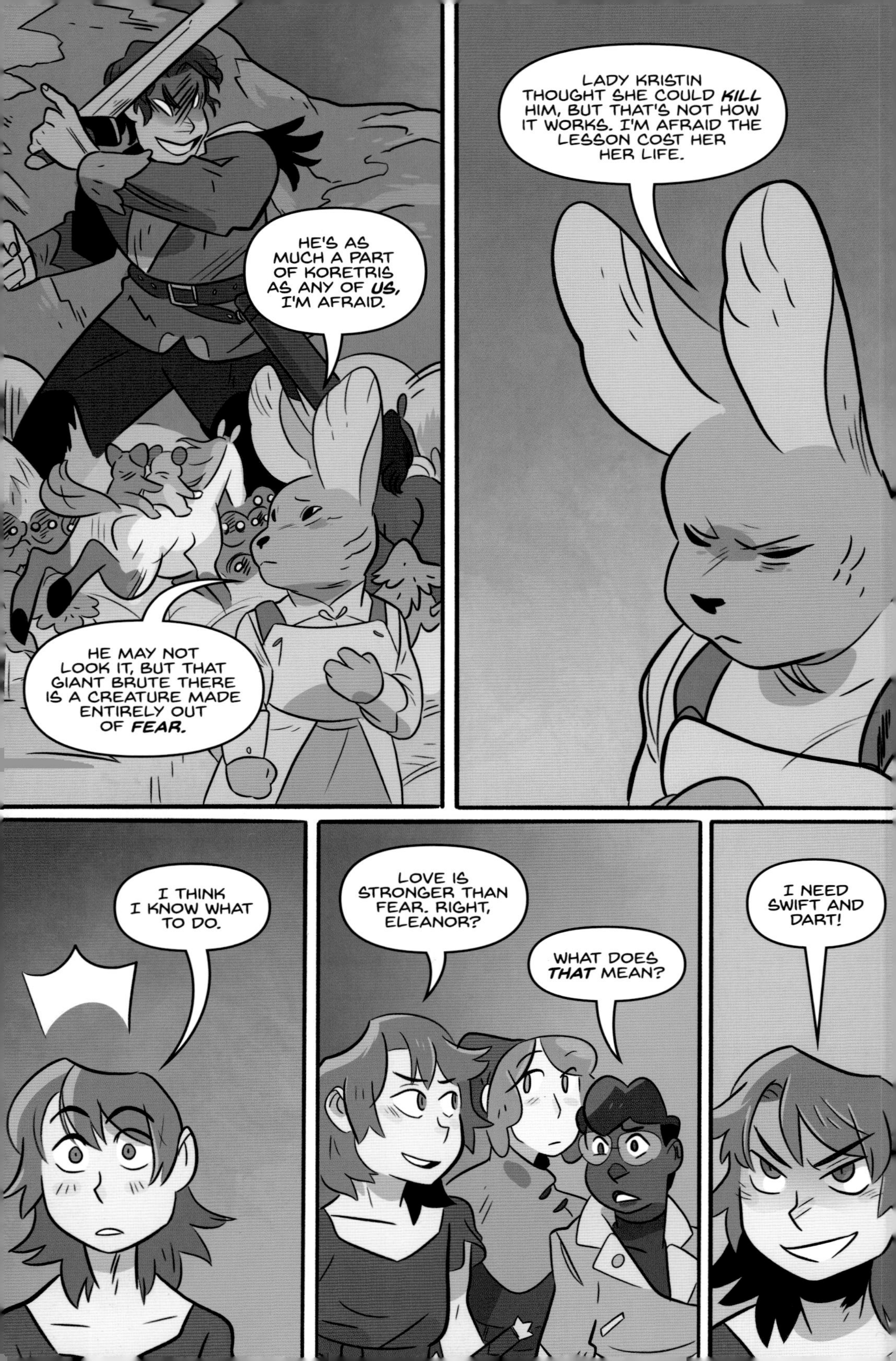
HE'S AS MUCH A PART OF KORETRIS AS ANY OF US, I'M AFRAID.
HE MAY NOT LOOK IT, BUT THAT GIANT BRUTE THERE IS A CREATURE MADE ENTIRELY OUT OF FEAR.
LADY KRISTIN THOUGHT SHE COULD KILL HIM, BUT THAT'S NOT HOW IT WORKS. I'M AFRAID THE LESSON COST HER HER LIFE.
I THINK I KNOW WHAT TO DO.
LOVE IS STRONGER THAN FEAR. RIGHT, ELEANOR?
WHAT DOES THAT MEAN?
I NEED SWIFT AND DART!

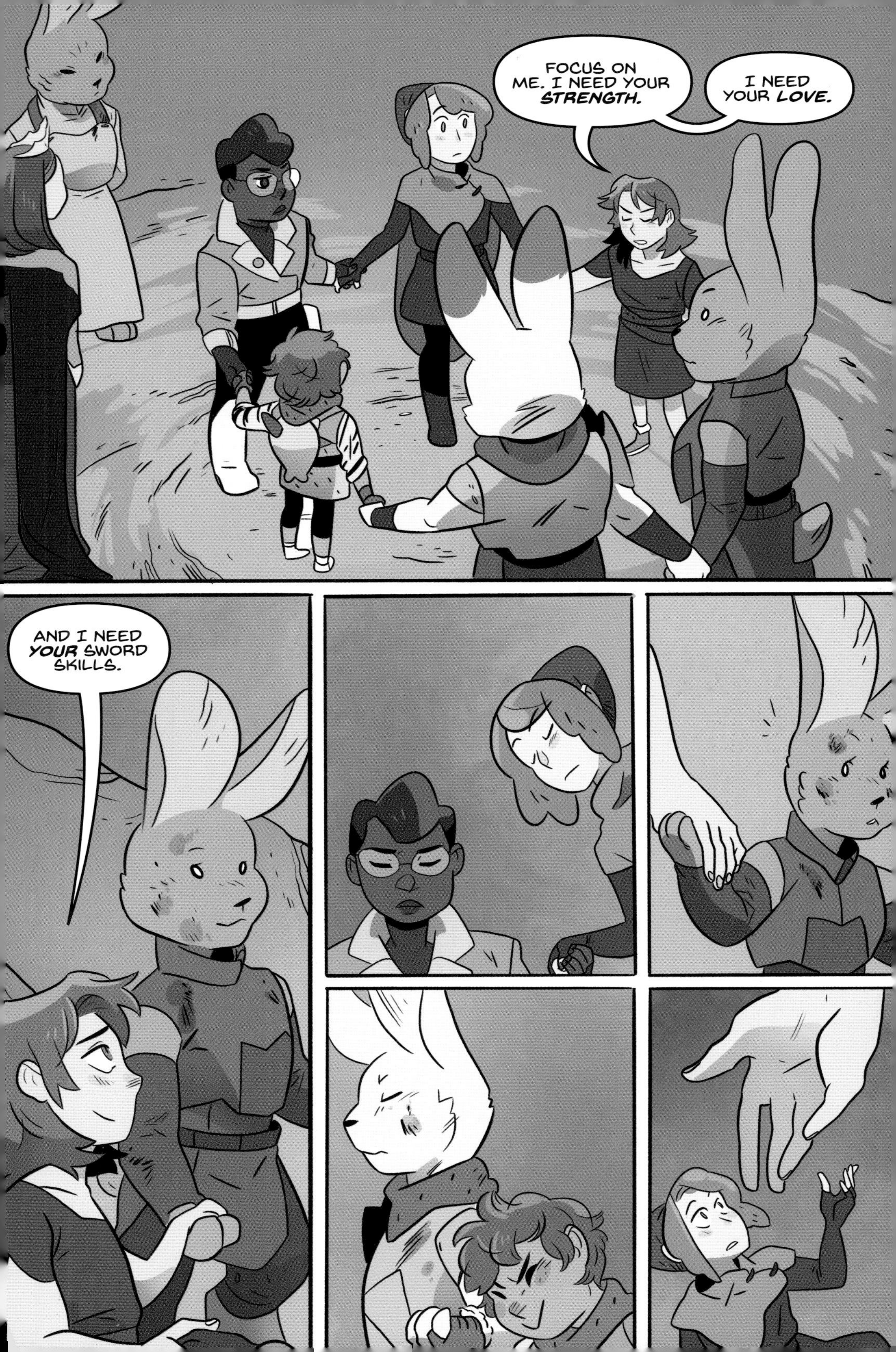
FOCUS ON ME. I NEED YOUR STRENGTH.
I NEED YOUR LOVE.
AND I NEED YOUR SWORD SKILLS.

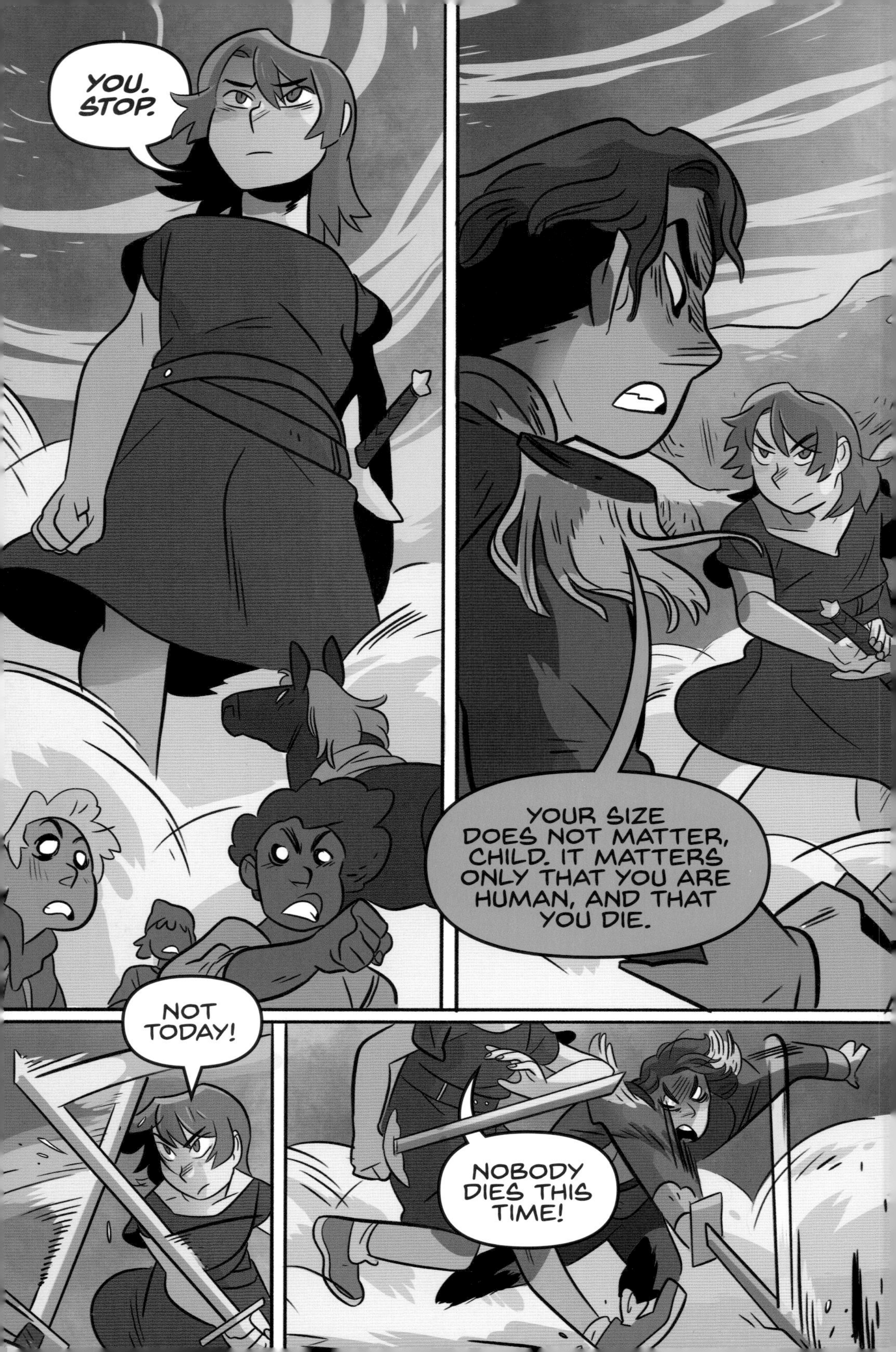
YOU. STOP.
YOUR SIZE DOES NOT MATTER, CHILD. IT MATTERS ONLY THAT YOU ARE HUMAN, AND THAT YOU DIE.
NOT TODAY!
NOBODY DIES THIS TIME!

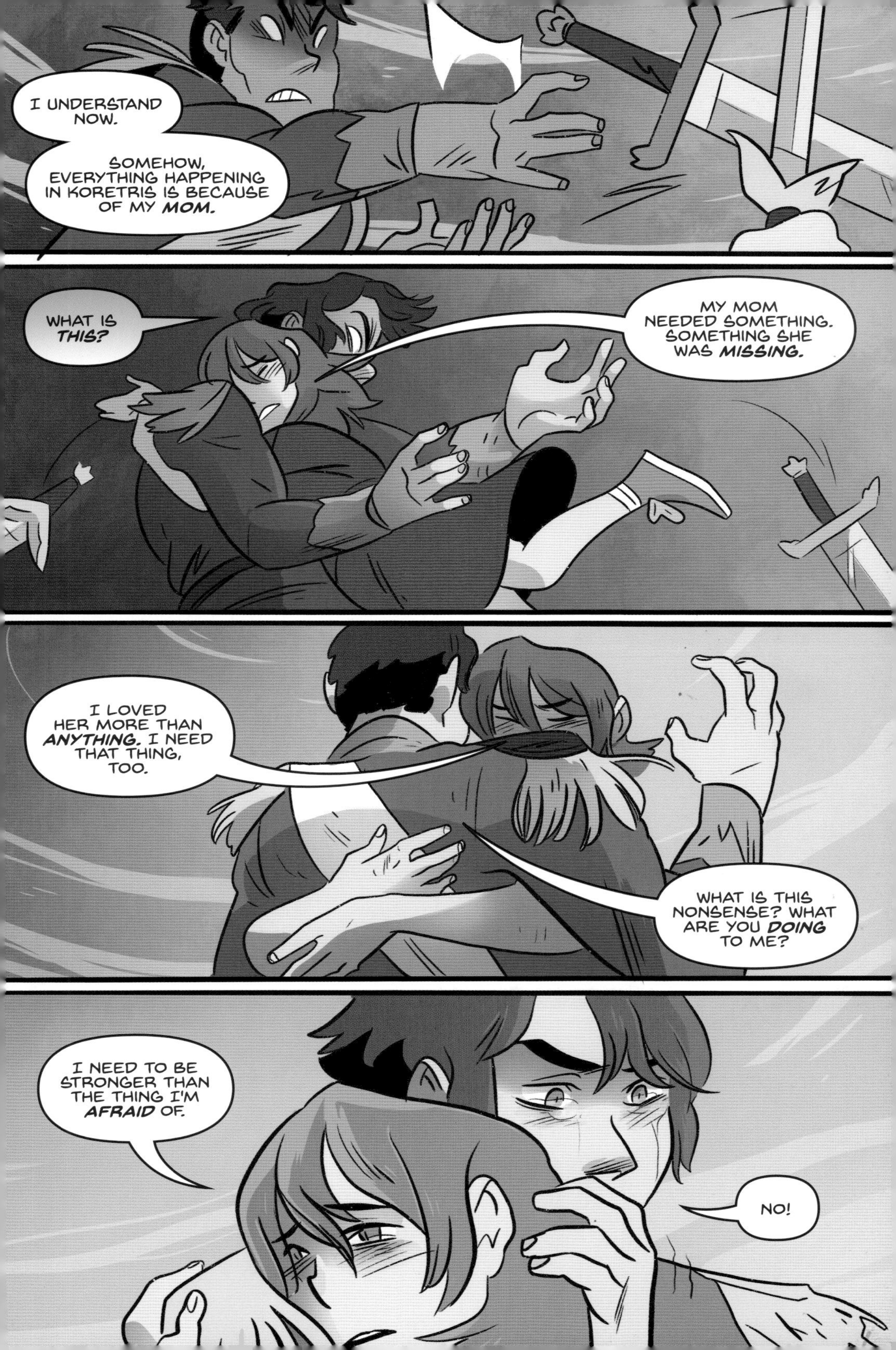
I UNDERSTAND NOW.
SOMEHOW, EVERYTHING HAPPENING IN KORETRIS IS BECAUSE OF MY MOM.
WHAT IS THIS?
MY MOM NEEDED SOMETHING. SOMETHING SHE WAS MISSING.
I LOVED HER MORE THAN ANYTHING. I NEED THAT THING, TOO.
WHAT IS THIS NONSENSE? WHAT ARE YOU DOING TO ME?
I NEED TO BE STRONGER THAN THE THING I'M AFRAID OF.
NO!

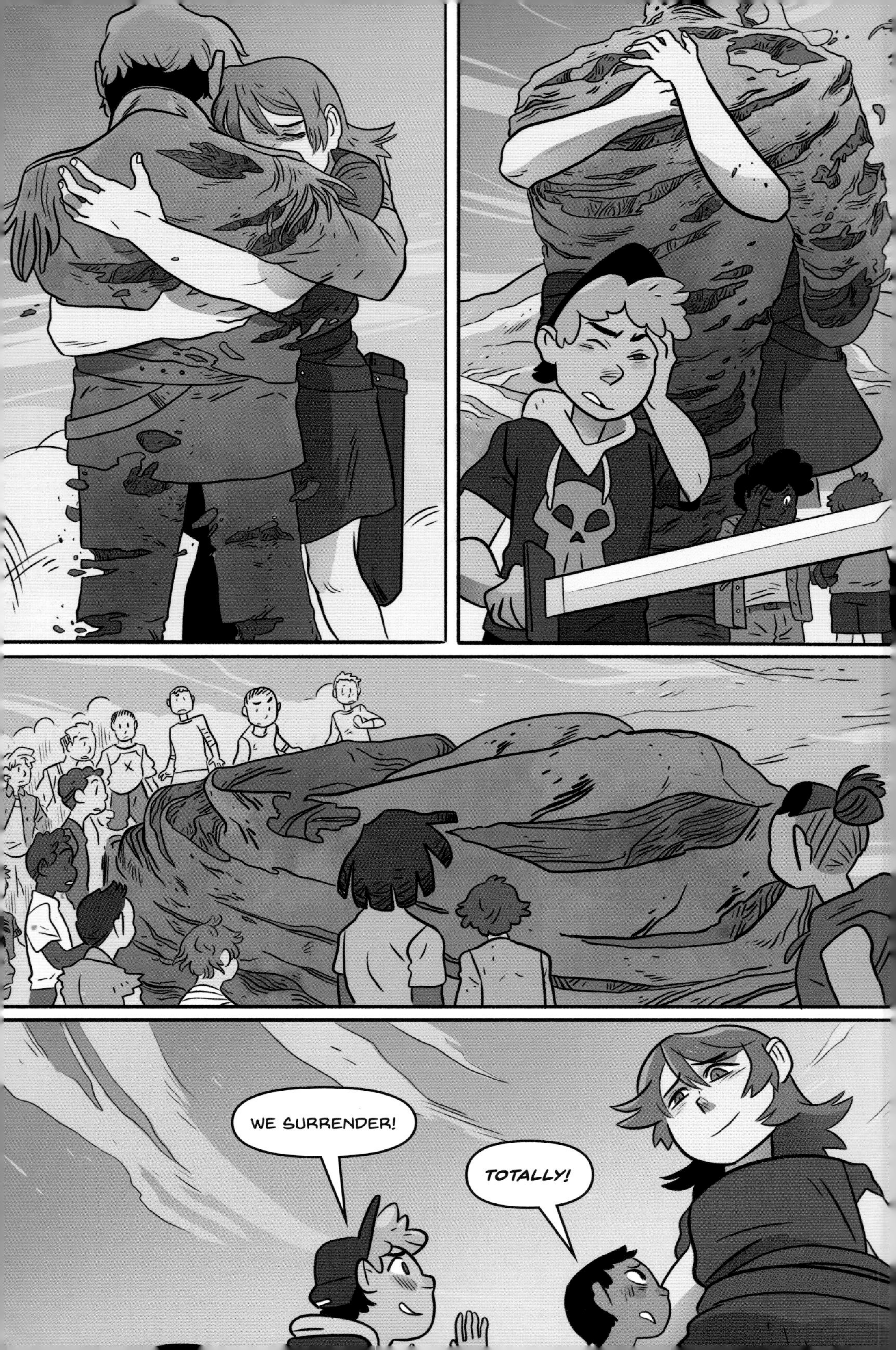
WE SURRENDER!
TOTALLY!

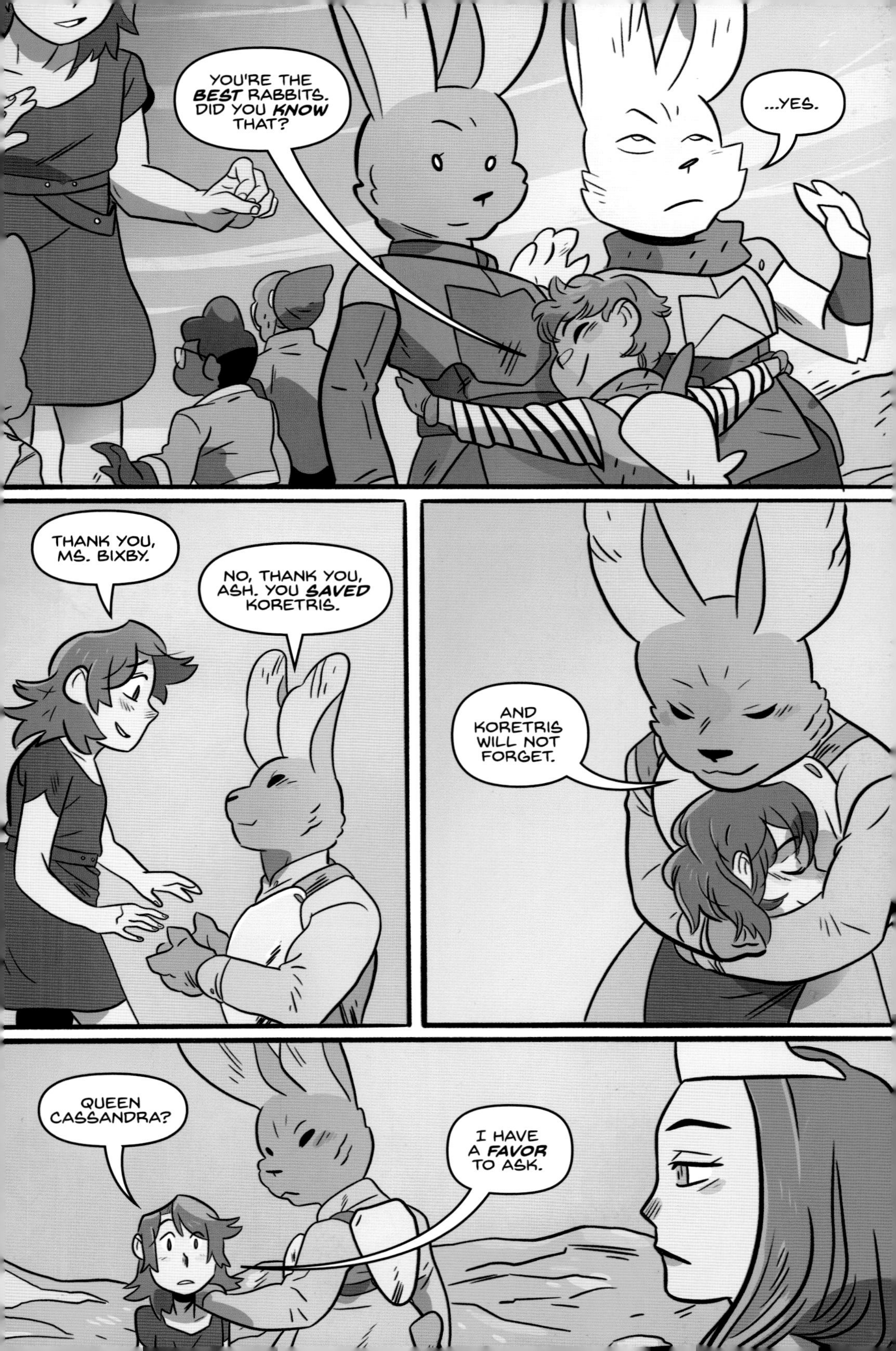
YOU'RE THE BEST RABBITS. DID YOU KNOW THAT?
...YES.
THANK YOU, MS. BIXBY.
NO, THANK YOU, ASH. YOU SAVED KORETRIS.
AND KORETRIS WILL NOT FORGET.
QUEEN CASSANDRA?
I HAVE A FAVOR TO ASK.

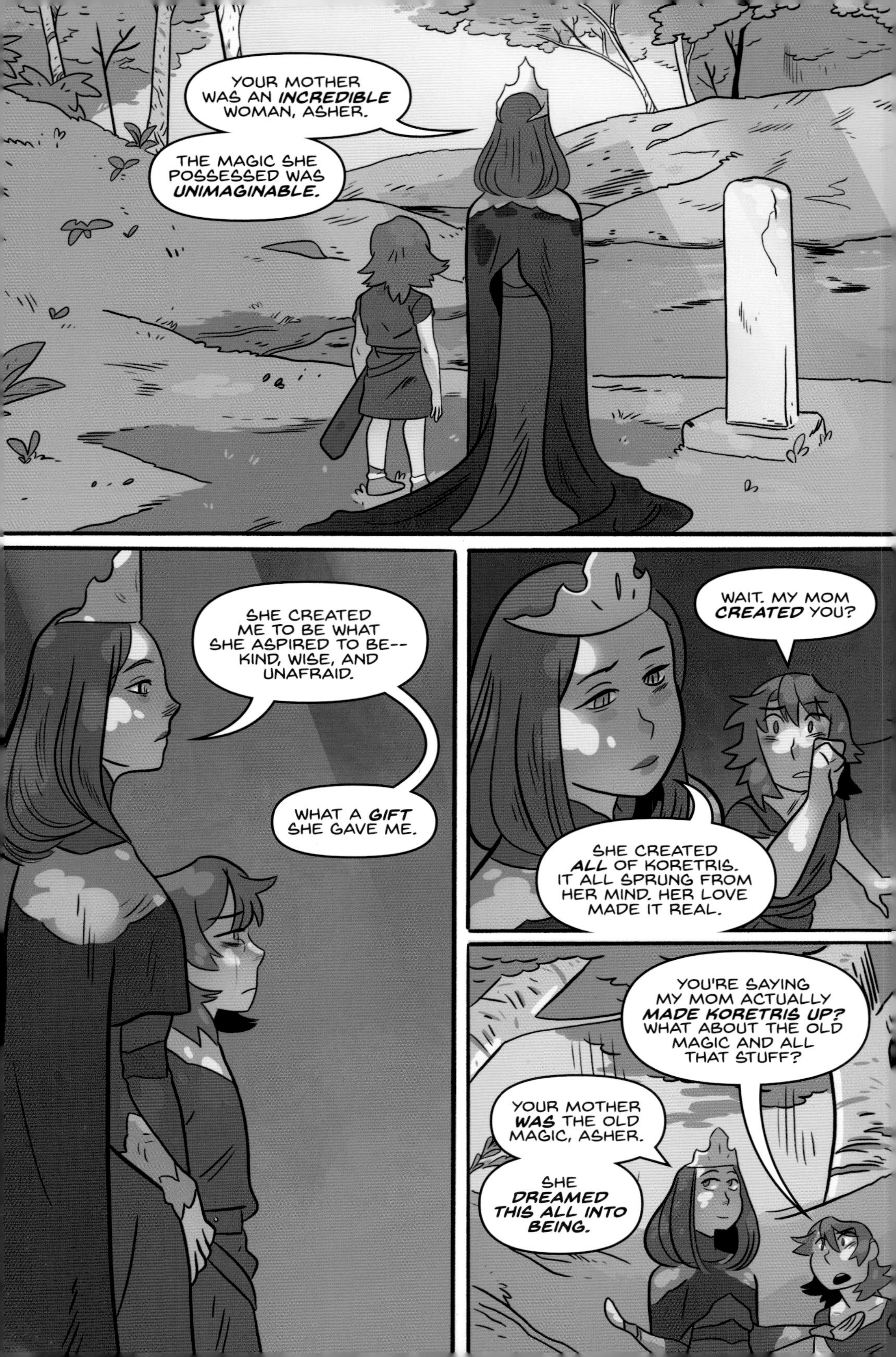
YOUR MOTHER WAS AN *INCREDIBLE* WOMAN, ASHER.
THE MAGIC SHE POSSESSED WAS ***UNIMAGINABLE.***
SHE CREATED ME TO BE WHAT SHE ASPIRED TO BE--KIND, WISE, AND UNAFRAID.
WHAT A ***GIFT*** SHE GAVE ME.
WAIT. MY MOM ***CREATED*** YOU?
SHE CREATED ***ALL*** OF KORETRIS. IT ALL SPRUNG FROM HER MIND. HER LOVE MADE IT REAL.
YOU'RE SAYING MY MOM ACTUALLY ***MADE KORETRIS UP?*** WHAT ABOUT THE OLD MAGIC AND ALL THAT STUFF?
YOUR MOTHER ***WAS*** THE OLD MAGIC, ASHER.
SHE ***DREAMED THIS ALL INTO BEING.***

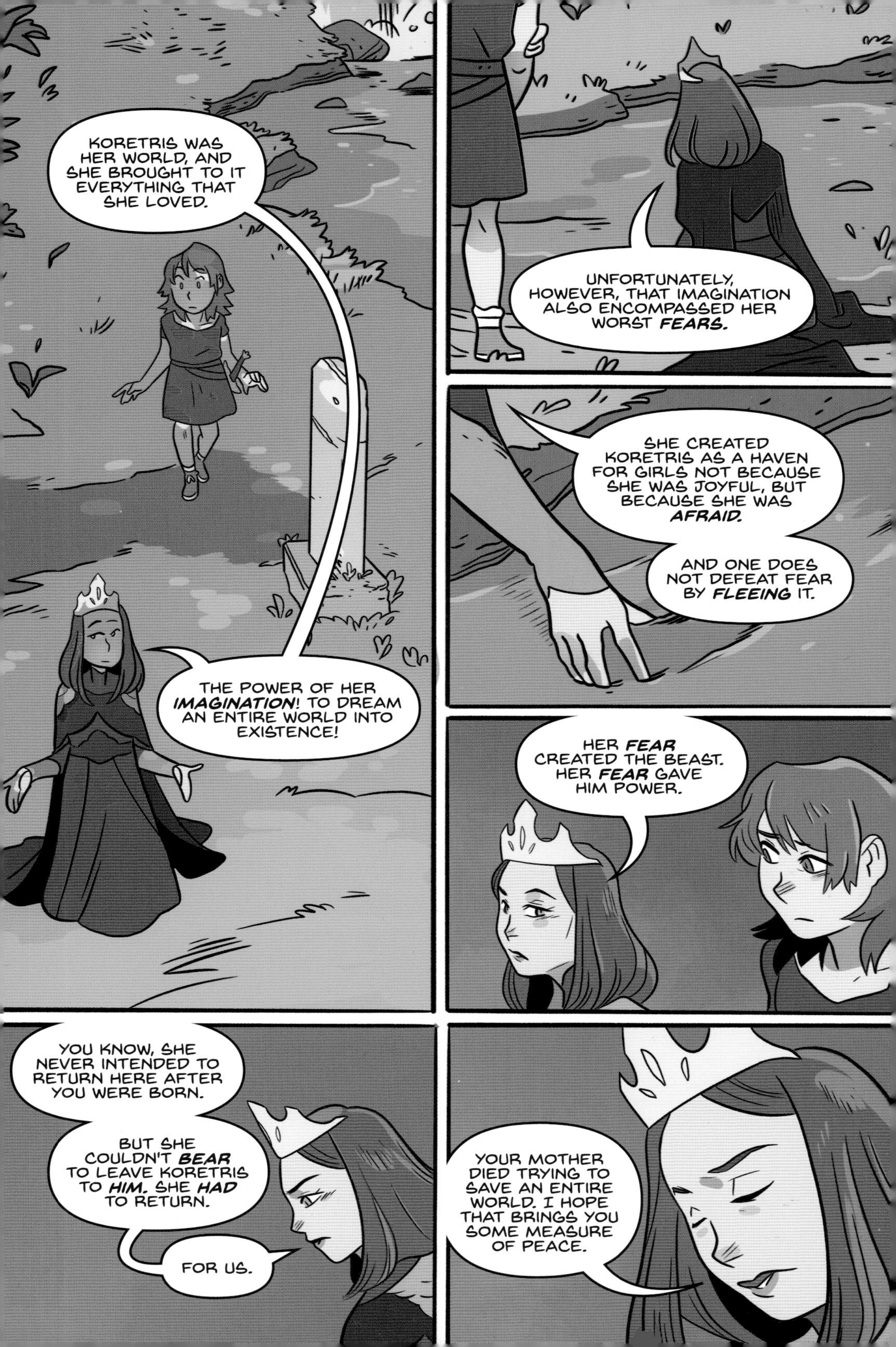
KORETRIS WAS HER WORLD, AND SHE BROUGHT TO IT EVERYTHING THAT SHE LOVED.
THE POWER OF HER *IMAGINATION*! TO DREAM AN ENTIRE WORLD INTO EXISTENCE!
UNFORTUNATELY, HOWEVER, THAT IMAGINATION ALSO ENCOMPASSED HER WORST ***FEARS.***
SHE CREATED KORETRIS AS A HAVEN FOR GIRLS NOT BECAUSE SHE WAS JOYFUL, BUT BECAUSE SHE WAS ***AFRAID.***
AND ONE DOES NOT DEFEAT FEAR BY ***FLEEING*** IT.
HER ***FEAR*** CREATED THE BEAST. HER ***FEAR*** GAVE HIM POWER.
YOU KNOW, SHE NEVER INTENDED TO RETURN HERE AFTER YOU WERE BORN.
BUT SHE COULDN'T ***BEAR*** TO LEAVE KORETRIS TO ***HIM.*** SHE ***HAD*** TO RETURN.
FOR US.
YOUR MOTHER DIED TRYING TO SAVE AN ENTIRE WORLD. I HOPE THAT BRINGS YOU SOME MEASURE OF PEACE.

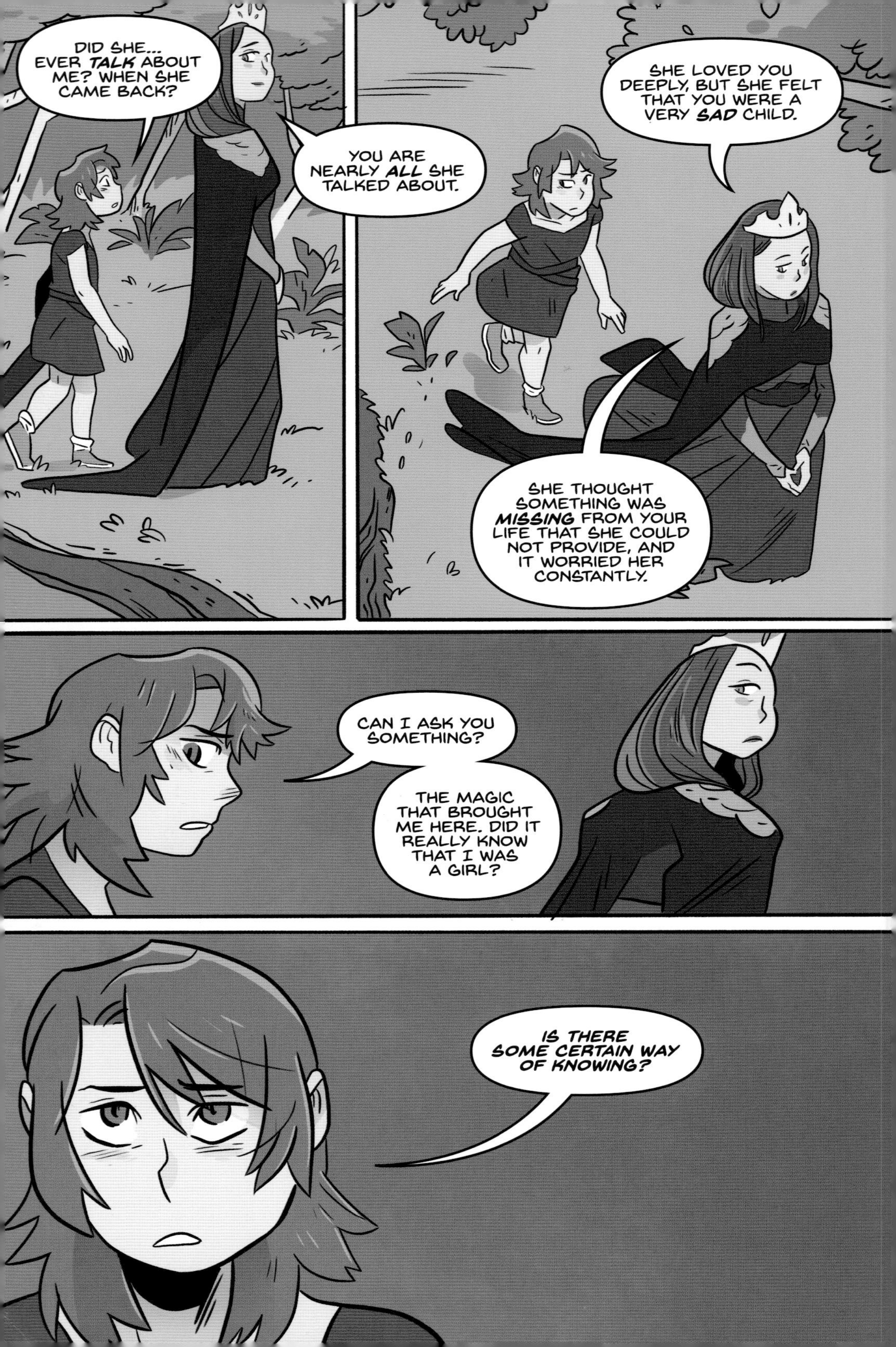
DID SHE... EVER *TALK* ABOUT ME? WHEN SHE CAME BACK?
YOU ARE NEARLY *ALL* SHE TALKED ABOUT.
SHE LOVED YOU DEEPLY, BUT SHE FELT THAT YOU WERE A VERY *SAD* CHILD.
SHE THOUGHT SOMETHING WAS *MISSING* FROM YOUR LIFE THAT SHE COULD NOT PROVIDE, AND IT WORRIED HER CONSTANTLY.
CAN I ASK YOU SOMETHING?
THE MAGIC THAT BROUGHT ME HERE. DID IT REALLY KNOW THAT I WAS A GIRL?
IS THERE SOME CERTAIN WAY OF KNOWING?

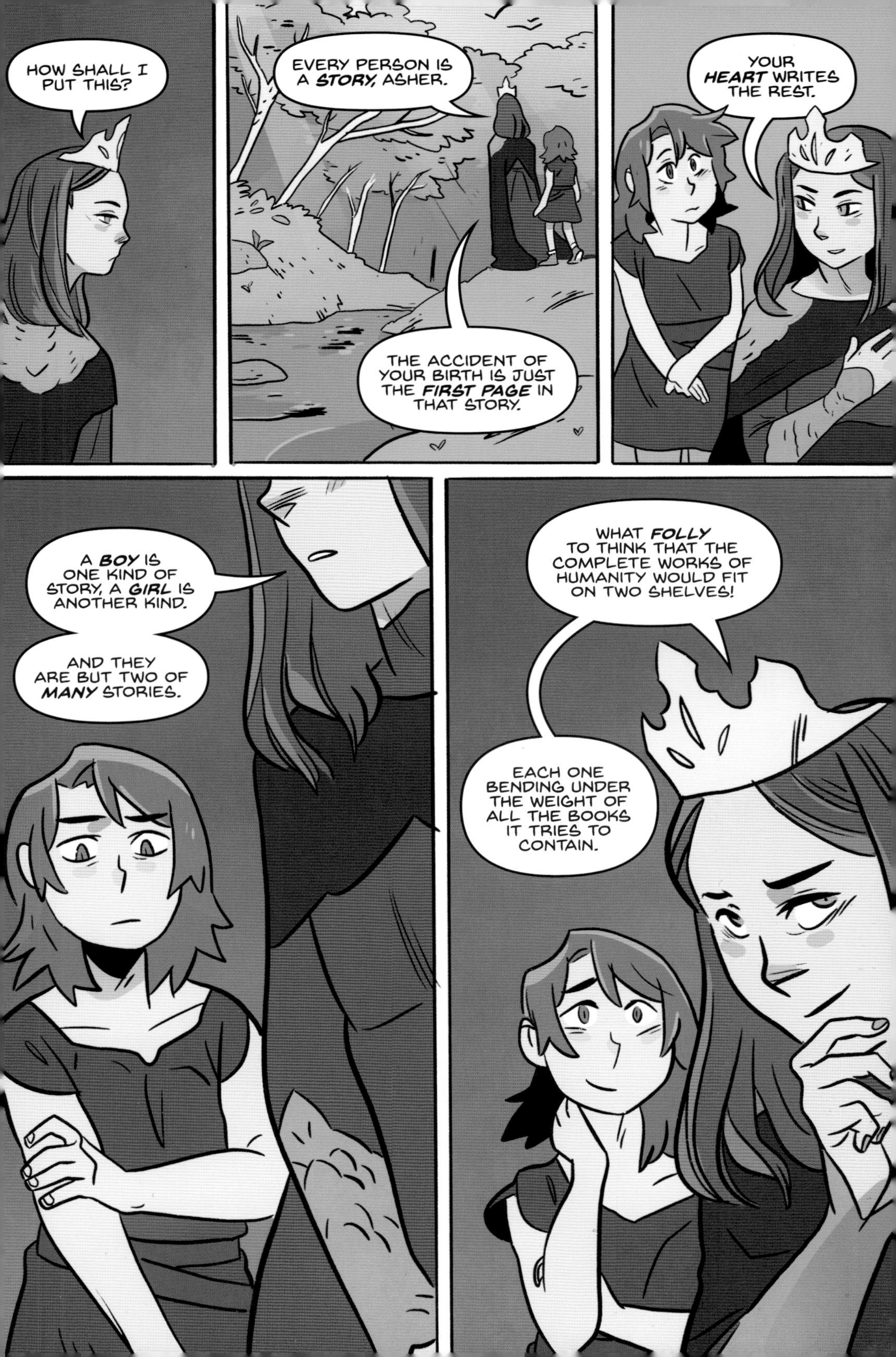
HOW SHALL I PUT THIS?
EVERY PERSON IS A *STORY,* ASHER.
THE ACCIDENT OF YOUR BIRTH IS JUST THE *FIRST PAGE* IN THAT STORY.
YOUR *HEART* WRITES THE REST.
A *BOY* IS ONE KIND OF STORY, A *GIRL* IS ANOTHER KIND.
AND THEY ARE BUT TWO OF *MANY* STORIES.
WHAT *FOLLY* TO THINK THAT THE COMPLETE WORKS OF HUMANITY WOULD FIT ON TWO SHELVES!
EACH ONE BENDING UNDER THE WEIGHT OF ALL THE BOOKS IT TRIES TO CONTAIN.

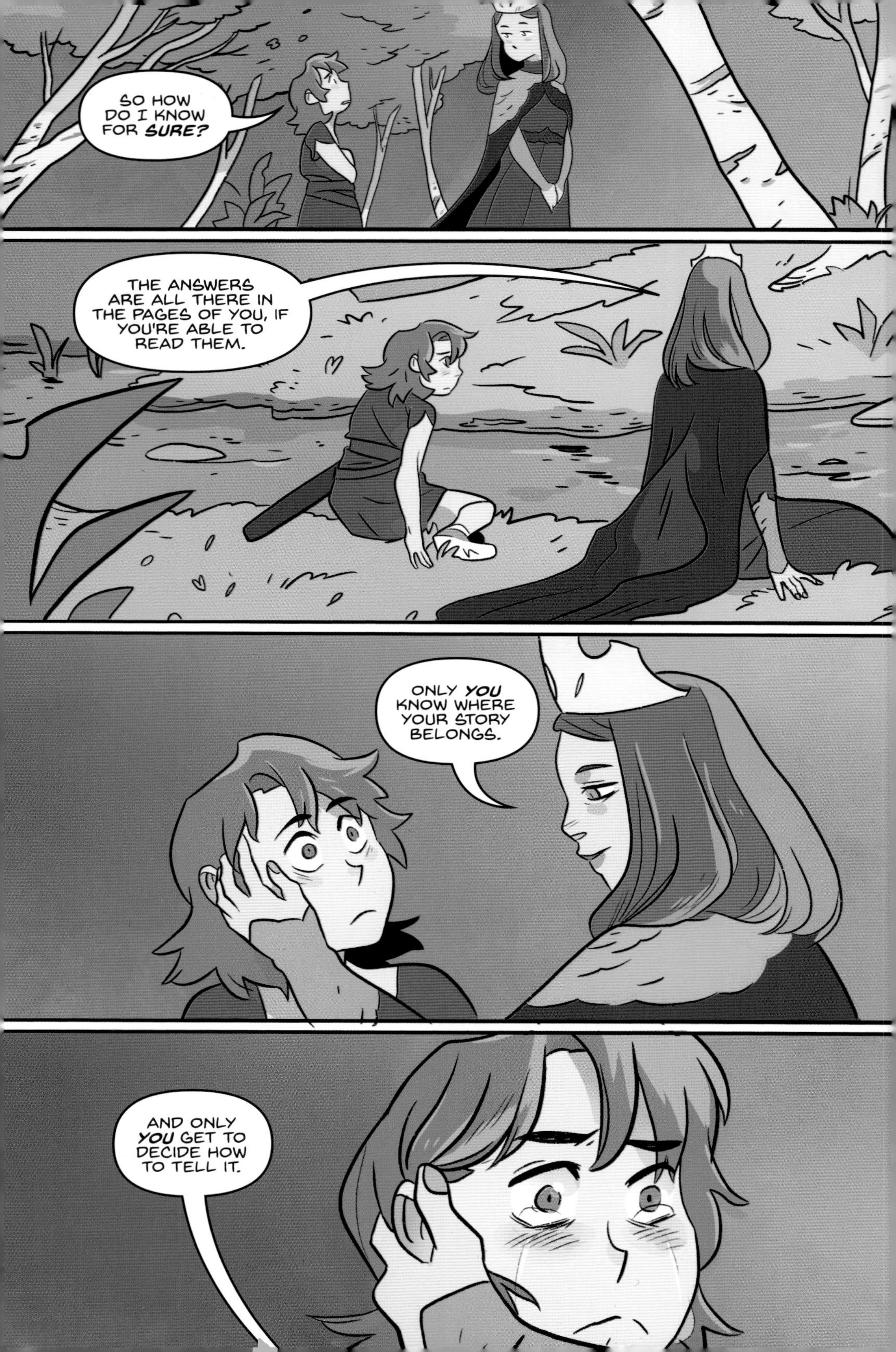
SO HOW DO I KNOW FOR SURE?
THE ANSWERS ARE ALL THERE IN THE PAGES OF YOU, IF YOU'RE ABLE TO READ THEM.
ONLY YOU KNOW WHERE YOUR STORY BELONGS.
AND ONLY YOU GET TO DECIDE HOW TO TELL IT.

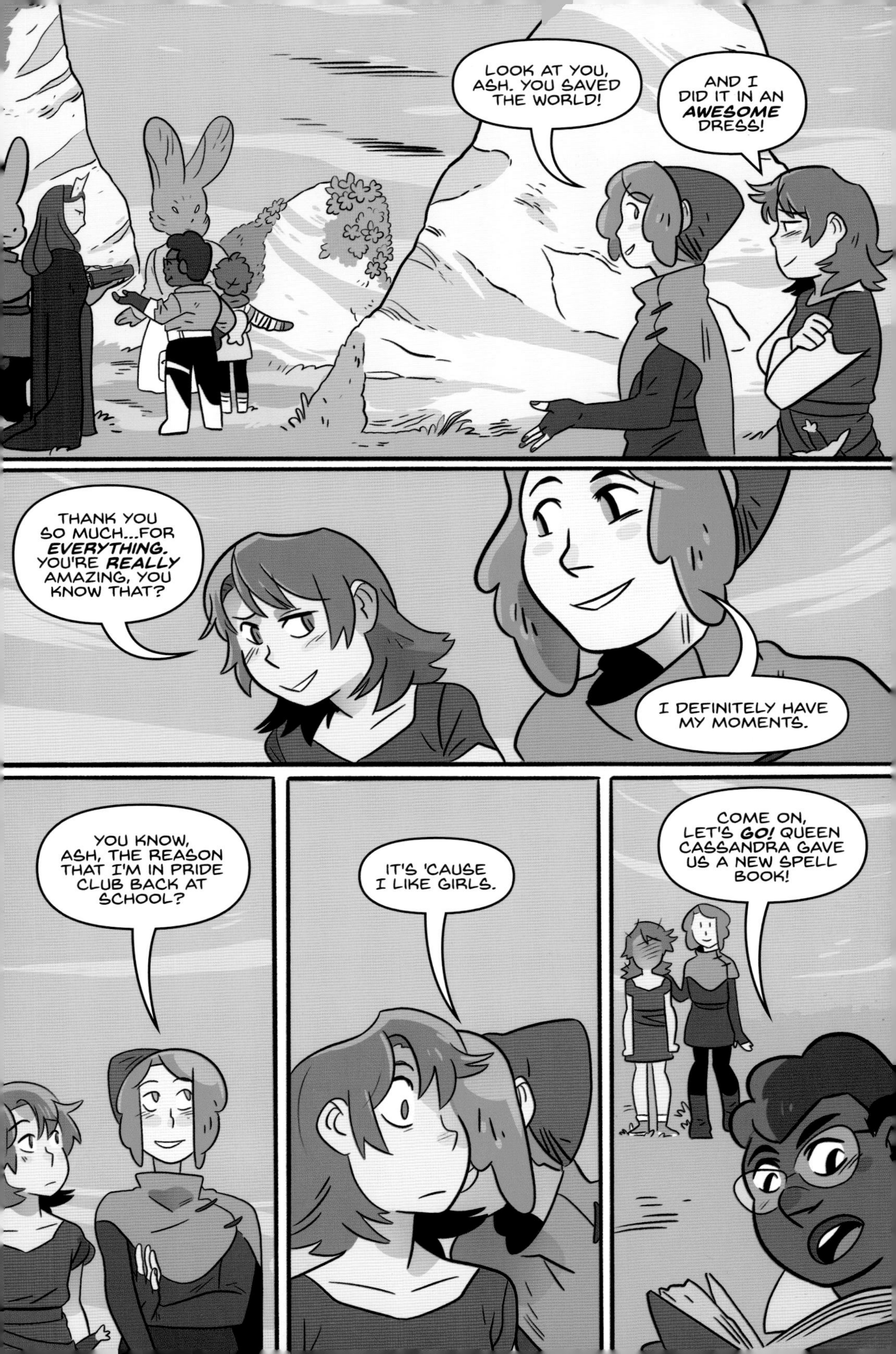
LOOK AT YOU, ASH. YOU SAVED THE WORLD!
AND I DID IT IN AN AWESOME DRESS!
THANK YOU SO MUCH...FOR EVERYTHING. YOU'RE REALLY AMAZING, YOU KNOW THAT?
I DEFINITELY HAVE MY MOMENTS.
YOU KNOW, ASH, THE REASON THAT I'M IN PRIDE CLUB BACK AT SCHOOL?
IT'S 'CAUSE I LIKE GIRLS.
COME ON, LET'S GO! QUEEN CASSANDRA GAVE US A NEW SPELL BOOK!

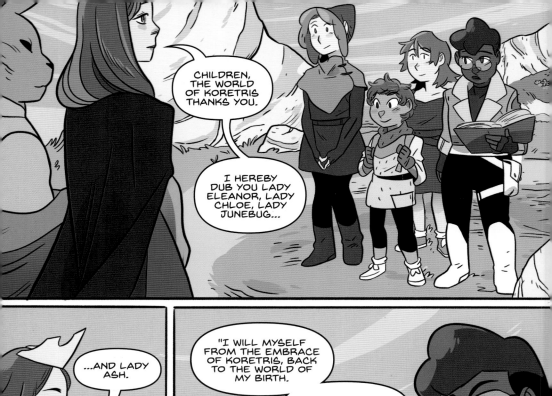

CHILDREN, THE WORLD OF KORETRIS THANKS YOU.

I HEREBY DUB YOU LADY ELEANOR, LADY CHLOE, LADY JUNEBUG...

...AND LADY ASH.

"I WILL MYSELF FROM THE EMBRACE OF KORETRIS, BACK TO THE WORLD OF MY BIRTH.

"LET THE SPACE BETWEEN WORLDS LIFT ME UP...

"...AND CARRY ME HOME."

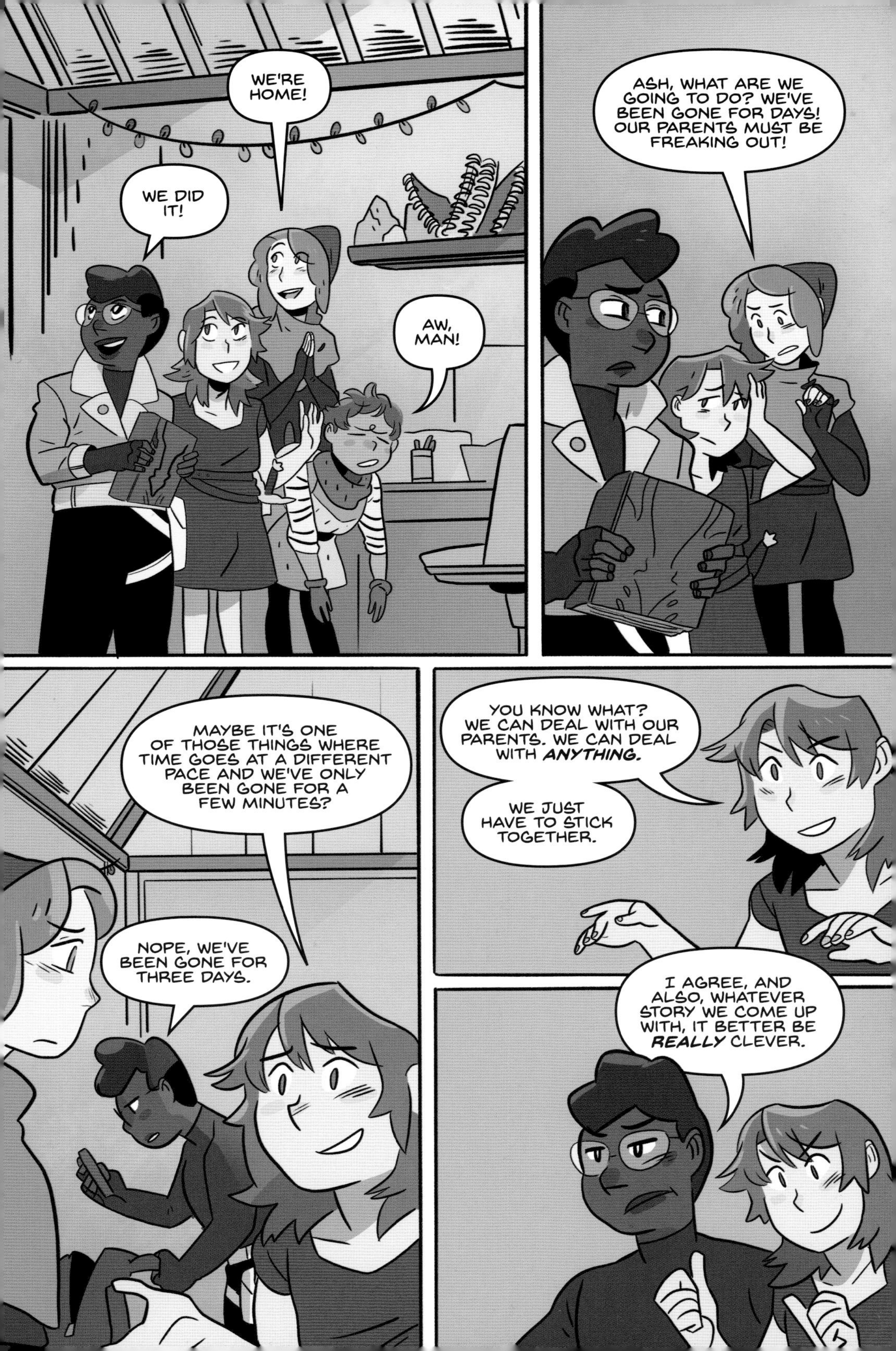
WE DID IT!
WE'RE HOME!
AW, MAN!
ASH, WHAT ARE WE GOING TO DO? WE'VE BEEN GONE FOR DAYS! OUR PARENTS MUST BE FREAKING OUT!
MAYBE IT'S ONE OF THOSE THINGS WHERE TIME GOES AT A DIFFERENT PACE AND WE'VE ONLY BEEN GONE FOR A FEW MINUTES?
NOPE, WE'VE BEEN GONE FOR THREE DAYS.
YOU KNOW WHAT? WE CAN DEAL WITH OUR PARENTS. WE CAN DEAL WITH *ANYTHING.*
WE JUST HAVE TO STICK TOGETHER.
I AGREE, AND ALSO, WHATEVER STORY WE COME UP WITH, IT BETTER BE *REALLY* CLEVER.

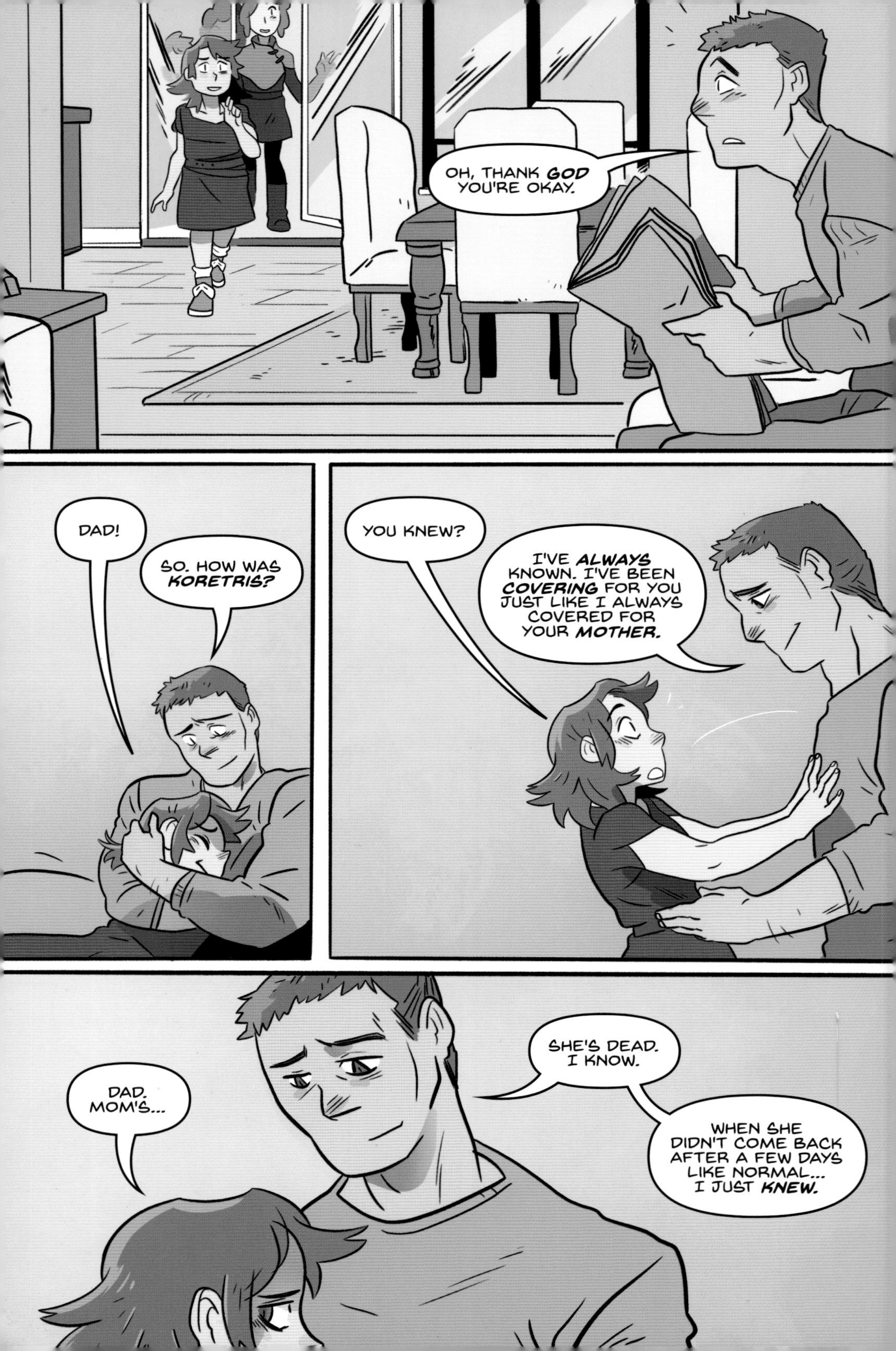
OH, THANK GOD YOU'RE OKAY.
DAD!
SO. HOW WAS KORETRIS?
YOU KNEW?
I'VE ALWAYS KNOWN. I'VE BEEN COVERING FOR YOU JUST LIKE I ALWAYS COVERED FOR YOUR MOTHER.
DAD. MOM'S...
SHE'S DEAD. I KNOW.
WHEN SHE DIDN'T COME BACK AFTER A FEW DAYS LIKE NORMAL... I JUST KNEW.

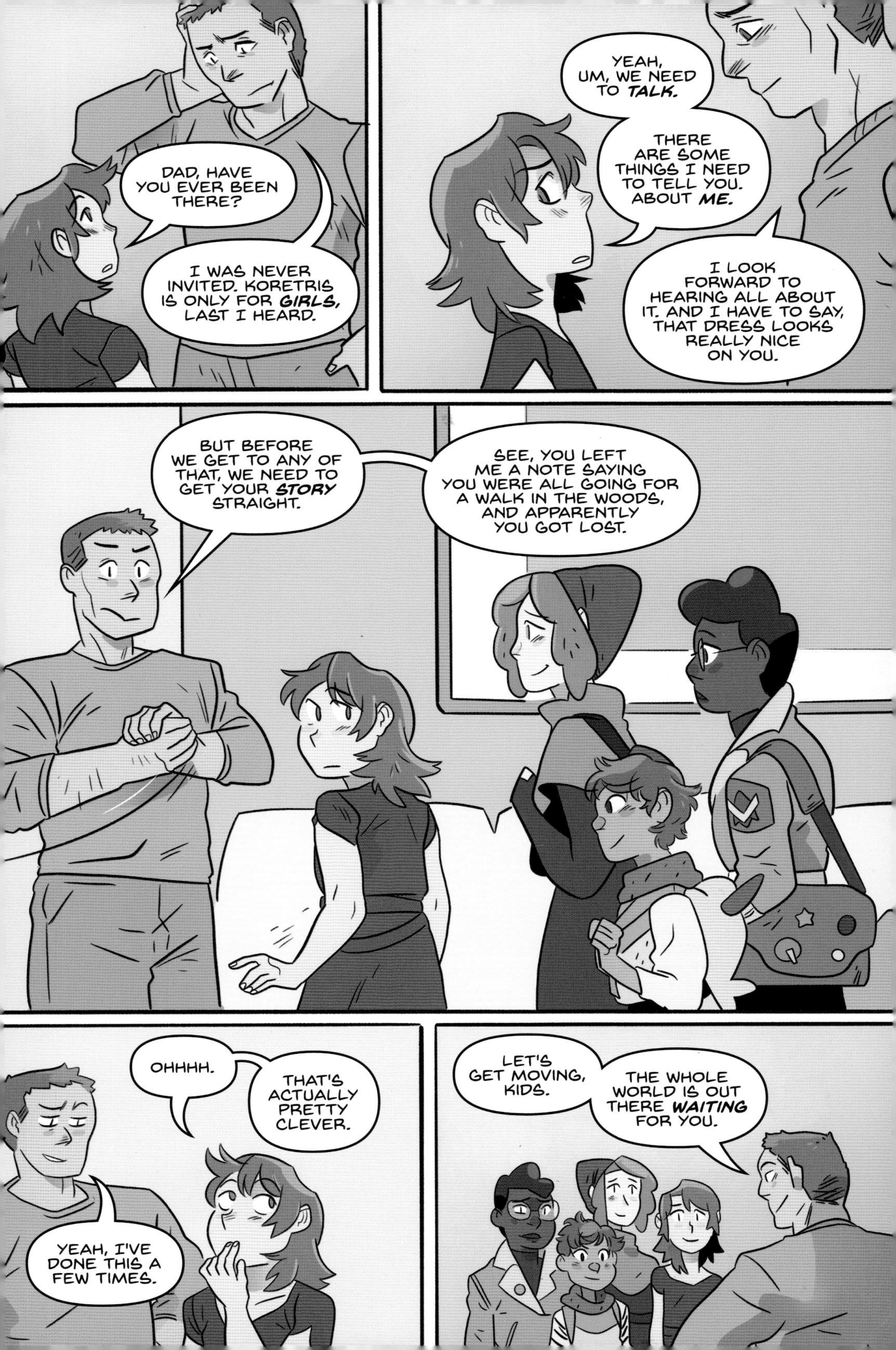
DAD, HAVE YOU EVER BEEN THERE?
I WAS NEVER INVITED. KORETRIS IS ONLY FOR GIRLS, LAST I HEARD.
YEAH, UM, WE NEED TO TALK.
THERE ARE SOME THINGS I NEED TO TELL YOU. ABOUT ME.
I LOOK FORWARD TO HEARING ALL ABOUT IT. AND I HAVE TO SAY, THAT DRESS LOOKS REALLY NICE ON YOU.
BUT BEFORE WE GET TO ANY OF THAT, WE NEED TO GET YOUR STORY STRAIGHT.
SEE, YOU LEFT ME A NOTE SAYING YOU WERE ALL GOING FOR A WALK IN THE WOODS, AND APPARENTLY YOU GOT LOST.
OHHHH.
THAT'S ACTUALLY PRETTY CLEVER.
YEAH, I'VE DONE THIS A FEW TIMES.
LET'S GET MOVING, KIDS.
THE WHOLE WORLD IS OUT THERE WAITING FOR YOU.

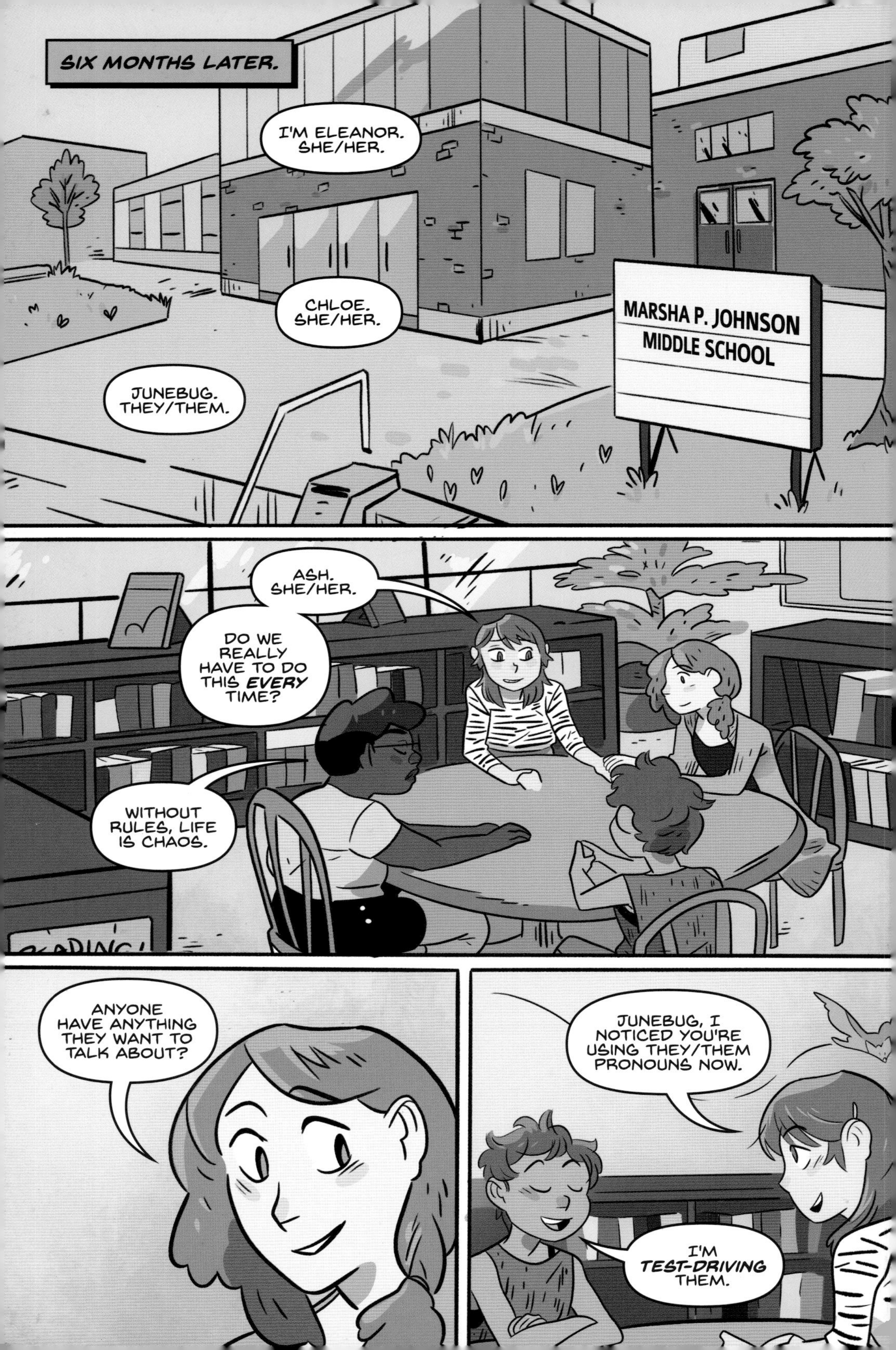
SIX MONTHS LATER.
I'M ELEANOR. SHE/HER.
CHLOE. SHE/HER.
MARSHA P. JOHNSON MIDDLE SCHOOL
JUNEBUG. THEY/THEM.
ASH. SHE/HER.
DO WE REALLY HAVE TO DO THIS *EVERY* TIME?
WITHOUT RULES, LIFE IS CHAOS.
ANYONE HAVE ANYTHING THEY WANT TO TALK ABOUT?
JUNEBUG, I NOTICED YOU'RE USING THEY/THEM PRONOUNS NOW.
I'M *TEST-DRIVING* THEM.

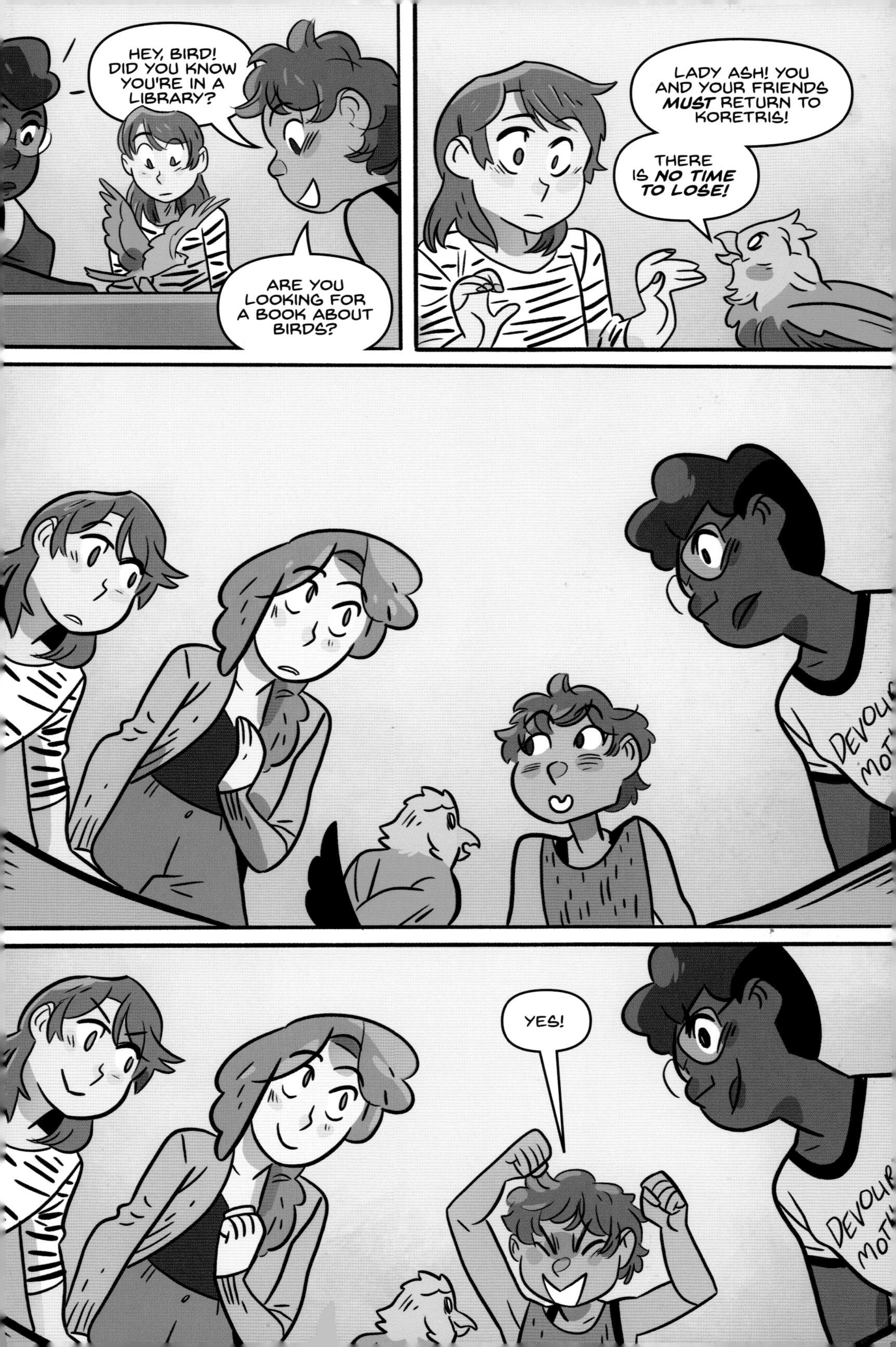
HEY, BIRD! DID YOU KNOW YOU'RE IN A LIBRARY?
ARE YOU LOOKING FOR A BOOK ABOUT BIRDS?
LADY ASH! YOU AND YOUR FRIENDS **MUST** RETURN TO KORETRIS!
THERE IS ***NO TIME TO LOSE!***
DEVOUR MOTH
YES!
DEVOUR MOTH

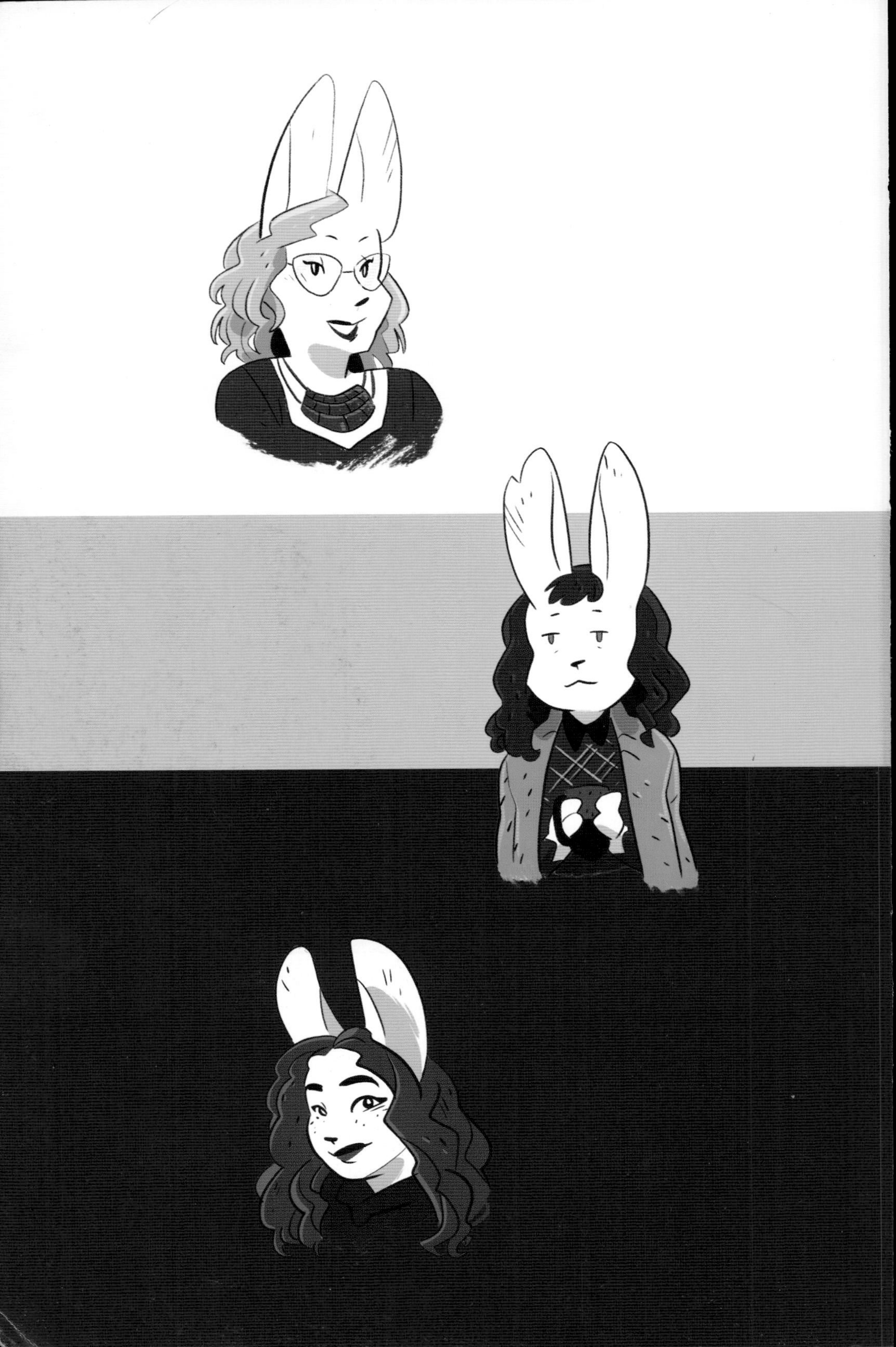

LILAH STURGES

Lilah Sturges is the author of many comic books. She lives
in Austin, Texas with two daughters and two cats.

MEAGHAN CARTER

Meaghan Carter is an illustrator with a love for shonen fighting spirit
and aggressive female leads. Since graduating in 2010, she's honed
her work with anthologies and webcomics. She lives with her
husband and three cats in Toronto.

JOAMETTE GIL

Joamette Gil is an award-winning editor, cartoonist, and letterer
extraordinaire. Her letters grace the pages of such titles as *Archival
Quality* (Oni Press) by Ivy Noelle Weir and Steenz, and *Mooncakes*
(Lion Forge) by Suzanne Walker and Wendy Xu. She's best known for
her groundbreaking imprint P&M Press, home to *Power & Magic: The
Queer Witch Comics Anthology* and *Heartwood: Non-binary Tales of
Sylvan Fantasy*.

A NOTE ABOUT IDENTITY

When talking about queer identity, we are primarily talking about differences in **gender, sex, and sexuality.**

Gender is how you identify in terms of masculinity and femininity. Like race, gender is a **social construct,** in that societies create ideas of what makes one "male" or "female" (for example, think about what are "boy colors" and what are "girl colors").

Gender Identity is associated with how you define your gender. However, gender is also performed; **Gender Expression** is how you behave, dress, and talk.

- People whose gender identity is the same as their sex may identify as **cisgender.**
- People whose gender identity is different from their sex may identify as **transgender.**
- Other gender identities include **nonbinary** (identifying as neither male nor female) and **gender fluid** (changing gender identity).
- **Sex Assigned at Birth** is determined by your anatomy and genetics. People can be **male, female, intersex** (having both male and female characteristics), or **transitioning.**
- When we say **sexuality** in this context, it is shorthand for **sexual orientation,** which usually refers to the gender(s)/sex(es) to which someone is attracted. Americans usually think in terms of **heterosexuality** (opposite-sex attraction), **homosexuality** (same-gender attraction), and **bisexuality** (attraction to one's own and other genders), but there are infinite forms of sexuality.

PRONOUNS MATTER!

Don't assume someone's sexuality, sex, or gender. Trans individuals often have specific pronouns they want people to use. If you are not sure what pronouns to use, they/them work as neutral terms until you know for sure. If you feel comfortable doing so, ask.

Adapted from The Anti-Defamation League, PFLAG National, & The University of Michigan International Spectrum Websites, and used with permission from Fred Fox.